Into the
Morning Mist

Into the Morning Mist

~

Robert Saur

ISBN: 1507564481
ISBN 13: 9781507564486
Library of Congress Control Number: 2015900780
CreateSpace Independent Publishing Platform
North Charleston, South Carolina

Prologue

~

JUNE 1

RON DOMBROWSKI DROVE SLOWLY OVER the winding country roads. The sky, with its cumulus clouds, providing a contrast against the lush green fields. Trees everywhere burst with newborn leaves, concealing their long skinny arms so noticeable during the endless winter months. All along the roadside, wildflowers bloomed, waving to all those who passed. With each turn, Ron spotted another farmer tending his fields, nurturing the rich soil. With luck, those freshly planted crops would grow in abundance. Ron breathed in deeply. The morning air felt crisp, yet comfortable. He kept his window cracked, enough to let in the fresh fragrant country air, but not so much to give a chill. It was a beautiful morning and set to be a beautiful day. On most occasions, the drive would be something Ron would relish, but today, on this day, nothing promised to be enjoyable.

For the last 30 years, Ron had worked as a loan officer with Finger Lakes Saving & Loan. Back when he started it was just a small local bank with a few branches throughout the Finger Lakes region of New York State. He and his fellow bankers had forged close relationships with many of the local farmers. They spent time with them, knew their families and when times got tough, they made sure the bank didn't abandon them. It was in those first few years at FLS&L that Ron met Jack O'Brien. Jack owned a horse farm in Hemlock, a sleepy lake town in the heart of the Finger Lakes, one of many picturesque towns in a valley carved out by glaciers thousands of years before. Like Jack, Ron had come back to the area after serving in Vietnam, trying to make sense of what he and his comrades had gone through and hopefully begin a new life. As with many vets, there existed a fragile mix of good days and bad. Both men were fortunate to meet the woman they would marry before the bad days over-took the good. Jack was one of Ron's first clients and their common past and no-nonsense approach made them a perfect fit from the start. Their relationship would only grow stronger as the years went by.

It was exactly this relationship that made this drive even more diffi-cult. Ron's mind continued to wander back to yesterday's meeting. All the major banking executives had traveled from New York City to meet and discuss the current state of affairs with the local offices. Some years ago, the locally owned bank sold out to one of the large banks headquartered in the City. Since then, closing loans far outweighed the importance of knowing and working hand in hand with your clients. Ron didn't like the new policy and knew his days were numbered, but he was hoping to hold on for a few more years and make it to retirement age. But after yesterday, that seemed a lot less desirable. It appeared that the Bank had been in-volved in a large amount of the sub-prime lending and now loss rates were skyrocketing. Even though nearly all of these sub-prime loans were gen-erated from branches in the New York City area, all branch locations were feeling the heat. At yesterday's meeting, Ron's boss informed the staff that all loans categorized as "not in good standing" were to be called. If the client was unable to pay the full balance in 90 days, then the bank would foreclose. One name jumped out at Ron on the list of delinquents, Jack O'Brien. Jack's farm had hit difficult times over the past year and Ron had agreed to suspend payments temporarily. Now Ron was forced to deliver the unwelcome news to Jack. Of course, the Bank had prepared a form letter that was available to all the loan officers. Ron read the letter before crumpling it in a ball and slamming it into the trash. As terrible as it was going to be telling Jack face to face, Ron couldn't consider sending such an impersonal letter. He owed it to Jack. 'Hell, not even my pains in the ass clients deserve that,' thought Ron. 'When did business relationships become so detached? Where had the days gone when a man's word was his bond? Where was the honor? Certainly not in a form letter.'

Letting his foot off the gas and gently applying pressure to the brakes, Ron began to slow the vehicle down. His 9-year-old Honda Accord, as sturdy and reliable as ever, came to a crawl before turning into the O'Briens' driveway. The O'Briens' property sloped at nearly a 45-degree angle as you entered. The pitch slowly eased as the driveway closed on their house, some 200 yards from the road. The driveway stopped at the house, a dirt and gravel road continuing down the hill toward the barn another couple hundred yards away. Ron chose to park near the house and walk, taking a quick view of the deep green pastures, extending to the woods on the opposite end of the farm, then sloping down toward the distant lake. He sighed, the disparity between the view and the job couldn't have been greater. Grabbing the knot of his tie, Ron pulled it tight and straightened his sport coat, formalities hard to shake. The coat and tie were a working-man's variety, serviceable and nothing special. And his shoes, well they were made to walk through farmland. Something he used to do quite often and something he wondered how much of he would do in the future.

Ron took a deep breath, let it all back out and then started toward the barn. He walked with all the enthusiasm of a man on his way to an IRS audit. It was hard to think of a time he had dreaded worse.

"Morning Jack."

"Ron, you must have an early tee time. I didn't think you bankers got up before 9."

Ron let out an uncomfortable chuckle, not being in the mood to laugh. "Jack," he said with a distinct seriousness in his voice, "I have some real bad news." Jack, realizing his friend was struggling with something, placed his bucket on the ground. "The bank has decided your loan is too risky and has called it in. They've given you until September 1st to pay it back."

Jack glanced down at the ground and thought a moment. "What happens if I can't pay it all back?"

"Then they will be forced to foreclose on it." Ron paused for only a moment, "Jack, I'll do everything I can to help you find another lender. I don't want them taking your farm. I'm so ticked off I'd leave the bastards today if I thought someone would hire me. It's not right Jack and they know it. But there is nothing I can do. I'm sorry." There, he'd got it out, told it like it is, knowing the quickest cut is the best cut. At least he could leave the farm with some semblance of integrity still intact.

Jack looked to his friend and spoke with resolve, "It's OK Ron, we'll figure something out."

With that, Ron lowered his head. He didn't know how to feel. Anger, frustration, sorrow, they were all there and yet Jack's calm demeanor only added to it. Ron's words should have sent his friend into a frenzy, but his friend did nothing. He knew Ron was merely the messenger and honorable men don't punish the messenger. Ron began walking back up the hill toward his car. He had only made it 10 or 15 feet when Jack called out to him. "Ron," he said. "Thanks for coming by in person." Ron slowly nodded and continued on his way, suddenly feeling worse than he had 15 feet before.

From out of the barn Margaret O'Brien, the woman who had stood by Jack for better than 37 years, appeared. "Was that Ron?" she asked Jack. "What's he doing out here," glancing at her watch, "especially at this hour?"

"The bank has called the note," Jack said, following Ron's lead of telling it straight. "We have until September 1st to come up with $400,000." The look on Margaret's face needed no words. She knew, like Jack, that they were in a bad spot. "Any thoughts?" she asked. Jack nodded, "Nope." With that, Margaret patted his back, kissed him on the cheek and headed for the house. Jack turned and picked up the muck bucket he'd set down. In one smooth motion, the aged farmer hoisted the over-laden bucket and deposited its contents in the waiting manure spreader. He stared into the rich smelling dung wondering where it had all gone wrong. The year had started out so promising. How could things have turned out so poorly? In and around the fresh new pile, flies buzzed about, happy with their new-found treasure. But to Jack, the spreader's contents, like this entire year, was a giant pile of shit.

Chapter 1

~⌒

IT WAS A BITTER DAY in Western New York. The temperatures weren't expected to get above freezing and the Great Lakes breeze made it feel even colder. "All right Manny, bring him out," yelled Jack, warm breath billowing from his mouth and rising into the cold air. Manuel Hernandez, or Manny as everyone called him, appeared from the barn with Sing So Long following on the leather shank. Without hesitation, the two moved up the ramp and into the trailer. Around the corner of the trailer came Michael O'Brien, the eldest of the O'Brien children at age 36. He stood almost a head taller than his father, with a slender build and a face that never seemed to smile. But as far as he was concerned, that seriousness came with the position of head trainer for O'Brien Racing. His father had noticed his training talent early and by age 25, Michael had taken over the reins, while Jack moved to the sidelines to enjoy his days away from the crowds back on the farm. Michael's win percentage had remained strong from the beginning, winning at nearly 30 % for the past 11 years, an outstanding percentage for the business. But the last couple of years his percentage had dropped, at first to the teens and then last year it was barely 10 percent. Michael's skills remained sharp, probably better than ever. The horses coming out of the farm on the other hand, were just not the same quality.

The O'Briens had always bred and raced their own stock. For the past 20 years they had been blessed to stand two decent stallions to go along with a fine group of 15 or so mares. In addition to breeding their own, the O'Briens would occasionally breed some of their mares to other stallions. With that approach, they were able to maintain a small, but competitive racing stable. But during the last few years, the O'Brien stallions were no longer producing the quality foals they once had. It forced the farm to increase the number of times they bred their mares to outside stallions. And this cost money, good money if you wanted to breed to proven stallions. Unfortunately, even a proven stallion doesn't always produce a great runner. The only horse that displayed any real talent in recent years was the horse currently settling himself in the van, Sing So Long. Sing, as they referred to him, displayed his ability very early in his training, his athleticism easy to spot, even to the untrained eye. He seemed to move so fluidly, almost effortlessly. His only real problem was his attitude. Thoroughbreds tend to be high strung, Sing took that to another level. Even Jack, the salty veteran, couldn't recall too many who could rival him in that department. They had raced him last year as a 2-year-old at Finger Lakes Race Track. It's considered a lower-level track, but Sing had run twice and won both races by large margins. He had also worked himself into a lather before each race, trying to buck off the jockey before one and nearly running off before the other. Luckily, during the latter, the jockey pulled him up with help from an outrider. The outriders follow along with the horses to make sure just such a thing doesn't happen. It was only because of Sing's immense talent that he had enough energy left to win both races. Michael didn't consider either jockey in those first two races to be top-flight and he blamed them in part for the problems. But it was enough to lead him to recommend castrating Sing in the fall before his 3-year-old year. Eliminating the hormonally driven behavior should result in a better mannered and less distracted horse. There were no arguments against it from anyone working at the O'Brien barn.

Since being gelded, Sing had been back at the farm resting. He seemed to be a calmer horse thus far. Once they had him back in training they would be able to tell just what the effect was. That day was coming soon as he and two of his stablemates, Mr. Nobody and Glitter, were on their way to Florida for winter racing. Normally the O'Briens would wait for Finger Lakes to open in April, but two things were prompting them to head for Florida this year. First, if Sing improved from last year, then he might be good enough to run in some of the more prestigious stakes races run during the winter and spring. The second thing was the money. Those stakes races had purses that far outweighed anything Finger Lakes could offer. And the farm was in need of some of that money.

The losses the operation had incurred over the last two years, along with the increase in the fees to breed, had hurt the farm. Added to that was the cost of refurbishing the barn and facilities. Jack had decided to get a loan from the bank to help manage the cash flow a few years back. The problem was that over the past year they were forced to lean more and more on that loan. The farm needed a good year and they were all hoping Sing would be the horse who brought it to them. Racehorse owners are dreamers, plain and simple. Even quintessential realists like Jack and Michael O'Brien. Sing stood quietly as Jack closed and latched the trailer doors. "All set back here," Jack said.

"OK," answered Michael, "where is James?" Hearing no response, Michael looked around. At the front of the property toward the road, he spotted the kids, his own Jack and Mary, and James' daughter Sydney. They were taking advantage of the steep slope as you come onto the farm. With several inches of snow on the ground, that area was perfect for sledding. It took Michael a minute to realize that there was one too many children up there. There was a fourth, a rather large 34-year-old child. "Come on James," Michael yelled, "get down here, we're ready to go."

When James heard Michael's call, he turned to the kids. "Well the fun is over, guess it's time to go." The three kids and James made their way down the hill toward the truck. The second son of Jack and Margaret, James was more fun-loving and optimistic as compared to his older brother. Physically, he gave Michael 6 inches, but outweighed him by a good 10 or 15 pounds. It had been that way since James was in 9th grade. Margaret couldn't count the number of times James would wrestle Michael to the ground for no other reason except that he could. Michael hated it, probably another reason James did it, and would curse and scream until Margaret broke it up. Michael and James' relationship back then was pure love-hate and it drove Margaret crazy. But in time, as with most brothers, the hate part faded and their relationship grew stronger. And James, like his brother, was a good horseman. Where Michael was organized and calculating, James was intuitive and philosophical. Although their differences still caused friction, they complimented one another perfectly while training horses. James reached down and grabbed a handful of snow. "Watch this guys."

The snowball fell at Michael's feet and splashed his pant legs. He looked up to see his brother's big grin. "It's gonna be a long trip," he mumbled under his breath. Just then Margaret, Michael's wife Janet and James' wife Lauren came walking out of the house toward the truck. Everyone converged on the heavily-laden vehicle. Michael kissed his wife and told her that he'd call her tonight. Then he turned and gave both kids a kiss and a hug and told them to be good for Mom.

James, always an entertainer, took hold of Lauren and gave her a long kiss which prompted an "alright already" from his father and an "eww" from Sydney. Of course, this did nothing more than bring a laugh from James. "Will you miss me?" he asked Lauren. "Of course," she responded, "who's going to shovel the driveway?" eliciting another laugh. "I'll miss you too Daddy," said Sydney. James bent down and gave her a hug. "You're my best girl," he whispered to her. Sydney smiled, "you're my best Dad." James returned the smile, patted her on the head and climbed into the truck.

Manny threw his bag into the back. Before getting in he said goodbye to Margaret and Jack. "Take care of these two for me Manny," Margaret said. Manny sort of laughed, not knowing exactly how he could do that. But he replied with a perfunctory "yes ma'am." With that, Manny grabbed his place in the back of the cab.

Michael, already buckled up in the driver's seat, put the truck in drive. Slowly the truck and trailer climbed the driveway, carrying the hopes and dreams of the O'Brien Stables with them.

James leaned forward trying to catch the name of the adult store they were passing as they cruised down Route 15 in Pennsylvania. Finally catching sight of the neon sign he eased himself back in his seat. "Hey Manny, should we turn around and stop at the Guilty Pleasures?" he said. "Maybe we can pick something up for one of those lady friends of yours. Although some of them probably have most of that stuff already."

"Whatever," Manny replied, "you know they're just my friends. I don't know why you insist on making a big deal out of it."

Of course, James loved teasing Manny and found it far more enjoyable getting Manny's goat rather than his permanently serious brother, the same brother taking great pains to ignore the present conversation. "Yes, I understand that "Backside Betty" has many friends." Finding humor in his own comment, James laughed.

"Where are you coming up with that from? I don't even talk to her."

"From what I've heard, there isn't much talking going on." Now James, enamored with his witty response, laughed harder and began poking at Michael. "You get it, you get it?"

Michael shook his head in disgust, attempting to ignore the adolescent behavior. James didn't care, he continued to revel in his own glory. Seeing James lean forward again, Michael glanced over at him, "what are you looking at now?" Then everyone heard the offensive noise, James wasn't looking at anything, he was adjusting his position. Manny and Michael cried in unison, lowering the windows as fast as the electric motors would allow, the foul odor beginning to envelope the cab.

James started laughing again. "I'm sorry guys, I'm sorry. That lunch is not sitting well. I don't know what made me think that a Mini-Mart burrito was the way to go."

Michael kept his head half out the window despite the biting cold air. "I knew this was going to be a brutal trip. We haven't even gotten out of Pennsylvania yet!"

"To the left," Manny cried pointing, his outstretched hand lunging from the back seat between Michael and James. "I see Number 17 over there."

Michael spotted it. Barn Number 17 at Maryland's Laurel Park Race Track, the overnight stop for Sing and his companions. As the van came to a halt, James grabbed for his jacket as he exited the cab. The cold late day air greeted him as a shock in contrast to the vehicle's warmth. But the ground was dry, no sign of the New York snow. He lifted the front seat forward allowing Manny to jump out. Both men stretched their arms and legs, having grown stiff over the last few hours, then made their way to the back of the trailer.

James pushed the latch up and out, a metallic sounding creak signifying the upper back doors were opening. Manny took one and secured it and James the other. Then both men grabbed their respective latches to the ramp, undid them and together slowly lowered it to the ground. The horses knew the trip ended and began to nicker, anxious to get out and stretch their own legs.

Manny walked up the ramp first as Michael met James at the back of the trailer. "The stalls are all ready" Michael said.

"Doors open?" asked James.

"Yeah, all set for them."

"OK Manny, go ahead and bring out Sing."

Manny clipped on Sing's shank and patted his nose. "Alright boy, back it up, there you go." He slowly pushed on Sing's chest, not too hard, just enough to let him know he needed to back his way out. Sing slowly began to move out of the 4-horse gooseneck, whose sides broadcast O'Brien Racing Stables in bold green letters. The slant load trailer was used mostly to shuttle horses from the farm to Finger Lakes Race Track and back again. Occasionally, Sarah, Michael and James' younger sister, used it for her horse show outings. It was a nice, well maintained trailer despite being a good 10 years old. And though nothing fancy, its 8 feet of living space certainly came in handy during those long horse show days.

Sing's ears rotated back and forth above his padded bumper helmet, the sound of his nickering buddies to his front and James and Michael waiting for him from behind. James and Michael were standing on either side of the ramp helping guide Sing down. Sing's back feet made contact with the pavement, his back shoes clanking on the hard surface. His eyes were large and his nostrils flared, excited by the unfamiliar surroundings. Manny tugged on his shank and Sing followed, only half paying attention. Into the stall they went, Michael closing the door behind them. As soon as Manny unhooked the shank Sing went directly to the stall door and stuck his head out, curious about this new place. Manny carefully removed Sing's leg wraps, bell boots and bumper helmet, making sure Sing came away from the trip unscathed. Only his blanket remained on. They were farther south, but temperatures still dropped into the 40's at night. Satisfied with Sing's condition, Manny pushed the horse out of the way so he could leave the stall with Sing's travel gear in tow.

In the next stall, James went through the same routine with Mr. Nobody. Manny placed the gear on the ground next to Sing's stall and followed behind Michael as he walked Glitter into his stall. Once inside Manny closed and latched the door behind them. Even though the horses were well mannered, nobody wanted to risk having one of them bolt out of their stall and start running loose on the backside.

Once Michael finished with Glitter, he re-checked Sing and Mr. Nobody, despite the fact that James and Manny had already examined their charges. But Michael knew the ultimate responsibility lay with him and he needed to be sure. After his own examination, Michael felt secure that all three horses took the trip well. "Let's get the gear in the truck, drop the trailer and head for the motel. We can come back over in a little bit and check on them. Maybe walk them around awhile," Michael said. Manny and James nodded their approval and put the plan in motion.

The clock on the wall said 12:30 a.m. Manny closed his eyes again hoping this time maybe he would fall asleep. He could hear James in one bed and Michael in the other snoring lightly. Not that that bothered him, and his pullout couch was certainly comfortable enough, but there was something else keeping him awake. For some reason, James' comment about the girlfriends kept running through his mind. At 26, Manny would've expected to be more experienced with women, even possibly married for that matter. But to date, he really hadn't even had a long-term serious relationship. And it bothered him, deep down in the subconscious mind, the place that keeps you awake at night, as he currently discovered.

His problem, as he figured it, revolved around his lifestyle. Manny was shy, and outside of anything equine, lacked in self-confidence. People like that rarely summon the courage to talk to a person of the opposite sex. And his workplace didn't exactly have much to offer. There were some nice women at the track, but most of them were, as Margaret put it, a little rough around the edges. Since Manny spent nearly all his waking time at either the track or the O'Briens' farm, he never met anyone. Generally speaking it didn't bother him, but every once in a while, now for example, he wondered when and how he would ever meet someone special. He longed for it, probably more than some because of the loss of his parents. It had been years since he'd felt an unconditional, unquestioning love. Maybe, he thought, flipping from his back to stomach, it'd been so long that *he* was actually the problem. Maybe he didn't know how to love. Maybe he remained distant from everyone because that's all he knew. Manny sighed. What was certain, was that he had no prospects, no idea what to do about it, and that, left him downtrodden.

The sound of Michael mumbling some sort of gibberish in his sleep prompted Manny to open his eyes again. He angled his head, arching his neck just so. 12:35 a.m. Well, at least all he expected to do tomorrow was hang out in the back of the truck. There should be plenty of time to take a nap.

Chapter 2

~

JANUARY 16

MANNY TRIED TO PUT THE lid on his coffee, his hand fumbling about the rim trying to get it secure. His eyes, rather than on his coffee, were watching James go from serving station to serving station grabbing anything and everything he felt would safely fit in his pockets without getting crushed. Banana, cereal, donut, nothing was safe. The man was a vulture.

"You think you have enough stuff there boss?" Manny asked.

"Hey, they said it was complimentary you know. It's gonna be a long trip."

"I thought you were going to steal that last chocolate donut from the poor little kid over there."

James looked over at the chubby little boy scarfing down the edible delight. "Well I considered it. He certainly doesn't need it."

Manny laughed, what a piece of work. "I hope none of that stuff is going to give you gas!"

James smiled, "We'll find out my friend, won't we. I make no guarantees."

As they were finishing up their gathering, Michael came into the small room that served as the breakfast area. Manny handed Michael one of the two coffees he'd prepared. "Thanks Manny. We all set?" said Michael. Manny and James each answered affirmatively. "OK, I've checked us out so let's get on the road. We've got a lot of ground to cover today."

Today was scheduled to be the longest leg of the three-day journey. The plan was to drive from Laurel, Maryland to Aiken, South Carolina. There they would stop at a friend of a friend's farm. Tom and Stephanie Marsh were longtime neighbors to Jack and Margaret and were also horse owners, but instead of racing they trained in eventing, the triathlon for horses combining dressage, show and cross-country jumping. When Jack said they were sending some of their horses to Florida for the winter, Tom mentioned they had friends in Aiken and if Jack needed a place to overnight during the trip, that might be a possibility. Jack indicated they would, so Tom called his friend and everything was arranged. Thus, their next stop, a friend's friend in Aiken, South Carolina. Michael expected this leg to take somewhere near 11 hours, a long day on the road for both man and beast.

Mile after mile after mile slowly ticked past. Michael sat in the passenger seat watching the lifeless scenery. Although driving can wear you out, being a spectator in country like this is worse. Michael leaned around his seat and looked into the back. Manny was completely passed out, his mouth wide open. He even had a little drool trickling down the side of his face. Michael smiled, 'looking good Manny, very nice.' Once again facing forward, he leaned over and picked up his portfolio from the floor by his feet. He unzipped and opened it up. Inside lay various charts, spreadsheets and the condition books for Tampa Bay Downs and Gulfstream Park Race Track.

He grabbed the top spreadsheet, which actually contained three sheets stapled together. Within each of those 8 ½ by 11 inch borders lay the workout, feeding and supplement schedule for Glitter for the next eight weeks, day by day. The distance of each workout, the varieties of feed, the grams per supplement and so on. It was this painstaking detail that made Michael successful in what he did. Few in the business could match the level of organization. But Michael knew exactly where he wanted his horses to be at any given time in their training. When things didn't go as planned, for whatever reason, he would refigure his calculations and go from there. He was always, always, on top of his horses.

For Glitter, if everything went according to the carefully planned schedule, he would be ready to run at the end of the eight weeks. Michael went through the schedule again, making it about the fifth or sixth time. He was anal; he knew it and didn't try to deny it.

After confirming the accuracy of the schedule Michael pulled out the condition book for Tampa. He looked for a race that would be the best fit for Glitter around the time he felt he'd be ready. Whether the race was an allowance race, running only for purse money, or a claiming race, which leaves your horse open to be claimed, or bought by another person, didn't matter to Michael. The purses for the claiming races were nearly as good as some of the allowance races and the chances of Glitter, or Mr. Nobody for that matter, getting claimed were pretty slim. They were both decent horses, but neither was stellar and no one would be familiar enough with them to take that chance.

Seeing a race Glitter might fit, Michael pulled out a red pen and circled it. Each horse had their name highlighted with a different color. Glitter was red, Mr. Nobody green and Sing yellow. If Michael looked at his condition book and saw a race circled in red, then he knew it was a suggested start for Glitter. As he admitted, he was anal. Once he completed his work on Glitter, he went through the same routine with Mr. Nobody. Again, he checked things over, circled a couple possible races and then turned his attention to Sing.

The schedule Michael set out for Sing differed slightly from his stablemates. His ultimate goal was to run in the Florida Derby at Gulfstream in early April. Knowing that was their aim, Michael backtracked. Sing would need at least three weeks between starts and Michael wanted to give Sing two starts prior to the Florida Derby. That meant going back six-plus weeks from the Derby to around the end of February. In order to accomplish this, Michael prepared Sing's schedule in December and began preparing the horse soon thereafter. By the time they left New York yesterday, Sing was already well into his assigned regimen. As long as the trip went well, there shouldn't be any interruption in his training.

Michael scanned the condition book for Gulfstream. Compared to Tampa, the purses were higher and the competition better. He needed an allowance race sometime near the end of February to start things. No chance they would risk losing Sing in a claiming race. There were two possible races. The first on February 22nd, which might be a little too soon, and a second on February 27th. That's the one to shoot for, Michael thought. Not only would it give them a few more days to get ready, but the race gave horses that hadn't won in three months a break on the weight they had to carry. Sing's last race was in September, so he would carry four pounds less than most of his rivals. Yes, this is the race; with any luck, the launching pad for a glorious campaign. He put down his pen, glanced out the window at the landscape rushing past, the endless flats of the Carolinas, but saw nothing. Not the grey skies, not the dormant brown grass, not even the leafless trees that dotted the countryside. His mind was lost on the Florida Derby.

It would be the biggest race he'd ever entered. A Grade 1 stakes race carrying a purse of $750,000, the winner netting 60 % of the purse, second place 20 %, as is customary. Not only tidy sums, but enough graded earnings to get you a spot in the Kentucky Derby, the race of all races. Even the 10 % that you would get for running third would be nice, though it probably wouldn't be enough to qualify for a trip to Kentucky.

Although it sounded hugely ambitious for such a small stable, Sing had shown every indication that he belonged with these horses, at least up to this point. In January every year, there are trainers and owners throughout the country who feel the same way. Dreamers. By the time the Kentucky Derby comes around in May most have had a change of heart, or more appropriately, have been forced to have a change of heart. But for now, for Michael, the O'Briens and many others, the dream lived on.

Chapter 3

~

"SLOW DOWN, SLOW DOWN," JAMES said, straining to see the road sign. The sun, what little there was, went down an hour ago making it difficult to navigate the foreign country roads. "This is it, Springhollow Lane. Turn right here. The house should be about a half mile on the right, 1040 Springhollow Lane."

All three passengers bobbed their heads back and forth trying to see something, anything, a house, a driveway, but there was nothing. Michael looked down at the odometer. "We're coming up on a half mile now." Sure enough, the reflectors the Johnsons placed on their mailbox were doing their job and the number 1040 appeared. Michael slowed the truck and trailer nearly to a stop as he turned into the driveway.

It was a nice wide drive meant for larger vehicles to come in and out. The darkness prevented anything from being seen except for the trees lining the driveway and the lights from the house a hundred yards away. The driveway went straight in from the road and then turned into a circle just before the house. Once the truck cleared the trees they could see barn lights off to the right. Michael started around the circle correctly assuming that there would be a driveway that continued on to the barn. He followed it down and came to a stop alongside the barn where the floodlights shown the best, figuring it would be the most well-lit spot to unload his cargo.

Inside the house, the foyer and front hall lit up. The lights from the approaching vehicle reflected off several mirrors strategically hung for incoming and outgoing individuals to appraise themselves. The reflections bounced all the way into the kitchen, where Matt Johnson stood talking to his wife of 30 years Claudia. "Looks like they made it. I'll head down to the barn and meet them," he said heading toward the front door. Matt grabbed his coat off the hallway rack, putting it on in one swift motion as he went. He barely opened the door when out of nowhere an 85-pound happy-go-lucky Labrador Retriever nearly knocked him over rushing out the door. "Easy boy, wait for me," he said closing the door behind him.

The three weary travelers disembarked from the truck and staggered around the vehicle. It had been several hours since their last stop and stiff legs greeted them all. Each man stood at a different part of the truck and trailer and looked around, all wondering where they could relieve themselves without being noticed. They heard and saw nothing.

"I sure hope this is the right place," Manny said, scanning the area for any sign of life.

"It's so quiet it's creepy," added James. Manny looking over the truck's engine nodded in agreement.

"Well, it's the correct address," Michael replied. "And it's a farm. Maybe we should go up to the house and...."

The sound of a dog barking broke the stillness, cutting off Michael in mid-sentence. Michael, James and Manny all turned toward the sound, not knowing what to expect. They sensed movement, but saw nothing, and became acutely aware they were standing in a well-lit area with no cover. The hunter could see the prey, but the prey was blind to the hunter. The barking continued, no one able to pinpoint its location, each bark nearer than the last. As if by instinct, each man took a step back toward the truck, still scanning the blackness.

The eyes appeared first from out of the shadows, each man certain they were locked on him. Then the body of the beast appeared, its tail wagging slowly from side to side. He added one more bark for good measure. Aimed at no one particular, it seemed far less threatening. Lester, it seemed, had found some new playmates.

"Hey big dog, come here," beckoned James, no longer preparing to dive back into the truck. The dog responded in kind and came straight at James. Arriving at James' feet still wagging his tail, the dog launched his two front legs into James' mid-section, nearly knocking him over.

"Lester, get down!" shouted a voice from the darkness. Lester paid no attention as his master came into view. "I'm sorry about him. He just loves company."

"Oh no problem," James replied, still rubbing Lester's head. "It's always nice to receive a warm greeting."

Seeing James had his hands full, Matt made his way to Michael. "I'm Matt Johnson. Welcome to our farm."

"Thank you very much," Michael said, shaking his outstretched hand. "I'm Michael," then he pointed toward the rear of the trailer where Manny waved, "that's Manny and this is James," he said pointing toward James and his new-found friend.

"Well, I hope you boys had a good trip."

"Yes sir. A little long, but everything has gone real well so far."

"Good," Matt said smiling, pleased with the response. "I thought we could unload the horses into the indoor ring. Give them time to move around a while. After dinner we can come back down. The wife is in the house preparing a nice authentic Brazilian dinner for you guys."

"I like the sound of that," James piped in, suddenly turning his attention away from Lester.

"Well good, I hope you boys brought your appetites along with the horses. My wife usually cooks for double the expected number, as you might notice," Matt said, simultaneously patting his belly.

"Don't worry," Manny quickly responded, nodding toward James. "He always brings his appetite."

Matt laughed, as did James. "As soon as you're ready bring them in. I have the ring all ready."

"Great, thanks Matt," Michael said.

"Certainly, I'll go get the lights."

James slid back in his chair. "That meal was absolutely awesome Mrs. Johnson. Thank you very much."

"Please James, call me Claudia and it was my pleasure." Claudia stood grabbing her empty plate, then Matt's and began heading toward the kitchen.

"Thanks, that was great honey," Matt said.

The clearing of plates prompted all three guests to simultaneously stand and grab for theirs. "Sit back down," Claudia said, "I'll take care of those. You guys just relax."

The boys remained standing, each with a 'are you sure?' look on their face, not knowing whether they should listen or disobey in an attempt to be polite. "Sit, sit," Matt said, motioning with his hands to be seated. "We had kids around here for years. She can't help herself, it's like a reflex." Michael, James and Manny sat down reluctantly.

"So, how do you know the Marsh's?" James asked, as Claudia re-entered the room collecting more plates.

"Tom and I went to school together at Penn State," Matt replied. "Seems like a lifetime ago. He and I were roommates the four years we were there." He smiled, "we had a lot of fun back then." He looked behind him to see if Claudia had left yet and seeing she was gone, continued. "Chased girls all over campus," he said, shaking his head at the foolishness.

Michael and James laughed, reflecting on similar endeavors. Manny smiled, but couldn't relate.

After a slight pause and another smile, Matt went on. "The first time I ever spent time around horses was at Tom's parents' place. Went up there a few times on break. I grew up in D.C. and had never been near a horse. Being on that horse farm opened up a new world for me," Matt said., "First time we went riding I almost got killed, had no idea what I was doing, but I loved it. Knew horses would be a part of my life from then on."

The boys smiled and nodded, including Manny, understanding the infectious passion.

"After college, I ended up in Atlanta and Tom went back to New York, though we've stayed close friends. First thing I did after finding a place to live was to find a stable and get riding lessons. And that's where I met Claudia," Matt said, wrapping his arm around her as she walked in from the kitchen.

"Best thing that ever happened to him!" she said with a smile.

James laughed, "Why do they always say that?"

"Because it's true," Claudia answered. "You guys would be lost without us."

"He's lost anyway," Manny said, sitting straight up, proud of his quick jab.

James snickered, "Well played Manny, well played."

"I'll tell you though," Matt said, looking at Claudia, "*we* almost didn't happen. Remember that phone call I had with your mom?"

"How could I forget!" she said, rolling her eyes.

The boys looked at them curiously, figuring a good story was forthcoming.

"So at this point we're engaged and living together," Matt begins. "And I haven't met or even spoken to her parents yet. They don't speak English and I know a little Spanish, but no Portuguese other than a few words Claudia's taught me. But I'm thinking, Spanish, Portuguese, same thing basically, right?" Matt pauses and looks to his listeners, as if pleading his case. "So I'm sitting around the house one day and the phone rings. Claudia's is out somewhere, who knows where, probably shopping," eliciting a quick smack from Claudia. "Anyway, I get up and answer it. It's her mom. That much I understood. I say hello in Portuguese. My first mistake because now she thinks I speak it. She starts talking a mile a minute and I can't understand almost anything she's saying. I think she's asking me if Claudia is out, so I say Si. Will she be back later, Si. Please have her call us, Si, no problema." Matt stopped to laugh.

"That's not what she was asking, was it?" Michael said.

"Noooo. Not even close." Everyone but the story teller began laughing, though he did crack a smile. "She's apparently expecting Claudia to be there, so when she's not, she thinks something might be wrong. So she's asking me, is something wrong with Claudia. My response, yes. Is she sick? Yes. Is she in the hospital? Yes." Matt gives an affirmative head shake, "damage done."

Unable to keep from laughing along with everyone else, Matt stopped the story, laughing at how badly he'd messed up. After regaining his composure, he began again. "So a couple hours later Claudia shows up and I tell her that her mom called. Meanwhile, back in Brazil, her family is going nuts thinking something terrible has happened. Claudia calls home and her brother answers because by now, her mom is nearly hysterical and bordering on heart failure. Eventually she's able to explain that nothing is wrong and that I am merely an idiot. Of course, she's shooting me dirty looks the whole time. I'm just sitting there thinking, 'what, what did I do?'" Matt glanced at his wife who was smiling and shaking her head. "It took, what, about a year before they forgave me. Man, for a while I thought they were going to send somebody up here to shoot me."

"You're lucky they didn't," Claudia said, before turning her attention to her guests. "I hope everyone has a little bit of room left. I've made Pave de Biscoito Maria, a layered cookie tart, for dessert. It's a recipe my mother gave me, before Matt nearly killed her."

JANUARY 17

With the early morning light, the three visitors saw what the darkness hid upon their arrival. The farm, which all three agreed was beautiful, sat on 100 mostly open acres. The driveway was lined on either side by trees and pastures. The house, made of brick and totaling probably 4,000 square feet, looked like something from the Civil War era. About 100 yards to the right of the house sat their extremely well maintained barn. The barn's center aisle was poured cement and each stall came equipped with its own fan and fly spray system. Attached to the structure was an indoor riding ring where the horses had spent several hours the evening before. From the barn the ground sloped gently downward. A tree lined path led to an oversized ring set up for both jumping and dressage. Standing just outside the barn's rear entrance, Manny had a perfect view of the ring and the finely groomed four-furlong dirt training track encircling it. On the ground within the ring large letters were posted equidistant apart. Manny knew it was for dressage, but thought it looked more like some sort of equine eye exam. Jumps, white, adorned with flowers and appearing as though they'd never been touched by an errant hoof, had been set off to the sides. A lone horse and rider trotted from one corner to another. The horse's legs the only movement.

"Wow, I wonder if they need any help?" Manny said jokingly.

"If they do, let me know," James quickly countered.

Manny opened Mr. Nobody's stall door, entered the 12' by 12' enclosure and attached his leather shank. They walked out of the stall and down the center aisle, Mr. Nobody's shoes clanking as they went. James followed behind as they left the barn and began moving toward the trailer some 15 feet away. Just as Mr. Nobody reached the ramp he planted his two front feet, bringing Manny to a quick halt. Manny looked back at the horse, made some clucking noises and asked Mr. Nobody to continue up the ramp. It fell on deaf ears. Mr. Nobody didn't move a muscle. Manny tried again. Again, not a step.

Manny turned away from the trailer and began walking in the opposite direction. For reasons known only to himself, Mr. Nobody accepted the change and followed. They walked about 10 feet or so and Manny again reversed his direction. Hoping that momentum might carry them up the ramp and in, Manny headed straight ahead. Mr. Nobody put his two front feet on the ramp and stopped. From behind, James and Michael clucked and waved their hands trying to get Mr. Nobody moving forward to no avail.

"Bring him back around," Michael said as he went and retrieved the lunge whip. Manny repeated his previous steps and came around again.

This time Michael stood behind them encouraging Mr. Nobody with a tap on the rear end. The tap had its intended effect and Mr. Nobody made it halfway up the ramp before stopping again. Michael moved forward as Manny held on tightly not wanting the horse to move backwards. Michael cracked the whip behind him, not hitting him but letting him know it was there. Mr. Nobody wasn't amused. He raised his rear and kicked out at the unseen threat. The kick threw Manny off balance and he lost a little of his grip. Realizing he had gained some freedom, Mr. Nobody threw his head in the air pulling Manny toward him. Now it was over, the shank went slack and Mr. Nobody had his whole head. He jumped to the right and off the ramp and there was nothing Manny, Michael or James could do. "Come on you damn horse!" Michael said. "Try it again Manny!"

Manny took a strong hold of the uncooperative animal and circled once more. This time Michael prompted Mr. Nobody with a heavier tap and continued it as the moved forward toward the ramp. But again forward progress stalled as they reached it. This time Mr. Nobody immediately began bucking. Time to take a break. After two long days on the road it appeared at least one of the travelers was in no hurry to continue the trek. In fact, they were all tired and patience ran thin.

"Hey Manny," James said. "Take him back to the barn entrance and just wait a couple minutes." Manny did as he was told and Mr. Nobody began to settle down. James walked to the truck, opened the front door and then the glove box. Inside sat a bag of hard candies, the mint kind, like the ones always around at Christmas time. He grabbed a couple and headed to the back of the trailer, hearing his dad's advice so many years ago, "Force is your last resort. Once you get the broom out, it's war. Try mints, try anything before the broom." He walked up the ramp and stood at the top. He looked toward Manny. "Has he calmed down?" Manny nodded his head yes. "OK, bring him forward slowly." Manny did so and as they reached the base of the ramp James began to unwrap the candies. Mr. Nobody pricked his ears and stared at the James' hands. "Come on boy, want some mints, come on."

Mr. Nobody cautiously put his two front feet on the ramp, stopped and then stretched out his neck as far as it would go. Unfortunately for him, it didn't reach. "Come on boy, a little farther." In the background Matt Johnson, with Lester at his side, watched the game, having been there more times than he could count himself. It was entertaining to watch, unless of course it's your own horse misbehaving. Mr. Nobody took a couple more steps forward and again stretched out for the candy. James rolled them around in his hand so his horse could hear them. Finally Mr. Nobody couldn't take it anymore and made his way up the ramp. James quickly backtracked until they were all well inside the trailer. Then he let him have them. "I thought this might work. He loves these things. It's like a Scooby Snack, he'd do anything for it." Manny smiled, glad to have finally gotten him in the trailer.

Once one horse was in, the other two went in without a fight. At last they were ready to begin their final leg. "Good luck gentlemen," Matt said shaking each of their hands. "Remember, all I want is Derby tickets."

"Thank you very much for everything Matt. It was a real pleasure meeting you and your wife," Michael said, the anger-induced sweat on his brow dissipating in the cool morning air. "If we get to the Derby, you'll be there." The doors to the truck closed, James put it in drive and away they went.

Chapter 4

~

THE SIGN POSTED ALONG INTERSTATE 95 declared "Welcome To Florida, The Sunshine State." In a few more hours they would be in Tampa, their final destination. Michael and Jack had decided to stable at Tampa Bay Downs since that's where Mr. Nobody and Glitter could compete. Sing would train there and, when ready, would travel the four hours to Gulfstream Park.

"Manny," James said as he rolled down his window, "how does it feel to be coming back here? It's been quite a while hasn't it?"

Manny stared out the truck window, the warm Florida air blowing through the cab. It sure had been a while, he thought. The palm trees looked familiar, but at the same time, it seemed like it had been a lifetime since he had lived here. So much had changed and yet so little. Manny had spent the better part of three years living in Florida, right in the Tampa area. He was just 16 when his father Ernesto was killed in a traffic accident. Having no relatives in the United States other than his aunt and uncle, the courts ordered Manny to go and live with them in Tampa.

Originally from Guatemala, Manny's father came to the United States through a Catholic mission group. His parents lived in a very poor area and this was an opportunity for Ernesto to make a better life for himself. After struggling through high school he went to work on a ranch where he learned to ride and break horses. His riding skills grew to be legendary in west Texas where he lived. The ranch's owner eventually encouraged

Ernesto to ride in the rodeo. His abilities would give him a chance to make a good living, much better than being a ranch hand. Ernesto agreed and became an instant success. But that was not enough. Ernesto's father taught him to always strive to improve himself and with that in mind, he began taking English lessons. It was there he met Susan, his teacher. Chemistry instantaneous, they tried to keep their feelings at bay, but in the end, neither succeeded. They began a relationship outside the classroom and within a year it blossomed into an undeniable love. Within 18 months, they married. A little over a year later, the two welcomed their first child, Manny.

Life was good in the Hernandez house. Ernesto made a nice living in the rodeo, allowing Susan to stay at home with Manny and letting them travel as a family when Ernesto had to go out of town. That all ended just after Manny turned 5. His mother became ill and was diagnosed with ovarian cancer. They initially reacted with shock, but quickly found their fighting spirit. "She will beat it Manny, don't worry," his dad used to tell him. Unfortunately, it didn't take long before the reality of the situation came to bear. His parents traveled from doctor to doctor, often times with Manny in tow. Though the doctors changed, the news never did. It was grim. The cancer had spread and the outlook was bleak. Vivid memories of his dad pleading with a doctor remained in Manny's head, despite his young age at the time. His dad's voice cracking as he spoke, "there must be something you can do, anything, please doctor, please." That image of his father, normally so strong, begging the doctors frightened Manny. It changed how he saw his dad, his superhero became human. In that moment his world changed. Even today, after all these years, that scene playing in his head made him shiver. But all the doctors could offer was their advice. Make the best of what time remains. But how do you watch your world collapse and still smile? How do you enjoy anything knowing you have a month, maybe two, before you say goodbye, never to see them again? It was impossible. Manny's mom fought hard and put up a strong front, but the sound of crying kept him awake at night. Sometimes his own, more often his dad.

As time went by, Susan spent more and more time in bed, each day growing weaker. She tried to give Manny as much time as her tired body would allow. Offering him every ounce of love she had, hoping it would last him through the years. But Manny was young, too young to understand and all that remained of those fateful days were faint recollections. The odd sight of a hospital bed parked smack dab in the middle of their living room. It seemed so weird, so out of place. He remembered holding her hand while she lay in that bed, her grip so weak, so different from before. He remembered the long tube flowing down from the clear bag into to his mom's arm, the steady drip, drip, drip. "Morphine," the nurse said, a hint of compassion in her voice. It meant nothing to a 5-year-old. He wondered if it hurt her, the tube stuck in her arm like that. And then of course the faint smile, the caring, gentle smile of a woman who would never, ever hold him again.

Three months after the initial diagnosis she died. Manny slept quietly in his own bed when it happened. His dad came in and woke him. They hugged and cried, for how long Manny couldn't say. It would turn out to be the second worst night of his life. Manny couldn't comprehend why his mom had been taken from him. To a 5-year-old, or even a 35-year-old, it just didn't seem fair. The laughter that always filled the house, the happiness that seemed to accompany their daily lives had disappeared. For what felt like an eternity there was nothing but tears. The heart of their family was gone.

With the help of friends and the church, Ernesto fought to overcome the devastation and go on with his life. There was no choice; he had a son who needed his care, a son who desperately needed to feel the love and happiness that so suddenly vanished. The entire church community helped out wherever they could. They would take turns watching Manny when Ernesto needed to travel. When Ernesto was in town, they made sure someone came by to visit, just to say hi.

Once Manny got older, Ernesto started taking him along once again. His grades suffered but his relationship with his father grew stronger. One night when Manny was 13 and they were out of town in some no-name motel Ernesto pulled out a letter. It was addressed to Manny. Manny could tell by the handwriting it was written by a woman.

"I think you're old enough to have this now," his dad said, handing the envelope to him.

Manny looked at it and then at his dad. Ernesto nodded, letting Manny know it was alright to open it. "This is from Mom, isn't it?"

"Yes. There was so much she wanted to tell you, but at your age..."

Manny looked back at the envelope, cautiously opening it. Inside was a message from a mother that existed only faintly in his mind. His heart raced and he trembled, struggling to hold it steady enough to read. The exquisite handwriting contained far more than words, it told of who she was, the person Manny never truly knew. How she met his father and how much she loved and admired him. How joyful they were the day she gave birth to Manny. How funny Manny was running through the house half naked, swinging his diaper as he went. Manny laughed, a tear falling down his cheek. The world around him disappeared as he went from page to page, trying desperately to go as slow as his racing mind would allow, savoring each word. She wrote so beautifully, he thought, so eloquently. Manny could hear her voice in each sentence, as if she were there, sitting with him, speaking softly.

The letter ran six pages, but nowhere near enough for the hole Manny needed to fill. She told him that he was the greatest son a mother could ever ask for and she would be watching him from above so he'd never be alone. His vision blurry with tears, Manny tried stoically to hold it together, but her final words were more than he could take.

"I pray every night that you will remember me. You have given me so much. I only hope that one day you will know how much you meant to me. Bringing you into this world was the greatest thing I ever did. I will love you forever, Mom."

Manny sat and cried, Ernesto hugging and crying with him. A father and his son, mourning a loss from which neither would fully recover. They talked into the early morning hours, Manny asking questions and Ernesto answering them, describing the greatest woman he'd ever known.

They laughed and they cried until they were emotionally spent, finally going to sleep, their bond stronger than ever before. When they arrived back home, a couple days later, Manny put the envelope in his drawer. Over the next few years he would look at it every day and every day he would think of his mother, wishing for more.

In the time that followed, Ernesto worked with Manny, teaching him how to care for the horses, both their physical and mental well-being and how to care for his tack; soaping, washing, even mending the leather. Of course, Manny also learned to ride and how to communicate with the horse using the gentle touch of his legs and hands. But just as important, his dad often told him, is learning to understand what the horse is telling you by his actions, how he moves, how he carries himself. And learn Manny did, with an ease that surprised his father. Though it may not have been traditional, it was indeed an education.

With only a couple more years of high school left, Manny and Ernesto began talking about the future. Manny wanted to join the rodeo like his dad, but Ernesto pushed for Manny to go to college. The conversations went round and round, usually ending with Manny out-talking his father.

"You should go to college," Ernesto would say.

"Why, you didn't go to college and you make lots of money."

"I make OK money. I'd probably make a lot more if I had a college degree."

"But God gave you a gift, a talent to ride. You said you should always use the gifts God gives you. If you worked in an office, you wouldn't be using your gift."

"But it would be safer. I wouldn't risk getting hurt all the time. Sometimes you have to think of your family."

"But I don't have a family."

"Well someday you will and you need to think ahead. Think about your long-term future. If you got hurt and couldn't ride, then you'd have no means of support."

"Yeah, but you've never been hurt."

"That's only because I've been very lucky. The sport is very dangerous and you know it."

"So, if you worked in an office every day, would you be happy?" Manny asked, knowing he was about to win the argument.

Ernesto paused ever so briefly before attempting to answer. But that pause was all Manny needed and he cut Ernesto off before Ernesto could begin. "No, see you wouldn't."

"Yes I would, yes I would."

"No you wouldn't Papa and you know it. And you wouldn't be using your God-given talent. And you told me never to make decisions based on money, money is not the most important thing. You told me that, remember? I should always follow my heart. You said that too."

Sufficiently flustered and without answers, Ernesto gave up. "You know, you are just like your mother. I could never win an argument with her either."

Manny smiled and waited for him to be almost out of earshot before adding sarcastically. "I love you Papa." Ernesto normally responded with a grumble and wave of his arms. Days, or maybe weeks later, Ernesto would think of some other way to phrase things and try again, but the outcome was always the same. The issue remained unresolved.

Chapter 5

~

MANNY WAITED AT SCHOOL FOR his dad, ready to be picked up for another weekend on the road. When his dad didn't show, Manny knew something was wrong. Maybe the truck broke down, he thought, it hadn't been running right lately. He wondered if his dad would get in trouble if they didn't hit the road on time. He sure hoped not. But then again he shouldn't, they just needed to get there in time for him to ride tomorrow morning. Feeling concerned, but comfortable that everything would be fine, Manny sat and waited and the hours ticked by. Finally at six o'clock, friends of the family came to get him. As they approached, their faces betrayed their emotions. Suddenly, a broken-down truck wasn't the worry. "What's going on?"

They looked at one another, pain radiating from their eyes. There were no words that could soften such a blow.

"What is it?"

Shedding tears of their own, they broke the news of the accident, the terrible accident. The shrieking brakes, the tractor-trailer ripping across the median, the collision. And then, having no alternative, the death. In an instant, Manny's life changed, again. A sharp, crippling pain swept up one side of him and then down the other. He felt drained of all his strength and his knees buckled, sending him falling to the ground. The others quickly helped him, trying to get him back to his feet.

"I need to see him!" Manny demanded, swaying slightly, trying to maintain his balance. "Where is he? WHERE IS HE?" They tried to explain, tried to say sorry, to touch and comfort him, but he was inconsolable. His eyes darted from person to person and then somewhere a thousand yards in the distance. Rational thought ceased, his mind was not willing to accept the outcome. "Somebody take me to him! Now, somebody! I need to see my dad right now. Where is he?" Manny tried to calm himself, convince himself that things weren't what they seemed. He just needed to see him, to talk to him. Then things would be back to normal. "He'll be OK, I know he will. I just need to see him." His father wasn't gone. It couldn't be true, it was a mistake. Maybe he was just hurt really bad and they were wrong. The others exchanged anguished glances, no one knowing how to respond.

"Take me to my father!!"

"OK Manny, OK. We'll take you there."

They drove to the morgue and brought Manny to his father. There had been no mistake. When Manny's mother died part of his soul died with her. The last 11 years with his father slowly, partially, refilled that vacancy. Now he was gone, forever, and without even a goodbye. Manny was without the only two people he had ever loved and without hope. To this day, he has no idea how long he stood by his dead father. At some point while standing there his mind shut down, his memory stopped recording. His next recollection wouldn't be until well after the funeral. A funeral he still has no memory of.

At first, friends of the family tried to take in Manny, but still being a child, the courts refused. Manny headed to Tampa to an aunt and uncle he didn't know and who had never raised any children. He started going to high school, but was slow to make friends. Nothing interested him. He never played traditional sports, felt no interest in any of the after-school clubs and knew that most of the kids not involved in activities usually found trouble. Then he discovered Tampa Bay Downs Race Track. There he found something familiar, the sound and smell of horses.

Having little money but plenty of time, Manny sought a part-time job on the backstretch. The transient nature of the backside worker aided him. There always seemed a need for someone who knew their way around horses and was responsible enough to show up day in and day out. It didn't take long before Manny's services were desired.

As time went by he began spending more time around the race track and less time at school. Being around the horses and the horse hands re-minded him of the rodeo. It was a comfortable feeling at a time when he had nothing else. He eventually dropped out of school and began working in the barns full time. His aunt and uncle, not really knowing what to do with him, let him go. He was staying out of trouble, so what more could they ask.

Things took a turn for Manny on what seemed another routine Monday morning. "Manny, we're going over to the backside kitchen to get some breakfast, you want to come along?" asked Oliver, one of the exercise riders.

"No, I brought something with me. Thanks."

"Are you sure? Ralph is cooking up his famous Jamaican Omelets. They're awful good," Oliver said with a big smile.

"That's OK, I'm good. Plus I'm trying to save up some money to buy a truck."

"Alright, have it your way. But you don't know what you're missing."

Manny smiled and continued cleaning his tack. An hour later he wan-dered over to the kitchen to get a cup of coffee.

"Hey Ralph, I hear you made the guys something special today," Manny said, looking into the outdoor kitchen which resembled more of an oversized snack stand than a kitchen.

Ralph approached slowly. "Hey Manny," he said, sweat beading on his head. "Made more omelets than I can count. The boys were hungry today."

"Ralph, you don't look so good, kind of pale. Are you feeling alright?"

"Yeah, yeah. I'm just a bit worn out. What can I get for you?"

"A cup of coffee please."

"Sure thing Manny."

The next day Manny arrived as usual. "Hey Manny."

Manny turned to see his friend sitting atop some nameless thoroughbred walking toward the track. "Hey Oliver, how's it going?"

Oliver grinned, "I hope you brought your breakfast this morning."

"Why?"

"Ralph is out sick today and nobody's manning the kitchen. We're all starving."

"I told him he didn't look good yesterday. I hope he's OK."

"I'm sure he'll be fine, "Oliver called out, now a good 15 yards from Manny. "The rest of us could be in trouble though if somebody doesn't fire up that kitchen."

"Ah, you'll survive," Manny yelled back. "You could stand to lose a few pounds anyway."

On Wednesday morning Manny showed up bright and early, and like the day before, Ralph was out sick. But this time he wasn't alone. Along with him was better than half of the backside workers, exercise riders included. A casual observer would have thought Tampa Bay Downs was getting ready to close for the year. The normal robust activity seemed to have ground to a halt. Horses waited patiently to be ridden and groomed. Trainers waited impatiently, wondering how their horses would keep to schedule. There existed a classic economic imbalance. Large demand, little supply.

Without Manny realizing it, a door opened for him. Thinking it might be fun, he volunteered to exercise the horses and given the situation, no one could say no. The horses were big, strong and fast, and Manny couldn't stop smiling the entire time he circled the track. The word fun didn't do it justice. Combining the animal he loved with a young man's need for speed, Manny found something special. He wasn't about to complain about being a groom, but this was definitely more stimulating. What's more, his ability was quickly recognized by the trainers. He rode the horses in the manner they wanted and came back with quality feedback. By the time the virus subsided, Manny had worked himself into a new position, exercise rider.

"Well?" said James, "what do you think?"

Realizing that he hadn't responded to James' question, Manny looked up, "Uh yeah, it has been a while." He paused for a moment, "I guess it feels a little strange."

"To me," James replied, "it just feels a little warm. And I think I like it!"

Manny laughed. James had become a brother to him and Manny felt very fortunate to have connected with the O'Briens. With the truck quiet again, Manny's mind wandered back once more, but not quite as far back this time.

Oliver had already dismounted when Manny came walking up atop his charge. "That was the last of them," Oliver said.

"OK." Manny took his feet out of the irons and slid off. Groom Jose Felix helped Manny slide the bridle off Harlandale's head and replace it with a halter and then paused as Manny removed his saddle. Once done, Felix and horse began walking circles around the shedrow. All part of the cool down process after a strong workout.

Oliver and Manny hung their bridles on the tack hooks and hoisted their saddles atop the saddle stand, then took a bucket full of soapy water and began cleaning the days grime. "Hey Manny, you've been exercising 'em for almost a year now, haven't you?" Oliver asked.

Manny tilted his head, looking off in the distance as he did so. "Yeah, I guess that seems about right."

"Did you ever think about becoming a jockey? You know, instead of just exercising."

Manny held the cheek piece of the bridle, but stopped soaping it, contemplating the question. He watched a trainer walk by, followed closely by a jockey's agent jabbering nonstop in his ear. "Sometimes..."

"Well you should," Oliver said before Manny had a chance to finish his thought. "You're a real good rider and the trainers think a lot of you. What are you weighing in at? You probably wouldn't even have to drop any weight."

"Yeah, it would be pretty cool, but I don't know," Manny said, shrugging his shoulders. "Who am I to think I'd be a decent jock? I'm just some kid riding horses in the morning."

"That's where you're wrong," Oliver said pointing at him, soapy water flinging off his hand at Manny. "Every one of those jocks was just some kid at one point. You got the smarts to do it. Hell, I bet you're smarter than half those guys riding this afternoon."

"You think?"

"Definitely," Oliver said. "You've seen what some of those guys are like. They couldn't think themselves out from under a blanket." Manny laughed but said nothing. "Go out and get your license. It couldn't do any harm and besides, you could still exercise in the mornings. Take a shot and see what happens."

"Well maybe, I don't know. What about you? Any thoughts on doing it yourself?"

"Manny, dude, look at the size of me." Oliver opened his arms as if Manny had never seen him before. "I'm 5' 7" and about 140 pounds. There's no way I could ever get near riding weight. No, I'm an exercise rider and that's all I'll ever be."

Manny flip-flopped for a week before he made up his mind to take that shot at race riding. Once decided, Manny forced Oliver to help him apply for a jockey license, although "forced" didn't quite fit the description. Oliver jumped at the chance and filled out the application for Manny with the exception of the signature. Oliver even went so far as to wrangle his cousin Charles into being Manny's agent. Charles already represented veteran rider Irwin Fletcher, but at his cousin's request, added Manny. There was no turning back.

As he sat in the O'Briens' truck, watching the palm trees fly past, he vividly recalled the first race he rode. Getting dressed in the jocks' room he was a bundle of nerves. Not that he expected to win and it certainly wasn't a big race, a maiden claimer if he remembered correctly. It was simply the excitement of his first time. Manny smiled thinking about it. He finished nearly last in that race, but it didn't matter, the adrenaline rush overwhelmed him. A week, and about 15 mounts later, he got his first winner.

The horse, Frau Blucher, was a big and gangly filly who had run a couple times as a 2-year-old without a win. Her body and mind hadn't caught up with her long legs, so her trainer, Britt Burns, opted to pull her out of training until she'd had a chance to grow. After a six-month hiatus, Frau Blucher returned and Manny had galloped her each morning since. For three months he worked her back into shape until she was ready to try her luck again. Now that Manny was a jockey and because Britt liked him, Manny got the mount in her return to the races.

It was a 6-furlong race and "die Frau" as they referred to her broke from the gate well. She settled in mid-pack, not too far from the leaders. As they came around the turn, Manny clucked and shook the reigns at her. She responded by picking up her pace. Knowing she was still a long-legged filly without much agility in her feet, Manny decided to send her wide and outside of the congested pack. With nothing to slow her momentum, die Frau rolled past the leaders and never looked back. After the race, the other jockeys doused Manny with buckets of ice water, a common ritual and one that no jockey ever complained about.

On his way back to the jocks' room, Manny shook hands, gave high fives and felt like the king of the world. The only thing that tempered his exhilaration was watching the race replay back in the jocks' room as they changed. Coming down the stretch Manny rode like it was life or death in the Kentucky Derby. Meanwhile, his horse was leading by about 10 lengths, surely an insurmountable lead. "I think you've got it about now, Manny," one of the other jockeys said as the others began to laugh. Manny put his hands in his face. It was so embarrassing. He looked so green. But he was green, and they were just teasing, and such is the life of a newbie.

Mounts came slowly at first, but his ability to judge the pace of the race and put his horse in a position to win eventually won over many of the trainers. More and better mounts began to show up. As the wins grew, so did his confidence. Every night he'd review the next day's races. He would study his rivals and make sure he knew his own horse. This preparation led to smart decisions during the race. And that led to wins. Success bred success, and with it, thoughts of his future.

Since moving to Florida, he'd been living with his aunt and uncle, although it was hard to call it "living" since he only showed up to sleep. And his achievements on the track meant money, money he used to buy the truck he wanted and money to put in savings for furnishing a place to live. The time had come to strike out on his own. The Tampa meet was coming to a close and Manny had done well. In fact, he'd become the leading apprentice jockey at the meet. Many of the trainers and horses were heading for Calder Race Course in Miami for the summer.

Manny watched as Oliver loaded another horse, leaving yet another empty stall. "When you guys heading out?" Manny asked.

"Most of the fellas are leaving now. I need to go home and pack before I leave. So, I'll probably take off some time this afternoon. How about you? I saw you have a mount tomorrow."

"Yeah, just the one. I'll probably take off after that. I took so long to decide if I was going that I haven't even looked for a place to live yet."

"Just stay with us. I think we've got an empty room, shouldn't be a problem."

"How much is the rent?"

"I think we're all paying about $250 a month, but I'm not sure if that's for the three of us or if that'd change if you come in. Either way, I'm sure a successful jock like yourself can afford it," Oliver said, laughing.

"Yeah, yeah, I hear you," Manny replied, slightly embarrassed by the comment.

"Seriously though, I told you you'd do great. You're a natural."

"You did say it and I owe you. I probably wouldn't have done it if you hadn't pushed me."

"Well, I take cash, check or money order. I'm not picky."

Manny laughed, "Thanks man, it's nice to know you're not particular."

Oliver smiled, "Good luck tomorrow."

"Thanks," Manny said, shaking Oliver's outstretched hand. "I'll see you some time tomorrow night."

Chapter 6

~

THE RACE UNFOLDED EXACTLY AS any other. The horses broke from the gate cleanly, a little jostling took place early and then everyone settled. Manny rated toward the rear of the field with his stretch-running mount, biding his time until later in the race. With about 3 furlongs, or three eighths of a mile, to go to the finish things began to go awry and as is usually the case, the change happened at lightning speed. Fellow apprentice jockey Carlos Santiago was trapped along the rail just behind the leaders. Rather than wait for something to open up, he decided to push his way out. As he angled off the rail, Carlos' horse suddenly clipped heels with the horse in front of him, dropping his horse to the ground in a heap and himself flying head first over the top.

The jockeys following behind, including Manny, braced, some veering in, others veering out, others frozen, everyone trying to avoid the fallen pair, but for some, there was no time and nowhere to go. A rail on one side, a wall of horses on the other. It was an accident you could see coming, but couldn't avoid. With no other options, Manny's mount attempted to jump the fallen horse who was now beginning to get up. Manny clutched, jamming his heels instinctively in his irons and dropping his ass to the back of the saddle, waiting to feel the collision, feel the bone-jarring thud of thousand-pound animals ramming one another. But it didn't happen. His horse cleared the animal by the narrowest of margins. Manny's eyes shifted back to the front and in that split second, his elation – his relief – disappeared.

Just beyond the rising horse lay Carlos, obscured from view until it was too late. The left front leg of Manny's horse came down on top of the fallen apprentice. The landing, awkward enough for Manny in the high stirrups, was made nearly impossible as his horse shifted quickly to evade Carlos. Manny couldn't hold on and tumbled to the ground, landing hard on his knee. The remainder of the horses and jockeys continued, the sound of their hoof-beats fading into the distance. Manny laid there in the sudden silence, writhing in pain, staring at the motionless body of his friend. Carlos was dead before they made it to the hospital.

After undergoing a series of tests, the doctors determined that the damage to his knee was only minor. But they never tested the damage to his psyche. Just days before, Manny had a clear path toward his future. Suddenly, he felt like someone had dropped him in the middle of a forest, trees and brush screening his view in every direction. He needed someone to talk to, to sort out his feelings. But Oliver and the rest of the guys were at Calder. And he barely spoke to his aunt and uncle. Of course, the man he really needed was gone, killed in his own accident, never to return. So Manny held it in and went back to grooming the horses while his knee mended.

At first, everything went fine, but as each month passed Manny began to feel more and more sullen. Most of the trainers and workers, and all the jockeys, were at Calder and those who stayed behind were what some might call the "B" team, not exactly the cream of the crop. Manny knew a few of them before and after a couple months, he figured he knew about enough. Too many of them represented the darker side of the track. Guys that got into trouble much too often. Guys his dad referred to as "unsavory characters." Manny went about his daily chores and that's what they'd become, daily chores. There was no fun, no banter with his pals, just work. The only thing that kept him going was knowing his buddies would eventually return.

It took six months before he could ride again, right about the time everyone was returning to Tampa. Manny looked forward to getting back to riding, but looked forward to his friends returning even more. As each van pulled in with more horses returning for the winter, Manny's spirits lifted. He wanted things back the way they were before the accident, though he knew that not everything could change right away. During his riding hiatus, Manny put on 10 pounds, along with growing about a half inch. He was still small by normal standards, standing 5'5", but his weight rose to 122 pounds, too heavy to be a jockey. Still being young, Manny could work himself back to racing weight. Injuries happen all the time and working themselves back into shape is what jockeys do. Moreover, it's what jockeys who want to ride again do. But mentally, Manny wasn't near where he'd been. His focus was solely on his returning friends, not race riding.

Manny turned the barn corner and spotted his friend wiping down his saddle. "Oliver, there you are. When did you get back?"

"Hey Manny, good to see you." Oliver wiped his wet hand off on his pants before shaking Manny's hand. "We got back a couple days ago."

"Oh, I hadn't seen you. Sure am glad you're back. This place was brutal with everyone gone."

"Probably real quiet I imagine."

"Quiet and boring. And most of the guys that stayed weren't worth anything. Screwed around a lot more than they worked."

"Knowing some of the guys that were here, that doesn't surprise me."

"So are you going to live in that place you were at before, or have you figured that out yet?"

"Yeah, actually Zeke, Frank and I got a place together. Had a little cook-out last night to christen the place."

"That sounds great," Manny said, the air going out of his voice.

"You still staying at your aunt and uncle's place?"

"Yes, but I was hoping to maybe get out of there soon."

"You definitely should." Oliver said, beginning to wipe down his saddle again. Manny stood and watched, his hands in his pockets, suddenly feeling awkward.

"You been riding again?" asked Oliver.

"Yeah, just started back. Knee's a little sore, but should be fine. Need to get used to riding again. How about you? I haven't seen you over at Britt's barn."

"I'm not really riding much for him anymore, mostly with Simmons and McMullan."

"Oh, no wonder I haven't seen you." Oliver nodded, knowing their barns would be on opposite ends of the facility. "You want to get some lunch after we're done this morning."

"Actually, I can't. I'm supposed to go with Zeke to look at a car he's thinking of buying. But definitely sometime."

"OK," Manny said. "Well, I'm gonna head back now. Good to see you Oliver."

"Alright Manny, I'm sure I'll be seeing you."

The racing may have returned to Tampa, but the fun and camaraderie didn't come back with it. Things had changed. Manny stuck it out for a few more months, but his old friends had moved on with their lives and it seemed time Manny did the same. Having reached 18, he was free to go wherever he chose. But he still liked exercising horses, even just being around the horses made him feel better. He realized he wanted to stay in the business, but the question was where to go. During the winter months, he had worked for some trainers who came from Finger Lakes Race Track in New York. That became his destination.

So Manny stood in his room, a room that was completely unchanged since he'd moved in a little more than 2 years before, and prepared to leave. A black and red Tampa Bay Buccaneers duffel bag and a light blue American Tourister suitcase lay on his bed. They contained everything he had in the world. Every piece of clothing, every official document and every family photo. Pictures of a family that no longer existed. He left his room and met his aunt and uncle in the kitchen. He told them of his plans and said goodbye. Then he was gone, as quickly as that. But as luck would have it, for a change, his timing was perfect.

For the last 40 years, Henry Williamson had been grooming and taking care of the O'Briens' horses. He finally decided it was time to call it quits, on a full time basis anyway. He promised to stick around long enough for Michael to find his replacement, which Michael figured to be a difficult task. And if it were just Michael doing the looking, it certainly would have been. But Henry knew everyone and everything going on along the backstretch. He was aware of the new guy and made a point to seek him out and talk to him. Henry liked what he saw and heard. The kid did what was needed without complaint. He understood the job, both horse and human elements. Most of all, the kid avoided the trouble makers. Henry knew Manny would be a good fit for an honest operation such as the O'Briens'. Like a good jocks' agent, Henry turned in his resignation and already had a replacement in mind. It was just a matter of introducing the two.

Michael had no idea who this Manny fellow was, but he trusted Henry's judgment when it came to people, as well as horses. Michael needed a groom and this kid needed a job and so began their association. The relationship, like most working relationships, started slowly as the individuals got to know one another. Personalities had to mesh and the O'Brien way needed to be learned. But the transition went well; the quality of those involved making it easy.

Each day Michael doled out his instructions and without fail Manny followed them swiftly and diligently, no questions asked. In Manny, Michael found a quiet, responsible kid, who stayed out of trouble and gave nice feedback after each ride. There was no drama, no trouble. It gave Michael one less thing to worry about.

James was also impressed by the kid's professionalism, but more than anything, he liked the fact that Manny laughed at his jokes. Henry was a great guy, but he was old and his sense of humor was lacking. And of course anything was better than Michael.

Jack recognized Manny for what he was, a diamond in the rough. He'd been around long enough to realize when you've got somebody good, take care of him. Following that logic, when Manny's apartment lease was up, Jack offered him the apartment above the barn. The only condition was that Manny had to finish high school. Nothing was free in life. Manny agreed and enrolled himself in night classes at nearby Livonia High School.

Of course Manny wasn't the most studious and when he began to struggle Margaret offered her services as a tutor. Having an empty nest, she enjoyed looking after him. And Manny definitely enjoyed the home-cooked meals. He made sure at least a couple times a week to request a little help in the hour just before dinner. It's funny how the timing always seemed to work out just right.

After two years of part-time classes Manny completed everything necessary and the high school allowed him to join the full-time students at the year-end ceremony. The commencement took place at an outdoor amphitheater on the campus of the local community college on a lovely June day. Manny felt out of place, being about four years older than any other graduate, but he was proud of what he'd accomplished and was thankful to the O'Briens for having pushed him to do it. And he was grateful to have the O'Brien family in attendance to see him receive his diploma. They cheered – James stood up and wailed, "Whoot. Whooot. Whoooot," as he made his way across the stage. It was a great moment for Manny. Although nothing could replace his mom and dad, the O'Briens gave him something he'd forgotten. Four years later, Manny still lived in the apartment above the barn and although he didn't need his tutor, he still found ways of being in the kitchen around dinner time.

Chapter 7

~

FEBRUARY 1

Jᴀᴄᴋ ꜱᴀᴛ ᴀᴛ ᴛʜᴇ ᴋɪᴛᴄʜᴇɴ table reviewing the pile of bills, sipping yet another cup of coffee. In front of him lay his version of a checkbook. An 8-column, green, accounting ledger pad – the type no longer sold in stores. When Staples listed it as discontinued, Jack bought the remaining 10 packs, 50 pads in total. Figured it would last him fifteen years or so and if he was still alive after that, he'd make a change.

Margaret walked into the kitchen and seeing what Jack was up to, reversed direction. Even when times were good, she wanted no part it. Jack cursed and complained after each check. Then he'd write them in the ledger, see the balance in the bank drop and curse again. If the cat walked by, he'd curse at the cat. If kid walked by, he'd give them chores and double it if they talked back. Even Margaret wasn't immune to the wrath, though Jack was careful not to push that too far. So when the phone rang Jack decided to get up and answer it. There are times when a distraction is welcomed, now being one. Jack grabbed the receiver and gave a quick, "Yeah."

"Dad, its Michael. Thought I'd give you a call and update you."

"Yeah good, so how's he doing so far?" There was no need to clarify the "he." Sing was the reason they were in Florida. His progress was all that really mattered.

"He's settling in really well. We've had him jogging around the track and taking things in. So far, he seems much calmer than last summer."

"Well let's hope that continues," said Jack. "I was just paying the bills and I don't like what I'm seeing."

With some hesitation in his voice, Michael felt inclined to pursue it further. "How bad is it?"

"It's not terrible yet, but we need that horse to run well, and sooner rather than later. With both you and your brother down there, it will be at least May before we have some regular runners at Finger Lakes." The Finger Lakes season began in April and James didn't plan on returning until mid-March. Michael and Manny would remain in Florida until sometime in April, hoping to run in the big race. Of course, Kentucky on the first Saturday in May was the ultimate goal, but nobody uttered that sentiment. After that, they would haul the horses back to New York. Once James returned it would be another six to eight weeks before the horses were race ready and until they could compete, there was no money coming into the O'Brien bank accounts.

Michael continued, "I expect, as long as everything goes smoothly, he should be ready to run by the end of the month."

"That sounds good," responded Jack. "And tell your brother this isn't some sort of vacation. I expect him to be working down there."

"Will do Dad," Michael said. Dad certainly knew his sons, he thought, knew them too well.

FEBRUARY 7

Manny patted Sing's neck as they walked back toward the barn. The sun, a vibrant orange color, was just breaking over the horizon. Sing was still puffing a little, not quite in shape yet, but getting there. He was making progress and acting like a pure gentleman. If things continued on this path, he should definitely be ready to race in a few weeks.

Although Manny enjoyed riding Sing and the other horses every day, being back at Tampa brought back conflicting memories. Some were good; like that special moment when he hit the wire in his first winning race, a jubilation he'd never experienced before and knew he'd never forget. Or the respect and acceptance he slowly but steadily gained from his fellow jockeys. And then of course there was the knowledge that he'd achieved it all on his own, through dedication and hard work. Those were fond memories.

But they weren't all like that, some unfortunately were bad; like the reason for being there in the first place, a feeling that never seemed to go away and then there was the race that ended things and the changes that followed. These reminiscences seemed to overshadow the good. Overall, a sense of loneliness, even during the good times, hung over him. It was the prevailing emotion. Those years in Florida were simply another difficult chapter in Manny's life. No other way to put it. Though his aunt and uncle were nice, decent people, Manny never knew them before that fateful day he arrived and they had never known him. That's tough stuff for a teenager, let alone someone who's just lost the only parent they had ever known.

But Manny was older now and those years after his father's death had forced him to grow up fast. The O'Briens planned on staying in Florida through the beginning of April. Even if being here made Manny uncomfortable, he could deal with it until then. He did look forward to getting back north though, no matter how cold. He missed his room above the barn, the sound of Jack growling at everyone and most of all he missed Margaret. She was the mother he never got to know. She would make special meals for him, attempt to speak Spanish with him, which was always comical because she wasn't very good at it, and made him feel like he was part of the family. A couple months he thought and we'll be heading back home. Manny could feel Sing's breathing returning to normal and he ran his hand through Sing's reddish brown mane. "What's a couple months, eh boy?"

FEBRUARY 13

"What's it look like?" James asked, leaning over the shedrow railing.

Michael continued to stare at the paperwork resting in his lap. His portable chair setup in front of the three stalls the O'Briens occupied. "He's right on schedule. I haven't had to adjust one thing." Raising his head, he looked at James, "He should be ready just as I projected."

"Excellent. I tell you, I really like his manner," James said, now pacing in front of the stalls. "He is definitely better now than he was last year. Whether it's being gelded or being more mature at 3, I don't know. But he certainly is acting the best he's ever been."

"Well, maybe all that work we've done with him is paying off," Michael dryly replied.

"Hopefully so. He's seems much more at ease. Things don't bother him like they did before. Remember last fall when that tarp blew off the manure pile?" Michael laughed, remembering the event. "God, he freaked out like there was no tomorrow. I think it took him a week to recover. I still can't get him to walk anywhere near that area."

"Yeah," Michael smiled, again laughing, no longer focused on his papers. "Poor, mental horse. He was completely stiff for about 15 minutes. Every muscle in his body was flexed tight."

"Let's hope those days are gone now. I really think he's got a great chance to be a Grade 1 horse. I mean, I hate to say it out loud, but man, he's something."

"Please don't say it out loud. Things are going too well. I don't want to jinx it."

"Too late, already said," James countered. "And you shouldn't be so superstitious. It makes you even more anal."

"Hey, you've been around this business long enough. Things could tank in an instant. I don't count my chickens before they hatch. That's all I'm saying."

James walked over to Sing's stall and glanced at the big chestnut gelding. Sing came to him and nudged him with his nose, hoping to prompt a treat. James petted Sing's forehead, running his hand through Sing's forelock. "You need to think more positively. All that negativity can affect the horses."

In the background, Michael turned his attention back to his papers while simultaneously shaking his head, an indiscernible "I'm sure" barely audible under his breath.

FEBRUARY 17

The apartment the O'Briens were renting wasn't more than 800 square feet, which at times seemed smaller than that. There wasn't much to do once you left the track, so quite often Michael, James and Manny found themselves cooped up together, trying not to get on one another's nerves. But at the moment no one was around, so James, sitting there alone, figured it was a good time to call home and check on the family. Lauren answered on the first ring and James led in with an overly enthusiastic "Hi honey!"

Lauren responded with "I told you never to call me here," which prompted a quick laugh from James. "Oh, it's you James," she said pausing for effect, "Awww, I knew that."

"It's OK honey, I actually thought I was calling my mistress. I must have dialed incorrectly."

"You wish!" She said, initiating another round of laughs from both sides. After going over the usual topics of work, the child and household issues, the conversation wound around to how things were with the horses and then how she was doing without James there. Lauren missed seeing and talking to him every day. His positive look on life, laid-back approach and sense of humor were the things she loved the most. It helped her decompress after long days at work. She was the breadwinner in the family, not that she cared. James was good at what he did and he worked hard. The fact that his job didn't come with a lot of money didn't bother her. What she wanted out of a man she'd spotted the first time they'd met.

It was the year after she graduated college. She and some of her girl-friends were attending the annual white water derby, a local charity event each spring that combines melting snow, a swollen creek and large group of lunatic rafters. The rafters are challenged with building a homemade seafaring vessel and then floating their way down the creek. Winners are judged on style, creativity and speed, though most are simply hoping to finish the course without sinking.

James and a couple of his buddies attended regularly, this year being no exception. They had created a lovely craft using an oversized bathtub as its centerpiece. Keeping it afloat was four empty 55 gallon drums, some two-by-fours and a lot of rope. The drums sat at the four corners with the two-by-fours and rope to secure them. The tub was lodged semi-securely in the middle. At the back of the tub, a couple more boards were nailed in place to create a pair of seats, one on either end. Two of the mariners would sit there and attempt to steer the vessel, while the third would stay up front and point out the obstacles.

About midway through the event, Lauren and her friends caught site of the guys. They were dressed as pirates and had the skull and crossbones flying from a makeshift mast. Two of the swashbucklers were paddling frantically trying to avoid a set of rocks protruding from the water directly in their path. James was standing in the front of the tub, but rather than assisting his mates, he was screaming he was the king of the world. That was, of course, until he saw Lauren and the girls. Then he lost focus.

He smiled, pointed at the girls and was midway through a long hello when the Tortuga Tub, as they had named her, hit the rocks at full speed. The three pirates were launched forward, James flipping head over heels out of the tub and landing in the water. The girls lost site of the crew as they floated downstream, trying desperately to get James out of the cold water and back aboard.

Later on that day, Lauren ran into James again when rafters and spectators gathered for drinks, a barbecue and the awards ceremony.

"I see you've changed into some dryer clothes after your little spill," Lauren said.

"Yes, that was a bit unfortunate. I blame my crew," James replied.

"Of course, of course. But aren't you supposed to be their captain. They follow your lead."

"Well they should, but really they're just two village idiots. It's very difficult to find a good crew."

"I see," Lauren laughed, "so, it sounds like it was a ship of fools."

James couldn't contain his smile. "Well, that's a bit harsh, but probably pretty accurate."

That started a conversation which lasted well into the evening. James even found a way to sneak "shiver me timber" in while describing how cold the water was. Counting that day, they'd been together for 10 years, married for seven and not one sense of regret for either in all that time.

Before they got off the phone Lauren made sure to put Sydney on to say hi to Daddy. Sydney, like many 4-year-old girls, had an endless supply of stories. She told him about the ice cream party they had at daycare, the tea party she was currently having with her Barbie's, the new Wiggles CD she got that mom made her turn off after playing ten times in a row, and then there was something about her friend Liesel's cat having its butt shaved. That one intrigued James, but rather than pressing Sydney, he decided to make a mental note and ask Lauren about it another time. Eventually Sydney ran out of steam.

James declared his love to his two best girls and told them he would see them in about a month. The warm weather felt nice, but he missed his girls and was looking forward to seeing them. As he hung up the phone he smiled. Life was pretty good, he thought, pretty good indeed.

FEBRUARY 23

While everyone else was thinking about home, Michael couldn't think of anything but Sing's upcoming race. He stood in the grandstand at Gulfstream Park, having just officially entered Sing in a race four days later. It would be the start to what everyone was hoping was a banner year. Sing had impressed them so much, that taking a shot at the biggest 3-year-old races in the country didn't seem that big a stretch. Although he didn't feel Sing was 100 percent yet, he did feel he was ready to run and they needed to get the show, his show, on the road.

Having taken in the view from the grandstand long enough, Michael decided to check the barn facilities, which was most of the reason he made the four-hour drive from Tampa. He could have entered Sing over the phone, but he figured it would be prudent to check out the place. No one wants any surprises come race day, especially with a nervous horse like Sing. Plus it would give him a chance to get out of the house and be alone for a while. He wasn't one for small talk and listening to James' and Manny's nonsensical conversations was quickly growing old. Although he missed home like the other two, it was more for the quiet than anything else. Sure he missed his wife and children, but he had a job to do and that was his focus.

Today that meant touring the barn area and checking out the facilities, which he did at as slow a pace as his type A personality would allow. It was a strange place compared to Finger Lakes, not that there was anything special about it. Maybe it was the palm trees and the sandy ground, or the smell of the ocean, itself not much more than a mile away. Whatever it was, it made you feel as though you were on vacation, or should be, especially if you came from western New York where the current temperatures hovered around the freezing mark. It occurred to Michael as he pondered it; he didn't feel the least bit like he was on vacation. If anything, he felt more stressed than normal.

He listened to the palm trees sway as a warm, pleasant breeze blew through. Letting the tropical air sweep over him, he envisioned a beach vacation. It'd been a few years since they'd had a getaway. A family trip to the ocean would be nice. He pictured himself and the kids playing in the surf and Janet sitting on a beach chair reading a book. Worry free, relaxing and fun. They'd done it before and needed to do it again. It was a great thought, unfortunately now was not the time. And just like that, his mind switched back to reality. He figured he'd seen what he needed to see, but the notion of making the drive back depressed Michael. Though the practical thing might be to start back now, he just couldn't do it. He wanted more time away, no, he needed more time away. Maybe a bite to eat and a beer, along with watching a few races might be just what the doctor ordered. Rushing back to their cramped quarters in Tampa certainly was not.

Chapter 8

~

FEBRUARY 27

MICHAEL, JAMES AND MANNY WERE up at 5 a.m., loaded Sing and were on their way by 6. They followed route 75 down the coast to Naples and then across the Everglades on the stretch known as Alligator Alley. James and Manny spent the next hour searching for an alligator. Whoever spotted one first earned themselves twenty dollars. Michael, being the driver, did not partake. There were several possible sightings, but none confirmed and in the end the bet went unclaimed. The one thing they did see was birds, lots and lots of birds. Mostly cranes, or at least that was the consensus, though nobody had any idea what kind. There wasn't much to see otherwise. It was wet, flat and boring. But with blue skies, pleasant temperatures and light traffic, no one complained. Traffic picked up once they hit the east coast, but there weren't any backups, nor were there any drivers attempting to text and drive simultaneously, which seemed to be a common trend on the Florida roadways.

By 10 a.m. they'd put Sing in the stall he would occupy at Gulfstream Park. There was nothing to do now but wait their turn. They were running in the 4th race which was scheduled to go off at 1:45. Sing appeared to be settled, so Michael grabbed a long straw of hay and broke it twice. He placed the three strands in his hand closing it into a fist, allowing the top of each strand to be visible. Looking at James and Manny he held his fist out. The two quickly grabbed for a strand, looked at it and then at the each others. Michael opened his fist to show the size of his straw. The decision was made.

"Damn!" James said. "I always get screwed doing these." He drew the short straw, first shift. Not that it mattered much, each of the three would eventually take their turn. Someone had to stay with Sing while they waited for their race. There was no chance they would leave him alone. Not that many trainers would. The shortest straw would go first, the next shortest second and the longest last. It made sense and meant they only had to play the game once.

In a huff James grabbed for the dusty fold-out chair still in its carrying case, leaning against the stall door. Sing looked on, his head stuck outside the stall door, as James fought to get the chair out of its protective shell. With one final yank, the chair flew out of the case. Sing bobbed his head up and down at the spastic motion. It was merely a reaction, though it looked like he was mocking James. James gazed back at Sing as he opened up the chair. "That's enough already."

Meanwhile, having drawn the larger straws, Manny and Michael wandered around, trying to find something entertaining. They walked from barn to barn checking things out. It seemed to both of them that if you've seen one backside, then you've seen them all, other than Saratoga or Keeneland, maybe. Most of the morning work was done except for some tack cleaning, gathering of the dirty towels and the occasional horse bath. Routine, boring and not at all entertaining.

"Now what?" Michael asked. Manny shrugged his shoulders. What do you do at a track when you have no horses? Without saying a word, the bored pair continued on their way toward the grandstand.

Although Manny was getting accustomed to being in Florida again, times like this, when there was nothing to do, no work to be done, his mind would start to wander. The warm breezes conjured up not so much thoughts of his father's death, but more of the life they had before. His dad was a true showman and beloved by all that met him. Manny could remember vividly his dad, after a really great ride, would turn to the crowd and pump his fist in the air, or grab his hat and wave it around, then toss it in the air. His dad would be smiling from ear to ear, bouncing up and down. The fans seemed to love his energy and enthusiasm. He wasn't a showboat. He just knew how to get the spectators excited. And after, as he was leaving the ring, he would always find Manny. He would point to him, wink and give him a thumbs-up. It was a moment between a father and his son. Thinking about it made Manny's heart ache. He wondered if his dad were watching him now and what he thought of his son. The question caused Manny to deliberate for a minute. He was an exercise rider, nothing more. Had he become a successful jockey, his dad certainly would have been proud. He was successful for a while. But then he stopped. Because of the accident, he stopped. He was too big now, what else could he do? The mind is a difficult thing to convince and Manny knew he was losing. He had quit and was now an exercise rider. Altogether not too impressive. Was there really anything to be proud of?

"Hey Michael, I'm going to head back now," Manny said.

Michael glanced at his watch. "You still have another 20 minutes you know."

"I know, but I'd just as soon go back and hang out with Sing." Realizing he may have insulted Michael, Manny quickly added, "Nothing personal, I didn't mean it like that."

Michael quickly cut him off. "Manny," he said lifting his hand in the universal halt position, "don't worry about it. I understand."

Manny smiled, still feeling uneasy. "Don't worry about coming over either. I'll stay over there until the race."

"Are you sure?"

"Yeah, it's no problem. There's nothing around here I care to see anyway."

"OK, well if that's what you want. I'll stop by around noon and bring you a hotdog or something. If you want to go somewhere then, just let me know."

"Alright, I'll see you then."

As Manny turned to go Michael added, "Tell James I'll be sitting in the stands." Manny said OK and continued on his way, still contemplating whether he'd accomplished anything to make his Dad proud.

As the horses ran past the grandstands, finishing the second race, Michael turned to James. "You ready?" he asked.

James slowly raised himself off his seat, "Yup," he said stretching out his arms. "It's about time. That was a long three hours." The two began the short trek back to the barns to collect Sing and Manny and prepare for the race.

As Michael and James turned the corner to barn 7, they could see Manny sitting on a chair in front of Sing's stall reading a book. Sing had his head drooping outside the stall door, almost as if he were resting on Manny's head and reading the book too. James, seeing a great opportunity, couldn't resist making a comment.

As they reached the stall he looked at Manny. "Is Sing helping you with some of the big words?" Manny laughed, responding with a curt "ha ha ha."

Michael ignored the commentary and went into Sing's stall. He bent over, slowly moving his hands up and down Sing's legs making sure everything felt right. He moved from one leg to another, just like he had before they left Tampa and again when they arrived at Gulfstream. Feeling no heat and seeing nothing unusual, he stood and made his way out of the stall. "All right, we've got about 15 minutes. Let's make sure everything is gathered and ready to go."

The journey from the barn to the paddock reminded Manny of the Macy's Day Parade. To the left, James held Sing with his shank. To the right, Michael held Sing with a second shank. He brought up the rear and in the middle of the three of them was their float. Sing bounced a bit as he went, his head swinging in each direction, taking in his surroundings.

Each swing prompted a light tug on the shank, both sides trying to keep the float centered and moving forward. It was delicate business. They needed to be gentle and keep Sing from getting ruffled. This was his first race away from Finger Lakes and his comfort zone. And it's not like he'd behaved there. But thus far, he seemed attentive and composed, and upon entering the paddock, James found his stall and led the group over.

After Michael cinched up Sing's girth, James walked him in circles, as much to keep him occupied as to stretch his legs. Manny stood apart from Michael, Sing and James, intermittently watching Sing and the other entrants. With about 15 minutes until post time Sing's jockey appeared. Fernando Torres, a young but up-and-coming jockey, waited to board Sing. Fernando came to Michael via several recommendations from trainers in Tampa. They liked to use him whenever they shipped over. What he lacked in experience, he made up for in his desire to win. He rode hard and would give you an honest effort. That was good enough for Michael.

From the corner of the paddock a woman holding a clipboard eyed the scene and then her watch. "Riders up," she yelled.

"OK, here we go," Michael said. Fernando, standing beside him, grabbed Sing's reins. Michael took hold of Fernando's now extended left leg and hoisted him up. As soon as Fernando hit Sing's back, Sing began to dance around, something obviously agitating him. James tried his best to keep him still and calm, but Sing would have none of it. He danced from side to side as James began to walk him toward the main track. They hadn't gotten very far when Sing reared up. Fernando, though young, wasn't dumb and decided to abandon ship, jumping off the skittish horse. Sing reared again. James held on to the shank trying desperately not to lose control, but also called on all his lifelong knowledge to not pull on the shank and make it worse. It proved an elusive balance. Sing began to stagger back, his two front legs punching out in front of him.

Michael saw it coming as if it were in slow motion. Sing was losing his balance. Manny, who had fallen in line behind Sing, scurried for cover, as did Fernando. With no chance of doing anything to help, Michael watched as the leather shank slid through James' hand. The sound of

James cursing filled the air, but nobody could hear it. Everyone's eyes focused on Sing, who staggered about like a hapless drunk. Then, in a grotesquely unusual motion, Sing toppled over backwards. It was an unnatural and sickening scene. A thousand-pound animal toppling over, legs flailing about, searching for some solid ground. The crowd gathered around the paddock gasped in horror as Sing landed with a thud. Sing pleaded for help, his shrill cry not even a resembling a whinny.

Manny cried out Sing's name. Having spent nearly every day grooming and riding him, Sing meant more to Manny than any horse he'd previously known. He was special to Manny and Manny was sensitive to his needs, probably too sensitive. Sing wasn't a horse, he was a friend and Manny's friend needed him now, but Manny could do nothing.

After hitting the ground Sing rolled to one side, trying to right himself. It took him a second to gather his wits before he stood up. He looked like the deer in headlights still trying to figure out what had just happened as Michael, James and Manny rushed to grab the shank and calm the dazed horse.

James grabbed the shank before Sing could consider bolting. Holding on tightly, he patted Sing's neck, trying to quiet him. Manny arrived moments later and also began stroking the horse's taut body. With Sing remaining relatively still, Michael approached and ran his hands once more over Sing's legs, feeling and looking for anything different. When nothing was found he asked James to walk him in a circle. The on-track veterinarian along with Michael watched carefully for any signs of lameness. Everyone, including the fans that remained in the paddock, was relieved to see Sing walking normally. He had come away unscathed. Dusty, but unscathed.

Michael and the veterinarian agreed that there were no physical effects from the fall. It was up to Michael whether or not they would scratch him from the race. His mind wrestled with the question, his hands resting on his hips, head bowed in thought. All eyes were on him, waiting for the verdict. He raised his head, looked at the horse, then at James, then at

Fernando Torres who stood there rubbing his elbow. "You OK to ride?" Michael asked.

"Sure, I'll be fine" Fernando replied.

"Alright then, let's get him out there. He needs to get a race in him." With that James quickly began walking him toward the track as Michael gave Fernando another leg up. Sing, still somewhat dazed from the incident, didn't fight back. Manny stayed close to his friend patting his neck and talking to him as they went. In less than a minute Sing and Fernando were on the track warming up for the fourth race.

Back in New York, Jack had just tuned in to the horse racing channel when they showed the footage of Sing's mishap. As the video rolled, the announcers noted the horse was fine and was on the track warming up. Jack was relieved to hear that, although he knew it probably compromised any chance Sing had of winning. As they neared the starting gate Jack could see Sing had been sweating profusely. Not a good sign. A horse that is calm and collected runs well. A horse that is washed out from sweat does not.

The race started almost directly in front of Michael and James. The two stood in the grandstands which allowed for a good view of the entire race. Manny had elected to stand near the rail. He always liked being close to the action and at the moment he preferred to be alone. The sound of Sing's cry continued to play in his head and left him unnerved. But it didn't matter which spot you were in, it was obvious Sing was strung out. As the gates flew open, Sing rushed out sprinting toward the lead. The race was just more than one lap around the oval, a total of one mile and a sixteenth. By the time they hit the first turn, Sing had captured the lead. Going around the turn his lead on the rest of the pack increased to about 3 horse lengths, the standard distance by which horses in a race are measured apart. After the first half mile, Sing continued to lead by 3 lengths, but there were no cheers from Michael and James. The announcer pointed out that they had run the first half mile in 46 seconds, a very quick time.

"He'll never make it at that pace," said Michael, as much to himself as to James. James said nothing, but figured he was right. As the field came around the far turn, the other horses began to close the gap. When they hit the straight away, Sing's lead had diminished to only 1 length. By the time they were at the eighth pole, Sing was done. Fernando did nothing to keep Sing going, knowing full well he was out of horse. He had let Sing run too fast too soon, well, there wasn't a lot of letting Sing do anything, today he was along for the ride, that's it. The other horses flew past. He eventually finished sixth in the field of nine. Manny quickly made his way onto the track to collect Sing and check on his condition. Michael and James followed soon thereafter. The horse looked exhausted, wide-eyed and spent from his paddock antics and a tough race. Slowly they walked him back to the barn area to cool him off before taking the long drive back to Tampa.

Jack watched as Sing faded down the home stretch. They'd thrown their horse in with the big boys and the big boys had bloodied their nose and sent them packing, like a bunch of hacks. He thought about giving Michael a call on his cell phone to find out what exactly happened, but decided against it. No one wants to get a call from the owner minutes after a race asking, 'What happened?' when you surely don't know what had happened. Plus, he knew Michael was certain to be upset and his own mood wasn't stellar. A call now would only make things worse. They would speak soon enough. As Jack turned off the television Margaret entered the room. "How'd he do?" she asked.

"He had a tough day today," responded Jack somewhat depressed, "a tough day. I guess we all did."

Chapter 9

~

February 28

As MICHAEL STEPPED ONTO THE deck of their apartment and slid the glass door shut, he heard a strange laugh emanate from the television followed by a burst of laughter from Manny. Having fully closed the door he turned to James, who sat, beer in hand, on one of the three patio chairs surrounding a small round patio table. "What's Manny watching?"

"Sponge Bob," James said with a smile. Michael raised his eyebrows as if to ask James if he was serious. "Oh man, that show is hysterical. Haven't you ever seen it?"

"No. It's a cartoon isn't it?"

"Yeah, and a good one at that. Sydney watches it. I usually sit and watch it with her."

"Why am I not surprised?" Michael said. James laughed, unbothered by the snide remark. "OK, before I call Dad," Michael continued, "do we have any idea what happened with the horse? You're supposed to be the intuitive one, what do you have for me?"

James became more serious. "Actually, nothing. I didn't notice anything. He'd been so good, I hadn't really paid that much attention."

"I haven't the slightest clue either. I guess we'll just chalk it up as an isolated incident." James nodded his head in agreement. "Alright, let's call him."

Michael put his Blackberry on speaker phone, dialed the number and then placed it on the table. Jack answered on the second ring. "Hello."

"Dad, its Michael and James," Michael said.

"Yeah, am I on speaker phone?"

"Yes."

"Good." For a man that rarely, if ever, turned on his own cell phone and who generally scoffed at technology, he loved the speaker phone. When someone asked him why, he responded because he hated to repeat himself. He could yell at everyone one time and be done with it. "Well, what happened?"

Michael glanced at James before answering. "We have no idea."

"None?" Jack said in disbelief. "Was it crowded in the paddock, maybe got him excited?"

"No," Michael replied. "It was relatively quiet."

"Something spooked him. Did any of the other horses act up?"

"No," Michael said again. "He was it."

"Well, I can't imagine he did it for nothing. Maybe a horsefly or something bit him."

"Trust me Dad, we've been over it and none of us remember anything. The jock…"

As if having a revelation, James cut him off. "Hey, you know, it was the first time in the paddock. We hadn't brought him over before the race. Maybe he suddenly spotted something and freaked out."

There was a moment of silence while they pondered the theory. Then, for a lack of alternative reasons, Michael and Jack agreed perhaps that was it. After a small pause, Jack spoke again. "He seems OK today though?"

Michael took charge once more. "Yeah, we gave him a little Bute and walked him today. He looks none the worse for wear. Wasn't lame or anything. Tired, but fine."

"That's good news anyway. Do you have another race on the schedule for him?"

"There's one in a couple of weeks. Assuming he picks up training where we left off, he should be ready," Michael said.

"OK. But I think you guys should definitely go a couple days in advance and school him in the paddock. Hell, school him in Tampa, it couldn't hurt. If he can't get out of the paddock, he ain't worth running, I know that."

Simultaneously, Michael and James agreed.

"Good enough. If anything comes up let me know."

"Alright Dad, we'll talk to you later," Michael said, before hanging up the call. He glanced at James as he got up from his chair and reached to open the sliding glass door. "Is there more beer in the fridge?"

"Yeah, a bunch."

"Good, I could use one." As Michael opened the door, he was greeted once again by the sound of Sponge Bob laughing, and Manny following soon thereafter.

MARCH 7

James and Michael stood near the stalls watching Manny and Sing casually make their way back to the barn. They gave Sing a couple days rest after their fiasco at Gulfstream, but were back to business now. Fortunately, Sing came away from the fall uninjured physically, but mentally, no one knew for sure.

"Well, how did it go?" Michael asked.

"Fine," Manny replied. "He's nice and fit and acted like a perfect gentleman."

"He didn't act screwy or anything?" James said, coming over and grabbing the reins, allowing Manny to dismount.

"Not in the least. Same as yesterday and the day before and the day before that. It's as if nothing at all happened. He's as relaxed and comfortable as he was before we left here. I think it was something at Gulfstream."

"I suppose that's good," said Michael pensively, still concerned they had no idea what set him off. But, as long as he was physically ready, they would go forward with the race as scheduled in just under two weeks. Depending upon how that race went, decisions would be made about whether to continue chasing the "big race" or limp back to Finger Lakes and a farm in distress.

MARCH 16

It was a beautiful afternoon, with temperatures in the 70s and not a cloud in sight. Michael, Manny and Sing cruised down the Interstate heading toward Gulfstream Park. Everything had gone according to Michael's pre-planned schedule and Sing was ready for his next race in two days. Everyone hoped this trip would go better than the last and despite the setback, expectations were still high. Because they were going to be gone for a couple days, the O'Briens agreed to have James stay behind and take care of Glitter and Mr. Nobody. Both had made their first start of the year a few days before, finishing third and fourth, respectively. Not too bad for first starts, at least they each collected a check. However small, it helped offset some of the mounting costs of being in Florida.

MARCH 17

The sound of a horse at full gallop normally wouldn't concern Manny. He kept Sing in the middle of the track for his morning jog allowing the horses having more strenuous works to stay along the rail. But the sound coming up rapidly from behind sounded much too far from the rail to be normal. An instant later Manny heard the irregular hoof beats of scurrying horses and the dreaded scream "loose horse." There is nothing worse than a loose horse on the track in the morning. With a large number of horses and riders coming and going, having a riderless horse charging through the mix is a recipe for disaster. With no time to think Manny pulled up Sing and swung his head around, grabbing a tight hold just as the wayward horse flew past. Coming no more than two feet from them, Manny could feel the after wind. Sing jumped and bucked, the excitement stirring his instinct to flee. Manny pulled at the reins forcing Sing to circle. "Ho boy, it's OK, it's OK," Manny yelled, trying to get Sing's attention. This is the last thing he needed. He was about to wrap up their jog and head for the paddock, the scene of the last race's debacle. Getting Sing all riled up before heading over was not what Manny hoped. Manny took a deep breath and loosened his grip of the leather yoke around Sing's neck, his heart still racing, the wayward horse now panicking others farther down the line. They had been fortunate, real fortunate. Sing continued to flare his nostrils, keeping his ears pricked at attention, but slowly he began to settle down, his breathing returning to normal. Giving him a pat, Manny turned Sing toward the paddock. "Let's get over there boy, before something else happens."

Sing and Manny spent nearly an hour wandering about the enclosure, the earlier excitement fading into memory. Sing sniffed and snorted at just about every bucket, bush, stall plaque or other insignificant object lying about the place. By the time they were done, they had visited every inch of ground at least once. "Alright big guy, our work here is done. Let's go home." Manny guided Sing out of the paddock and back toward the barn, confident the exercise had succeeded. The test would be tomorrow.

MARCH 18

With 20 minutes to post time Manny slowly walked Sing around the paddock waiting for the jockey to arrive. The hour spent there the day before appeared to have done the trick. Sing showed no signs of being nervous or ill at ease. Michael standing in Sing's temporary stall breathed a sigh of relief, though he knew it wasn't time to celebrate yet. And he wasn't alone;

back in Tampa, James watched the action via simulcast trying to maintain his anxiety. Phil Teator arrived moments later. A veteran journeyman jockey who Michael thought might better handle Sing's unpredictable nature. Not that anyone blamed the younger Fernando Torres for the previous race's problems, but his youth probably didn't help things. After a brief discussion with Michael, it was time for Phil to mount. Michael, James and Manny all held their collective breath as the new rider was lifted atop Sing. They waited, fearing the worst, but nothing happened. Sing didn't seem to care at all. For a moment Manny just stood there as if he wasn't sure what to do next. Then, regaining his head, quickly realized he needed to follow the other horses exiting the paddock. Manny brought Sing in line and headed toward the track. Crisis averted.

Pulling out his binoculars Michael scanned the field of horses searching for Sing. From his grandstand perch, he had a good view of the entire oval. Manny had once again chosen to stay down along the rail, balancing his need to be close to the horses and the dirt and his need for solitude all at the same time. After bouncing from horse to horse Michael spotted Sing. Almost immediately the relief he previously felt disappeared. Sing was throwing his head back and forth, fighting his jockey's commands. It was a different jockey than the last race, but this horse couldn't be that temperamental thought Michael, could he? Sing continued his dreadful behavior even as the assistant starter loaded him in the gate.

Jack turned on the television just in time to see the horses break from the starting gate. The first thing he noticed once he caught site of Sing was the veteran jockey fighting to keep him from sprinting to the lead. Sing's head shook up and down, a sign he was lodging a complaint. Sing continued his complaint the entire first quarter of a mile. It wasn't until they hit the backstretch that he finally gave up. By that time Phil had him settled in mid pack, covered up behind horses, roughly an equal number in front and behind him. The horses coasted smoothly, their positions remaining unchanged. As they began to go around the far turn Phil saw his chance and leaned slightly forward, giving Sing his cue to pick up his pace, which he happily did. The turn gave way to a straightaway, the home stretch. With it a wall of horses came bounding toward the finish line. The announcer took note of the scene declaring it was anybody's race.

Michael's spot in the grandstands offered the best vantage point to monitor the race. He could see Sing and one other horse beginning to break away from the rest of the pack. The two horses ran neck and neck pulling away from the field. Phil hit Sing left handed, trying to get Sing to switch his lead leg. Race horses are taught to lead with their left front leg on the turns and switch to their right leg on the straightaways. For humans it would be similar to shoveling snow or raking leaves and holding the shovel or rake in the same hand the whole time, one arm eventually begins to wear out. Shifting to the other can give you renewed energy. Sing, unfortunately, would have nothing to do with it. Michael could see what was happening and feared the inevitable outcome. Sing began to slow down. The other horse edged away and won by half a length. It was a disappointing finish for Michael. He knew he had the better horse. Sing's head tossing before and during the race and his failure to switch leads cost him the victory. Had either one not occurred, Sing most certainly would have won. In his own mind the decision was clear. They would not try to run Sing in the Florida Derby. He simply wasn't ready. The bigger question was would he ever be?

Jack and James, despite watching in two different cities 1,200 hundred miles apart, saw the same thing Michael did. They knew that Sing was a long way from being a good race horse, let alone the great one they all thought he could be. Only Manny was encouraged by what he saw. Of course at this point the troubled condition of the farm was unknown to Manny. To him, Sing gave a good effort and that's all that counted. The other stuff could be fixed in time. He was confident the O'Briens would work out that part. It was a confidence they weren't currently sharing.

Chapter 10

~

MARCH 19

JAMES SAT IN THE AIRPORT awaiting the call to board his flight. He just sat there staring at his beat-up blue duffle bag until he noticed a set of eyes looking back at him. Sydney had placed a princess sticker on his bag and it miraculously remained affixed, despite the banging the bag had taken over the past couple of months. Seeing the little princess prompted James to smile, regardless of his mood. His mind was awash with mixed emotions. He was certainly glad to be going home. He missed his wife and daughter even more than he expected he would. Not seeing their smiling faces every day was tough. Having been away made him realize even more just how good a life he had. In that respect, it would be good to be back. But what bothered him was having failed to accomplish anything since arriving in Florida. They had failed to win a race, failed to get Sing to settle and the dreams of running in one of the premier races had died with those failures.

James had never been the most ambitious of people and he knew it, but he also had found success in whatever he really put his heart into. At this moment, for the first time in his life, he felt as though *he* had failed. He had nothing to offer. When Michael and Manny returned from Gulfstream, the three sat down and hashed out the race. Sing hadn't thrown his head about or failed to change leads since he was a 2-year-old in training. Why now? Michael leaned on James for some ideas, some insight, but James came up empty. James was supposed to be the perceptive one, the one that had the answers when it came to a horse's strange behavior. But James had no clue and he could sense Michael's disappointment. It gave him a feeling of uselessness he'd never encountered before today. As he sat there waiting for his flight, still gazing at a little princess, it hit him, he'd done virtually nothing on this trip that was of any value. He could've stayed behind and saved the family money. He should've stayed behind. This was not how he envisioned the trip or returning home. Two months ago he pictured himself heading out on a crusade and returning home as a conquering hero, having helped put Sing on a path to glory. Instead, he would have to try and explain why things were going so poorly. It was a question for which he had no answer. But it did raise one other. He was scheduled to begin getting the other horses ready for the Finger Lakes meet. The question now was whether he had the ability to do so. With his confidence heading south, he wasn't so sure.

MARCH 20

Margaret stood by the stove as Jack came stomping into the kitchen from the outside, cursing under his breath. "Jack, we don't use that kind of language in this house," she said sternly. Margaret's words had a parental air about them which Jack, at this moment in time, did not appreciate. Of course he knew full well that out on the farm he was in charge, but inside the house, well that was Margaret's domain. He said nothing. His repentant look was apology enough. With that settled, Margaret asked the logical question. "What's the matter?"

"The daa..." Jack was able to stop before he got himself in trouble again. Margaret just looked at him with raised eyebrows. Carefully choosing his words he started up again. "The darn tractor broke down. And I'm not too excited about spending the money to get it fixed."

"Do you know what's wrong with it?"

"I think so, and if I'm right, it's not going to be cheap." Jack took off his gloves and dialed the phone. Margaret turned and attended to the pot she had on the stove. After a couple minutes Jack hung up the phone. Margaret, hearing her cue, turned and looked at him.

"Well?"

"Bill thinks it's the same thing as me." Bill was Bill Smith, owner of the local tractor dealership. In a small community such as theirs, he was also the tractor salesman and knew more about repairing them than even the farmers who bought from him. "He should be coming out with some parts in about an hour. When he gets here, send him out to the lower field." Jack paused on his way out the door, realizing he'd forgotten something. "Please."

Margaret smiled and nodded.

Jack reentered the house a few hours later as the sun began to set. "Perfect timing," Margaret told him, as he was taking off his overalls. "Dinner is almost ready. How is the tractor?"

"She's up and running again." He waited a moment before adding, "five grand later."

Margaret winced as she heard the amount. "Five thousand dollars?! Whew, looks like we may need to sell that knife collection of yours." She smiled after adding the knife collection comment. She said it in an attempt to add some levity to the situation. She knew full well that he would never sell them. Every man brings something into the house that makes his wife cringe. For Jack and Margaret, it was Jack's collection of fighting knives he'd collected while seeing the world compliments of the U.S. military.

Jack, having traveled this path before, made sure to respond to Margaret's comment. "I'm taking those knives to the grave."

Margaret, ready as always, offered a quick retort. "Trust me Jack, when you go, those knives go with you."

The two exchanged smiles and after Jack washed his hands, sat down to eat. They were a team, each trusting the other unconditionally. That support, now as much as any time during their marriage, was critical. Things weren't going in the right direction and Jack wasn't sure what he could do to turn that around. After a few minutes of quiet eating Jack lifted his head.

"I think I'll call Ron down at the bank tomorrow and ask him if we can postpone the interest payments for a few months. It'll give us a chance to take care of the tractor." Jack took another spoonful of stew but stopped just short of putting it in his mouth. "And save my knife collection."

MARCH 21

"I'll take care of it Jack. We'll suspend payments for 90 days. The interest will be added to the overall balance. If I run into any trouble, I'll give you a call." With that, Ron Dombrowski hung up the phone. Eight months ago he had arranged to have the O'Briens' loan change from principal and interest to interest only. That one wasn't too hard. The O'Briens were longstanding clients and always good for anything they borrowed. But times had changed and this one might prove to be a little more difficult. Fortunately for Ron, the man who would be making the ultimate decision owed him. The regional manager, Henry A. Livingston III, had come up through the ranks, but his path had already been paved. His father, like his father before him, was part owner of the bank. Henry the Ain't, as he was known behind his back, was destined to run the place. Even after they sold out to the "giant" downstate, Henry the Ain't continued to run operations for the local branches. Now the fortunate part for Ron was that Henry, while climbing the latter, often messed up things. Like many born with a silver spoon, Henry focused more on play than on work. When that lack of focus led to errors, Henry scrambled around attempting to correct the mistakes before his father found out. That's where Ron came in. Ron couldn't count the number of times his quick thinking saved Henry from certain embarrassment. Now it was time Henry repaid some of that debt. Ron stood up from his desk and walked into Henry's office, closing the door behind him.

It took some "encouragement" from Ron before Henry caved in, but Henry's backbone had never been his strength. "Alright, I'll give them 90 days, but that's it. I've got headquarters breathing down my neck. Too many loans going bad."

"Thanks Henry." Ron got up from his chair and left Henry's corner office, smiling from ear to ear.

Chapter 11

~

MARCH 30

THE CALENDAR THAT HUNG ON the kitchen wall informed Manny that he had been back in Tampa for two and a half months now. As he stared at it, listening to the hum of the refrigerator behind him, he tried to rationalize why, in all that time, he hadn't called his aunt and uncle. He conjured up various reasons; too busy, too difficult to get to their house, never a good time to call, and so on, but none stuck. His most plausible reason was perhaps it was still difficult to think back to that time in his life. That would be natural, he thought, but somehow that wasn't it either. Maybe it was the way he left.

When the day came and Manny decided to leave for New York, there was no party, no tearful hugs goodbye. One day he simply came home, packed up his belongings and let his aunt and uncle know he was heading to Western New York in hopes of hitching on with some people there. Not having any idea of what to do or say, they wished him good luck and told him to keep in touch. Something he never really bothered to do. As he stood before the calendar, the real reason he was afraid to call was growing clearer. Deep down Manny knew his actions back then weren't right. His guilt was undeniable. He tried to suppress those feelings, convince himself otherwise, but he couldn't. It was a poor way to say goodbye to the people who had taken you in and given up their home for you. Quite frankly, it was embarrassing to have behaved so ungratefully. And now, after all these years, Manny was afraid of what they might say to him. He also knew he needed to face that fear. He needed to thank them for what they'd given him and let them know he was alright. Regardless of what they might say, Manny had no choice but to pick up the phone.

APRIL 1

Manny and his aunt spoke cordially, but nothing more. It seemed as though neither person had any idea of what to say. As Manny drove Michael's truck down the highway toward his aunt and uncle's house he began to wonder if he was making a mistake. In the 15 minutes he'd driven, he had probably thought up 20 different scenarios, all awkward. What if they just sit there, staring at one another with nothing to say. The thought of three people, supposedly related, sitting on fine living room furniture, filling their time with nothing more than a prolonged awkward pause made Manny cringe. He glanced down at his watch. He was looking to see what the time was, but noticed the date. April 1st, April Fools Day. Instantly a thought crossed Manny's mind, "Am I the fool here?" He didn't have to ponder the question long. Things began to look strangely familiar. The house leading into their neighborhood. A white stucco one-story with a red tiled roof, black shutters, a red door that matched the roof and three large palm trees smack in the middle of their front yard. Exactly the same. The park at the end of their street. The baseball field, the basketball court, the soccer field, the playground. Manny watched the kids scamper about. There always seemed to be kids, no matter what day or what time. Their driveway. The cars, they were different, but otherwise it was the same. Nothing had changed.

Exiting the truck Manny began to feel the anxiety that always accompanies entering the unknown. The fear of what lies in wait. Horses he understood, people he didn't. He started to panic. He could feel his body temperature rising and a wave of nausea swept over him. Great, he thought, I finally get the guts to come over and I end up puking on their driveway. Beads of sweat formed on his forehead and streaked down his sideburns. He could taste the bile coming up his throat. He staggered slightly, resting his hand on the truck to steady himself. Luckily, the near-by ocean became Manny's ally. A cool breeze kicked up, sending a chill across his sweat-filled body and his temperature down to a normal level. "Alright, let's get this over with," he said to himself. He double timed it up the walkway and knocked on the door, still trying to steady himself after his short bout with nausea. The door opened and a well-known face appeared from behind. Perhaps it was a little older, but it was the same nonetheless. And with it came a soft welcoming smile.

"Manny, oh my gosh, it's so wonderful to see you." She reached out and embraced him. It was heartfelt and comfortable. Any doubts he'd had about coming melted away as he entered the house, still held tightly by the aunt he hadn't seen in over seven years.

As he walked through the front entrance, the first thing Manny no-ticed was the pictures that lined the walls. They were mostly of his aunt and uncle visiting places, and some of other people Manny didn't know, but there was one he found immediately recognizable. It was a picture of his mother, father and himself as a baby. He was taken aback at first at how pretty his mother looked. As a child it's not something you notice, but now, as a grown adult, Manny saw her for more than just a mother, but as a wom-an. The woman who married his father. An individual in her own right. Admiring her soft features, Manny could see why his dad was attracted to her. Her smile, exactly how Manny remembered it, warm and welcoming. It was a strange realization, suddenly discovering that your mom was a per-son like anyone else. What was her life like before she met Dad? Was her childhood nice? Was she always as happy as when they were a family? So many questions thought Manny, and nowhere to find the answers.

Manny's eyes shifted off his mother to his father. Even in the pic-ture, Manny could see the self confidence in his father's face and in his stance. He was an impressive man, thought Manny, in his flashy Western shirt. Manny looked down at his own shirt, also a flashy Western style.

He smiled, in some way proud that he dressed like his father, the man he wanted so much to be like.

Entering the living room, it was just as Manny recalled it, very neat and orderly. His uncle was already waiting and shook Manny's hand. His aunt quickly headed for the kitchen and asked Manny if he'd like something to drink. "Water would be just fine, thank you."

"So Manny," his uncle started as his aunt brought the drinks and some cookies and set them on the coffee table. "As you can see," waving his hands around the room as if showing it off, "things haven't changed much around here for us, but we're dying to hear what you've been up to these last few years. Where are you living? What do you do? We want to hear everything." Manny's aunt sat down next to his uncle and they both looked at Manny with great expectation.

Manny paused a moment trying to figure out where to start. Then he began telling them about meeting the O'Briens, who they were, that he groomed and exercised horses for them and that he lived above their barn in an apartment. He told them about completing high school and how Mrs. O'Brien helped him study. And of course he told them about Sing and what they were doing in Florida. All along the way, his aunt and uncle would ask questions and it was obvious they weren't just being nice, but that they were genuinely interested in Manny's life.

When Manny finished bringing his aunt and uncle up to date, the room suddenly went silent. 'Oh man, here it is,' Manny thought, 'the dreaded awkward pause.' Then his aunt reached down to the foot of the sofa and picked up a shoebox. She lifted the top off and inside was dozens of letters.

"Manny, did you know before your mom died that she and I used to write back and forth all the time?"

"No," Manny said, very surprised, "I didn't know that at all." Manny looked at the letters, not unlike the one he had. His eyes were wide and his face blank. They were a link to an unknown world. A world Manny longed to discover.

"After our conversation yesterday, I pulled these out and started to read them again. Would you like me to show you some of them?"

'Some, not some, all,' Manny thought to himself. 'I want to touch them, smell them, read every last line.' But he couldn't quite say that. "Yes, please."

"Let me read you this one first," she said, pulling one from the box. "I read this one last night and really got a kick out of it. You had just turned 4." As she began reading, Manny realized that as much as he wanted every single letter for himself, these were her treasures. Treasures of a sister she lost. Manny quickly understood how lucky he was that she was willing to share them. "And since his birthday, Manny just runs around wearing his new cowboy hat, trying to lasso anything in sight. I think we've had about a dozen visits from neighbors each asking that he leave their dog alone."

Manny smiled and blushed, not knowing what to say.

Reaching down into the box, his aunt grabbed another letter and glanced over it. She smiled. "This is one of my favorites, but I don't think you'd be quite as interested. It was just after your parent's second anniversary. Your dad took your mom out for dinner and bought her flowers." She paused a moment, thinking, of what Manny wasn't really sure, then abruptly she continued, her voice somewhat shaken. "Your dad was really good to your mom. He was a wonderful man."

Manny could see a tear well up in her eye and he suddenly understood her thought. The tragedy. The pure tragedy of it all. A good man gone. A loving sister gone. Two beautiful people. People *we* lost.

She regained her composure, not wanting to dampen the mood and pulled out yet another. "Oh you'll love this one," she said, a small sniffle still apparent. "It seems you had quite an adventure while visiting the zoo."

The letters and stories went on for a while, an awkward pause the last thing on anyone's mind. This time around, Manny interjected, asking questions and soaking up answers. Come to find out, they knew more about Manny, and his mom, than he'd realized. Not that anyone wished it, but had Manny's father's passing happened earlier in his life, when Manny was a little younger, who knows how close Manny might have become with his aunt and uncle. Regardless, that was the past and Manny was ready to start anew. And his aunt and uncle, equally as excited, welcomed this new beginning with open arms.

Driving home, Manny felt a huge sense of relief, and joy. He also felt a pang of embarrassment over how he had fretted about the meeting. As it turned out, his aunt and uncle had longed to find out how he was doing. They told him they were never really comfortable with how they were supposed to have treated him during his years with them. With his age and the fact they hadn't raised any of their own children, it was all very foreign. When that fateful day came and Manny told them he was leaving, they really didn't know if they should try to talk to him about it. In the end, they felt as badly about his departure as Manny did.

But that was behind them and after four very short hours of talk and laughter, their relationship had found a fresh start. Manny vowed to keep in touch this time and his aunt and uncle did the same. Cruising down the highway, Manny put the windows down and let the warm Florida air run through the cab. It was a refreshing feeling. At that moment, he didn't have a care in the world. It would've been impossible to wipe the smile from his face. Somewhere inside him a portion of the void disappeared, however small. And even though Manny didn't consider them to be his real family, they were blood relatives and it was wonderful to have them. His real family, he thought, was waiting for him on a little farm in Western New York.

Manny looked at his watch, just as he had on the trip out hours before. Once again he noticed the date. This time he laughed. He was no fool today, no not at all; he was the luckiest guy around. He found an Aunt and Uncle that loved him. And he found someone he could love back. Yes, today was a day to remember. Luck wasn't something plentiful in Manny's life. Sure, he was fortunate to have met the O'Briens, but beyond that, it seemed life had dealt him more than his share of misfortune. His mother contracting cancer at such a young age, his father's untimely death and the tragic spill that ended his riding career. For one of these things to happen, it might be considered bad luck, but for all of them, that was simply cruel, too cruel to be bad luck. Manny was due. The gods of fate owed him and Manny was more than happy to collect. He felt a surge of confidence he hadn't felt in some time. As if his life was finally beginning to take direction. The sound of a horn blaring startled Manny back to reality. He shot a glance to his right, his heart skipping a beat. It was nothing, just one driver upset with another. This Florida traffic is wild, thought Manny, a far cry from the peaceful country driving back in New York. I need to get off this road, before the gods change their fickle minds.

Chapter 12

~

APRIL 7

THE ROOM WAS SHROUDED IN darkness. Only the light from a small desk lamp, illuminating the area directly in front of James, shone through, trying hopelessly to keep the blackness at bay. The piece of paper lying before James was titled 'accomplishments,' it's heading written in all capital letters and underlined. Farther down the page was the number 1, followed by a horse's name, Kentucky Crown and then some scribbled notes. The notes, though not decipherable to anyone but James, indicated that James had uncovered Kentucky Crown's need for a demanding schedule. When he was in training, he needed an arduous regimen and to race often. Once James discovered this, Kentucky Crown turned into a very happy and productive Thoroughbred, and made the farm a great deal of money along with it.

Below the number 1, was the number 2. Again the name of a horse, Deputy Dancer, and various illegible notes. This time, the notes described a horse in need of more attention, more care and handling. James' intuition revealed the reason behind Deputy Dancer's antipathy toward things. Under James' watchful eye and constant attention, she blossomed both as a runner and a horse.

They were two major breakthroughs James could point to, but he could find no more. He sat there in silence, searching his brain for something else. His list of life's accomplishments could go no further than number 2.

Surely there must be more. He had been training horses full-time for 13 years, 18 years if you count the part-time work before he finished college, but in his mind he had nothing to show for it. He scanned the years in his head, tried to remember the horses, the races, anything to spark a positive memory. But nothing surfaced. It was as if he'd been nothing more than a stable boy in all those years. There was nothing to validate the countless time and effort. Two accomplishments, a pathetic display. His mind began to sink.

The silence was suddenly broken as a cat jumped onto James' lap, surprising him. James looked down and ran his hand across the cat's back, eliciting a soft purr from the feline. "What are you doing up at this hour Bullwinkle?" he asked. A more vocal purr, the only response. James looked back at his short list. "Can you come up with anything Bully? I've got nothing, not a thing." His eyes shifted back at Bullwinkle. "Your Dad's not worth much, do you know that?" His voice hushed and without hope, "not worth much at all." Bullwinkle offered no rebuttal. James grabbed the paper and crumpled it into a ball, dropping it into the waste basket. "OK Bully, enough of this. Let's just go back to bed." His futile exercise finished, James reached up and flipped the switch, lights out, perhaps on a career.

APRIL 8

James stood at the kitchen window watching the sun set in the western sky. "What's going on honey?" The words startled James, not having heard Lauren enter the room. Without turning he quietly replied "nothing." Lauren knew better. Since James had returned from Florida he hadn't been the same. She knew something was eating at him. She had waited until now to see if he would voluntarily offer it, but he hadn't. It was time to take matters into her own hands. "You've been awful quiet ever since you got back. What's bothering you?" Her words were soft and gentle. There was no hint of the usual sarcasm they always seem to enjoy heaping upon one another. For James, that kindness made it even more difficult to let out what he was feeling. But he had bottled it up too long.

"Why do you love me? I mean really….what do I do? I help train horses, make only a modest income and I'm really not even that good at it. What can I give you?" James barely took a breath as he let it out. An outburst of feelings. A release. A relief.

Perceptive, like most women, Lauren quickly identified the heart of the problem. It was the part about being good at what he does. Why would he say that? He's never shown a lack of confidence before. She closed in on James pressing her chest against his back, her hands on his shoulders, while he continued to gaze out the window.

"Well," she said, pausing as if needing time to think of the reasons, "you are one of the nicest, most gentle, caring men I've ever met." She paused again allowing it to sink in. "You make me feel like the most special woman in the world and," changing her tone for effect, "it doesn't hurt that you're quite good looking." This last part brought a faint smile to James' lips. "And as far as your ability to train horses, you have an ability to understand those animals like no one I've ever known."

With that James turned abruptly toward Lauren, breaking their contact just enough so their faces were mere inches apart. "Then why can't I figure out what is up with this horse?" The real issue had finally surfaced. She knew he'd been frustrated by Sing, but didn't realize just how much.

Lauren reached out gently, grabbing each of James' hands. Her eyes slowly moved from his hands to his eyes. In a voice that was calm and sincere she began to speak. "James, you have always been able to diagnose these horses without any problem. It's come naturally, easily. Now, for the first time, *this* horse has you stumped." James stood there, his eyes glued on his wife, thinking about what she'd said, trying to decide whether it was true. But as his mind wrestled, she continued. "You can figure this guy out, just like you've done with the others. But *he* is going to take a little more. You're going to have to study him, watch him, take time to understand who he is. I have faith in you. You just need to have a little faith in yourself."

"But what if I can't?" he softly begged, no longer certain of his skills. "There's no rhyme or reason why this horse does what he does."

James' confidence may have been hurting, but Lauren's confidence in her husband was unshakable and the determination in her voice was undeniable. "You can and you will. You're the one who always says as a trainer you're expected to find the map for each horse…," she softened her tone as she went on, "I have no doubt in my mind, if anyone can, it's you."

"I'm not so sure," James said, shaking his head. "Michael and I talked at length about it when I was down there. I was completely clueless. Sing doesn't act like other horses. I don't even know where to begin." James lowered his voice, "You should have seen the look on Michael's face." He turned away from Lauren and gazed out the window, staring at nothing.

Lauren stood back, her arms folded. Her husband was feeling sorry for himself. It was time to get tough. "So what are you going to do? Give up?" No response. "Maybe things have been too easy for you. I hope you're not about to back down because things have gotten tough. I didn't figure you to be one to back away from a fight." It was a play to his manhood. James knew it and didn't like it, but couldn't help but take the bait.

"Of course not," he said, turning to face his accuser. "But I have virtually nothing to go on. The horse is completely unpredictable," he continued, his voice raised. "How am I supposed to figure out what's wrong with him?"

That's right, Lauren thought to herself, fight back, show me what you're made of. "Find out what's wrong with the horse, figure it out, don't quit on him. Think about that, maybe he needs you as much as you need him," she said. "I don't know, but I'm tired of watching you mope around this house like a lost puppy. I didn't marry some lame-o. Enough with the pity party."

The words angered James, but they were meant to and he knew it. He wanted to fight back, but she was right. He knew that too. And she'd said it for the sole reason of waking him out of his stupor. Of course, that ticked him off as much as what she'd said. Nobody likes it when their spouse is right and they're wrong. Instead, he just stood there in silence.

Lauren knew she had James beaten. It was time to back-off and help build him up. "There must be something you could do. Start with when and where the episodes happened. Maybe you should jot down notes on everything and see if something starts to come out. Ask Michael for his notes, God knows he takes a lot of notes."

"And if nothing comes out?"

"Then so be it. All you can do is try. It's not like anyone else is coming up with anything. Everybody is in the dark with this horse, what's to lose?"

James nodded his head. The fear of failure had gripped him, but the worst-case scenario was already present. How much worse could it get?

Realizing James had acknowledged his need to stand and fight, Lauren spoke, "You ready to take this horse on?"

James waited a couple of seconds, still somewhat miffed at her method. But the battle was over, it was time to concede. "Yeah, I'm ready," he said in a quiet, yet thankful tone. "And by the way, I hate you."

Lauren smiled at her man, who slowly turned his head away, pretending not to look at her in a fake effort to hide the smirk on his own face. "There's the man I married." She opened her arms and hugged him.

As their embrace ended, James subtly laughed. "You know, last night I tried to come up with a list of things I've accomplished since I'd been training and all I could come up with was two."

Without being able to stop, Lauren broke into a laugh. "Are you kidding me, two things, that's it!" She could see by James' facial expression that he wasn't amused. "Seriously," Lauren said, staring straight into James' eyes, "I think you need to take a step back and think, truly think about your abilities. I can't tell you the number of times I've heard both Michael and your Dad talk about how important you are to the operation. How well you compliment your brother. Even your Mom has made mention of it." She paused a moment for effect. "They wouldn't just say those things, they're not like that. Well, I guess your Mom might, but not the other two."

James laughed at the comment. "That's true," he said, "definitely the part about my Mom." He smiled and pulled his wife close again, thankful to have her. She was right again he thought. Deep down he'd probably always known it, but it's human nature to occasionally doubt oneself, especially in the horse business. Sometimes you merely need someone you trust, someone you love, to jolt you back to reality. Lauren was there and had done her job perfectly. James knew what needed to be done. Quite simply, it was time to stop feeling sorry for himself and start making sense of this crazy animal. His energy was renewed.

"So, just two huh? That's all you could get," Lauren said, returning to her sarcastic operandi.

James nodded his head, and grinned. "Yup, it started get a little rough. I even had Bullwinkle helping me."

Lauren laughed. "Oh yeah, good luck with that," she said. "This morning I found him sitting in the bathroom staring at the wall. Probably not your best choice for an advisor."

Chapter 13

~

APRIL 9

Michael stood along the rail as Manny and Sing made their way past. "How'd he do?" Michael asked, now walking in stride with them.

"Fine, he changed easily, both on the backstretch and coming for home. I think he was just being ornery last race." Manny leaned in and patted Sing's neck, "You were you just a little ornery last race. Weren't you boy?"

"OK. That makes every day this week he changed like we trained him. He better not pull that bit again."

"He's still learning," Manny said, defending his friend. "I'm sure he'll do fine next out. You guys have him on the right track."

"Yeah, let's hope," Michael said, "cause his next out is only six days away."

"Oh, you found a spot for him?"

"Yeah, it wasn't too hard since he hasn't won a race in so long. He fits an awful lot of conditions."

"Well, he'll be ready," Manny said, stroking Sing's mane. Michael nodded like someone not quite as sure.

"I'll meet you back there." Manny clucked at Sing, asking him for a trot and they started their way toward the barn.

Michael kept his eyes on Sing as he and Manny began to outpace him. Sing looked fit and ready. He moved with a graceful gait, like a top-class show horse, which was a career he was quickly closing in on. Michael wasn't so sure anything they were doing was the answer. Sure, Sing changed his leads now, but why does he always wait until the race to mess up?

For a man like Michael, this type of horse presented a big problem. Michael needed definite issues that were easy to pinpoint, even if they were tough to correct. The horse that wouldn't change leads, he could fix. But Sing would do it fine one day and then refuse during the race. That made no sense to Michael. He could take the horse that always broke slowly and work with him in the gate until he came out like a shot. He could take the speed horse and train him to sit behind horses, take dirt in his face and then be ready to run when they turned for home. These were problems he could fix. This mental horse that was one day on, one day off, was beyond his understanding. Michael was left brained and this just didn't compute.

APRIL 12

Michael looked at the *Daily Racing Form*, studying Sing's competition. He certainly had every chance to win this race based on who he would run against, Michael thought. They were a moderately accomplished bunch, at best. Of course, God only knew what Sing had planned for his next 'adventure.' Somewhere inside that horse was a runner, a potentially great one at that, but so far, how to draw it out remained a mystery. His race was scheduled in three days. One last attempt before they wrapped up their stay in the Sunshine State. A day or two after the race they would retrace their path back to New York. Michael hoped at least they could end the trip on a winning note, as did the rest of the team. The trip would still be seen as a failure, but less so anyway. Perhaps a win could become the springboard of success for the remainder of the year.

After all, Sing's first race was a complete throw out. The paddock debacle left Sing no chance of doing well, let alone winning. In his second race, Sing gave a good effort. He obviously had issues, but overall he ran well and was only beaten by one horse. If Sing could overcome some of those issues and win this race, then Michael could feel good about Sing's direction. He needed to know Sing was improving. He needed to keep positive. The same sense of frustration manifesting itself in James was beginning to grow in Michael. A win, even if it wasn't a stakes race, would do well to quell those feelings.

APRIL 15

Manny scurried about the Gulfstream Park barn area ensuring everything was in order. This being his third trip there, he was getting quite familiar with the place. So much so, he had gotten to the point he would stop and talk to some of the locals. Regardless, Manny looked forward to heading home to New York after this one. They had been gone for three months now and that was more than enough. He longed for his cozy room above the barn, some privacy and some good home cooking. Manny was just about ready when Michael arrived at Sing's stall.

"We about ready?"

Manny grabbed the bucket and sponge and took a quick look around. "All set." Hearing the OK, Michael attached the shank to Sing and they began the trek to the paddock. Michael had made the decision to travel from Tampa to Gulfstream the day before the race this time. The first time they came the day of the race and it was a disaster. Last time they came two days in advance and it seemed to give Sing time to get comfortable with his surroundings. This time Michael chose to compromise between the two. Of course with James in New York he didn't have anyone to stay with the other horses for two days. He arranged for a fellow Finger Lakes trainer, also spending a few months in Tampa, to take care of them for the day.

Scotty Ash came down every year. Why exactly, Michael didn't know. Scotty's horse stock wasn't all that good and he never fared well down here. Michael figured it was probably to get away from his wife. Rumor had it in the years prior to him heading for Florida, Scotty and his wife would be at the brink of divorce by the end of each cold winter. Too much time cooped up together. No matter what the reason, Scotty was a good guy and kind enough to watch the horses. Not that Michael felt they needed more than one day. The only thing they really needed was a victory.

Led by Manny, Sing casually strolled around the paddock. Watching him, Michael had to wonder what exactly set him off that first day. Sometimes he acted like nothing bothered him and other times he would spook at virtually nothing. He was still contemplating the matter when the jockey, Sergio Ramos, came up beside him. It was unfortunately the third jockey in as many races. It would be nice to maintain some consistency, but the last jockey, Phil Teator, already had a mount for Joe Jones, a trainer he rode regularly for and the first jockey, Fernando Torres, well, that just didn't feel right to Michael. Regardless, Sergio was a solid rider with experience and had been riding the Florida circuit for years. He'd learned his trade on the unsanctioned and wild bush tracks in Panama as a youngster and still rode with that same reckless abandon. Knowing Sergio would give him all he had, Michael felt comfortable giving him the mount for today's race. The two watched Sing while Michael tried to fill him in on some of Sing's tendencies. Sergio listened, nodding his understanding, but never said anything in response. After the short one-way conversation, it crossed Michael's mind that he hadn't inquired as to how well Sergio spoke English and he wondered if he'd understood a word Michael had said. 'Too late now,' Michael thought to himself as the paddock judge called for riders' up. Sing accepted his new rider with no qualms and Manny led the duo toward the track.

Michael and Manny took their respective positions to watch the race, Michael in the grandstand and Manny by the rail. Michael stood watching Sing intently through his binoculars. Sing threw his head again during post parade, but not to the extent he had last time. An encouraging sign, thought Michael, maybe their training was making progress. Maybe this time he would show them he was a genuine race horse.

James stood alone in front of his parents' television, glued to the set. He wanted to catch any and every glimpse of Sing. If Sing acted up, he wanted to see exactly when. It might give him that little clue that would help him understand why. Somewhere out there was the answer to the mystery, an answer James was determined to find. But whenever they showed Sing, outside of a little head tossing, he seemed fine. He acted alright in the paddock, again in the post parade and he seemed to warm up well. Deep down James actually felt a twinge of disappointment, followed quickly thereafter by a shot of guilt. He certainly didn't want Sing to act up, but Sing always does something. Why not today? Why should today be any different? Maybe this meant something, James thought. Could his lack of trouble hold the clue he'd been searching for? It suddenly occurred to him that he wasn't there today. Maybe he was the problem. As quickly as that thought arose, he remembered that he hadn't been there for the last race either. 'Good,' James thought, breathing a sigh of relief, 'I'd hate to discover that problem was actually me.'

Hearing the clang of closing gates, James brought his attention back to the present. "Dad, they're going in the gate," he yelled to his father. Jack strolled out of the kitchen and into the family room, cup of coffee in hand. He was never one to arrive before it was absolutely necessary, partly to calm his nerves. The last horse moved in and they were ready for the start.

Having watched Sing in the paddock and warming up, Michael felt certain this race would be different. Sing broke well and the jockey positioned him just behind the leaders. He was anxious, but not overly so. Of course, Michael thought to himself keeping his binoculars fixed on Sing, I don't think he's ever not been anxious. That thought suddenly drew Michael's attention away from the race, scanning his memory for a time when Sing wasn't so excitable. It dawned on him that Sing had never had a race without some sort of incident. He had probably been his best behaved in this race. Hearing the announcer call Sing's name brought Michael back to the present. The horses were rounding the far turn. Sing had joined the leaders and was beginning to move past. The jockey had yet to ask him for his best run. Michael continued to keep his binoculars trained on Sing as they entered the stretch.

With an eighth of a mile to go Sing looked like a winner. He had taken a clear lead and behind him only two horses continued to run well. The remainder of the pack was slowing down. He even begrudgingly changed leads as they hit the stretch. As long as he could keep moving at this pace for the next 12 seconds, he was home free. But it was Jack who noticed first. "He's shortening his stride," which in horse racing means he's running out of steam. Sing's breeding was laden with stamina. This race was a mile and an eighth. A sixteenth of a mile longer than his previous two, but well within Sing's limits. The fact he was running out of gas meant something was wrong. By the time he passed the sixteenth pole, he was running on nothing but fumes. Sergio tried in vain to keep Sing moving, hitting him right-handed and then switching to his left hand, but Sing had nothing left to give. Both Jack's and James' heart sank as those same two horses charged passed Sing toward the finish. Sing managed to hang on for a disappointing third. As they stood there dumbfounded, James voiced what they both were thinking, "what the hell just happened?" There was naturally no answer.

From the grandstand, Michael couldn't see anything that looked out of the ordinary, watching Sing gallop out and pull up to a jog. Sing hadn't taken a bad step and didn't appear lame in any way. Heading down the steps toward the track Michael cursed, loud enough for himself to hear but nobody else. Normally he would have kept them under his breath completely, but he was unable to hold it in any longer. It seemed as though absolutely nothing went their way. The racing gods were against them and sometimes you have no choice but to curse them.

Standing along the fence for a race usually limits the amount you can see. You have to rely on the call of the announcer. But in this instance because of his proximity to the track and horses, Manny had an advantage when determining why Sing had faltered. As the horses ran past him Manny could hear Sing struggling to breathe. He wasn't sure why, but he knew Sing wasn't getting the oxygen he needed to carry that speed, or at least that's what he thought. That's what cost him the race. The question was what was inhibiting his breathing.

Back at the barn, Michael cringed at the computer monitor as he watched the snake-like tube slither its way through Sing's respiratory tract. Even if it didn't bother the recipient, it gave Michael the willies. It reminded him of some of the medical shows his wife finds so fascinating. Quite frankly, he finds them revolting and refuses to be in the same room when she's watching them. Unfortunately, on this occasion, he had no choice.

After the race, Michael and Manny had readily concluded they needed to call the vet. Michael would've preferred they did it in Tampa, with a vet he knew well, but now was the best time. So Manny, with his new found local contacts, got a good recommendation and Michael called. The vet came out immediately and with Michael and Manny watching, initiated a procedure known as endoscopy on Sing, commonly referred to as scoping.

The fiber optic cable poked and weaved its way until it found an answer. It turned out Sing had a fair amount of mucus in his lungs brought on by some sort of infection. Dr. Mosey showed it to Manny and Michael, pointing out the blemish on the screen. They nodded and acted like they could see it, neither wanting to admit they couldn't make heads or tails of what appeared before them. But it certainly became understandable, after watching the procedure and listening to Dr. Mosey, why Sing couldn't hold the lead in the stretch. Actually, how he had run as well as he did was a testament to his courage and ability. Once the diagnosis was complete Michael gave Jack a call. The two horsemen concluded that remaining in the warmer Florida temperature would be better for Sing. The trip home would be postponed for a couple weeks to allow Sing time to get healthy, warm weather and a round of anti-biotics hopefully doing the trick. And that was yet one more disappointment for Manny, Michael and the rest of the O'Brien team. The deep water felt deeper.

Chapter 14

⁓

MAY 1

THE TRUCK STARTED DOWN THE Johnsons' long driveway toward the house before veering right and heading for the barn. Better than three months had passed since they were there and the Aiken farm blossomed with the sights of spring. Previously barren trees now overflowed with new leaves, the spring rains had turned the pastures a lush and deep green, and all along the house and barn flowers bloomed in bright colors. It was in sharp contrast to the bland winter landscape that greeted them on their way down to Florida. A contrast that was shared in the attitudes of Michael and Manny. The one-time excited travelers, filled with anticipation, were now beaten down by the long and fruitless journey.

Matt Johnson and his faithful dog Lester exited the barn and headed toward the truck came as Michael brought it to a halt. After turning off the truck, Michael opened his door to see Lester wagging his tail and looking up at him. But after getting a good look at the driver Lester decided to head to the other side. Manny was just stepping down from the cab when Lester came scurrying around.

"Hey boy, how you doing?" Manny asked. Lester continued to wag his tail, but didn't come to Manny. Instead, he angled his head around Manny and gazed into the truck. Manny turned, following Lester's gaze and looked into the empty vehicle. It took a second, but then it dawned on Manny what the dog was doing. "Awe, I'm sorry buddy, James isn't with us," Manny said apologetically. "He's already home." Lester just stood there waiting, not understanding a word Manny said. But no one emerged. The sound of trailer doors opening sent Lester running to the back. But alas, no friend, only horses. The trip's disappointment, like some entity let loose by the truck's open doors, spilled out to envelop even Lester.

About the time Lester's tail stopped wagging, Matt reached the truck and greeted Michael and Manny. He could tell by their appearance they were worn out. "You boys look like you've been ridden hard and put away wet."

Michael smiled knowingly. "It's been a long three months since we've seen you last. And suffice to say it didn't go as well as we'd hoped."

"Well, let's get the horses put away and get you guys inside. We can grab some beers and I'll fire up the grill." They were welcome words from a gracious host.

"Thank you Matt," Michael said. "That sounds awful good right about now."

Michael stared at his beer, St. Pauli Girl, taking notice of cute barmaid donning the label. Looking at it, he realized he'd drunk down to her im-possible-to-miss chest, making the bottle half empty. Catching the sweet scent of blooming lilacs, Michael picked up his head and surveyed his sur-roundings. The evening air felt quite cool, yet had a comfortable feeling about it. It was good to be outside, with open space, having been confined to that apartment in Tampa for so long. Add to that a couple of beers and he was nice and relaxed.

"Ready for another?" Matt asked.

"No thanks, I think I'm good," Michael said.

Matt glanced at Manny with inquiring eyes, but was turned down there as well. "OK. Well I think I might get one more."

"This is nice," Manny said.

"It is," Michael replied, as he watched Lester roll over onto his side.

Matt returned moments later with a fresh beer and cracked it open. The men sat on their Adirondack chairs and gazed at the fields. To their left were the open pastures and to the right the riding ring and training track. The horses were put up for the night, leaving the countryside peacefully still. The sun was just about down leaving an orange glow over the distant tree-line, melting away any stress the day may have brought.

The three horsemen sat and shared horse stories and enjoyed the serenity of country living. For Michael, at least for tonight, it helped relieve some of the pressure he'd been feeling. Life is short and things have a way of working themselves out and sometimes you lose that in the daily details. He finished his beer and set it aside his chair. "This is a wonderful place you have here Matt."

"Thank you Michael. We really love it. I remember years ago when we were still living in Atlanta, we had gone to New York to visit the Marsh's and while we were there we went to your folks farm for a cookout. I absolutely loved it. The setting was idyllic. Before we had left for the evening, my mind was made up. The next day I told Claudia it was time to get out of Atlanta and move to the country. Within two years, I quit my job and we moved here. I haven't looked back since, she neither. That's been about 12 years now."

Michael smiled. He heard the sound of steak juice popping on hot coals and glanced at the smoking grill. He looked out over the quiet pastures and watched a hawk coast by. How nice it would be to feel that way, content. To wake up each day and not have to worry. Maybe one day, he hoped, but not now. He was much too far from it.

MAY 3

The stay at the Johnsons' farm served as a pleasant reminder of what lay a couple days drive away. The next morning the boys left early and drove for what seemed like an eternity before once again stopping in Laurel, Maryland where they bedded down their horses in Tim Keefe's barn, another friend of a friend of a friend. After some greasy fast food and a bad night's sleep, they got up, loaded the horses and began the final leg. As they passed through Harrisburg, Pennsylvania, traveling route 15 toward New York, they knew home was but a few hours away. Neither Manny nor Michael had much to say. Both just looked forward to getting there. Once they crossed the border into New York snow flurries began to fall. A cold front had come in and the temperatures fell unseasonably low. It made Michael feel like even the elements were disenchanted with them. "This weather almost seems appropriate," said Michael. Manny nodded his agreement. "When we get there," Michael continued, "let's just put them out in the small field for a little while. Give 'em a chance to stretch their legs and get Sing's head down, it couldn't hurt his lungs, that's for sure. Hopefully Mom has some dinner cooking for us."

Manny smiled with a big grin. It had been a long time since he'd sat in Margaret's kitchen and enjoyed one of her meals. "That sounds real good to me."

About an hour later, they drove down the sloping driveway of the O'Briens' farm. They'd made it home. Manny and Michael unloaded the horses and some of the integral equipment and left the rest. It was cold and it was miserable. Their sullen looks and slow movements reminded Michael of a sports team who had played hard and lost. They were tired, their spirits were broken and they just wanted to get done with the business at hand. As they finished unloading the last horse, Jack appeared.

"How's our champion?" he said with a certain sarcastic tone.

"He's doing alright," replied Michael. "He should be ready to start training again in a couple days."

Jack nodded as Manny came walking up. Manny smiled at Jack and let them know he had put all the horses where they needed to be. Jack grabbed Manny by the back of the neck and gave him a friendly shake. "Well, it's good to have you boys back. Why don't you go inside and get something to eat. Mom has a nice hot meal for you. I'll take care of things out here." Both smiled and thanked Jack. As Michael passed, Jack gave him a pat on his shoulder. It was the proverbial "good game" given after a failed effort. Michael sure didn't feel like it had been a "good game." Nonetheless, he welcomed his Dad's consolation.

Chapter 15

~

MAY 5

THE COLD FRONT THAT HAD so rudely greeted the gang returning from Florida had moved out and was replaced by pleasant spring temperatures. It was Kentucky Derby Day and tradition mandated an O'Brien family Derby picnic. Michael with his family and James with his family arrived in early afternoon to begin the festivities. Even Daniel and his wife Nicole attended, arriving a little while later. Daniel – son number three, was four years younger than James. He and Nicole lived in Rochester, about 30 minutes from the farm, where they maintained professional careers. As a youngster Daniel saw work around the farm as nothing more than a chore. It was no surprise that when he was old enough to choose a profession, his choice had nothing to do with horses or farming. His father liked to joke with him that his hands were too tender for farming, which usually elicited a "whatever" response from Daniel. Today's presence meant that the entire family, including "adopted" member Manny, was there with the exception of the boys' sister Sarah. She would be returning home the following week after finishing her final year at Cazenovia College.

The tradition called for a cookout of some sort, usually a game or two of cards and culminated with the race itself. Not the most exciting of traditions, but it was a great reason to get the family together. At least that's what Margaret thought anyway. Today's event looked just like those of year's past, but under the surface lingered a seriousness that betrayed the games and banter. Vanished hopes, failed expectations, made this year different. There were no side bets, no picking of horses, none of the usual who could or couldn't get the Derby distance. They were out because their horse didn't perform when it counted. And that cloud of disappointment hung with them. Their one and probably only chance to ever get the Derby went all wrong. So around the time the men would usually call for a deck of cards, the discussion began to drift toward the source of those failed expectations; what to do about the horse?

Even after the debacle of a trip to Florida everyone still believed in Sing's talent. Not one of the team had given up on him yet. Only Daniel, having virtually no personal investment in the animal, thought they should consider selling him. Let someone else frustrate themselves trying to figure the horse out, he suggested. It caused the group to pause, but within a minute or two they dismissed the idea. Each of the group had a different reason, but none were willing to quit at this point. For Michael, it was a test of wills, his against the horse. For James, Sing represented a giant riddle he couldn't quite figure out, but knew the answer was out there somewhere. For Jack, years of experience told him this horse was special, they just hadn't mastered how to draw it out of him. And for Manny, it was as simple as he loved the horse. Each day highlighted by his morning workout on the greatest horse he had ever ridden.

In the end, they decided the best approach would be to nurse him back to health and run him at Finger Lakes. With the lower level of competition he should be able to win easily. Perhaps if he won a couple of races, it would build up his confidence and then maybe his skittish attitude might begin to disappear. It was a theory anyway.

From the family room Margaret yelled that the horses were on the track for the Derby. Putting the theory into practice would have to wait; it was time to watch horses that had already proven their worth.

Five minutes after Margaret's announcement the horses were standing in the gate. Two minutes and 3 seconds later The Sarge sprinted under the finish line and the horse racing world crowned a new champion.

"There goes the Florida Derby winner," James said, referring to The Sarge's previous race.

Michael looked at James. "And your point?"

"That horse never scared me. Sing could have taken him."

"Sing hasn't *taken* anyone. What are you thinking?"

"I'm saying he's got it in him," James said, much louder than necessary.

Michael was about to lay into James when Jack interceded. "Enough already," he said, eyeing both boys. "I've heard as much as I care to about that horse. The past is the past and we all know what needs to be done. We are where we are. No more discussion on it. Got it? No more."

MAY 12

Most college students when moving their belongings into or out of the dorms use the family car or, more likely, the family SUV. Not Sarah O'Brien, she was lucky enough to have her family show up with a horse trailer in tow. Thank God they had at least given it a good cleaning beforehand, she thought. Today was graduation day and she was graduating with honors in Farm Management. As the youngest of the O'Briens, she was a full eight years younger than her next sibling. Her three older brothers loved to tease her about being an "accident," which her parents vehemently denied despite the fact that it was true. Even though she was an unplanned event, Jack and Margaret were thrilled when the day came and a girl popped out. After three boys, having a girl was a gift from above.

Sarah was born to be a farm girl. While most girls in high school were out looking for parties and boys, Sarah preferred to stay at home, ride horses and even muck stalls. Her parents actually had to push her to accept a date and go to her prom. It wasn't that she was unattractive; there were a number of the boys in her class vying for her attention. But she, like her dad, enjoyed being in the company of equines more than humans. And when Margaret pushed her to be more social, she would search out and try to enlist the help of her dad. Jack, knowing his daughter was just like he and seeing nothing wrong with it, would usually beat a hasty retreat. It was a no-win situation for him and he didn't want to come between his two favorite ladies. In those instances he found his tractor to be a safe refuge.

Having loaded the final piece of furniture, Jack latched the trailer door shut. He scanned the area looking for Sarah, as Manny, who had come along to help with the bigger pieces, came around the trailer. "You see her?" Jack asked.

Kids and parents scurried about the place creating a hectic scene, everyone trying to pack up and say goodbye at the same time. Manny looked dazed and confused. "No, and I'm not sure I'd spot her if she were right in front of me."

OK, not much help there, Jack thought to himself. Finally, in the distance, across the parking lot, Jack spotted her, hugging one of her classmates and smiling from ear to ear. Seeing her smile made him smile. It would be good to have her home again. Her energy could liven up a room and would be welcomed back at the house. But as glad as he was to see his daughter coming home, it reinforced the need to get the farm back making money. She was one more person who hoped to make a living through O'Brien Racing. This summer was going to be an important one for the future of the operation, no doubt about it. And as he stood there, waiting for his daughter to eventually make her way back, a group of men were meeting in a large conference room in a giant skyscraper in New York City, men who were putting a plan in motion that would jeopardize the very existence of Jack's beloved farm.

MAY 19

The combination of liniment and hay filled the air of Sing's stall, as Manny rubbed the remaining oil on Sing's skin, messaging it in. The mid-day sun, high in the sky, shone through the stall door. Where the light beams came through, particles of dust could be seen gently floating down. It was quiet and peaceful as Manny went about his business. Manny had already pulled Sing's mane, and even considered banging his tail like the Europeans do, but then figured Michael wouldn't care for that. No sense ticking off the boss. Groomed and muscled, Sing looked phenomenal. Add in his perfect conformation and bright chestnut coloring, Sing appeared ready for a portrait and the Hall of Fame.

Manny took a step back and stared at him, using his pants to wipe the oil from his hands. It was difficult not to love this animal. Between his ability and looks, he was everything you could ask for in a horse. It's why Manny spent so much time with him. No one asked Manny to rub him down again, or trim his mane, or clip his whiskers. It wasn't a part of his job. But he had no pets to go home to, no blood relatives nearby to visit, not even a girlfriend. Perhaps Sing made up for those things, though Manny didn't spend much time psychoanalyzing it. The reason was irrelevant. All that mattered was the enjoyment his time with Sing brought him. So he spent his mornings riding him and his afternoons showering him with attention. And that combination worked, for both horse and rider.

MAY 21

"What are you doing?" Mary asked, entering her dad's study.

"Well," replied Michael. "I'm looking at how the horses are doing and if there are any races coming up that they could race in."

Mary gazed down at the sheets spread across the table, then at the computer and then at her dad. None of it made any sense to her, but it didn't stop her from asking more questions. "Which horse are you looking at now?"

"Right at the moment I am reviewing Sing So Long's charts."

Mary looked at the spreadsheet, still didn't mean anything. So, she decided she would have to take her dad's word for it and moved on to her next question. "What does it tell you?"

Michael, accustomed to the relentless questioning from his daughter, exhibited a father's patience. "It tells me he's almost ready to race again.

So I'm looking at the computer because it tells me the different races and then I can determine if any would be just right for Sing."

Now Mary was intrigued, though she hadn't figured out what her next question should be. While the wheels in her head were turning, Michael went back to the computer, scrolled through his options and waited for the inevitable. It didn't take long.

"Maybe I can pick one out for you."

Michael looked at his daughter and knew he would have to at least partially indulge her, otherwise she might turn on the little girl drama. He'd seen it before and it wasn't pretty. "Alright," he said with a smile, "let's take a look at some of these races." Michael moved his mouse over the Finger Lakes Condition Book and opened it up. It listed the races available for the next three weeks. "OK, we need an allowance race going more than a mile." Mary stared at Michael as if he spoke a foreign language.

Realizing she had no idea what that meant, Michael tried a new approach. He spotted a race that could work and pointed to it. "Now this race might work. It's a mile and a sixteenth with a purse of $18,000. Although, it's coming up next week and that might be too soon." Michael turned his head toward Mary. It was time to include her. "That one's not bad, but maybe we should look for another one. What do you think?" It was a leading question which worked perfectly.

"Yeah, we should look for another," Mary answered.

Michael scanned further and quickly found what he wanted. "Hey, there we are." He pointed to the race for Mary to see, not that she understood the combination of letters and numbers. "This race is a mile and an eighth, with a purse of $20,000, for horses who haven't won a race in three months and it's not for another two weeks. I think that would be just the thing." Michael gazed over at his daughter. "Do you think we should enter him in this one?"

Mary felt confident in her answer. "Yes, that's the one Dad. Enter him in that one."

"OK, good idea. I'll do that," Michael said, giving her a soft pat on the head.

Mary grinned, her work now complete. She turned and strutted out of the study, secure in the knowledge that she had solved her father's dilemma.

Chapter 16

~

MAY 31

RON DOMBROWSKI SAT IN THE corner of the conference rooming fuming as he listened to the Bank's Vice President's diatribe. What a bunch of crap he thought. In Ron's mind, it was definitely us and them. What was left of the old western New York FLS&L was the "us" and those yahoos from downstate New York, the bank that bought them out, were the "them." *They* had made the questionable loans. *They* had made the bad judgment calls, not us. But to listen to the speech, it seemed as though *we* were in this together and *we* had to make some tough choices. Had it not been for the piece of paper Ron held containing the names of the condemned, he probably would have stopped listening long ago. But one name on that list made Ron livid. Just over two months ago Ron persuaded Henry Livingston to suspend the O'Briens' payments for a few months. Now that choice had come back to bite him. The loan was considered delinquent, so it made the list. Henry the Ain't could have easily had it removed, Ron was sure of that. But he didn't. All during the meeting Ron glared at Henry, but Henry refused to glance anywhere near where Ron was seated. So Ron waited, his anger growing as each minute passed.

As the meeting ended, Ron noticed Henry make a quick move to the door. That bastard is trying to bolt out of here, he thought. Ron quickened his pace brushing a couple other distraught lenders out of the way. As he finally made it to the door, he saw Henry retreating into his office, closing the door behind him. Ron sped up his pace blowing by the secretary's desk.

Henry liked to use his personal secretary as his first line of defense. She jumped up hoping to halt the onrushing train. "Mr. Livingston isn't to be disturbed." She stood no chance. Ron was past her before she finished her sentence.

Knowing what was coming, Henry picked up his phone hoping to quickly find someone, anyone with which to start a conversion, but he was too late. Ron came barging in before he could dial the last couple numbers. Ron was holding the list above his head, waving it about.

"This is total bullshit Henry. There is no way the O'Briens should be on this list."

Henry slowly hung up the receiver and looked up at the madman before him. "Ron, you need to calm down."

"Calm down, are you kidding me? You're about to take down their entire operation. They've been with me for over 30 years, with the bank for over 60."

"There is nothing I can do Ron. Corporate is calling all the shots on this one."

Ron cut him off before he could continue his bailout. "Did you even try to talk to them about this one? Did you talk to them about any of these?" Ron paused long enough to tell nothing was forthcoming. "That's what I thought." He threw the list onto Henry's desk, sending a cup filled with pens and pencils flying about. Disgusted, though pleased at least with having disturbed Henry's overly neat desk, Ron turned and headed for the door. At the doorway he turned back around. "Henry, you're a coward. Do you know that? I don't know why I ever helped you." Ron shook his head and continued to his desk.

Arriving at his desk he noticed a sheet of paper laid atop his keyboard. It was a form letter Corporate prepared for the lenders to give their condemned clients. "Are you fucking kidding me," Ron said aloud, speaking to everyone and no one. He crumpled it up and threw it against the wall. "To hell with this place." Grabbing his coat, he stormed out, knocking over a pile of mail that sat on the corner of his desk. Tomorrow was going to be a bad day.

Chapter 17

~

JUNE 2

THE NEWS RON BROUGHT HIT Jack with a force not even he could've expected. It angered him that a bank his family had dealt with for over 60 years, better than 30 of which were directly with himself, could so easily sweep them aside. He certainly didn't blame Ron, which is why he refrained from cursing him out on the spot yesterday. Besides, Jack thought, we are a good client, somebody out there must be interested in having our business. He figured on Monday he'd call around and get something set up. Take care of that problem and then turn his attention to the other problem, the horse. Though he hoped the horse problem was already on the road to being fixed.

Once Sing recovered from the lung infection, Michael brought him over to Finger Lakes and re-started his conditioning pattern. The weather was good, helping keep his workout regimen on schedule, and Sing seemed to thrive being back on familiar ground. Michael and James were pleased with his progress and his attitude.

Today, Sing was entered to run in an allowance race against a field of lesser accomplished horses. He was also being reunited with the jockey who'd ridden him in his first two starts, Johnnie Joyce. Both of which were wins. By all accounts, he should get an easy victory under his belt. And being only a 25 minute ride to the track, Jack could've easily gone but instead decided to stay at home. After yesterday's news Jack simply didn't feel like venturing out and to date, his watching Sing hadn't provided any racing luck. Maybe staying away would change things. Not that Jack was superstitious by nature, but for anyone involved in sports of any kind, superstition is just the norm. It happens to all types, from the professional athlete all the way down to the weekend hacker at the local golf course, everyone has their superstitions. Naturally the horse business is no different and, like it or not, no one involved can escape it.

Back in his training days, Jack had an old baseball cap that served as his good luck charm. He got the cap years before while coaching Michael's little league baseball team. He liked it enough to wear it nearly every morning during the training hours. It wasn't anything to look at, a simple red front and brim with a white mesh back, but it fit with the comfort of an old shoe. Most days he'd put it away after the morning session, but sometimes, when he knew they needed some good fortune, he would pull it out and wear it for the races. Whether it actually worked was debatable, but Jack thought so. There were plenty of win pictures at the O'Brien house with that cap in the photo. Either way, he felt that doing something different today might help put the O'Briens back in the winner's circle.

From inside the barn Jack could hear a truck coming down the driveway. Wrapping up the evening feeding ritual, he walked out to see Michael's truck and trailer pulling up near the barn. He didn't expect to see Michael this evening so he wondered if the visit was for pleasure or something of a less enjoyable nature. As Michael exited the cab Jack could see his facial expression. Michael wasn't there for pleasure.

"Toss him in his stall," Michael yelled to Manny. Out of the trailer came Sing and Manny. Even a novice could have spotted the fact that Sing was lame on his right front leg.

Jack let out a sigh, "What happened now?"

Michael took a deep breath and began his story. "Well, he decided to change it up a little this time. He actually did real well in the paddock and warming up, a nice change from the last three. Then during the race he rated behind the leaders and made his move on the far turn. He was the only horse moving as they came down the lane. The lead horse was tiring badly, so it looked like he had it in the bag." Michael paused a moment, as if wanting to distinguish the good news from the upcoming bad news. "Then the jock on the lead horse gave his mount a strong left-handed whip. So at this point his horse veers out real sharply just as Sing is about to go past. He basically cut him off right when Sing was on top of him." Becoming more and more animated, Michael continued. "Sing clipped heels with the other horse and it looked like he was going down. How he stayed up I'm not sure. Unfortunately, Johnnie couldn't hold on. He went tumbling off, race over!"

Margaret, who had arrived near the beginning of the story, spoke up first. "I thought you guys were supposed to be Irish? What ever happened to having the luck of the Irish? A bunch of hooey I think." As it were, her family bloodlines led back to Denmark and Italy. On occasion she enjoyed teasing Jack about his Irish heritage and the children as well, who were all very proud of being part Irish. Knowing she had the attention of the two O'Briens she gave an over-emphatic sigh and shrugged her shoulders, then began walking back to the house. Jack wasn't so amused, but it brought a smile to Michael's face.

Jack turned his attention back to Michael. "Is Johnnie OK?"

"Yeah, he's fine. He didn't land too hard and the rest of the pack was back far enough they avoided him pretty easily." Beginning to walk into the barn he added "a lot better than the horse anyway."

Concerned, Jack asked, "How bad is the horse?"

"Actually he's not that bad," conceded Michael. "He's got a nice-sized gash on his right front cannon and it's swelled up quite a bit, but it doesn't look like there's any real damage. The vet stitched him up and we took a couple x-rays. After that we iced him down. He should be fine, but…"

Jack cut him off, finishing what Michael was surely going to say. "But he'll be out of action for a while, again." Jack made sure to overemphasize the word again. So much for bringing a little racing luck, Jack thought, wondering out of the blue about an old red and white mesh ball cap.

Chapter 18

~

JUNE 3

JUST AS THEY DID MOST nights, Margaret and Jack ate dinner in near silence. With as many years of marriage as they had, no one felt the need to talk unless there was good reason. They spent most days together, or at least saw one another multiple times in passing. If anything needed to be discussed, they had ample opportunity to do so.

Their quiet routine had changed slightly with Sarah returning from college. Instead of just the two of them, they were now three. Not that there was suddenly a great deal of chatter at the table, Sarah also tended to speak only when spoken to – something she learned as a child and hadn't outgrown. Tonight though, it was back to only Margaret and Jack.

"No Sarah tonight?" Jack asked.

"No. Jenny is in town tonight so they decided to go out for a bite and talk. Since they never get to see each other anymore, Jenny being in Albany and all, and with the marriage next summer, it was nice they both had time. I know Sarah misses seeing her. She's really a nice girl." Jack sat there, shoveling his dinner and not saying a word, a clueless look plastered on his face. "You have no idea who Jenny is, do you?"

His eyebrows raised and he let out a big breath of air. "No, I haven't the slightest."

"Jack, I swear. Jenny? Little Jenny Duncan? Lived at the edge of town on Buffalo Street?" Margaret could tell by Jack's face that he still had no idea. "They were in Brownies together. Played soccer in high school together." She continued to study his face, hoping something would ring a bell. Still nothing. "Ugh, you're unbelievable."

"What do you want me to say? We had four kids. There were more kids coming and going around here than you could shake a stick at," Jack said, waving his fork about.

"I bet if I said the name of a horse you'd remember it, wouldn't you?" Margaret countered, with a bit of attitude to boot.

"How am I supposed to respond to that?" Jack said, knowing full well he probably would. Margaret replied with only a huff.

Having 'resolved' Sarah's whereabouts, but not dinner itself, Margaret figured it was a good time to clear her mind of nagging thoughts.

"You didn't mention anything to the boys did you?" she inquired.

Jack had debated yesterday whether or not he should say something to Michael. But heaping bad news upon bad news wasn't Jack's style, and besides, he was planning on calling the other banks tomorrow. As long as someone picked up their business, then it wouldn't be any big deal. "Nope. No sense worrying the kids at this point."

"I agree," responded Margaret. Of course Margaret, like all women, excelled when it came to worrying. Jack's answer was what she expected, she surely would have known if indeed he'd said something, but that wasn't really where she was aiming. She allowed Jack to get another bite before she followed up her first question with the one she couldn't shake out of her mind. "So what happens if tomorrow no one can help us? I've been thinking about it and have no idea what, outside of selling the place, we could do."

Jack looked up from his plate to see the worried look in Margaret's eyes. He knew he needed to respond to her request. The only problem was his answer offered no real solutions. "I really don't know dear. Tomorrow, if I get shot down, then I guess we'll have to cross that bridge. Until then I'd like to ask you to not worry about it, but I know that would be wasted on deaf ears." Jack smiled at her. It was his way of giving some sort of reassurance where none could be found.

Margaret appreciated the gesture, as she always did, and returned Jack's smile. Inside, her gut was telling her tomorrow would not bring good news. For now, she would try to play along with Jack and pretend his words had soothed her. "OK dear, I'll put it out of my mind and wait and see what happens tomorrow." She could lie for the good of the game, if needed. It was a funny game they played. She knew Jack didn't believe her and Jack knew she knew he didn't believe her, but none of that mattered. Trying to explain it to an outsider was like reciting an Abbott and Costello routine, but to Jack and Margaret, it was their way of letting the other know they understood.

JUNE 4

Banks are funny sorts of institutions. If you were to talk to a businessman, he's likely to tell you that as long as you have plenty of money and little need, then most banks are more than willing to give you a loan. In fact, they will probably actively pursue you, offering to give you anything you'd desire. On the other hand, if you're struggling and needed funds to help run your business, then those same banks assuredly won't have anything for you. If they were to find a little something for you, then chances are they would require at least your first born as collateral, possibly a second born as well depending upon the size of the loan. Though they would never ask you to have a second child for their sake; that would be going too far.

As far as Jack O'Brien could tell, banks were pretty much useless. He'd spent the better part of two hours this morning sitting in the den, calling around to various banks trying to secure financing for the farm. It was two of the longest hours of his life. Of the four, only one would consider taking them in and the interest rate and terms of the agreement, should it go through, were, according to Jack, outrageous. After finishing his conversation with the last of the four, Jack slumped in his chair, massaging his face with his old farm hands. Margaret walked into the den to see a worn-out farmer.

"You look worse than if you'd been Christmas shopping with me."

Jack smiled. "If given the choice, I would go shopping with you in a heartbeat rather than talk to these banking morons."

Although it was obvious the calls didn't go well, Margaret still felt the need to ask the question. "What'd they say?"

Jack, never one to mince words, gave it to her straight. "Well, of the four only Lincoln Bank will even consider us. Their terms and rates are ridiculous, but they may be our only choice. We should hear something back from them by tomorrow afternoon."

Margaret took it in and nodded her understanding. "Let's keep our fingers crossed and hope for the best," she said. Then, with their business concluded, she turned and left the room leaving Jack still motionless in his chair.

As he sat there, unable to move, Jack whispered to himself, "And what the hell happens if these clowns turn us down too?" The bridge was getting closer.

Chapter 19

~

JUNE 5

FOR ANYONE WHO'S HAD TO wait for something important, especially when you know it's coming soon, but aren't sure exactly when, time can tick by excruciatingly slow. The best thing to do is keep as busy as possible, for as long as possible. By doing so, the theory maintains, your mind will focus on the task at hand and not on whatever it is hanging over you. The theory works occasionally, but not always. Some things are just too heavy. The life and death of a farm, a perfect example.

By 9:00 a.m., Jack was back in the house refreshing his mug of coffee, the morning chores complete. Margaret entered wearing a light coat and carrying her purse. "I'm heading for the bank and grocery store, need anything."

"Yeah, if they have any more of those plums, pick some up."

"OK," Margaret said, making a mental note, "anything else?"

"No, not that I can think of," answered Jack. They each looked at their watches, the hands within moving at an agonizingly slow pace, and then at each other. They both thought it, but neither said it. 'Only eight more hours until the end of the business day, eight long hours.' One after the other they headed out the door, both moving at what was for them a dawdling pace.

As Jack cruised in his tractor along the north western side of the fence line, he spotted Margaret's car pulling in the driveway. He glanced at his watch, 10:35. Not bad, he thought, she drug that out about as long as she possibly could. Jack's eyes turned back toward the fence, hoping against hope that somewhere amongst its wooden planks he'd find a problem. Something in need of addressing. He began to think he was too diligent with the property. Whenever something needed fixing, he took care of it right away. Normally, that would be considered a good thing, but not to-day. Today, it meant less work, which was not what he wanted. Efficiency had a price. Then, a crazy thought entered his mind. Run into the fence with the tractor. That should give him several hours' worth of work. He took a look at the fence before quickly coming to his senses. Instead of breaking a few boards, he'd probably end up damaging the tractor and cost himself several hundred dollars in tractor repairs. Maybe not, but with his current run of luck, who knew? It certainly wasn't worth the risk. So instead, Jack continued on, his eyes scanning the landscape for anything that would put keep him busy.

Noon arrived with Jack and Margaret back in the house for lunch, glad to have made it to this point in the day and hoping the call would come soon, ending the torture. By the time Jack had cleaned himself up, lunch was prepared and waiting. Neither spoke until the meal was complete.

"Excellent pasta salad, dear," said Jack.

"Thank you, I'm glad you like it. We hadn't had it in a while so I made a whole batch," Margaret said, pointing to the large bowl sitting on the kitchen counter. "We might be eating it for a while unless we have the kids over."

Jack raised his eyebrows and looked at the bowl. "Alright by me if it's only us. I'm sure I can put a dent in it."

Margaret stood up, collected both plates and headed for the sink. "What do you have planned for the afternoon?"

"Unfortunately, not much. I've pretty much run myself out of things to do." Margaret nodded her head in agreement, having run into the same problem. "I'll probably head down to the barn and putter around. At least it will keep me out of the house."

"I'm not sure what I'll do," Margaret said. What she didn't say, was that she was glad Jack wouldn't be hanging around the house. Being cooped up together, with the stress level increasing, would surely make things worse. "God I hope this call comes soon."

As if her plea had been heard in the heavens, the shrill cry of a phone suddenly echoed through the kitchen. Jack looked at Margaret and she at him, their faces surprised and anxious. Jack waited for her to give him the nod to go ahead and answer it. Once she did, he walked to the phone and slowly picked up the receiver. "O'Brien residence, Jack O'Brien speaking." Silence descended upon the O'Brien house as Lincoln Bank's Ed Spivey informed Jack of their decision. Margaret studied Jack's face hoping to discern whether the news was good or bad. His expression displayed nothing; it was the perfect poker face. For two long minutes Jack listened silently. Then as abruptly as the call came in, it ended. "Thank you very much for your time, goodbye." Jack turned and hung up the phone. Not wanting to drag things out, he turned toward Margaret and shook his head no. They both stood their quietly for a moment, letting the gravity of their situation sink in before Jack spoke up. "It looks like we've crossed the bridge."

Margaret stood there sullen in her disbelief, "I don't think I like this side of the river."

Chapter 20

~

JUNE 6

THE AROMA OF BACON, EGGS and coffee filled the O'Briens' kitchen. It was a comfortable smell, which belied the mood that hung over the house. Sarah and Margaret were eating at the table when Jack walked into the kitchen. For the first time since Margaret could remember Jack had slept in. Of course, sleeping in meant he was still up by 7 a.m., but for Jack, wake up was usually at 5:30 a.m. Sarah, who was accustomed to her father coming in from the outside to get breakfast rather than the bedroom, was taken aback. She knew something must be amiss for him to be getting up now. She could tell her mother had something on her mind simply because she was being so quiet. Being quiet was a normal occurrence for her dad, not her mom.

Jack went straight to the cupboard and grabbed his travel mug. It was a mug he'd won while he and Margaret were on vacation in Niagara Falls years ago, Jack hit knocked six milk jugs off their platform or something. It was a beat up old mug that Jack refused to throw out. According to Jack, it was the only thing he had ever won in his life, therefore he was keeping it. Plus, as he put it, "it was a crusty old mug for a crusty old man." Margaret said she couldn't argue with logic like that.

With mug in hand, Jack poured as much coffee as it would hold – he always took it black - and secured the top. Looking at Margaret he said, "I'm going to head for the track and talk to the boys." Sarah, already feeling ill at ease with the unusual morning events, gave her dad a questioning look. Jack, not wanting to give things away, gave her a hushed, "Good morning, honey," and made his way out the door. He knew as soon as he left Sarah would press Margaret until she was given the news. Better to have Margaret do it, thought Jack, she has a much gentler way about communicating these kinds of things. Telling the boys was one thing, but to have to tell his baby girl. Well, that would just be too difficult on a proud old father.

Before the door had closed Sarah was staring intently at her mom. Margaret returned the glance and waited. As expected, it didn't take more than a couple of seconds. "Mom, what's going on?"

While Margaret tried to soothe a worried Sarah, Jack pulled onto the backside of Finger Lakes. He could've made the trip blindfolded. The horses were stabled in the same barn they'd been in for years. Jack had made this same trek every day for years and years until Michael took over. The barns looked the same, despite having aged another 10-plus years. They used to be blue, but were now a light gray with red gutters running the length of the barns. Jack noticed the neatness of the paint. He guessed they had been re-painted within the last year or two. It looked good, he thought. Better than the old days.

As he got out of his truck, part of him actually missed the old routine. The camaraderie amongst the trainers. The uniqueness of sharing such an unusual profession. Depending upon how the next few months went, Jack thought, 'I might be back here looking for work'. He always figured he'd end up where he started, walking hot horses around a hot shedrow. That less than glorious thought quickly disappeared when he saw Michael, James and Manny standing in front of one of the stalls, looking in at its occupant. Perfect he thought, at least now I won't have to do this more than once.

"Gentlemen, got things straightened out yet?"

The three men all turned abruptly, shocked to see Jack closing on them. "Dad, what are you doing here?" asked Michael. "Haven't seen you around here in ages."

Jack put his hands in the pockets his old work coat and closed in on the boys. The smile he had as he walked up soon disappeared. "I'm glad you're all here."

All three, including Manny, knew Jack well enough to know something wasn't right. The tone in which he had addressed the three and the fact he had come all the way to the track to talk to them, meant whatever was on his mind must be important. It was Michael who again spoke up. "What's going on Dad?"

"Last Friday, Ron Dombrowski from the bank came out to see your mother and me. He informed us the bank was giving us 90 days to pay back the loan we had with them. Otherwise they would foreclose on the farm." Jack paused momentarily, looking at all three, waiting to see if they had anything to say. When nothing more than a look of horror came from each of them, Jack opted to continue. "We decided not to say anything until we had a chance to call some other banks and try to make other arrangements." A glimmer of hope rose from each face only to be dashed by Jack's next sentence. "Unfortunately, no one wanted to work with us. At this point neither your mother nor I have any idea what exactly we'll do. But if nothing else, we thought you boys should know."

The three stood there in stunned silence, not sure what to say. Each was trying to digest what it all meant. It seemed impossible for James and Michael to fathom, the farm, their livelihoods, the entire world they knew, appeared to be in jeopardy of crashing and burning. That 50-acre plot of land wasn't just a piece of property, it was the center of their very universe.

Even Manny, who'd finally found stability in his life couldn't believe it. Deep inside him a fear began to well up. A fear that he would be once again cast out on his own. 'God not again', thought Manny, 'please don't let it happen again.' The sound of someone finally speaking snapped Manny back to reality.

"How's Mom doing?" asked James.

"She's hanging in there. Exactly what you'd expect from her. She's a tough girl, that mother of yours."

"Well, what do you think we should do now?" asked Michael, always taking an objective view of things.

Knowing Michael may ask such a question, Jack was ready with a response. "Right at the moment, nothing. Let's just keep the operation going as before. If we have to sell some horses, or drop some down in class, we can do that, but for now, just do what you've been doing. I'm going to look at what our other options are and run some numbers. We'll figure something out."

Both Michael and James were curious as to what exactly those other options might be, but knew deep down if they did exist, they probably weren't something that provided for a happy ending.

Realizing he'd said enough and not wanting to answer any more questions, Jack excused himself. "Time to head back to the farm. I've got work to do." Each of the boys said goodbye. The three, not sure of what to do next, just stood there, each lost in their own haze.

That evening the effects of Jack's news began to ripple through the family. James held it in only until they were sitting down to eat. Lauren said nothing at first, but the look on her face was, as they say, worth a thousand words. It dawned on James as he sat there looking at her that that was probably the exact same expression he had given his father earlier that morning. After absorbing what James had said for a minute or two, Lauren spoke up.

"Do you think they will actually lose the farm?"

James wasn't able to respond before Sydney, not fully understanding what was going on, had to pipe in. "How do you lose a farm? Do you lose a barn? I lost a baby doll once, but Mom found it. Maybe Mom can find the farm."

James and Lauren just looked at one another. As serious as the events were, it was hard not to laugh at the insights of a 4-year-old. Realizing they had no chance of explaining the farm wasn't missing, they decided instead just to agree with her and move on. "OK honey, maybe tomorrow I'll go over and help Grandma find the farm. How's that?"

"That would be very helpful Mommy," replied Sydney, prompting a laugh from James.

"Sounds like she's heard that phrase before." Lauren smiled, knowing that if she'd said it to her once, she'd said it a million times. Now able, James answered Lauren's original question. "At this point, Dad said he was going to run some numbers and look at their other options. Neither Michael, nor I, have any idea what those might be. I kind of think he was just making that up to make us feel better. I honestly have no earthly idea where they could come up with that much money without selling it off." James made sure to say "it" rather than "farm," lest Sydney jump back into the middle of the conversation.

"Are you kidding me?!" Lauren said, the whites of her eyes suddenly visible. "I can't believe the bank would do that. It just doesn't seem fair. Have they tried talking to someone else at the bank?"

"Well, the guy who's their contact isn't pulling the strings. Michael spoke to Mom later on and according to her, the head of the local office won't deal with it. The decisions are coming from their corporate offices and this clown is unwilling to try to step in."

It was obvious to Lauren, based on James' tone that he had nothing but disgust for the man. Then it dawned on Lauren she actually knew who the man was. "Isn't that Henry Livingston?" Surprised that Lauren had any idea who this evil banker might be, James gave her the double take. Seeing James' quizzical look, Lauren realized she needed to expand on her comment. "He's the same age as my sister. They went to college together. From what she told me, he was a real...", she paused for a moment and gazed over to see whether Sydney was paying attention. Sydney looked to be conducting a game of field hockey with her peas, so Lauren felt safe to continue. Picking up where she left off, she said softly "a real ass." Then she increased her volume to a normal tone to add "just real arrogant."

"Well," James said, "I don't know the guy, but I can tell you, he's not doing much to help us."

The dinner continued as usual until Lauren chose to ask one more question. She was hesitant, but opted to go ahead anyway. "They'd have to get rid of all the horses then, wouldn't they?"

"Yeah," James said without flinching, "they would probably have to sell them. Nowhere to keep them if the farm's gone."

Lauren quickly put two and two together. "Any thoughts on what you would do with yourself if things don't work out?"

James continued eating as he spoke. "Not really. Michael figured he would try to take on new clients, basically open it up as a public stable. He didn't say anything, but there's no way he could afford to hire me as an assistant. He'd probably have a tough time making it on his own for a while."

James was about to keep going when Sydney cut him off.

"Daddy, don't talk with your mouth full. It's not polite."

James gave Sydney an apologetic glance. "I'm sorry dear." Then he turned his head back to Lauren. Lauren just smiled at him with raised eyebrows. That daughter of theirs was certainly a tough one. Having lost his train of thought, it took James a minute to figure out where he'd left off. "Anyway, I could probably check around to see if any of the other trainers needed help. To be honest, I have no idea what I would do otherwise."

"Have you thought about opening your own stable?"

The question forced James to stop in his tracks. "I have," he said pausing to play with the food on his plate. "I couldn't do it." Lauren, listening intently to the comment, was about to reassure him of his abilities when James realized what exactly he had said. "No, no, no. I don't mean that I don't have the ability. I mean I just couldn't do that to Michael. If I were to open a stable too, then we would be forced to compete against one another for new owners." Lauren eased back in her chair understanding what James was saying. She was big on family and knew how close James and his family were. "There's simply no way I could do that to him."

"Yeah, you're right" Lauren agreed. "I hadn't thought about that." She got up from her chair and began to clear the table before adding "Let's just hope it doesn't come to that."

Michael chose to wait until the kids were tucked into bed before informing Janet of the news. It came as a jolt. Living in a one-income household can make things much easier when it comes to taking care of kids and doing all the things to keep a house running. One person is charged with working a "normal" job and earning the money. The other person becomes the house's "operations manager." This person makes sure the house activities and all the people in it, run smoothly. As long as it is financially doable, it can make everyone's life easier. The risk, as Michael and Janet were finding out, was that if something happened to the one income, it could wreak havoc on the entire family.

As a trainer, Michael had the opportunity to open his barn to the public. He could take in horses from anyone looking to have their horse trained to race. It's not something he wanted to do, but it looked like it may become a necessity. The only real problem he saw was that it would probably take a year or two before he had a full barn, well, a full barn of decent horses. There were always owners with horses out there, but they were mostly the owners that stick you with bad horses nobody else wants to train. And of course, the fewer the number of horses, the less he made. As he explained all this to Janet, she was quick to point out she could look for some part-time work at least to help make ends meet. Hearing the words "make ends meet" sent Michael's blood pressure rushing. He was a good trainer and, like his father, a proud man. He liked having his wife at home to raise the kids. It was the way he grew up. It wasn't that he minded Janet going to work; it was more he felt an obligation as the man of the house to be able to support his family. Thoughts of his own failings were becoming too prevalent in his life.

His inability to turn Sing around was a frustration which had been growing steadily throughout the year. The horse was talented with huge potential and Michael had no capacity to control him. Now, his ability to support his family seemed less than certain. This was not how it was supposed to be. He was losing control.

"You don't need to get a job," Michael said.

"No, I don't need to get a job at this moment. But a few months from now I may."

"I'll get things figured out," he said, rubbing his face. "I'll get this damn horse figured out. We don't need you taking some shit job for pennies!"

"Why would it be for pennies and what makes you think I couldn't find a decent job? I used to work remember. I do have skills," she said before pausing. "Maybe I'd like to contribute more. Maybe I want to do this. It's not always about you, you know."

"I'm not saying it's about me. All I'm saying is we need you here taking care of the kids."

"That's bullshit and you know it. This is about your ego and nothing else."

Michael began to get more and more pissed. Realizing that further dialog might cause him to attack Janet, he left the room. "I need to get out of here."

Janet knew him well enough to let him go. His level of intensity, at this moment, was much too high for rational conversation. She could wait.

Years ago Michael had spent time with a therapist discussing how intense he often got. As much as he despised the thought of seeing a therapist, he understood in the end, it could not only make his life better, but the lives of his family, too. One recommendation the therapist made was to take a walk – actually she had said to run – when he felt the pressure build and do it outside in the fresh air, no matter the weather. And for Michael, this usually worked, much better than counting to 10, which he tried and instantly dismissed as crap.

His walk would last as long as needed to quell his anger, not that it would fully go away. The issues were there and weren't going to get resolved overnight. But tonight, his anger would be held in check. Not everyone was so lucky. Some knew exactly where they wanted to direct their growing fury.

Chapter 21

~

JUNE 8

SARAH AND MARGARET WERE QUIETLY going about the business of cleaning stalls. It was a beautiful summer morning; the sweet smell of fresh hay permeated the barn. The horses that weren't at the track were out in the pastures doing what horses do best – grazing. The only other creatures in the barn with Sarah and Margaret were a couple of barn cats. They sat perched on a mountain of bailed hay watching the cleaning crew, digging out the old and laying down the new. It was tedious but offered instant gratification at least until the next morning when you were faced with the same task. Sarah took a break from picking out one of the stalls and looked up at the feline spectators.

"What will happen to Dixie and Parkway?" she said in a hushed tone.

It was a simple question whose depth went well beyond two cats. Margaret knew her daughter needed to release some of the emotions built up over the last couple of days. Her method of drawing out that emotion was as simple as her daughter's initial question. "What do you mean honey?" she asked, as if she failed to understand the question, knowing full well it would force Sarah to continue.

"Well if we lose the farm, what will happen to them? This is their home too. They'll have nowhere to go. How will they live?"

Although what she said was true, it paled in comparison to the overall situation. The family was on the verge of losing their home, their life savings, their livelihood, their dreams. A couple of barn cats weren't exactly the top priority. But yes, the cats' world was unquestionably in danger, though the cats had one advantage on their human companions, they had no idea what was happening. Margaret stopped and leaned on her pitch fork. As she did, she gazed up at the cats. Sarah followed her lead and stared at them as well. The cats, apparently growing bored with the show, stopped paying attention. Dixie yawned and began circling for a good sleep spot, while Parkway opted to do a little cleaning of his own. "I guess they've lost interest in us," joked Margaret. Sarah let out a little snicker. "They'll be OK dear, we'll all be OK," Margaret said in a motherly voice.

It had been less than a month since Sarah had come home from college. College, that world that allows us to dream about the future and its infinite possibilities. Unfortunately for Sarah, her dream world had vanished and she was ill-prepared for life's sometimes harsh reality. Not fully buying into her mother's comment, Sarah pressed her further. "But how? You and dad don't have that kind of money."

"You're right honey, we don't. Perhaps in the end we will have to move. At this point I don't know, but I don't want to give up hope yet." Margaret spoke strongly and held conviction, whether she herself believed it or not.

The words did little to quell Sarah's anxiety. She began to tear up, struggling to keep from losing it all together, her face awash with fear. Giving off the impression of hyperventilating, she spoke only in single words, sobbing intermittently between them. "This...this...is...our home...our farm." As she was trying to get it all out Margaret walked to her and wrapped her arms around her distraught daughter. It was a hug Sarah needed, but it opened a waterfall of emotions. The tears that had been welling up came gushing out. Margaret tried to whisper reassuring words as she stroked Sarah's hair. It's easier for some to face crisis than it is for others. Sarah was young and hadn't known anything but stability. She had been the sheltered baby girl and paid the price for it now.

After a few minutes Sarah pulled herself together. When she did, Margaret's motherly instinct took hold of the situation. "Now, you listen up my girl. No one has taken this farm from us yet and I have faith in the end, no one will. You need to be strong. Your father will think of something, he always does. Until then, we have to support him and press on. Understood?"

Sarah sheepishly looked at her mother still wiping the tears from her face. "Understood."

With that the two O'Brien women continued to muck out the stalls. Above them, two cats, oblivious to the plight of the farm, dozed quietly on a bale of hay.

Just outside the barn doors, unseen by the women inside, stood Jack O'Brien. Although he hadn't heard the entire conversation, he'd heard enough. Enough to know his only daughter had been reduced to tears, terrified of an uncertain future. Not only that, but hearing his wife's unshakable faith in him, when in fact he had no idea how to change the course they were on, left him feeling angry. Angry and bitterly frustrated. His therapist, if he had a therapist, would have told him to go for a walk. A long, long walk. But he had no therapist and what he overheard was more fuel to a fire that was growing bigger by the day.

JUNE 10

It was a quiet Sunday afternoon when Manny licked the seal of the envelope, finishing another letter to his aunt and uncle in Florida. He had promised to stay in touch and thus far he'd stayed true to his word. Of course now it wasn't so much an obligation as it was a desire. They had written Manny not long after he arrived back in New York. It was the first piece of "real" mail Manny could remember receiving. Needless to say it was a great feeling. He made sure to follow with a return letter soon thereafter.

This time he decided to write them first. He wanted to let them know what was happening with the farm. It was a nice outlet for him. He didn't feel it was his place to discuss it with James or Michael, or even Jack and Margaret for that matter. He wasn't family and wasn't sure if it was his business to talk about it. With his aunt and uncle he felt it was alright to open up about how he felt. His desk sat against the wall and was aside one of his two windows. Looking out the window as he wrote, it hit home just how hard it would be to leave this place.

Even though the apartment wasn't more than 300 square feet, it was perfect for Manny. He was close to the horses, in fact he could hear them below sometimes if they were in their stalls. In the morning he could start his day by going downstairs and greeting them. Stop by each stall, give them a pat on the head and then make his way out into the world. It was a nice way to start the day. It also didn't hurt that Jack and Margaret didn't charge him anything to live there. If he was forced to move, he was certain his rent would increase. Then of course there was the view.

It was hard for Manny to imagine any other place that would afford him this view, certainly not one he could manage to rent or buy. From either of his two windows Manny overlooked the majority of the pastures. So when the horses grazed in the fields Manny could sit and watch them roam, he knew all the mares, all the foals, all their habits, all their moves. They were an extension of the family. Bucknrun - a fitting name for the precocious youngster who made a habit of pulling on other halters and then squealing and bolting. Ayr Apparent – the tough old mare who kept everyone in line with just a look. When she made her way across the pasture no one got in her way. Rosie's a Tiger – an anomaly of a name for a filly afraid of almost everything. They all had their own personalities. Who needed a television when you had a pasture of entertainment.

If that weren't enough, Manny could also see a fair portion of the lake off in the distance and regularly marveled at the setting sun cascading off the water. It was everything he could ask for, and there wasn't a house or another human to be seen anywhere, except possibly Jack who Manny suddenly spotted driving through the fields in his tractor. 'God how he loves driving around in that tractor,' thought Manny.

Jack sat behind the wheel of his tractor thinking about the place he had called home his entire life. If someone asked him to list all the things he loved, it wouldn't take him long to answer the question. For Jack, the only things he truly loved were his wife, his kids and the patch of land he called home. OK, maybe a few horses, but that was it. It was simple and that's how Jack liked it. It was his own little kingdom. Having spent his whole life there, he knew every square inch of the property. In the old days, the ranch hands would ride the fence line looking for spots in need of repair. Jack preferred to ride fences atop his trusty old tractor. Though no one in their right mind would agree, to Jack, that tractor seat was his version of a Lazy Boy recliner. He would spend hours riding from one end of the farm to the other. When the kids were little they would ask Margaret what exactly Dad was doing. She would usually reply by saying she had no idea, but he seems to be enjoying himself.

Jack stopped the tractor along the far edge of the property. He climbed out and looked around. Not a sole to be seen. He bent down on one knee, took off his gloves and sifted through the dirt beneath him. Perhaps there was another love in Jack's life, the smell of the earth. It's a cool smell, fresh, even at times rich smelling. One could say that it's something that keeps you grounded, at the risk of making a pun of course. To work the land, treat the soil with care and then reap the benefits is something few in the present-day world can understand. Jack was one of the few. Standing up, he surveyed the fence line and saw nothing in need of work. Time to move on down the line he thought. As he was climbing back into his "recliner" Jack began to wonder what he would do if they were to sell. Looking for things to fix around the farm was how he spent his time. If he were forced to live in some small house, what could he find to fix besides a sink or faucet or something trivial? The tractor, what would he do without his tractor? He recalled one stretch where the weather was so bad that he was stuck inside with Margaret for four or five days, barely leaving the house to check on the horses. By the time the front had passed, the divorce papers were being drafted. Not really, but the truth was that Jack was unbearable if he was forced inside for long stretches. For the sake of his marriage, Jack knew he had to find some way to keep the farm.

It had been nine days since Ron brought the news and less than a week since being turned down by every bank. With each day Jack's frame of mind grew worse. Spotting a branch that must have fallen from one of the trees outside the fence line, Jack stopped the tractor and climbed down. He yawned as he bent over and picked up the stick. With so much on his mind, Jack was having difficulty sleeping, which just added to his foul mood, eroding his mental well-being. Although he laid part of the blame on himself for getting the farm in this predicament, his thoughts kept going back to the bank and their failure to help, or even to simply warn him about what may lie on the horizon. Looking around, he took in the splendor of his home. But as he finished admiring it, a scowl came over his face. "You really think you're going to get this place?" He laughed, a cynical, psychotic laugh, "My ass, you're getting this farm." Holding the stick with two hands, Jack, in a rapid, violent motion, snapped it in half over his knee. "No way in hell, you bastards." He threw one side over the fence and looked down at the other, gripping it like you would a club. "Not over my dead body," he said harshly. And with that, he launched the other half deep into the woods, sending a startled group of birds airborne.

Chapter 22

⁓

JUNE 13

ONCE YOU'VE LIVED WITH SOMEONE for 30-plus years you pretty much know exactly how they are doing just by observation. What Margaret O'Brien observed could only be described as unsettling. She was helplessly watching as Jack flip flopped between being depressed and enraged. His mood seemed to be growing worse as each day passed. It occurred to Margaret that maybe if she had the kids and grandkids come by, it might help snap him out of his doldrums. It was worth a shot anyway and if nothing else, she and Sarah would enjoy the distraction. She picked up the phone and dialed her son's number.

Michael answered on the first ring. "Hi Michael, it's your Mother."

"Hey Mom, how are things at the house?" He and James were very curious how their father was dealing with the situation.

"Actually, I'm a little worried about your father. He's been..." she paused for a moment. She wanted to tell Michael what she was feeling, how he'd been acting, but to do so somehow felt like she was betraying her husband. She was growing increasingly worried about his behavior, but just couldn't come to say it. "Well, let's just say he's been a little out of sorts. I was wondering if you, Janet and the kids could come by for dinner tomorrow? It might help him take his mind off things."

"Hold on just a minute Mom and I'll check." In the background Margaret could hear Michael and Janet talking. "We can't make it tomorrow night, but how about Friday instead?"

What was one more night thought Margaret. "Sure that sounds great. We'll see you then." This will be good, Jack loves seeing his grandchildren. Hopefully it will be just what the doctor ordered.

JUNE 14

Jack gently hung up the phone. It was the last of the calls he was expecting to receive. One of the options Jack thought of to help save the farm was to get other local farmers to buy into his property. He thought perhaps he could sell the rights to farm his land for a certain period of time. For $100,000, you had the rights to farm 20 acres for the next 25 years. He had enough open land to sell the rights to two plots. If he could do it and then sell all the horse stock, including Sing, he could probably raise $300,000. That would leave him $100,000 short, but he figured once he got that close someone might give him a loan for that remaining portion. He would lose his basic livelihood, but would keep the farm and the home where he had lived most of his life. Unfortunately, none of the local farmers could capitalize on Jack's offer. All had sympathy, but none had money. Jack stared at the phone for a moment before turning and walking out the door.

As he slowly walked down to the barn the heat resonating inside his belly began to spread throughout his body. He had had enough. That failed attempt extinguished what little hope remained. He could no longer contain himself. The anger, searing and relentless, now overwhelmed him. People's lives were crashing down and the bank simply shrugged it off. What could they do, they said, they had a business to run. Lives were being traded for profits. The people, the farmers, his friends, were expendable. It brought Jack back to a time and place he'd previously pushed to the recesses of his mind. A time when he'd spent his days in uniform, hunting for those our country called the enemy.

Back then, he was young and naïve. He trusted those in power to make decisions knowing lives lay in the balance. But he learned very early in his tour of duty, things aren't always as they should be. They'd been sent into a valley that according to Division Headquarters had "some" enemy activity. Jack's 50-man platoon was airlifted in and told to scout around and try to make contact. They did. But what they ran into wasn't just "some" enemy. They'd crossed paths with an entire North Vietnamese regiment of about 4,000 men. It wasn't long before Jack realized they were in danger of being wiped out. He quickly found a piece of high ground and formed a defensive perimeter. As the enemy sent wave after wave at them, Jack's men fought back with everything they had. Jack screamed into his hand-held radio time after time for air and artillery strikes. He called them in so close to his own position he himself needed to take cover, lest he get hit. Their perimeter grew smaller and smaller, their numbers dwindling and it looked like the end was near when suddenly the enemy withdrew. Jack had no idea why or what happened, but he was happy. That was until he found out what had really transpired.

After Jack, and what was left of his troopers, made it back, he went to Headquarters to give his report. It was there he discovered how much Division knew, but never told. It seemed that Division HQ figured there was at least a battalion or more of enemy soldiers stationed somewhere in the vicinity they sent Jack and his men. That's better than a thousand men. They were using Jack's platoon as bait. Division had readied several of their own battalions assuming contact was made. But the thing was, those battalions weren't there to rescue Jack's men, they were used to attack the enemy from other positions. Jack and his men were on their own. They were deemed expendable, or to put it another way, left to die. Luckily for Jack, the Divisions other battalions had forced the North Vietnamese to turn away from Jack's platoon just in time to keep them from being overrun. As Jack finished giving his report, he could hear several high-ranking officers in another part of the tent cheerfully bragging about enemy body counts. 'This will boost the career' he heard one say. No one mentioned the American dead that lay on the battlefield. And that's what it came down to. While Jack had to go write letters to the parents of his fallen soldiers, explaining how and why their boys died, men in the rear smiled, pointed to numbers and advanced their careers.

By the time Jack's tour of Vietnam ended, he'd learned one of life's bitter lessons the hard way. Decisions are made for many reasons, but all too often, those reasons are selfish. What is best becomes what is best for me and my career. It took years before Jack overcame his hatred for the "establishment," though he never completely got over it. Now the bank, and its unfeeling son-of-a-bitch executives, reawakened those feelings.

And this hatred, this rage, woke up a man in him who was frightening, frightening for anyone who dared cross him. A man who'd seen and done things that most couldn't understand. Not even Jack could realize how far he had fallen because Jack the husband, Jack the father, had disappeared. Somewhere on his walk from the house to the barn a switch had flipped and the content old man was gone. In his place stood a man 35 years his junior, ready once again to stalk his enemy, prepared to lash out in anger. The bank had awoken a killer.

As Jack made his way down the aisle, the horses knew something was up. They watched as he went about feeding them. Their sixth sense, perceptive to the fury inside him. It made them agitated. There was danger in the air. They stirred in their stalls, dancing back and forth, not knowing what to do or where to go. They felt the urge to flee, but like Jack, were trapped, unable to find safe refuge.

Years before it was the horses, different from the current batch, but still, it was the horses that heard the stories. They listened as their master told them of the death and destruction. Stories of fear, terror-filled nights and men dying for no cause. Stories of no homecoming, no thank you for your service, only pain and suffering. They were the outlet that somehow absorbed his negative energy and helped him get on with his life. Their physical strength transforming over time into his mental strength. Today, the horses felt it anew. Only now, they didn't have enough time to make a difference. Like a grenade whose pin had been pulled, it was only matter of time before the inevitable explosion.

Ron leaned over and kissed his wife goodbye, then softly said he loved her. It was a ritual that had been practiced nearly every day of their married lives, yet somehow, something seemed different today, thought Anne. She was right. All morning, while Ron was getting ready for work, he kept experiencing a feeling of foreboding, a premonition of bad things. He couldn't put his finger on it, but there was something in the air. He wanted his kiss this morning to have more feeling than the normal peck, just in case. In case of what, he didn't know.

Henry Livingston walked out of the quick mart with an extra-large cup of coffee in hand. He gazed down at the hood of his BMW as he prepared to open its door. "Man," he said disgustedly, staring at the large bird dropping that now graced his sports car, "right in the middle of the hood, damn birds." He scanned the sky as if to see the culprits. After spotting none, he opened his door and sat down. His watch said 8:20, no time to get it washed now, he thought. The meeting he was supposed to be in started in 10 minutes and he figured he'd be lucky get there on time. "That'll have to wait until tonight," he muttered to himself. Having meetings scheduled throughout most of the day, he knew he'd be stuck in the office until evening.

It wasn't until Margaret turned off the vacuum that she realized Jack was inside and on the phone. And it didn't take more than a few seconds later to know the call was not a pleasant one. She heard more than a few expletives fly as Jack's voice echoed throughout the house. She wanted to go and check exactly what was going on, but was afraid. Then it dawned on her, for the first time in all the years she'd known Jack, she was actually afraid to approach him. He hadn't been himself lately and the sound of this conversation only heightened her concern.

Ron sat on the other end of the line, slumped in his chair, taking the abuse. It wasn't his fault this happened, but he was the connection to the bank. He knew his friend needed to vent at someone and he was it. While Jack rained blow after blow upon him, his mind began to wander. Ron had given up, surrendered. He no longer had the strength to fight back, not that he wanted to with Jack, but he didn't have it in him to fight the bank that was so callously leaving his clients out to dry. How long the conversation lasted Ron couldn't have said, his mind had long since gone numb.

"A BUNCH OF GOD DAMN BASTARDS, AND THAT'S ALL YOU PEOPLE WILL EVER BE. I OUGHTA COME DOWN THERE AND RIP SOMEBODY A NEW ASSHOLE." Ending his tirade, Jack slammed down the phone and stormed out of the house toward the barn.

Lunchtime at the O'Brien house was always at noon. Noon came and went and Jack never showed. At 1 o'clock Margaret heard the door open and thought 'finally.' But she watched as Jack passed through the kitchen on his way upstairs. "Jack, do you want something for lunch?" she asked. "No." That was it. No explanation, no apology. For Jack to miss his midday meal meant something, not that it's a big deal to most of the world, but Jack was like clockwork. Margaret used to joke that you could set your watch by it. This is bad, Margaret said to herself, this is real bad.

Jack tossed his oil stained jeans into the dirty laundry and began rummaging through his dresser for another pair. After locating the correct drawer and pulling out a new pair, Jack sat on the bed and put a leg through one side. Glancing up at the chest of drawers in front of him, he paused. He sat there staring at the top drawer. What he had said to Ron at the end of their conversation started running through his head. Once he finished putting on his clean pair of pants, Jack stepped slowly toward the dresser grabbing the handle to its top drawer. He opened it up, looked around and brushed aside some letters, a handkerchief, some cufflinks he'd never worn and a handful of coins. Underneath, laid a cold reminder of days gone by. It was his military issue 45-caliber pistol. It had been so long since he'd thought about the gun that he'd forgotten it was there until just now. He reached into the drawer and pulled it out. It was still in its holster so he unbuckled the leather strap and drew out the weapon. He hadn't held it in probably 20 years, but it felt good in his hands. The sense of power and control were undeniable. A surge swept through his whole body. For a man who had felt so helpless in recent days it was a tremendous rush. He put the gun back into its holster, reached again into the drawer and grabbed a pair of clips of ammunition. He put the clips into his pants pocket and tucked the gun under his shirt. Turning away from the dresser, he walked out of the bedroom leaving the top drawer still opened.

Jack continued methodically down the stairs, his gait with purpose. Through the kitchen and out of the house he went, not saying a word. He walked to his truck, opened the passenger door and then the glove box. The pistol and ammunition fit snuggly inside concealed from any passerby's view. He would finish fixing the stall door he thought, and then perhaps, pay his friends at the bank a little visit.

The stall door moved smoothly on its new hinge and all traces of spilled oil had disappeared, but Jack's foul mood lingered. And his intention of driving down to the bank after he'd finished remained as well. In fact, he was probably more determined now than the half hour ago when he put the gun in his truck. While he fixed the stall door, he pictured the bankers, laughing and joking in their expensive suits and cars, like those company men in Vietnam. They're smug attitudes, thinking only of their paychecks. They needed to feel the pain they were so callously heaping upon others. Looking at the door and tools, Jack couldn't help but remember his own father and watching him do some of the same work around the barn. That memory only reinforced his feelings of failing not only his wife and children, but the generations of O'Briens that had come before him and watched over the land. He began to think if it came to it, he would prefer to be dead than to live the rest of his life in some small house on no land, knowing he'd let them all down. And if he took some of those arrogant bankers with him, so be it.

Chapter 23

GRABBING THE SHANK THAT HUNG over the fence, Manny unlatched the gate and walked into the pen that temporarily housed Sing. Sing's leg had healed enough to allow him to spend most of the day in the small pen. There he could move around and increase the leg's blood flow, thereby aiding the healing process. They didn't want him romping through the pastures with any of the other horses yet, lest he re-injure the leg. And with his luck, that was a strong possibility. In another week or so they could bring him back to the track and put him in training again. Even though he couldn't ride him, Manny made sure to say hi to Sing every day. Of course, living right above him certainly made that easy. Sing spotted Manny coming over with the shank and started walking toward him. Manny noticed Sing approaching and smiled. "Want to play a little tug of war there big guy?" Although Manny knew it wasn't the smartest thing to do, he chose to keep doing it anyway. Letting Sing play tug of war with his shank had a tendency to make him want to do it all the time. Even if someone were actually trying to attach it to his halter and lead him somewhere. But Manny always figured it wasn't that big a deal and it was more important to enjoy life than to worry about such trivial things, whether you're horse or human.

They were in the middle of their game when Jack emerged from the barn carrying old wood from the stall. Hearing the commotion Jack looked over to see Manny and Sing playing. Manny spotted Jack about the same time and was going to say something when Sing, as if noticing

Manny had lost his concentration, gave the line a sharp tug. Manny was taken completely off guard. By the time he realized he needed to let go, it was too late. He landed with a loud thud at Sing's feet, face first no less. The pain radiated throughout his body as he laid there. Sing, seeing the lump of human flesh at his feet, lowered his head and gave Manny a big sniff, adding insult to injury. Slowly Manny raised himself up spitting out some of the blood he now tasted running through his mouth.

From the scrap pile Jack shook his head 'stupid boy.' After tossing a couple more slabs on top he turned to walk into the barn. Gazing back at the scene, Jack noticed that Manny was limping his way out of the pen with Sing following behind him, the shank still in his mouth. When Sing nickered, Manny turned around. Sing shook his head up and down as if begging Manny to play some more. Jack stopped walking and continued to watch, what a peculiar site he thought. Manny smiled at Sing and reached once again for the rope. The game picked up where it'd left off. It took Jack a moment to realize it, but he was smiling too. Something he hadn't done in days. It was like watching a boy and his dog playing, except this was a horse. Horses didn't respond like this to humans. Jack recognized there was an unusual bond that existed between these two.

As if catching himself doing something he shouldn't, Jack quickly wiped the smile from his face. He didn't want to feel better. He didn't want to smile. There was hate in his gut and a gun in his truck, there was no room for anything else. He pictured the bankers again in his mind. *They* were stealing his land, destroying his livelihood and by God he was going to make them pay. No dumb kid and lame horse could change that. He wouldn't allow it. He had to stay focused. The bank was the enemy. They were smart and wealthy and Jack was nothing more than a dumb farmer, that's what they thought. The pompous bastards felt nothing for him. Jack stoked the fire inside himself. Let it build, let it grow.

Having re-energized his anger, Jack quickly put away his tools and headed for the truck. Behind him, Manny and Sing continued their friendly competition. Jack could hear them, but refused to turn and look. Subconsciously, he knew watching them play lessened his desire to exact revenge and that had to be avoided at all cost. Reaching the truck, Jack slid into the front seat and reached his hands to the ignition. The key was there, like always. With one rapid motion, he turned the key and the truck jumped to life. He jerked the handle to reverse and without haste, backed the vehicle up. Coming to a sharp halt, he put the truck in drive and sped away, never once looking in his rear view mirror. Behind him, the horses, the barn and his house, faded into the distance.

Across four lanes of highway from the local branch of Finger Lakes Savings and Loan a lone truck waited in an otherwise empty parking lot. Inside that truck, Jack O'Brien sat expressionless, holding his 45-caliber pistol. He stared at the bank, watching an occasional customer enter or leave. Parked several spots down the entrance was a BMW. Jack looked down at his watch, 2:30. He'd been sitting there for 30 minutes. That BMW was there when Jack arrived and if it had belonged to a customer, they surely would have left by now. 'That belongs to the bastard that runs this place,' Jack thought, 'it has to.'

Jack looked down at the gun resting in his lap. His eyes studied the contours of the gun, moving his gaze from one end to the other. The pebbled grip, well-worn from many years of hard use, offered a slightly different shade of black from the rest of weapon. And it was heavy, heavier than Jack remembered. Of course he was younger back then and stronger, not the worn out old man he was today. Jack continued to stare at the gun. This trusty black weapon had accompanied him on many missions during the war. It had been fired in anger countless times before and taken the lives of several men. Today, Jack thought, would be its final mission. It would be their final mission together.

From the kitchen window Margaret could see Jack's truck was missing. He hadn't said anything and she couldn't recall anything he needed to pick up. 'Where could he have gone?' she wondered. Jack always told her when he was leaving, he was very thoughtful that way. She had no reason to think anything was wrong, but instinct told her otherwise.

She began to fill with a profound sense of worry. Searching her mind, she tried to think of someone she should call. She needed to talk to someone to quell her anxiety. But who? And why? Jack left without lunch, hardly an emergency. No, there was no one she could explain this to. It made no sense. She was panicking over nothing. But even so, the fear was real, and it stemmed from a place that knows. It stemmed from a wife's intuition.

The elderly couple slowly made their way out the door and to their over-sized boat of a car. Scanning the parking lot, Jack determined they should be the last of the customers. Anyone left must be a bank employee. Just like in Vietnam, collateral damage should be avoided, Jack thought, they, the customers at least, are innocent. Jack searched the parking lot one more time, making sure there were no other new vehicles he'd missed. At the far end of the lot Jack spotted a Honda Accord, gold, late modeled. It looked familiar, but he was pretty sure it wasn't a customer. What was it about that car? Then it hit him, that's Ron's car. How had he not realized it before? How could he have been watching the bank for nearly 45 minutes, seen the cars and not even thought of Ron? His mind was fixated on the bank, on the owner of the BMW, on his own plight, on everything but his friend sitting inside.

Jack looked away from the car and back at the BMW. He needed to remain focused on the enemy. 'Maybe that isn't Ron's car,' Jack thought and glanced at it again. It was. He'd seen it enough times in his life to know. He didn't want it to be, but it was. "Damn it Ron, why do you have to be in there?" Jack's mind raced. 'Of course where else would Ron be,' Jack thought, scolding himself, 'he works there, dumb-ass.' He thought about Ron, his friend. The cookouts they'd shared. Jack didn't want to face Ron inside the bank. The thought of coming face to face with his friend made Jack feel ashamed. He thought again about the cookouts and Margaret and how she loved being a hostess during those cookouts. The fun they used to have. He thought about the farm, the wonderful sloping land and the horses and the magnificent sun sets.

The weight of his 45 increased with every moment, now his hand seemed barely able to support it. He felt so tired, so exhausted. He searched his mind for a way out, a way to fix everything. There had to be an answer. Nothing. Nothing. His mind raced back and forth, no thought staying more than a split second. He couldn't focus. The cars rushed by, blurred, one, then another, then another. They must be going a hundred miles an hour. He felt trapped, his head wouldn't stop spinning. There were no alternatives, none. He couldn't find a way out. Tears began to stream down Jack's face, running over his lip and onto his shirt. He lifted his hand, the gun held tightly, wiping the tears and snot from his face. "FUCKERS, MOTHER FUCKERS!" he yelled, banging the gun against the steering wheel over and over again.

They laughed at me, I know they did, Jack thought, suddenly calm. They thought I was nothing, nobody. They smiled when they talked about carving up my land, our land. The land my father and grandfather and great-grandfather worked and sweated over. Death, they deserve death. Jack grabbed for the door handle. He tried to pull it open, but couldn't. He couldn't muster the strength, his arm suddenly limp. What was wrong? Why can't I do this? "OPEN THE DOOR JACK, OPEN IT GOD DAMN IT."

His head rocked back and Jack screamed, though no sound could be heard. He wanted to get out and run to the bank, to charge in and blow away the bastard who caused this pain. He could picture the scene, the son-of-a-bitch groveling for his life. Who has the power now? What do you think of me now? Jack could feel the satisfaction, ending his worthless life. But he couldn't do it. He couldn't even get the door open. With his free left hand, he pounded the door, three, four, five times until his hand ached with pain. For the first time in more than 30 years he cried. That man, the one who could kill was gone. As much as Jack wanted to believe he still existed, he didn't. A wife and kids and a life filled with love had eventually changed the soldier. That person was gone forever and Jack hated himself for it, but taking another person's life, no matter how much the person deserved it, was no longer an option.

He suddenly felt drained of all energy, overcome by sleepless nights, fits of rage, confusion, dead-end options. His heart beats seemed to slow with each passing beat. At that moment, Jack felt he could sleep forever. He breathed deep, taking in as much oxygen as his lungs would allow. His mind no longer raced, but rather, was the picture of clarity. He knew what needed to be done.

Jack raised the gun until it was level with his face. He looked at it, knowing the power it held. He wiped the tears from his eyes to see it more clearly. It was so close to his nose he could smell the steel; acrid, cold, lifeless. The gun no longer felt heavy. It was light, like a plastic toy gun the boys used to play with when they were kids. He thought of the boys, but felt no emotion. All emotions were drained. He looked out the window. Cars and people, coming and going. But Jack's eyes looked right through them as if they didn't exist. He saw the bank, but no longer had any hate. It was done, he was done. With the ease of a man who'd done it hundreds of times before, Jack finger's moved into firing position. So much emotion, so much pain. Somehow it had to end. He took a deep breath. Then, without looking at the weapon, he flipped the lever, depressing the magazine release. The ammunition clip slid from the gun and landed in Jack's lap. It was over.

Jack sat there exhausted, staring straight ahead, wondering why he couldn't do it, but far too tired to understand his mind's behavior. He wasn't the man from 35 years ago. He knew it all along and tried to suppress it. But there was too much in his life he loved and there were too many people who loved him. He wanted to be the Ripper, to hate and kill and seek revenge. But his wife made sure he wasn't that man, his beautiful, caring, lovely wife. Jack reached over and placed the gun back in the glove box, followed by the clip. He closed it and turned the ignition as a final tear welled up in his eye. The engine hummed as he put the truck in reverse and looked in the rear view mirror, an empty parking lot behind him. The stray tear trickled down his face. There would be no killing today. It was time to go home.

The truck pulled into the space it had vacated an hour and a half before. Jack put the truck in park and turned it off. Reaching across the seat, he opened the glove box, grabbed the pistol and ammunition and headed inside the house. He saw Margaret and Sarah in the living room, but said nothing. Afraid that Margaret might follow him up the stairs Jack hurriedly went to the dresser. He noticed he'd never closed it from before and hoped nobody had realized anything. He quickly put the items back and closed the drawer. Feeling as though he may have gotten away with it, he let out a sigh, his head bowed. Gently raising his head he gazed at the top of the dresser. He saw something then he hadn't noticed earlier. He wondered how he could have been standing there before and not seen it looking right back at him. It was a picture, but not just any picture. It was of eight men in uniform. It was a picture of Jack and his squad in Vietnam. How ironic he thought. Recent events had put him in a mental state that sent him back to that agonizing period of his life. And now, here he stood, staring at this picture of that exact time. He looked into the eyes of the men in the picture. They were strong men, honorable men, men for which Jack had the utmost respect, men who made it home, men who didn't get out alive. Jack couldn't pull his eyes away. He was proud to have stood with such men. His recent actions would have let those men down. He thought of Ron, thought of facing him with a gun in the bank and the shame came rushing back. That's not what gallant men stand for. That's not what these men would have done. Now, the shame came in measured waves, sweeping over top of him.

There are moments in life you know you will never forget. Moments that alter who we are and what we're made of. This was one of those moments. Jack had sunk to a depth that eclipsed any before and he knew it. He was ashamed to admit he could reach such a place, but in the same breath he realized there would be no more sinking and as each second passed, his inner strength, so prevalent throughout his life, gained power. He was reborn standing there, holding the photo, staring at the men within. Their eyes met his, he could hear their voices as if they were speaking to him. "Stay strong Jack, stand tall. We're with you. We'll always be with you."

As if absorbing their strength, Jack straightened himself, correcting his slouched posture. He placed the picture back on the dresser and took a step back, nodding acknowledgement to the soldiers. Then he quietly repeated a phrase from a creed he'd known by heart. "Never shall I fail my comrades. I will always keep myself mentally alert, physically strong and morally straight and I will shoulder more than my share of the task whatever it may be, one-hundred-percent and then some." It felt good to repeat those words, because to Jack and those men in the picture, they weren't just words; they were a way of life. If the day came and he was forced from his land, then he would go with his head held high. Until that time, he was going to fight with all he had. Jack O'Brien had reached bottom and survived. Now it was time to start crawling out of the pit that had nearly cost him his life.

Margaret heard him coming down the stairs, but chose not to get up and say something. She was thankful he'd returned home and didn't want to upset him by asking questions. She knew her nerves were beginning to fray. Years of marriage told her discussing things at this moment, when they both were on edge, could do far more harm than good. 'Be happy he's back,' she told herself, 'and pray something positive happens soon.'

By 4:30 Ron had had enough. Another painful day at the office. It was getting to where he couldn't stand coming to work. Packing up his laptop and paperwork for the day he wondered back at the sense of foreboding he'd had earlier this morning. Nothing happened that realized those fears. He'd had the call from Jack and that was bad, but that wasn't it. Whatever it was that had spooked him, he figured, didn't happen. So he stood up, put on his sport coat and grabbed his computer bag. Glancing around the office he could see the place was already thinning out. As he made his way to the door, Ron could hear only one voice, Henry's. "Asshole," mumbled Ron.

He walked out the front door and looked at the traffic rushing past. Others trying to get home, getting away from the grind of another day. Pushing the unlock button on his car key, it hit Ron that his day wasn't completely over and maybe he still had something to fear. "Well, if nothing else, I'd better drive carefully on the way home."

Sitting in his office with his feet on his desk, Henry Livingston took a peek at his watch, barely listening to the person on the other end of the line. It was nothing more than another useless conversation with another useless employee to Henry. All he could think was please wrap this up so I can get out of here. "Listen Bob, I understand, but there's nothing I can do about it today. It's not that big a deal, alright? Now I've got to get out of here and get my car washed, unless you plan on coming over here to do it for me." Hearing no response on the other end, Henry assumed he accomplished ending the phone call. "I'll see what I can do tomorrow morning when I get in." Henry hung up the phone and muttered "finally." He grabbed his keys and made his way toward the door wondering how these sniveling people made it through life every day. "Henry the Ain't" was focused on his own world, completely oblivious to Jack O'Brien's anger, Ron Dombrowski's premonition and the violent ending that might have been.

About the same time the two bankers drove away from their office, Jack trudged inside his house. Since he'd been back, he'd spent his time outside, letting the fresh air clear his mind. Despite being exhausted, it seemed to do the trick. Mentally, he could feel his old self returning. Margaret heard the back door open and went to see if it was him. He looked worn out, like a man who'd plowed their 50 acres by hand.

Looking up at his wife, Jack quietly asked if she would prepare dinner a little early this evening.

"Certainly dear, why don't you go and get cleaned up and I'll get things started." Jack nodded and slowly began his way to the stairs. Seeing his subdued manner, Margaret summoned the courage to ask a question she needed to know, but feared the answer to. "Are you going to be OK honey?" she asked.

Knowing how he had behaved recently, Jack made sure to turn around and make eye contact before responding. "Yes," he said, struggling with how much or how little to tell her. In the end he decided to just leave it at that, repeating it one more time so she knew he meant it. "Yes, I will."

Chapter 24

~

JUNE 15

THE SOUND OF THE PHONE broke Ron from his daydream. It was a wonderful trip to Europe with his wife that he was hoping to take. They both dreamt of seeing the Alps and talked about planning a trip, but with Ron's job situation, they thought it best if they wait a while. The line rang a second time and Ron let out a sigh. "That can't be the Alps calling." Then it dawned on him it was about this time yesterday Jack O'Brien called and reamed him out. He became filled with dread, but felt an obligation to answer it anyway. "Ron Dombrowski."

"Ron, Jack O'Brien here." Jack waited to see if Ron would say anything, but there was only silence on the other end. Taking that as his cue, Jack spoke. "Listen, about yesterday, I wanted to call and apologize. I had no right whatsoever to call and lay into you like that. I'm sorry, I feel..."

Ron cut him off, as a friend he understood and didn't want Jack to have to continue. Ron was sure a call such as this must be a painful thing to swallow, letting it drag out would only make it worse. "Jack it's OK. I don't blame you. Hell, if it was me I would've done the same thing, which is why I didn't try to stop you." With that simple, sincere apology, two old friends came together again. After this phone call, they'd never talk about it again. The conversation continued as Jack updated Ron on everything he'd tried thus far. Ron empathized with him but unfortunately could offer little.

"Ron, again I apologize and appreciate you taking the time to talk to me."

"Like I said Jack, don't worry about it. It's actually kind of funny. It reminded me of my drill sergeant back in basic training." Ron could hear Jack laugh into the phone. "That guy used to scare the shit out of me," Ron said, now laughing alongside Jack.

"Well if things don't work out, I guess I could re-enlist," Jack said.

Feeling as though what needed to be said had been said, Ron let Jack go. "Take care Jack and say hello to Margaret for me."

"Will do Ron, you do the same." Hanging up the phone Jack noticed Margaret leaning on the doorway. He smiled at her, a quiet smile.

Margaret knew Jack was a proud man who didn't like to admit his errors. She also knew that phone call couldn't have been easy. In a quiet, assuring tone, she spoke to him. "You're a good man Jack O'Brien. You always have been and you always will be, regardless of where we lay our heads."

Jack looked at Margaret like an addict ashamed of his recent behavior. But like the addict fulfilling his 12 steps to recovery, Jack felt a need to apologize. "I'm sorry dear. The way I've acted lately, well, it's been poor to say the least." Margaret's eyes remained focused on Jack, but she said nothing, allowing him to get out everything he needed to. "I've let myself down. And more than that, I've let you and the kids down. But that's over now and I won't let it happen again."

Sensing he'd finished saying his peace, Margaret spoke. "Jack, there's nothing to apologize for. I love you. The kids love you. And I realize you have a thick skull, but you need to understand this," she paused, making sure to have his focus, "we'll be OK, no matter what happens, we'll survive this."

"But I can't help but feel that this mess is my fault."

"I understand that, but none of us have disagreed with anything you've done. Given the same circumstances, if it were our decision to make, we'd have done the same, each one of us." Jack acknowledged the truth in her statement with a nod of his head, but he still had his doubts. Margaret sensed it and searched her brain for an answer. "Do you remember when James was 15 and playing JV football? The last game of the year that season?"

Jack looked at her quizzically, not really sure where she was going, "Yeah, I remember him playing."

"That last game of the year, when they had a chance to win the league."

Then it hit Jack what she was talking about. James had had a chance at an interception that would've probably won the game. It was wet and the ball went right through his hands. The opposing team caught it and went for a touchdown.

"James was devastated," Margaret continued. Jack agreed with another nod of the head. "Do you remember what you said to him after that game?"

Jack shrugged his shoulders, "I know I tried to console him, but I don't remember exactly what I said."

"Well I do," Margaret said. "James kept saying he should've just knocked the ball to the ground instead of trying to catch it. But you told him he was wrong. You told him he had a chance to get it, or pick it, or something and take it all the way. You said he had a chance to win the game on that play and that the ball was wet and the guy from the other team made a lucky grab after he missed it. You said he made the right decision at the time and that sometimes things don't go your way. Sometimes, the right decision now, turns out to be the wrong decision in the end. You told him he did what he should have done and that you would've done the same."

Jack smiled, his own words were being used against him. Now, he couldn't help but accept the fact that she had a point. "How do you remember these things?"

Margaret walked toward Jack. "I'm a woman Jack. It's what we do." She hugged him. "Do you understand now?"

"Yes, I understand," Jack conceded. "And by the way, I would've said picked it off, not get it or pick it."

"Not the point, Jack."

Jack held her a little tighter. "I know, I know. I'm just saying…"

Around 6:00 that evening a van pulled up and two young children bolted out followed by their parents. The kids hugged grandma before Michael and Janet entered the house. Michael walked over and kissed his mother.

"How are you doing?" he asked. When Margaret responded with a simple "good," Michael asked the next, more important question. "How's Dad doing?"

"He seems to be doing much better. I'm not sure what happened, but he's definitely better. I was a little worried about him earlier." Finishing her sentence Margaret thought about how much of an understatement that was.

Feeling satisfied things were in order Michael decided to change topics and was about to ask where his sister was when she entered the room. "Hey Sis, how's everything?"

"Hey Michael, not bad. How are things with you?" Just then the two kids came running through the room screaming as they went. Waiting for the sudden interruption to pass, she continued on, angling her head toward the door through which the kids had just run, "and the family?"

Michael laughed, being accustomed to such behavior. "We're hanging in there, circumstances and all." Sarah nodded her understanding. The two had never been close growing up because of their age difference, but over the last couple of years they had begun to close that gap. Their mutual love of horses had done a lot to make that happen. "I guess we're all hoping for a miracle to keep the family business going."

"Yeah, you're right about that," replied Sarah. "Some of us are merely getting started."

Just then, Sarah and Michael spotted Jack lumbering down the stairs. When he reached the bottom, he spoke in a voice much louder than necessary if he were speaking to his two children seated before him. "What's all this noise I'm hearing?" Within seconds "little" Jack and Mary came sprinting into the room yelling "Grandpa" on the way. Jack knelt down and the two young kids ran straight into his arms. Jack rose to his feet lifting both kids off the ground. "Oh, it's good to see you two." Little Jack and Sarah began hammering Jack with questions one after another. "Did you fix anything today?" "Can I help you fix something?" "Can we ride the tractor?" Unfortunately, the children never once left Grandpa Jack near enough time to answer even one of them.

Janet strolled into the room and laughed at the scene. "OK you two, give Grandpa a chance to answer something."

While her grandchildren were pressing their grandfather for information, Margaret was trying to put the finishing touches on dinner.

"Anything I can do to help Mom?" asked Sarah who opted to leave the chaos in the other room.

"Not at the moment. I've got about five more minutes and we'll be ready." As she finished, Manny entered through the back entrance. "Well it's about time young man."

"I'm sorry Margaret. I wanted to say hello to the horses on my way up."

Margaret gave Manny the "that's a legitimate excuse, but..." look and then glanced at his hands. "You probably touched those animals didn't you?" Manny smiled a guilty smile. "Alright, lavos sus hermanos."

Manny laughed, he loved it when Margaret tried her Spanish. "I'll go and wash my hands, but I don't have any brothers." Margaret looked at him quizzically and then at Sarah. Sarah was also laughing, being nearly fluent in Spanish. Still holding her mother's gaze, she raised her hands and said "manos, Mom, manos." Margaret, realizing her mistake, laughed along with Manny and Sarah.

Within a few minutes the whole group gathered in the dining room and began choosing seats. Manny stood in the back waiting to see where the children would end up. As he stood there, Jack came over and put his hand on Manny's shoulder. "How's everything Manny?"

"It's going real good Jack," he said. "Hopefully Sing will be ready to start training again soon."

Michael overheard and quickly piped in, "Yeah, I figure next week we should get him back at the track to begin jogging."

"Good," said Jack, "that's real good news." Once again Jack focused on Manny, looking into his eyes. He could never tell Manny what happened the day before or what role Manny played in helping him through it, but as it was with Ron and Margaret, Jack felt the need to say something. "I want to thank you for everything you do for the family. It means a lot to us," Jack paused for a moment, "to me."

Manny stood there somewhat dumbfounded. Jack wasn't the sensitive type and usually didn't make comments like that. "Ahh, it's no problem Jack. I'm happy to do it." For a moment, Manny wished he would have called him Mr. O'Brien, or sir, or something less casual, then dismissed the thought. Still, he felt the need to say more, to thank him for all he'd done for him. But the moment had passed.

Everyone finally settled in to their seats and looked toward the head of the table. Normally Jack would give the nod for everyone to start, but today he felt something else was needed. "I think before we begin tonight, it would be nice to have a blessing."

James and Michael looked at each other, thinking, 'A blessing...?

Suddenly little Mary raised her hand, emphatically waving it. "Can I do it, can I do it?"

Jack smiled at his granddaughter. "Of course you can. I think that would be great." And so the eldest member at the table called for a blessing and the youngest member gave one. Mary clasped her hands, closed her eyes and bowed her head. The others seated around the table followed suit. 'God is good, God is great...' She thanked God for all the wonderful food, health and happiness they had, a sentiment everyone shared and perhaps some even more than others. Once Mary had finished, everyone reached for the nearest dish.

Only Margaret waited. She sat at the opposite end of the table, gazing its length at Jack. She smiled, her first smile in days. The man she loved, strong yet caring, who had so recently disappeared, was once again sitting before her and that, she thought, was truly a blessing.

Chapter 25

~

JUNE 20

THE STORM CLOUDS HOVERING OVER the O'Briens' farm finally began to recede and along with it the sense of foreboding. To know the family's patriarch was once again at the helm meant a lot to each of the O'Briens. The reality of the situation endured, but the stout leadership Jack projected took measured amounts of stress away from the rest of the family. It gave everyone a sense of security and allowed Margaret and the children to deal with what anxiety remained in their own way. For James and Lauren, humor usually prevailed as the mechanism of choice. This day would be no different.

Lauren and Sydney made their way through the grocery store, cruising up and down the aisles. It was as routine as it gets. Lauren looked down at the can of Spaghetti O's with Meatballs, shaking her head, as she placed it alongside another in the cart.

"Hey, Daddy's favorite," exclaimed Sydney.

"Yes," Lauren replied in a huff, "since he's been about your age. Someday we're hoping he grows out of it." With her business in the aisle concluded, Lauren began to push the cart forward continuing the zig zag pattern she was setting from one aisle to the next. Abruptly, she brought the cart to a stop.

Sydney looked up at her. "What are you doing Mom?"

There, no more than 15 feet away, stood Henry Livingston. Lauren could hardly believe it. She hadn't seen or heard one word about him in years. Then suddenly he turns out to be the guy who may take down her husband's entire family and now, less than two weeks later, she comes face to face with him in the grocery store.

Observant as always, Sydney took notice that mom was staring at someone and turned to look. "Who's that guy, Mommy?"

Lauren leaned toward Sydney, made a face and said "He's someone who thinks his poop doesn't stink." Not wanting to be recognized, Lauren quickly began pushing the cart again, this time with a bit more pace. She was afraid if he recognized her and they began to talk, she might say something she'd regret. She'd done it before. She nearly passed by him unnoticed when Sydney opened her mouth.

"Hey mister, your poop stinks too you know."

Lauren lowered her head and pushed the cart, aghast at Sydney's comment. She didn't bother to apologize at the risk of being found out.

Henry was reading a label when he heard a little girl's voice, though he wasn't exactly sure what she'd said. It did sound like she mentioned something about poop stinking, but whatever it was, it didn't seem appropriate for a child to be saying such things. 'Probably the parents' fault,' Henry thought, they really should give a test to anyone considering having a child.

Lauren sped along until they made it to the aisle with the feminine products. She turned the cart sharply tipping it momentarily on two wheels. Sydney, enjoying the ride, let out a "whoopee," as they careened down the aisle. About the middle of the aisle Lauren slowed the cart to a crawl. She wasn't sure what else George might be shopping for today, but feminine products were probably not amongst them. They'd found their bunker. Lauren and Sydney lingered for 15 minutes before Lauren figured it was safe to continue, keeping a wary eye out for an unsuspecting banker.

James arrived home just as Lauren was finishing putting away the groceries. Sydney spotted James coming up the driveway and ran to meet him at the door.

"Daddy!" she cried out as James walked into the house. James picked up his daughter and gave her a big hug before putting her back down.

"How was your day today?" he asked, walking toward the kitchen.

Sydney followed in tow. "Good. We went grocery shopping and got you Spaghetti O's."

"Oh you did. Thank you very much."

"And I told the man his poop stinks."

The comment made James do a double take and glance over at Lauren, who was already cringing. Meanwhile Sydney, having given her news of the day, took interest in what was on television and left the room. James, realizing the adults could speak freely, sat down on one of the kitchen chairs. "Care to explain that one?" he asked with a broad smile.

"Yeah," Lauren replied ever so slowly. "Next time I tell you to watch what you say to her, remind me to do the same." James began to laugh, but said nothing knowing what comes around goes around. When Lauren realized no wisecrack was forthcoming, she continued. "So we're in the grocery store and who do I suddenly see? None other than Henry Livingston."

"No kidding," James answered back. "Isn't that strange? I figured he had his own personal shopper."

"Exactly! Anyway, of course Sydney sees me staring at him and wants to know who he is. I, like an idiot, tell her he is someone who thinks his poop doesn't stink."

James laughs again. "Good line, Mom."

"Yes I know, not one of my best moments. So I decide to try to get out of there fast before he recognizes me. We're just about past him when your daughter decides she's going to take matters into her own hands." Anticipating what was coming, James began to laugh harder. "Yes you guessed it. She says, 'Hey mister, your poop stinks too you know.' As you might imagine, I didn't stick around to see if he heard it."

After a few minutes James settled down. "What am I going to do with you two?" he joked, smiling at his wife. "And I thought I had to worry about bringing her to the track."

Chapter 26

~

JUNE 21

IT WAS THE LAST DAY of school, a day for kids across the land to celebrate. Janet O'Brien pulled into the school parking lot to pick up her two elementary-school students, Jack and Mary. As she walked toward the staging area where kids who are driven home gather, she was amazed at how fast the year went. Part of her was hoping the summer at home with the kids would go just as fast. But then again she thought, that would mean summer was over and in western New York, you live for summer.

As she approached the hectic scene she noticed one of her old friends Denise, a school administrative assistant, watching over the kids with her clipboard in hand.

"Denise, how's it going? A little chaotic around here, huh?"

"Hey Janet, great to see you. Yeah, you could say it's a bit out of control. Here to pick up your two?" she said, scanning the masses for the two O'Brien children.

"Yup. The start of another summer vacation. I'm sure I'll be ready to send them back here by mid-July at the latest."

Denise laughed. Having two of her own, she knew exactly what Janet meant. "Say, have you ever considered going back to work at all? One of our part-time office workers has decided to retire and we're going to start looking for someone to replace her. Have any interest?"

Janet thought about the conversation she'd had with Michael only two weeks before. "What would the hours be?" she asked with a hint of enthusiasm.

"Basically, it would be the normal school hours, three days a week. I think the total number of hours is around 18," Denise said, waving at some kids and pointing the way to others.

"That would be perfect. Of course, as long as they don't make me do this," she said gesturing at the mass of kids Denise was trying to keep corralled. Meanwhile Jack and Mary, having spotted their mom, dashed over. "Looks like I have my two. So if I'm interested in the position is there someone I should contact?" Janet asked.

"They probably won't even start the process until sometime in July. If you like, I'll mention it to the woman in charge of personnel. I'll tell her to give you a call when the time comes."

"That would be great, thanks Denise and good luck."

Denise smiled, "Thanks, I need it today."

With that, Janet and the kids made their way back to the van to head home and kick off summer recess. Janet drifted in thought about the potential new job when she felt Mary tugging at her sleeve.

"What were you and that woman talking about?"

Although it was an innocent question, Janet knew if she told the kids, then they would surely pass the information to their dad. At this point in time, that's not really what Janet wanted. "Oh, nothing. We're just old friends." Fortunately that sufficed and she was left to think about what a great opportunity she may have stumbled upon, and along with that, what Michael's reaction might be.

JUNE 24

James held onto the reins as Manny cinched up Sing's girth. Once secure, Manny patted Sing on his neck. It had been three weeks since Manny sat atop the big chestnut gelding. "It's been too long," Manny quietly said to Sing, who shook his head, rattling the metal bit in his mouth.

"Do you think that means he's glad to be back or not so much?" asked James, handing Manny the reins.

Manny laughed as James gave him a leg up. "I believe he said he was very excited about being here with me today."

Now it was James' turn to laugh. "You got all that from that little nicker? I've got Monty Roberts galloping my horse. I'd like to see an actual translation on that." Manny just smiled and turned Sing toward the track for their morning workout, arriving at the backstretch just as the tractors finished harrowing it. The freshly groomed surface looked wonderful, the same way a ski slope looks after a new fallen snow, surface pure and untouched, like an invitation. It's almost a shame to disturb it, but a day's work must go on, so off they went.

Traveling down the backstretch at a slow canter Manny began to reflect on the previous 12 months he'd spent aboard Sing. The first time he had ridden him was just about a year ago. It was a ride Manny wouldn't forget. He had ridden many horses, but none like this one. Sing's motion was fluid and strong, even as a 2-year-old in training. Sitting atop him, moving at a gallop, felt like getting behind the wheel of a Porsche after driving a Yugo all your life. Manny had never driven a Porsche, hell, he had never driven a Toyota, but the power underneath him was unmistakable. According to James, when Manny returned from his first trip with Sing, he could barely contain himself. He smiled from ear to ear and you would have thought he'd won the lottery. And although he rode Sing nearly every day since then, Manny's heart would still beat slightly faster each time he was lofted atop the athletic animal.

It was a short ride today. Being out of action for three weeks took its toll on Sing's conditioning. As they walked back to the barn Manny stroked Sing's mane. "Don't worry chico, I'll get you back in shape. Rapido." Sing just kept on walking while Manny kept on talking. "I know you can do it chico grande. There are big things in your future. One of these days you'll show 'em, I can feel it. It just hasn't been the right time yet." The pair turned the corner to see Michael and James waiting near Sing's stall for their return. "And you'd better believe I'll be there to see it."

Chapter 27

◡

JULY 2

EVEN WITH THE REAL ESTATE market in decline a good piece of property was a good piece of property. When one of his fellow bankers gave Ron the number to Benson Realty, he felt an obligation to Jack to give them a call. They were a local real estate development company. Their niche was purchasing old farm land and turning it into new housing developments. With recent events in the mortgage world, Benson Realty was keeping very busy. It made Ron wonder if someone at FLS&L had struck a deal with the developer. Maybe get a commission on the purchase or subsequent development of the properties that were forced to sell. He certainly hoped not, but at this point nothing would surprise him.

"Thank you very much for the referral, Mr. Dombrowski. We'll have one of our agents drive by and take a quick look at the property. If it's something we might be interested in, then we'll give you a call and set up a time to take a closer look."

The woman on the other end of the phone was extremely courteous, thought Ron. They're probably getting their pick of prime real estate all over the Finger Lakes, why shouldn't she be? "Thank you. I'll wait to hear back from you," Ron said in his most polite, professional voice.

Ron debated on whether or not to mention the developer to Jack. If they weren't interested, then why even bring it up? But Ron knew deep down that would never be the case. Jack's farm was beautiful. It sloped downhill with a few rolling hills dotting the 50 acres. Most of the property offered a nice view of the lake which sat a couple miles to the south. Hills rose slowly on either side of the lake, as if they were two hands cupped together. The unspoiled, deep blue water within shimmered in the sunlight; its waves gently lapping the lake's pebbled shore. 'Heck,' Ron thought, 'if I were to build a house, that's where I'd want to be.' He envisioned possible names of the new development, 'Deer Meadows...Rolling Plains...O'Briens' Hills...' So it didn't take Ron long to reach his conclusion. He picked up the receiver and dialed Jack's number.

It was Margaret who answered the phone. After respectfully asking her how she was doing Ron got to the point of the call. "Is Jack around? I've contacted someone about your land and just wanted to make him aware of it. Hopefully, it will never come to that, but I thought we should begin the process anyway." The comment didn't seem to faze Margaret, for which Ron was thankful.

"Yes he is, in fact," she paused momentarily, "he just came out of his office."

Ron had been to their house a ton of times, but couldn't recall noticing an office. He paused a moment, amazed at his own ignorance, "I never knew you guys had an office in the house."

"Well, let me put it this way," Margaret said. "I wouldn't recommend going in his *office* until he's been out of there for about 20 or 30 minutes."

Ron was still laughing when Margaret handed Jack the phone. "Hey Ron, how's it going?"

Ron was finally able to curtail the laughing enough to speak. "Not too bad Jack," he said regaining his composure. "I'll tell you, that wife of yours is a real pistol."

Having no idea what it was Margaret said, Jack glanced at her and agreed with Ron. "That's one word for her.' Margaret gave Jack a look like she had no earthly idea what he was talking about.

Once again composed, Ron let Jack know about the developers and the conversation he'd had with them. Jack understood the need to get that ball rolling, 'damn wrecking ball,' he thought to himself. To date no other options seemed to be panning out and there was nothing on the horizon. They talked a little bit about what a ballpark figure might be for the acreage, based on what Ron knew. If nothing else, it would give Jack a chance to run some numbers and determine how much, or if all of the land, would need to be sold. Not a pleasant task, but a necessary one. At the end of the conversation Jack let him know he appreciated the help.

"No problem Jack," Ron said, "I'm not done fighting yet." Even if he couldn't solve the problem, Ron wanted to let Jack know he was with him in spirit.

JULY 4

The knock on the door startled Jack, who was focused solely on the numbers jotted on the paper in front of him. "Yeah," he said without raising his head.

"The kids should be here shortly," Margaret yelled, not bothering to open the door.

"Alright, just let me know when they arrive." Jack was too deep into his figuring to stop now without good cause. He stared at the numbers before him, analyzing the estimated selling price of most of the stock of horses they owned. Another sheet of paper contained a list of equipment and its approximate value. By calculating what he could sell these assets for Jack got an indication as to how much more he would need to pay off the loan. Or, to put it another way, how much of his land he needed to sell. He hoped, under a worst-case scenario, they could sell part of the property and still retain the house and some acreage. The only asset he couldn't figure a price for yet was Sing. Sing's worth rested in their ability to get him into the winner's circle. A trip to the winner's circle would boost his value substantially. Saratoga opened in three weeks and a trip to the winner's circle there would increase his value by three to four times. Jack knew Sing's success could change the amount of acreage they could keep by a dozen or more. They needed to run him at Saratoga next time out.

Just north of Albany in New York lies the quiet town of Saratoga Springs. Within the town limit stands America's oldest race track and for six weeks starting the end of July and running until Labor Day, the town springs to life. During that time, the country's best horses, owners, trainers and jockeys converge to match skills. Name a famous horse and he has probably run there at least once. Everyone wants to win at Saratoga, whether you're a big gun or a small-time player like the O'Briens. Usually the prestige is worth as much as the increased purse money, but in this case, the opportunity to increase his horse's value took precedence.

Of course, Jack knew a little something about sending a horse to Saratoga. Over the years he'd sent a number of horses east down the New York State Thruway, always making sure to pick his spots carefully. Jack never entered a horse just to say he ran one. If you saw the entrant was an O'Brien trainee, you could bet your life he had a shot. Jack actually believed there was something about the place that brought them luck. As if there was some sort of aura that followed the O'Briens to the grandiose track. He never mentioned it to anyone, including Margaret, but he always, always felt they would win. Jack loved the feeling of being the underdog, the overlooked little guy against the big name players. He reveled in taking them down. Jack was in the midst of recalling a previous trip to Saratoga's winner's circle when Margaret yelled again.

"They're here."

"OK, I'll be right out," Jack said. He stood up continuing to gaze down at the numbers before him. They unfortunately didn't look as good as he would've liked. As if speaking to the numbers Jack pleaded, "Alright, see if you can multiply a little while I'm gone." Jack shook his head and made his way toward the door. He could already hear the sound of grandchildren running amuck.

Margaret stood in the kitchen fixing drinks for the kids and adults, preparing food for the grill and doing whatever anyone needed at that moment. It was utter chaos and Margaret loved it. The entire family attended to, which according to Margaret, is how it should be. As she handed glasses of lemonade to Sydney and Mary, Daniel and Nicole entered the kitchen, almost getting run over as the two kids scampered back outside.

"Man, those kids are everywhere," Daniel said.

"Yes they are," Margaret agreed. "But there's always room for more," she added with a sly smile. Both Daniel and Nicole looked at one another and winced.

"I don't think so Mom. We can't even commit to getting a puppy let alone having a child."

"Listen, you two," Margaret said bluntly, "you're never ready for having a child. When they arrive, you just deal with it. It's not rocket science you know."

Having heard this spiel before, Daniel nodded his head, "Yes Mom, I know," while grabbing for a couple of glasses of lemonade. Then, as Margaret turned to tend to one of the dishes she was preparing, he and Nicole retreated out the door.

Realizing Daniel had beat a hasty exit Margaret ran to the door and yelled. "I know where you two live you know."

James and Lauren passed through the open door as Margaret was finishing. "You give it to him Mom!" James told her.

Finding a new target Margaret turned toward son number 2. "Don't make me start on you now. I'm expecting more than one grandchild from the two of you."

"Mom please, we've tried. Lauren's gone baron on us. There's nothing we can do," James said. "Thanks for making Lauren feel really uncomfortable."

"Oh she is not," Margaret said. She shot a glance at Lauren. "You're not are you?"

"No I'm not, don't worry. He's just trying to make a joke. And not a good one at that," Lauren said, slapping James on the side of the head.

"Owww. That's not very nice," he said, holding the side of his head.

Margaret jumped to the aide of her daughter-in-law. "You deserved it my dear. Good for her to give it to you."

James laughed knowing he'd received his just desserts.

"This is why I hate the holidays," James said, a sly smile aimed at his mom.

Margaret stopped, raised her eyebrows and pointed her finger at him, chastising him without speaking as only a mother could.

Out by the giant oak tree, Jack prepared the grill. He slid his hand over the coals to feel the heat, then yanked it back. Definitely hot. He grabbed a brush off the side of the grill and scraped away the remnants of a previous dinner. The bits and pieces made a sizzling sound as they fell from the rack onto the hot coals. Back and forth Jack went, up one side, down the other. No different than working the fields. After a few minutes he stopped brushing and took a look. Satisfied, he placed the brush back. The grill was ready for the impending feast.

A game of horse shoes had begun nearby. It was close enough so Jack could not only watch, but hear the game, which was the real entertainment. Strangely enough, it was Sarah, the youngest of the siblings and only female, that turned out to be the best thrower. Jack always got a kick out of watching them play and watching the boys get frazzled when she beat them. Presently Sarah and Manny were beating Michael and Daniel without mercy.

"Nice shot Sarah," Manny said, bending over to pick up two shoes. "That makes it 18 to 4. You guys are in trouble."

As Michael was preparing to throw, James came strolling up. "Did I hear that right, 18 to 4? What's up with that? Now, I can understand Daniel stinking up the place, the only thing he's used to throwing these days is his bear-claw wrapper in the garbage." After allowing a moment for laughter, James kept going. "Seriously dude, you look like you're chunking up a bit. You may want to skip a meal now and then."

"Shut up already," said Daniel. "Nobody invited you over here."

Tuning out James' discourse, Michael let fly his first horse shoe which landed about two feet short. Sarah took a step forward, pretending to measure the distance from the shoe to the stake, which needed to be about a foot and a half closer to get a point. "Nice arm Alice, I think you left it just a hair short."

"Quiet down, before I wrap this next one around your neck," replied Michael, as he lined up for his second shot. He made sure not to leave this one short, heaving it at the metal stake. Unfortunately, he didn't fare much better this time either. It ricocheted off the stake and began rolling end over end away from the target causing Daniel to jump for cover.

"Good Lord man, you trying to knock that thing over," James said, laughing. "Hey Daniel, you're pretty nimble for a big guy."

Daniel smiled at James as he began picking up Michael's errant tosses. "You might want to think about leaving my friend. As bad as I am, who knows where my throws will end up and I'd *hate* to accidently hit you."

"Probably best if I stand right next to the stake then, isn't it," James said.

The banter became background noise as Jack scanned the property. What more could anyone want? The sight of the horses grazing in the fields and the lake in the distance looked like something out of a postcard. But it wasn't a postcard; it was his home, precious and peaceful. A small breeze kicked up and the branches and leaves rustled in the wind. Jack could recall a picture of his grandfather as a young man standing in front of this same tree. Back then, the tree couldn't have been much more than 6 feet tall, barely taller than his grandfather. He looked up again as the leaves fluttered once more. It's amazing how things change, he thought.

"Here's the chicken and hamburgers."

Jack turned to see Margaret approaching with a tray in hand. No time to dwell on things now. "OK the grill is ready. Let's load her up."

After dinner Jack excused himself, though no one really noticed him leaving, and headed toward the barn. Within a couple of minutes, he re-emerged sitting atop his tractor with an old flatbed trailer in tow, loaded from one end to the other with straw. Giving three good honks of the horn, Jack signaled it was time to head for the lake.

From in and around the house, kids scampered and adults walked toward their makeshift chariot. Jack stood at the back, ready to assist the smaller members of the clan. One by one Jack tossed his grandchildren into the back of the trailer, each one landing gently on a fluffy bed of straw, each one laughing as they flew up and in. Once the adults had climbed aboard, Jack returned to his place at the wheel. "Are we all ready to go?" he said. "Yessssss…." Jack put the tractor in gear and with a sudden jerk, off they went.

Every Fourth of July the town launched fireworks over the lake. The O'Briens would tractor their way to a boat launch along the lake's western shore, singing songs and throwing straw along the way. There they would meet up with other families who lived along that side of the lake. Friends would share drinks and desserts and enjoy the evening together. It was one of those things that made living in a small town pleasurable. Tonight, despite the circumstances, was no different. In fact, as the tractor chugged its way along the path, it occurred to most of the adult members of the O'Brien family that this particular Fourth of July was one to savor even more than normal, though no one actually verbalized it. They were all aware of what loomed. For all they knew, this could be their last time. But that disparaging thought remained in the background and as the tractor came to a halt, the only thing on anyone's mind was fun and fireworks, the fun part already being in full swing.

The boat launch and parking lot, which could fit about 80 or 90 vehicles, was filled to capacity. It was a full-fledged tailgate party. The only thing missing was some sort of sporting event. Everyone mingled from truck to truck to car to table. "What's mine is yours." And if they weren't acquainted before tonight, they would be by night's end.

An hour into the night, Michael with Janet and James with Lauren crossed paths, having taken different routes around the parking lot. Their kids had long since left their sides and were running wild as a gaggle of kids might. The chit chat between parents stopped suddenly as they all heard the sound of Jack laughing and telling someone they were crazy. Following the sound, they spotted him and Margaret with several other adults about their age, Jack's face lit up with a broad smile, the likes of which none of them had seen in quite some time.

"It's good to see him laugh like that again," James said.

"Yeah," Michael said, "it reminds me of all those years, back when we were kids. God, he loved these gatherings."

Somewhat surprised that their father-in-law would ever act so social and jovial, both wives gave their husbands questioning looks.

Michael understood their surprise, but had no good reason, "I don't know, we never could figure it out either. Maybe it's the beer, but he always was happy and go-lucky whenever we came down here for one of these." With raised eyebrows, the women accepted Michael's explanation, understanding it was one of life's great mysteries.

"Speaking of beer," James said, turning toward Lauren, "what do you say we go find us one." Lauren nodded and they said their goodbyes.

The laughter and games slowed, interrupted by "oohs and ahhs" at the sight and sound of the bursts overhead. Even after the display had ended most people stuck around to enjoy the moment, soaking up every ounce, friends enjoying friends. Eventually the kids slowed down and the grown-ups grew weary, so as night descended upon them Jack started the tractor and gently helped the children into the old hay wagon. No one spoke on the ride back. They sat in the straw and stared up at the stars sparkling in the clear sky. Siblings, cousins, husbands and wives, arm-in-arm, all hoping the ride would last a little longer. It was a wonderful end to a great Fourth of July. One they all hoped wouldn't be the last.

Chapter 28

~

JULY 11

THREE COLLABORATORS PARTNER EACH TIME a horse steps foot on the racetrack. One is of course the owner of the horse. This may be a single individual or a group of individuals. The owner, or owners as it may be, employs a trainer, the second collaborator, to prepare the horse for the races. The third collaborator is the person who will ride the horse in those races, the jockey.

The trainers of those horses make their money two ways. They have a daily rate they are paid by the owner, which most will tell you does nothing more than break even, and they also get 10 percent of the horse's winnings. So it's in the best interest of the owner and the trainer to find the best jockey each time one of their horses race. Jockeys earn a flat fee for a losing mount but rely on 10 percent of the earnings to make a living. The jockey naturally wants to ride the best horse in each race. The best jockeys have the greatest number of horses from which to choose. Whoever trains the best horse in any particular race usually has a number of jockeys interested in gaining the mount. Because of this scenario, loyalty is not usually expected, not to say it doesn't happen. If a particular trainer has a number of good horses, a good jockey will often ride some of his lesser performers in order to secure the mounts on his better stock. For years the O'Briens had quality horses and never had problems finding good jockeys. They held the fleeting loyalty of some of the best local jocks. But times had changed, the quality of the horses was down and the loyalty had long since disappeared.

Today's race card exemplified that point. The O'Briens had two horses entered at Finger Lakes in two races. Neither horse was expected to win. As the entries came out a few days in advance of the races, no one approached Michael to secure the mounts. Not even the jockeys who were struggling for mounts. When Michael mentioned it to Jack, Jack recommended they give the mounts to Manny. Each year the O'Briens would give Manny a few mounts as a "gift" for his hard work and dedication. Usually the horses he were given weren't the cream of the crop and they often had to carry extra weight because of Manny's size. But Manny always gave them a good ride and if nothing else, he appreciated the gesture. Despite knowing he would never be a full-time jockey again, he still had that competitive spark that lives in all athletes and it felt good to exercise it. Michael wasn't expecting much out of the horses anyway, so he figured 'why not?'

Manny stood in front of the mirror in the jockey's room admiring how he looked in the familiar green and white silks of the O'Brien Racing Stable. It had been almost 10 months since Manny's last mount and it felt good to suit up again. Securing his sleeves, Manny took four rubber bands and wrapped two around his right wrist and two around his left. Then he extended his arms making sure the sleeve length was comfortable and the bands would remain in place. With no buttons to secure the end of the sleeve at the wrist, rubber bands are the jockey's method of choice. Next, Manny grabbed for his helmet, its green helmet cover secured in place by an even larger rubber band. He slowly placed it on his head, fitting it snugly. His gaze returned to the mirror. He withheld the urge to smile, excited and anxious to get out there. For a split second he felt the yearning, wishing he could drop those 10 pounds and be a jockey again. But he knew that wasn't his reality. 'Enjoy what you have,' Manny told himself, 'it's a good life.'

"Hey Manny, looking good."

Manny abruptly turned around to see Chico dressed and ready for his next mount. Chico was a veteran jockey who'd been riding at Finger Lakes for years. His real name was Javier Cesar, though no one actually called him that. He picked up the name Chico nearly 30 years ago when he started in the business. At the time, no one cared to know Javier, he was just another young Hispanic kid trying to make it, so rather than fret about his real name, they simply called him Chico. Actually, as the story goes, it tended to be "hey Chico," more often than not. Eventually he found success, but the nickname stuck and he never insisted on being called Javier. Manny ran into him most mornings and knew him well. For despite being one of the more sought-after jockeys, Chico came out to the track every day to work horses and make sure he kept his business. "Chico, good to see you. I saw you had a ride in this race."

"Yeah, it looks like you, me, Johnny and Phil all have speed this race. Should be interesting to see who gets the jump. I'm hoping Phil's connections stiff their horse, otherwise he'll probably run us all into the ground." Chico looked across the jockey's room toward where Phil McDonough sat, then back at Manny. "I asked him, but he ain't talking."

"Well, it probably won't matter for me. I don't think we have much of a chance in this one, but who knows," Manny said.

"Hey now, none of that negative thinking," the crafty veteran said. "Ride every race like it's your last. You'd be amazed at how many races I've won that looked impossible. This is horse racing after all."

"You're right Chico," Manny said with a smile, "you never know." Manny reached out and bumped fists with Chico, as they headed for the exit, "Thanks for the advice and good luck. I hope you finish second behind us."

Chico laughed. "I meant you might be lucky enough to finish second behind me. Let's not get carried away now."

Manny laughed at Chico's rebuke and the two made their way to the paddock. On the way, Manny tightened his chinstrap and smacked his whip against his highly polished boots, now ready to put the power of positive thinking to the test.

He met Michael and James in the paddock and the three discussed the strategy, of which there was little. Their horse was outclassed and because of Manny's size, he would be carrying 4 pounds more than he was assigned. But Ramblin Rudy was a gutsy horse who tried every time and like Chico said, you never know when it comes to horse racing. After they watched Rudy circle the walking ring several times, Manny mounted up and horse and rider walked to the track. Just before they were snatched up by the pony boy, James patted Rudy's neck and gave Manny a wink. "Go get em Manny."

Manny smiled back at James just as the pony boy whisked them away. The butterflies in his stomach began to flicker. The race meant virtually nothing, but it had been a while for Manny and like any athlete, if you can't get excited before a game, you probably shouldn't be playing.

In the corner of the grandstand stood Jack O'Brien, unannounced to the three boys. He hadn't been to the track since the day he told his boys the farm was in trouble and hadn't seen Manny ride in almost two years. So, he figured, this would be a good day to get out. Why he didn't tell the boys, he was coming he wasn't sure. Part of him just wanted to watch them, the way he had when they were kids. Let them do their own thing without worrying about Dad being there.

Looking down at his program he noticed their horse was listed at 20-1 on the morning line. As he scanned the tote board he laughed seeing the odds were currently 37-1. Apparently nobody liked their horse. He was a little hard to like in this race. The horse likes the lead, but he was not only facing better competition than his recent races, there were several other horses in the race who also like the lead. Hence the odds. The race was three quarters of a mile, or six furlongs in racing terms, starting on the backside and going around one turn.

Ramblin Rudy broke well from the starting gate, but as expected, several other horses dashed toward the lead. Manny saw them rush up and tried to hold his mount back. The three horses, including Chico's, sped away as Manny settled Rudy in behind them. Despite not being on the lead, where he likes to be, Rudy seemed to be moving comfortably and that's what's important. The race continued this way for the first half mile until the breakneck speed of the front three began to exact its toll. As they came around the turn the leaders began to slow down. Manny saw his opportunity and angled his horse off the rail and around the leaders. Chico, riding the outermost of the three lead horses, looked to his right to see a horse getting ready to pass him. Chico was already working hard to keep his mount going and knew he had no chance to win. When he realized it was Manny preparing to take the lead, he smiled. "Take it to em Manny," he yelled. "Bring him home, Manny, bring him home."

A surge of adrenaline coursed through Manny's veins hearing Chico cheer him on. He knew he was a long shot and that things were going bad for the farm. If he could win this he thought, it would be a great shot in the arm. He looked up and saw the eighth pole. One eighth of a mile to go.

What Manny couldn't see, but was clear to Jack high above, was the favorite in the race, a big grey named Abucktwenty, was uncorking a huge rally from the back of the pack. The speed at which he was closing on Manny was too much. Manny didn't stand a chance.

Manny heard the pounding of hooves coming fast behind him. He turned to look back and saw a horse and rider coming quickly to his outside. Manny smacked Rudy with two sharp cracks with his whip in an effort to get everything he could. It was for naught as the big grey flew past them leaving Manny to finish second. His heart sank as they galloped out after the finish line. Finishing second certainly wasn't bad, but he'd thought he had it won. How great it would have been to go back to the farm tonight and share the news with Jack and Margaret. Some things, he guessed, simply weren't meant to be. 'Horse racing is not Hollywood' Manny said to himself.

James and Michael greeted Manny as he dismounted. "Man, we almost had it," James said.

Manny smiled and shrugged his shoulders. "Almost," he quietly repeated as he began to make his way to the jocks' room. He had made it only a few feet when he heard James yell "hey." He turned to see James pointing at him.

"Nice ride."

From the grandstand Jack watched as another jockey caught up to Manny and gave him a pat on the back just before they went underneath the stands and out of view. Not bad, he thought, not too bad at all. He started down the steps and headed for the parking lot, his curiosity satisfied. Later that night Michael called and gave him the day's results. Their other horse, also hopelessly outclassed, managed to finish third. The purses weren't going to save the farm, but might buy some diesel fuel for the tractor. Not a bad day all things considered, Michael told him. Jack agreed.

Chapter 29

~

JULY 13

It was Friday the 13th, a fitting day to receive such a call thought Ron, despite the fact that it was a call he knew was coming. He still wasn't sure if he should consider it good news or bad. It was Benson Realty and, as he had expected, they loved the property. A couple of their agents had driven past earlier in the week and were excited to pursue it further. One would suppose that someone looking to buy your property would temper their enthusiasm when discussing it. You never want to let on how much you want something. It gives the seller too much power. Apparently in this case, they either felt as though they held all the chips, or just didn't care. It also dawned on Ron that he wasn't the seller and these vultures probably figured it didn't matter much to him. Of course they were wrong. If they wanted that land half as badly as it sounded like they did, well Ron was sure he would help Jack squeeze every last nickel out of them.

They wanted to schedule a time to survey the land and asked if he could set it up for them, which he naturally agreed. As it was, they wouldn't be ready to do it until the beginning of August. Business must be good, Ron imagined. The thought made his stomach turn. He wondered how many other families' lives were being turned upside down. He decided he didn't want to think about it. It was time to go home and spend a nice evening with the wife.

JULY 15

It had been three months since Lauren snapped James from his brief bout with depression. Since that time James had studied and watched Sing. He spent time reviewing the video replays of each race. He took note of when Sing was comfortable, what made him nervous, who the people were around him, and he even took a closer look at Sing's diet. Each race seemed to throw out a different twist. Sometimes it was the paddock, sometimes after the jockey climbed aboard and occasionally he waited until they were on track warming up before the race. Unfortunately, nothing gave him a true indication. The only time he never had any problems was in the morning. Each morning he always went about his business like a professional. But why, wondered James. That, in itself, had to be some type of indicator. Something always heightened his level of anxiety come race time. It had to be something they were doing, but what?

Since James' research project had begun, Sing had only raced one time. To really understand the issue he knew he would have to wait for Sing to get back to the races. Race day always seemed to pose the big problem. What James had noticed through all this was that there wasn't something particular that made him nervous, but more, certain things seemed to put him at ease. A theory was beginning to take shape in James' mind. He just needed a chance to test it.

JULY 17

Michael, James and Manny stood outside their barn at Finger Lakes cleaning tack and enjoying the pleasant weather. All the horses had been worked and were now resting in their stalls. It promised to be a quiet day as the O'Briens didn't have any horses entered on today's card. Thus far, the farm had faired reasonably well winning at a 13 percent clip. Not as well as in the past, but a little better than the last couple of years. Of course, none of that mattered if the farm went under. If that happened, then all the horses currently under Michael's care would be dispersed in a sale, with the exception of a possible few. So Michael decided to spread the word he was accepting new clients. Max Bellows, a fellow trainer and friend, who wasn't taking on any new clients, had received a call from an owner looking for a trainer. He passed the number to Michael and recommended he give him a call. "I don't know the guy, but it might work. I think he had some horses at Belmont but they weren't good enough. As long as he pays the bills, what the hell, right." That was two days ago and so far, Michael refused to pull the trigger.

"Well, you ever gonna call this guy?" blurted James out of nowhere. Michael looked at him and turned back to the bridle he was soaping. "This guy isn't going to wait forever and we both know you need to do this."

Unfortunately, Michael knew every word James had spoken was true. Still, making that call, in Michael's eyes, meant admitting he couldn't make it on his own without outside assistance. But he knew he needed to get over that. The success they'd had in the past was gone now and changes needed to be made. This was the start. "Alright, alright I'll do it. I'd prefer doing that to sitting here with you clowns and cleaning tack anyway." So Michael got up and headed into his office at the end of the barn to make the call.

James sat there acting as if Michael's words hurt him. "What's up with that brother? Where's the love, man?" James began to crack a smile as he finished, flashing a wink at Manny. Manny laughed at the nonsense and thought about how much he enjoyed simply hanging around these guys.

About 15 minutes later Michael emerged from his little corner office. His manner gave no indication as to how the conversation went.

"Well, what's the story?" pleaded James.

"We should be getting three new horses some time in about a week or so."

"Excellent, excellent. You're quite a salesman there Mr. O'Brien," said James. "Do we know anything about these horses? Can they run, are they mares, colts, or like my friend Manny here, geldings?" James smiled and pointed at Manny.

Manny was used to the ribbing so he took it in stride and answered James back in Spanish. "Eso no es lo que su mujer dijo."

James had no idea what Manny had said, but laughed anyway, figuring it was an insult of some kind. "Hey, hey, hey, no speaking Spanish here."

Michael stood there shaking his head. "If you two are through, then I'll answer the question." Like two school kids caught fooling around, both James and Manny straightened up. "There are two colts and one mare. They've been running down at Aqueduct and Belmont and have fared OK, but the owner thought they might do better up here."

"Sounds good to me," said James. "I'll make sure we've got the stalls ready for them."

Chapter 30

~

JULY 22

"Manny," Michael yelled as Manny and Sing began to make their way to the track. Manny turned to acknowledge he'd heard him. "Do me a favor and take your time warming him up. I need to stop by the Racing Office real quick and I want to be in the stands when you go. I shouldn't be long. I'll call James on the walkie-talkie when I'm set. And remember, 5 furlongs out of the gate, nice and easy."

"OK," Manny bellowed back.

"James is already out there on Mac."

Manny nodded his understanding. Once they made it to the track, Manny started jogging Sing. He felt good, his leg had healed nicely and his conditioning was right on target for another race in a week or so, a couple of races in the Saratoga condition book circled. This workout would let them know exactly where they stood and based on how Sing was warming up, Manny expected it to be a good one.

The assistant starter looped his leather shank through Sing's bit and walked him into the starting gate. Sing entered easily having done this same thing 100 times before. The assistant then slid the shank from the bit, while holding onto the cheek piece of the bridle, perched himself alongside Sing while another assistant latched the gate door behind them. Manny buried his right hand into Sing's mane at the base of the neck and loosened up his left, then shifted his weight deep into his stirrups, positioning his toes and heels just the way he wanted them. He could feel his heart ticking a shade faster. No matter how many times Manny had done this, the adrenaline rushed all over again. The assistant starter shook Sing's bridle, making sure his head pointed forward, and then looked at Manny. Manny saw the man looking at him from the corner of his eye, but made no attempt to make eye contact. Silence means ready in the gate. Manny remained focused straight ahead and the assistant starter scanned the turn to see if any horses were galloping, seeing none, he bellowed, "Gonnnnna break." The starter standing about 15 feet in front of the gate heard his compatriot, waited a second and then pressed the button. The magnet holding the front gate doors together released and the doors swung open.

Sing shot out, with Manny holding on tight. The plan was to merely breeze Sing, so Manny crouched low and went along for the ride. He would make no effort to encourage Sing forward and as it were, he didn't need to. Sing moved well, gliding over the track and Manny could feel he had a lot of horse underneath him.

From the stands Michael watched Sing move easily down the backstretch and around the turn. As Sing passed each pole indicating another eighth of a mile Michael would glance down at his stopwatch, 'Perfect.' So far Sing was taking each eighth in a consistent twelve-second clip. After each furlong, Michael muttered, 'Perfect.'

At the end of the stretch, James sat on his pony and watched Sing and Manny coming down the stretch. Without conscious effort a smile formed on James' face. The horse was an athlete, simply put. The fluidity of his gait made it look so effortless, it was impressive to watch. James couldn't tell what his time was, but he anticipated it would be right on target. He focused on Sing's stride and listened for any noise as they galloped passed where he was stationed. Sing sounded and appeared like a horse ready for his next race. James clucked at Mac and the old bronc loped into a canter toward where Sing would pull up, keeping an eye on Sing and Manny as they began to ease.

Michael arrived from the grandstand and saw James exiting his pony's stall. "Well what'd you think?"

"I think we're ready to go," James answered. "How was the time?"

"Good, one minute and a fifth. Basically he went 12-second eighths the entire way."

"Nice. He galloped out real well also."

Just then Manny and Sing came walking around the corner. "How did he feel?" asked Michael.

"Perfect," replied Manny. "He did it real easy like. Simpatico," he said, smiling at James. "He feels ready to me."

Michael stood straight up, "Well, I guess that makes it unanimous. I'll make the call and enter him."

"Saratoga?" James inquired.

"Yup. For some reason Dad really wants his next start there. So, Saratoga it is."

Jack sat at the kitchen table with Margaret when they heard Michael's truck coming down the driveway. A few moments later Michael entered the kitchen.

"Hi Dear," said Margaret. "How's everything?"

"Not too bad Mom," Michael replied as he bent over and gave his mom a kiss. "How's everything here?"

"Good. We're just having our afternoon coffee."

Michael could smell the aroma of coffee, an almost permanent scent in his parent's house. "It smells like French vanilla, something new?"

Jack looked up at his son and crinkled his nose. "That would be your mother's idea."

"Hey, I'm trying to give your father a little culture," Margaret said. "I kind of like it."

Jack stood and brought his coffee cup to the sink, "She thinks anything with French in it is culture." As he passed Michael he mouthed the word 'terrible' and then poured the remainder down the drain. After rinsing out the cup he turned back toward his son. "Why don't you come down to the barn for a minute and give me a hand?"

"Sure thing Dad," Michael said.

Jack then turned his attention toward Margaret. "We'll be back in a few minutes Mother."

"Oui, oui," answered Margaret, eliciting a smile from Michael and a shake of the head from Jack.

Once the two had left the house Michael shot his dad a quizzical look knowing his dad had just made an excuse to get the two of them alone.

"I didn't want to talk about this in front of your mother. Not that it's that big a deal, but anyway," Jack said, responding to the look. Michael said nothing, but continued to keep his eyes locked on his dad both curious and nervous about what may come next. "I wanted to make sure I talked to you about it because it affects you the most and I suppose your brother as well."

"Sure Dad, what's up," Michael said in the manner you'd expect from a supportive son.

"I want to run Sing at Saratoga because I feel like, if he runs a good race, then we might be able to get a good amount for him. At least a lot more than we would if we just ran him here. No damn money here, we all know that." Jack breathed heavy before continuing. "At this point, it doesn't appear as though we will have any choice but to sell off part of the farm anyway. I'm hoping maybe we can keep a few acres and the house. But the horses, well, I think they're all going to have to go."

Hearing his dad voice what he and his siblings feared hit Michael hard.

"Yeah, we all figured that might be the case. We're all hoping it won't be, but we've always known there was a good chance."

Michael's realistic view on life could be a party killer at times, but Jack was thankful for it now. It made this conversation much easier. "I think you need to start opening up the stable to outside owners, if you haven't already."

"Funny you say that, I just spoke to a new owner the other day. We're expecting to get three coming in next week." Michael had debated when to tell his dad and was still wrestling with it before he came over. It was a relief to finally let it out. Not that it would've been that big a deal. Jack was a realist like Michael and knew it had to be done. I guess in the end, what bothered Michael was that by saying it out loud it brought home the realization that it was almost over. They were planning for the death of a loved one.

"Good, good," said Jack. "When is Sing's race anyway?"

"He's entered in the third race August 2nd. An allowance race, going a mile and an eighth. The purse is fifty-two thousand."

"He's ready to go?"

Michael gave him an affirmative nod. "He worked 5 out of the gate this morning, breezing, we timed him in one minute and a fifth."

"Sounds like you have him set. Who'd you get to ride him?"

"We picked up Rafael Bejarano," replied Michael.

"Nice," said Jack with a hint of surprise in his voice, "he's a darn good jockey." By now the two had made their way into the barn. The horses stood quietly in their stalls resting for the evening. A couple popped their heads out to see who the visitors were and whether they'd brought any treats.

"Dad," Michael asked, "are there any other possibilities? I just can't imagine you giving this up." Michael opened up his arms indicating that it was the entire barn, or more specifically, the barn life, he was speaking of.

"Thus far, no" Jack said. "Every angle I've tried has come up empty. We'll have the developers out here shortly and they'll give me a price. I hate like hell to have to sell to them, but I'm about out of options." Michael shook his head in disappointment. Not even so much for his own self, but for his father. Jack was a good man and Michael was afraid this could have lasting effects on his life. But what Michael didn't know was deep down Jack still felt he had one more card to play. It would be a long shot, but the more he thought about it the more he gained confidence in it. It was such a long shot that he'd decided not even to mention it to Margaret. It was something he was cooking up on his own. If it came to it, he wanted to be the one to pull the trigger. This was his kingdom and he wanted to call the shots for the last battle. But first, he would wait to see how things faired in this next race and then he would make his decision.

"Well," Michael said as he gazed from one end of the barn to the other, "I should probably get going."

"Yeah, get home to the family. Say hi for us."

"Will do Dad. Oh, and by the way, if the day comes and they're tearing down this barn, let me know. I want to make sure I'm far, far away. I don't think I could stand to be anywhere near when it happens."

"Don't worry, I will. And chances are I'll be joining you wherever you are."

Chapter 31

～

JULY 26

THE SOUND OF THE PHONE ringing was barely audible over the chaos at Janet O'Brien's house. "OK, everyone out of the house," she yelled. "Out back, let's go, let's go." A stampede ensued as the chaos began to make its way outside. As the last of the five children left, two of which were hers and three of which were over for a play-date, Janet picked up the phone. Her calm voice gave no indication of the mayhem, "O'Brien residence."

"Hi, this is Betty Shannon from the elementary school. May I speak with Janet?"

"This is she," Janet replied enthusiastically.

"Denise Calabrese gave me your name and number and said you might be interested in working part time once school opens again in September."

"Yes I did," she said tailing off toward the end as she watched the children jumping off the top of the slide.

"Is this something you're still interested in?"

Realizing that her response didn't indicate the true level of interest she had, Janet turned away from the children in an effort to remain focused on the call. "Oh yes, I'm sorry, I'm definitely still interested."

"Great, that's great news. Would you be able to come in for an interview next Monday the 30th at about 9:30?"

Hearing the screaming behind her, but refusing to turn toward it, Janet answered. "That would be no problem at all."

"Super. We look forward to seeing you then."

"OK. Thank you so much for the call. Goodbye." She smiled, still holding the disconnected phone in her hand. Only the sudden sound of screaming broke her enjoyment of the moment. Janet slowly turned around to see what they were up to now. To her amazement she watched three children in one giant heap come crashing down the slide together. They hit the ground in a tangled mass, all laughing. Janet let out a sigh and glanced over at the calendar. Still over a month to go before school starts. It's going to be a long month, she thought.

While Janet was keeping tabs on the five animals in the backyard, her husband watched as a trailer pulled up to their barn, prepared to deliver three animals of the equine variety. For the first time Michael was taking on horses someone else owned. He stood near his truck, nervously, and watched as the driver emerged from the cab. Manny and James stood together near the stalls, watching as well.

As the driver crawled out of the truck and to the ground, James let out an abrupt laugh only Manny could hear. "What time machine did this guy step out of?" Manny looked in amazement as the driver reached high in the air, stretching out his sore back. He wore a pair of vintage red Chuck Taylor canvas sneakers, cutoff jean shorts, a black Def Leppard tank top, which had to date back to the 80's, and a large gold chain to top it off. Naturally, his hair extended well below his shoulders. James smiled and looked at Manny. "I have *got* to talk to this guy." Manny, not sure what to make of him, decided to remain back near the stalls.

"Dude, how's it going? Have a delivery for us?" James said, approaching the man.

"Yeah, I think so. You M. O'Brien?" the driver asked.

"No, I'm J. O'Brien." James turned toward Michael, who was making his way over, and said, "He's M. O'Brien."

The driver pulled a piece of paper from his back pocket. "I have three horses for M. O'Brien, Finger Lakes Race Track, Barn 27."

Michael approached the driver, "I'm Michael O'Brien and those would be mine," he said, as he grabbed the paperwork from the driver.

"OK, where do you want them?"

"We have stalls ready for each of them," Michael said, pointing to where Manny stood. "Manny, open up the stall doors."

The driver began walking toward the trailer's side door with James right behind him. "Dude," James said, "I love Def Leppard."

The driver turned toward James, "Well all right, awesome man."

James extended his arm. "I'm James O'Brien."

The driver shook James' hand. "Nice to meet you man, I'm Sammy Biasi."

James pointed over at Manny, "he's a big fan of their rock ballads." Sammy glanced over at Manny and gave him a thumbs up. Manny, not having heard any of the conversation, gave the two a confused look.

"What about you?" the driver asked. "What's your favorite?"

James quickly tried to pull a Def Leppard song from memory. Though he liked them, he wasn't truly a devoted fan. "Ahh, probably be Armageddon It."

"Hey, good tune," Sammy said, strumming an air guitar along his hip.

James smiled, relieved he'd come up with something good. He and his new friend Sammy proceeded to open the trailer's doors and let the ramp down. James walked up the ramp, untied the first horse and led him out of the trailer. Michael stood close by, carefully studying the horse's conformation. James took the horse into his stall, unhooked the shank and then walked out, with Manny closing the stall door behind him. These simple steps were repeated for each horse until all three stood safely in their own stall.

Their ears were pricked and they whinnied to one another, excited by their new surroundings. They looked good – they usually did going from Belmont to Finger Lakes – thought Michael, hopefully they will be competitive at this level. Although the purses were less at Finger Lakes than they were at Belmont and Aqueduct, so were the day-to-day costs of having your horse trained. If the horses performed better here, then the owner would probably be financially better off.

With the unloading process complete, Michael entered each stall and went through his routine. It's the same routine he had with all his horses virtually every day of the year. He would look and feel his way up and down every horse. His hands slowly moving over the contours of each of the horse's legs. Lifting each hoof, picking it out and examining the soul. There is an old saying that says no hoof, no horse and bad feet can turn the best runner into a spectator. In time Michael would become intimately familiar with the feel of each one of these horses. So much so that if even the slightest thing weren't right, he'd know. Today, everyone checked out fine and started Michael thinking about a few changes and tweaks that might help.

While Michael analyzed the new horses, James chatted with Sammy, discussing the merits of rock music from the 1980's. After the two concluded that the 80's were the greatest rock decade of all time, Sammy the driver jumped back in his truck and drove away. James made his way back to where Manny stood in front of the stalls.

"That guy was priceless. I would've invited him to dinner at our house, if I didn't think Lauren would kill me."

Manny laughed, "Good move."

As Michael left the last of his new horses' stall, he began to think maybe it wasn't so bad opening up his stable. The new horses looked fit, they should be competitive and being able to bill someone a daily rate would be nice, which reminded Michael that he needed to come up with a day rate to charge new clients. While he was basking in this new-found circumstance, and wondering why James had such a broad smile, his cell phone rang. The number didn't appear familiar at first and then it dawned on him it was the new horses' owner. At that moment his euphoria began to dissipate. They weren't Michael's horses and there was someone else, the guy who pays the bill, who is going to be interested in everything that happens with his horses. Michael knew he couldn't blow off the call.

"Michael O'Brien. Yes Mr. Harvey, they arrived and I've put them in their stalls." James and Manny stood by and listened to one side of the conversation, deducing what the person on the other end of the line was saying. "No, no problems at all. They look good and seem to have taken the trip fine. I'll probably leave them in the stalls for a bit and then walk them around the backside to get them used to the place. Sure that's no problem; I'll give you a call tomorrow and update you. OK, talk to you then. OK. Thanks. Bye."

James wanted to make some wisecrack about sucking up to an owner, but thought better of it. Truth be told, he hoped these horses would really work. If Michael could find success with them, then other owners would follow and maybe they could grow the stable. Time was ticking and about a month from now James had no idea who he would call his boss. It would be awful nice if that person was his brother, even if he didn't have a sense of humor. James looked at the three new horses, all of which had their head stretched out of their stall taking everything in. He quietly whispered to himself, "You guys better be runners, some of us are really counting on you."

JULY 27

Sarah trotted down the stairs and into the kitchen seeing Manny finishing a ham and cheese sandwich and a Snapple. "Hey Manny, want to go for a ride down to the lake?"

It was your typical day in Western New York at the end of July, nice and sunny though a little hot. "Sure, that would be great," he said, shoving the last bite of sandwich into his mouth.

"OK, I'll go tack up Blaze and Kitty. Come out when you're finished." Manny nodded his approval, not wanting to speak with his mouth full. Manners matter as Margaret always said. Blaze and Kitty were two Quarter Horses the O'Briens owned for pleasure and to pony the younger Thoroughbreds in training. When not being worked, they made great trail horses. Out on the trail they often came across deer and other animals and nothing ever spooked them. They were also not afraid to cross a stream or large puddle, something that terrified many of the high strung Thoroughbreds.

"We're almost ready," Sarah said cinching up Kitty's girth. "I thought we would head down to the boat landing. Maybe take a quick dip and then come back. I threw a couple of towels in the saddle bag for us." The same place the family had been to watch the Fourth of July fireworks, the boat landing provided an easy spot to get to and offered a perfect fence for tying up the horses.

"Sounds perfect to me," Manny said, swinging into the western saddle.

They ambled down the trail, a country lane, unpaved and narrow. It was meant for those on horseback or perhaps those with a horse and buggy, although a tractor and trailer fit quite nicely on national holidays. With trees lining the pathway it kept the trail mostly shaded which was a blessing on days like today. Neither Sarah nor Manny were big talkers, so it wasn't unusual for them to take a trail ride and barely speak. Both enjoyed quietly communing with nature and their animals. But today, like this whole summer, was different.

"Well," said Sarah, "what do you think will happen?"

Manny didn't need to ask about what, it was the same thing he was debating asking her. Manny sighed, "I'm afraid to think about it. I haven't heard anything good, have you?"

Now Sarah sighed. "No, nothing. Hopefully Dad will think of something. Neither he nor Mom has told me anything, which makes me think that so far, they have nothing."

"Yeah, James and Michael haven't said anything either. I don't think they know anything," Manny added.

As the two continued down the trail they spotted a pair of deer standing in the middle of the path. The horses pricked their ears, but kept on walking. The deer, equally as interested, stared at the oncoming intruders before turning tail and bounding into the forest. The deer's ability to jump and sail through the air seemed effortless and became the next topic of conversation. Manny and Sarah shared stories of previous encounters with the graceful animals, some funny, some frightening. The deer talk carried on until the tree-lined trail opened to a clearing, giving way to a wonderful view of the lake. The sunshine glistened off the waves. The pair of riders took the horses down to the water line allowing them to drink before tying them to the fencepost. The quick dip turned into a 45 minute frolic in the water.

"So much for a quick dip," said Manny, drying himself with one of the towels.

"Oh well, what can you do?" countered Sarah doing likewise. "I don't know about you, but I don't have anywhere to be until feeding time, so we might just as well enjoy this now, we may not get a chance again."

Manny smiled, "Good point." Then he looked back at the horses. "Want to bring them in the water?"

"Sure, why not."

So Manny and Sarah removed the saddles, mounted bareback and walked them in the water. The horses took to the moment, as if they too understood its significance. After wading in a few feet, Kitty stopped and started pawing at the water. Each time she pawed a cascade of water shot into the air causing her to shake her head up and down. Seemingly finding enjoyment from it, she repeated the process over and over, the game never growing old. Blaze opted for more movement and greater splashing. He trotted back and forth along the water's edge, allowing the splashing water to hit the underside of his belly and fly out in front of him. Their eyes were wide and their motions animated. And Manny swore he could see them smiling. As long as time allowed, the foursome basked in the sun and surf. Eventually Manny and Sarah re-saddled and began the trek back. As they left the clearing and entered onto the trail they halted the horses, turned and looked at the lake. No words were spoken, merely a goodbye gaze, just in case it was their last.

Chapter 32

∼

JULY 30

BETTY SHANNON WALKED JANET TO the door and continued on with her for another 10 feet. "Janet, thanks a bunch for coming in."

"Thank you for giving me the opportunity," Janet said.

"No problem and just so you know, their expecting to give a formal offer at the end of the week."

"OK, thanks."

"And this is off the record of course, but you're the leading candidate."

"Really?"

"Oh, God yes. You were overqualified to begin with and I'm pretty sure you just knocked there socks off."

Janet thanked Betty again and headed for her car. A wave of euphoria swept over Janet as she did. Her smile extending ear to ear. The position was nothing more than an office assistant, but it had been years since Janet needed to conduct herself in a businesslike manner and it felt good to know she still could. And it felt great to know she had impressed the various school officials she'd met. She had no doubt she could do a great job and based on what Betty said, she'd left the interviewers feeling the same. There was no cockiness, it was the certainty of being tested and knowing you'd nailed the answers.

So now she would wait and see what happens. Yes, she was the leading candidate, but it wasn't a certainty. The big question at this point was whether to tell Michael or continue holding out until she was sure the job was hers. Waiting would certainly be the easier thing to do. Who knows, maybe she wouldn't get it and there wouldn't be a need to have that conversation, at least at the moment anyway. But after that interview, Janet made up her mind. It was time to rejoin the working world, even if it were just part-time.

Driving away, she realized there was actually another question that needed answering. She'd left the kids with her neighbors. The question was, should she go out and spend a little time by herself, shopping perhaps, or should she go back and relieve her helpful neighbor. 'She'll be alright for another hour,' thought Janet, turning toward the shopping center, 'I need a break from those two.'

While some people were excited about the possibility of re-entering the workforce, others were wishing they had the means to call it quits. Such was the case for Ron Dombrowski. He hadn't thought too much about the O'Briens over the last couple of weeks. Not because he was insensitive of course, but mostly because it was summer in upstate New York and you try to squeeze as much activity as possible before the long cold winter comes back around. Unfortunately, the phone call Ron just ended brought him back to reality. Benson Realty called and was ready to set up a day to come out to the O'Briens' farm and survey the land. Or, to put it more aptly, they were ready to cut Jack's farm into pieces and reap the financial benefits. Ron appreciated loyalty, this made him feel like a traitor. It was time to call Jack and make sure it was OK for them to come out.

Knowing Jack as well as he did, Ron waited until mid-day to call the house figuring that Jack would have come inside for lunch. Sure enough, after two rings Jack answered.

"Jack, Ron Dombrowski here, how's everything?"

"Hey Ron, not too bad," Jack said, which naturally was a lie, but there was no sense saying anything else. Everyone knew the date and that they had one month before they would be booted from their property. Whining wasn't going to change it. "What's going on?"

"I just got off the phone with Benson Realty and they would like to come out to the farm next Tuesday, the 7th and survey the land."

The comment offered a hard dose of reality to a man who was himself a realist. "Well, I guess it needs to be done." Jack paused for a moment before continuing. "Tell them that's fine."

Ron could feel the pain in Jack's voice. "Listen Jack, I can come out there and show them around. You don't have to be there, you know. I don't mind doing it."

Jack cut off Ron. "Ron, I appreciate the gesture but this is still my home and I do what needs to be done, at least for the time being."

The words hit Ron hard, 'my home, at least for the time being.' God, he thought, there has to be something that can be done. It was beginning to dawn on Ron this was affecting him more than he realized. For the first time, he recognized if the O'Briens did lose their farm, he would probably carry a certain level of guilt with him for the rest of his life. He didn't directly cause them to lose it, but he played a major role and worse yet, did nothing to stop it from happening.

The two men hung up the phone, both hoping the next month would go by fast and end this misery. Some sort of miracle would be better, but the reality of the situation said something different.

JULY 31

Manny held Sing with as tight a rein as he could, straining to control the head-strong horse. The weather had been abnormally warm the previous two weeks, but finally broke when a cold front blew through last night. This morning horse and human awoke to much cooler temperatures. The humidity, which always seemed present, had all but disappeared and the air felt crisp and fresh. And this welcomed change wasn't lost on the horses. To say they were feeling full of themselves would be an understatement, Sing included. Of course, Michael also had him wound tight for his next race, so between that and the friskiness, Manny had his work cut out for him. "Easy boy, will you? You're going to pull my arms right out of the sockets."

Sing paid no attention. He had already bucked twice on the way to the track for their morning jog and was threatening to do it again, despite the jog. He wanted to run. He wanted to break loose and take off. Manny, on the other hand, was under strict orders to do no such thing. Sing was a coiled spring, ready to be released in two days' time in Saratoga. Until then, he was to remain coiled, much to his and Manny's dismay, the latter of whose arms were beginning to turn to rubber.

As they made their way around the oval, Manny watched as another exercise rider trying to get his mount from the barn to the track was tossed off. It was the second rider he'd seen come off today, along with several other incidents that almost resulted in the same. "Man it's like a rodeo around here," Manny said to himself. The comment, made without thinking, suddenly reminded him of his father. His mind drifted back to his childhood, picturing his dad in the middle of the ring, hanging on a bucking bronco for dear life. The vision didn't last long. Without warning Sing veered sharply to the left as if trying to avoid something in his path, of which there was nothing. The sudden shift caused Manny to lose his balance. Fortunately, he recovered quickly and refocused on the task-at-hand. "Sing, would you take it easy, you're killing me this morning."

For days now Lauren had been feeling poor. It wasn't that she felt sick exactly, it was more like a general malaise with a bit of nausea mixed in. As she wandered around the drug store looking for something to help alleviate her symptoms, something dawned on her.

Overall, Lauren had always been healthy, so getting sick was not something she had to deal with very often. Scanning the various over-the-counter medications, she thought about her symptoms and the last time she had felt like this. She was trying to recall what she had done then, whether it worked and if it had, get the same medication now. And that's when it struck her, 'the last time I felt like this...' she recalled, 'I ended up giving birth to our daughter about eight months later.' Lauren did some quick math in her head and realized she should have had her period several days before. "Ohhh, now that's interesting," she said aloud. Just then she realized there was an elderly couple standing a few feet away staring at her, wondering what she found so interesting. She smiled at the couple, "medicines fascinate me." The couple smiled and nodded at the strange woman, then scurried away. Not that Lauren cared, she was never too concerned about what others thought and she was far too engrossed in her own situation, recognizing the strange recipe of glee and dismay.

Browsing the aisle a little farther she found the home-pregnancy tests. "Well, I guess I should bring one of these home and see what happens."

Driving home after picking up Sydney from daycare, Lauren couldn't stop thinking about the possibilities, and of course when this curious set of circumstances had occurred. Occasionally she would nod and acknowledge Sydney while Sydney rambled on and on about the day's events in the fascinating world of 4-year-old daycare. Lauren wasn't sure whether to be excited or frightened about the results. She and James wanted another child, but with everything going on with the farm and James possibly losing his livelihood, now just wasn't the best time. Of course, anyone with children will tell you, there never really is a perfect time. They show up and you go from there, ready or not.

As she was thinking about the current family dynamic she began to wonder what exactly James would think. He seemed to have overcome the funk he was in a few months ago, but the farm situation was weighing on him, even though he didn't let on. How would the news of another mouth to feed hit him. Suddenly she began to feel extremely anxious and the more she thought about it the less she wanted to take the test. 'I'm sure I'm not pregnant,' she thought, 'my period will come tonight or tomorrow.' Sometimes the best way to deal with a situation is to head straight for denial. Forget about the facts and go with what makes you feel better. It's a strategy that rarely works, but is often tried. 'I'll wait a couple more days,' she thought, 'and if it doesn't arrive by then, well I guess I'll have no other choice.'

Returning to the world around her Lauren noticed that Sydney was still talking. Looking at her in the rear-view mirror, Lauren nodded and acknowledged she was listening once again. Then she smiled and thought to herself, if we do end up having another, let's hope this one is a little less of a talker than the one we already have.

Chapter 33

~

AUGUST 1

Jack pulled past the main entrance of Finger Lakes and kept going toward the barns. This was the fourth time he'd been here in the past couple of months, which was more than the previous five years put together. 'Well,' he thought, 'I might as well get used to going out and about. If all those houses go up around ours, then I won't have my little hideaway anymore.'

The three boys were pleasantly surprised to see Jack pulling up to the barn. "Gentlemen, how is our boy doing? Ready to go for tomorrow?" Jack asked as he exited the truck.

Manny and James deferred the question to Michael, though they could've answered just as easily. "He's ready to go. We were just discussing the details."

"Yeah, what's the plan?" Jack asked.

"We plan to pull out about 5:30 which should get us there around 9:00. Hopefully that will give us a little time to maybe take him to the paddock and stretch his legs."

Normally in a situation like this Michael would take the horse and Manny would go with him. James would be in charge of staying behind and making sure the other horses followed their prescribed regimen. But it dawned on James that in order to test the theory he'd been developing he would need to go with Michael and have Manny stay behind. "Michael,"

James interrupted, "I'd like to go with you this time. Dad do you think you could come over and help out tomorrow morning?" Jack was taken slightly aback but answered that it shouldn't be a problem.

Michael, also taken off guard by the comment, normally would've told James it was dumb for him to go when Manny was more than capable, but with the situation as it was, Michael found it difficult to say no. The way things looked, about a month from now James might be out of a job and allowing him this little thing, seemed to Michael, like granting James one last request. "If you don't mind Dad, then I guess it's alright by me."

James glanced back to his father. "Are you sure Dad?" he asked like a child who'd just been invited swimming at a friend's pool. The only thing missing was a "please, please, please."

"No, it's no problem. It'll be fun to come over and shake some of the rust off. It's been a long time."

"Alright then we're all set," James said quickly, putting a conclusion on the conversation. "Tomorrow I put the theory to test," he muttered to himself.

Manny stood in front of the stall door. He'd been there for the entire discussion, but said nothing. His heart sank at the point things were decided. He'd never seen Saratoga and his desire to go had grown greatly over the past several years. All the stories he'd heard of the grand old track and the races he'd seen on television made him long to see it. When they'd decided a week or so ago that they would run Sing there, Manny thought his chance to see the place had finally come. To be left out was devastating and he couldn't understand why James was so set on being the one to tag along with Michael. James had been there several times and never indicated that he was overly excited to return. He also knew what it meant to Manny and that's the part that really hurt. But Manny said nothing. He would do his job. The track certainly wasn't going anywhere and maybe he'd get an opportunity another day.

Jack left the boys for home not long after the plan was set. On the way he made a couple detours stopping at Wager's Farm and Garden for a new hose, a pair of gloves and a couple of feed buckets and then stopping at The Italian Deli for lunchmeat and much to Margaret's chagrin, limburger cheese.

After a tasty, if not smelly, lunch, Jack went into his office and pulled out his old-fashioned rolodex. It had been a while since he'd looked at it, having memorized nearly all the numbers he called regularly. Thumbing through became a trip down memory lane, each card representing some contact, some event from his past. Amazed at how far back some of the cards went, Jack smiled, that is, up until he came across a certain card, Pete Lynch – Lynch's Tractors. Wow, Jack thought, I guess it's been a while since I cleaned this baby out. Pete had sold Jack his first tractor. It was so long ago, Jack couldn't even remember what year it was. But what was still fresh in his memory, was Pete's death 10 years ago.

Pete was already up there in years when Jack met him, but he loved the business and kept on plugging, all the way until his heart said no more and quit on him. The day of his funeral the church was packed with farmers from all over the county. Each one dressed in their regular farm gear, overalls, boots and so on, just the way Pete would have wanted. He was one of them. A man of the land, through and through. It was a sad day when he passed, but worse yet, his death marked the end of an era. Lynch's Tractors had been around for better than 40 years, but since none of his kids took to the business, when he died, it just folded up. Everything he had worked his whole life for was gone. It was like losing a friend, twice over. And that notion hit Jack a little too close to home.

Trying to shake the depressing thought, Jack continued scrolling until eventually he found the number he was searching for, a number of an old friend and fellow trainer. He didn't like making the call, not because of who he was calling, but rather why he was calling, but he knew it had to be done. The voice on the other end of the line sounded older, though unquestionably familiar. "Bobby, it's Jack O'Brien here. It's been a long time."

"Jack, how on earth are you? You still hiding away on that farm of yours?"

Jack laughed, "As much as possible. You still training the ponies down there?"

"Sure am. Have no idea what I would do otherwise." Jack thought to himself how true that was and how close he was to finding out what the "otherwise" might be. "We're in Saratoga now. Beautiful up here, wish we could stay up here longer."

"Actually that's why I'm calling. We have a horse running tomorrow in the third race over there. He's got real potential but unfortunately we're considering selling him. I thought maybe you might have some clients who'd be interested in him. He needs a hands-on trainer and I know you'd do him right."

"Hmm, that's interesting. I might have some clients who'd be interested, yeah definitely. I appreciate the call Jack. I'll take a look at him tomorrow and let you know."

"Alright Bobby, good luck over there this summer and I'll talk to you soon."

The two men hung up the phone. Jack sat there recognizing the process to sell out had begun. It was the beginning of the end. A mere 30 days stood between him and the end of the farm.

Chapter 34

~

AUGUST 2

IT WAS 5 A.M. AND the sun remained absent. Darkness blanketed the grounds, except where the street lamps stood illuminating small patches of ground below them, or the odd few barns whose workers had arrived early. Michael and James quietly went about hooking up the trailer and making sure everything was safe and secure. When both were satisfied that their transportation was ready, they pulled Sing out of his stall. He balked a couple of times at the shadows before finally walking up the ramp and into position. The hesitation didn't cause any alarm to the trainers, it happens all the time and is generally anticipated. In fact, it's kind of a nice surprise when it doesn't. Having loaded the horse, the two men scanned the ground around the barn to make sure nothing was left behind. After everything checked out, they hopped into the truck and slowly pulled away. It would be a four hour trip, most of which was down the New York State Thruway. The final leg would take them from the sleepy town of Amsterdam, where they exited the thruway, along the back roads to Saratoga. Altogether it was a pleasant journey. As they drove along the road leaving the barn area, Michael and James could see more workers filtering in and going about their daily routines. The racetrack's backside was quietly coming to life.

It wasn't more than a half hour later that Jack and Manny pulled into Finger Lakes. They had decided to save a little gas and drive together. As they got out of the truck Jack looked around. "Well no sign of their truck or the trailer. Hopefully that means things went smoothly and they're on their way."

Manny agreed, "I'm sure we would've heard if something wasn't right."

"Yeah, you're right," Jack said. Although you couldn't tell, Jack had a case of the nerves. This was an important race for Sing today. Jack wanted to see him do well for several reasons, one of which was the thought of a prospective buyer watching. The clock was ticking and several critical decisions loomed on the horizon. Sing could do a lot to help the situation if he were to have a good race today. "Alright Manny, you're certainly more familiar with this routine than I am. Why don't you just let me know what you want me to do."

"Yes sir," responded Manny and the two began to go about the O'Brien Racing's morning ritual. Manny let Jack know what needed to be done and which horse to get ready next. One by one Manny would take them out, walk, jog, canter or gallop depending upon the schedule that was laid out for them.

While Manny rode, Jack prepared the next horse, cleaned the stalls, made notes for Michael regarding each horse and to his own surprise, thoroughly enjoyed the morning. He even took the time to clean some tack, a chore he always dreaded. The work was a nice distraction and Jack knew it. Something different, yet familiar and comfortable. As the morning wore on, a couple of the old timers Jack knew years ago stopped by to say hi. They were old and grumpy, just like Jack. Jack missed that camaraderie and it planted a small seed somewhere inside him.

For Manny, it turned out to be a routine day, less one horse, his favorite. That horse was on the way to Saratoga, where Manny had hoped to be going too. He tried not to dwell on it, to do so made the morning's chores difficult to get through. The thought crossed his mind that maybe he would ask James about it when they returned. But then again, with the situation they were in, nobody needed him stirring anything up. They were beginning to finish when Manny's cell phone rang.

Standing underneath one of the large trees that dotted the Saratoga paddock, Michael dialed Manny's number.

"Hello."

"Manny, how are things going?" Michael said, recognizing Manny's familiar accented voice.

Manny, having seen the number calling in, knew beforehand who it was. "Hey Michael, everything's going well. No problems at all. How about with you guys?"

"So far so good. We're in the paddock at the moment. James is walking him around, letting him check everything out. Is my dad around?"

"Yeah, hold on just a minute."

Michael could hear Manny yelling for Jack and then several moments of silence. When Jack answered the phone there was no doubt who was on the other line.

"Michael, what's it look like over there?" Jack said in his normal gruff tone.

"All is well thus far. The trip went well and he's interested in everything, but not overanxious. I wanted to let him settle a bit before I called you. Also give you guys a chance to finish your work."

"Yeah, I figured as much. What have you done with him so far?"

"Well, after we got here we let him hang out in his stall for a half hour and sniff the place out. Once he seemed adjusted, we started walking him around. Now we're in the paddock." The paddock at Saratoga was a big change from Finger Lakes. You could probably fit about 25 Finger Lakes paddocks inside the one at Saratoga. "We'll spend a little more time here and then head back to the receiving barn and wait our turn."

"That sounds good. We'll be done here soon, so if anything comes up call me at the house."

"Will do, Dad." Michael paused for a second hearing James saying something in the background. "Hey Dad, James wants to know if you've enjoyed yourself this morning."

"Tell your brother this is a cakewalk. I don't understand why he's always whining about how hard he works."

Michael laughed. "I'll make sure to let him know what you said. Wish us luck."

With a distinct sincerity in his voice, Jack replied, "Yeah, good luck."

Satisfied that Sing was comfortable with the paddock, Michael and James walked him to his temporary stall to await the race. The two trainers decided to stick around the barn area for a while and watch the other horses and grooms come and go. Even though Sing rested quietly, taking a nap in fact, neither Michael nor James felt secure enough to leave at the same time. So after a while, and one at a time, they left the barn and wandered about the old track.

Unlike most tracks, Saratoga had been built for its patrons to take pleasure in both the horse and the wonderful Adirondack summer weather. Behind the track's main structure, Saratoga's park-like setting invited the masses to relax and enjoy. Everywhere you looked there were trees, picnic tables and people set to have a great day at the races. A three-man band played inside a pavilion for the passing crowds and a five-piece old-style band worked the picnic areas. As James wandered about looking for a cheap meal, which he struggled to find, he couldn't help but think if you couldn't enjoy a day at the races here, then you probably couldn't anywhere. A grand place. Certainly a place time had forgotten. A thought which lent itself to a bit of irony, because before James knew it, it was 1:00 and the horses for the first race were sprinting down the stretch. Time to head back to the barn.

Sing was entered in the third, an allowance race for 3-year-olds who hadn't won a race in two months. It drew a very deep and strong field. Not exactly what Jack and Michael wanted, but they couldn't choose their competition. When the first race ended Michael made sure Sing was awake and began putting everything in order. That of course didn't take long, one horse doesn't require but so much equipment. Within 20 minutes they were ready to roll. Feeling prepared, Michael and James walked to a television and watched the second race go off. About five minutes later, the call came to begin bringing the horses over for the third race.

The walk from the assembly barn to the paddock cuts directly through the picnicking crowd. Michael remained nervous about how Sing might react to the throngs of people lining the white-fenced path, but it didn't seem to bother Sing. They made it to the paddock and began circling the same tree they had several hours before. Sing bounced on his toes, but didn't appear overanxious. Five minutes on and Rafael Bejarano's valet arrived with his tack. So James held Sing as Michael cinched up the girth, straightened his saddle cloth and prepared Sing for Bejarano, his newest jockey. Once set, James continued to walk Sing around the big elm.

Within a few minutes Bejarano arrived at Sing's tree, Bejarano hopped on his toes, a ball of muscle and energy. He and Michael discussed Sing's tendency to be headstrong early in the race. The new jock let Michael know he would do his best to keep him relaxed and hold something back for the stretch. Then the paddock judge called for riders' up. Game time.

Rather than hang out at the O'Briens' house and watch the race, Manny opted to return to Finger Lakes and watch the simulcast. He was watching the horses begin to leave the paddock when he caught a horse off in the distance beginning to act up. The camera quickly focused on the horse ahead of Sing. The horse had spooked at something and turned toward Sing as if he were going to run in that direction. The groom holding the horse spun him around in short order and regained control. But the horse's actions sent Sing into a frenzy and triggered his instinct to flee. James held on and in an effort to escape, Sing bucked sending Bejarano flying. Fortunately, the jockey hit the ground, rolled and bounced right up. He took a look at himself and dusted off his silks. It wasn't the first time such a thing had happened and it assuredly wouldn't be the last. One of the hazards of the profession.

James tried to settle Sing as Michael gave Bejarano another leg up. They quickly caught up to the post parade and made it onto the track, the cameras keeping close tabs on the two riled horses.

Normally Michael would have been livid at such an event, but by now, it was merely expected. He looked at James, who shook his head before turning to make his way to their seats.

Jack hovered in front of the television having seen the same coverage as Manny. Margaret sat on the couch having chosen to watch the race this time around. "Mother," Jack moaned, "Can we catch a break just once? Just once, that's all I'm asking." Margaret wanted to offer some conciliatory words, but even she was thinking the same thing.

Along the paddock fence, Bobby Gillner stood and watched the big chestnut dump his jockey. A little skittish he thought, but otherwise a goodlooking animal. Not that he expected different. His old friend Jack knew his horseflesh and wouldn't have called unless the animal had value. That was for certain. Bobby looked at his *Daily Racing Form*, scanning the past performances of the individual participants. Tough race, he thought. "Well," he said aloud, though to himself, "this will be perfect. This race should be a great test to see if you're worth the money." He raised his head from the paper and watched the last horse leave the paddock. Turning away from the fence, Bobby joined the other patrons heading for the tellers to make their wagers and watch the race. Time to find out if this guy can run.

Rafael Bejarano knew his trade and took his time warming up Sing. He allowed Sing to take it at his own pace not wanting to upset the animal. And for the most part it worked. The race started directly in front of the grandstands, going one mile and an eighth, giving Michael and James a perfect view. Sing appeared anxious, but that was relative when Sing was involved. As the gates opened Sing bolted forward, gunning for the lead, but Bejarano leaned back in the saddle and held the reins tight. He knew if he loosened his grip and gave Sing his head, the horse would sprint forward. Sing resented it for a moment, then relented, knowing it wasn't time to run yet.

Another horse to Sing's inside went to the lead and Bejarano eased Sing, resting just off the flank of the leader as they went around the first turn. The heavy favorite, Upandover, sat in mid-pack about 3 lengths behind the two front runners. Trained by the meet's leading trainer Todd Pletcher, Upandover came into the race off a 5-month layoff. A minor injury had forced him off the Kentucky Derby trail, but according to his trainer, he was ready to pick up where he'd left off. If that were the case, he would be awful tough to beat.

Everyone appeared content with their respective positions which remained about the same until they made their way around the far turn. The pace had been fast, though not unreasonable, but Sing's constant pressure finally wore out the pacesetter. Without being asked Sing slowly passed the fading leader as the turn became the homestretch. Behind him Upandover made his move and began gaining ground. By the time Sing reached the eighth pole, Upandover had closed to within 1 length. Knowing he needed to get more out of his horse, Bejarano tried to get him to change leads, but Sing refused. The battle between jockey and horse continued down the stretch all the while Sing's lead diminished.

"He won't switch leads again," Michael said disgustedly. "Come on horse, for once in your life do what you're supposed to do."

There was no need for James to add anything, he could see it for his own eyes. All looked lost as the other horse overtook Sing with each stride. When Sing's competition was almost a length in front he finally switched to his right lead.

Even though most of the people watching didn't see the lead change occur, the result of that change wasn't lost on anyone. Normally this late in the race, when one horse passes another, the horse being passed usually lessens their effort. They continue to run, but their heart is gone. When Sing changed his lead, he found another gear. Back he came, ears pinned, not ready to give up just yet. The term used to describe such an effort is "game" and Sing was just that for the first time in his life. Watching the seemingly beaten horse re-rally and sensing an exciting finish, the crowd roared to life.

Manny's eyes were affixed to the television above him. The building around him could've tumbled to the ground and he wouldn't have noticed. He watched, as the best horse he'd ever ridden refused to give up the fight. Though mild mannered and quiet, Manny couldn't help but yell to the television as if Sing could hear. "COME ON SING, DIG IN, DIG IN, GET UP THERE."

Inch by inch, Sing clawed his way back to the leader until they were once again on even terms, neither competitor giving in. As they crossed the wire the two horses were locked together. On different strides, their heads were bobbing in separate intervals up and down. With the speed they hit the wire it was impossible to tell who'd won. Everyone watching the television turned to one another "who was it?", "who got it?" Manny couldn't tell and hoped it was Sing, but no matter what the outcome, he was proud. His horse showed a tremendous amount of heart and courage and it made Manny revere him even more.

About 20 or 30 seconds after the race, a video replay of the race's final 50 yards came on the televisions. They showed it in slow motion to make it easier to tell who'd won. One head up, one head down, one head up, one head down. Down you win. Up you lose. Stride after stride this continued to the finish line. The video slowed as the horses crossed the wire. Viewers leaned, then celebrated or cursed. With the slower speed it was easy to tell whose head was down, who was the winner.

"Damn!" cursed Margaret slapping her knee. She rose from the couch and walked out of the room.

Taken aback by the sudden burst, Jack stood there in silence. He couldn't recall the last time he'd heard Margaret curse. And that, if nothing else, indicated the level of frustration this family had reached. Jack stuck around and watched the replay a couple more times. "God, when are we going to catch a break?"

Michael and James flanked the chestnut gelding on their way to the test barn. Having finished second, Sing was subject to a drug test. He would be cooled out, allowed to drink some water and then everyone would wait for him to give a urine sample. It was post-race routine procedure. Unless you gave your horse a little something "extra" to increase his chances, it shouldn't be a problem. As they made their way toward the barn, Michael, as frustrated as ever, looked into Sing's eyes. "Why do you have to be so mental? Don't you realize how good you could be?" Sing returned Michael's gaze and blew out his nose sending dirt and "other" things in Michael's direction. Even Michael had to laugh, though it did nothing to curb his frustration. "Exactly," he uttered, wiping the nastiness from his shirt.

Along the rail Bobby reached into his pocket and pulled out his cell phone. Hopefully his client had been watching the race. This horse had some issues, but definitely had talent. Being gelded and only 3, Bobby knew if he could get this horse into his barn, chances were he would have him around for a long time. And hopefully they would win a lot of races together.

Bobby's owner picked up the phone on the first ring and the trainer opted to skip the formalities and jump right in. "Did you see that? I think we've got a good one here."

The O'Briens' truck cruised along the Thruway heading west into the setting sun. In the front seat sat two men whose moods had hit polar opposites. In the driver's seat Michael ran the day's events through his mind. He could come up with nothing, no idea why Sing does what he does. He was ready to send up the white flag, ready to surrender.

Sitting in the passenger seat next to him, James, on the other hand, felt as though he'd had a revelation. He had been studying Sing for months now, thanks to his wife's encouragement, and now it appeared he'd put all the puzzle pieces together and the picture was as clear as day. This has to be the key he thought to himself. Though now was not the time to bring it up as Michael treaded in a funk. The theory wasn't way out there, but he knew he would probably get some resistance, well actually, probably a lot of resistance. So he would wait for the right time. At least he could tell Lauren tonight, he thought, she would certainly be excited for him.

By the time James walked in the door Sydney had long since gone to bed. Lauren sat in the living room reading a book as James entered. "Hey Honey, how did it go? Did Sydney treat you alright?"

"Oh yeah, she was her usual self," Lauren said in a somewhat distracted manner. "How did the horse do? I completely forgot about turning it on."

"He finished second. Lost on a head bob," James said, in a way that struck Lauren as odd.

"You don't seem too upset by it."

"Well, it would have been nice if he won, but I think I finally figured him out," he said, his voice rising at the end. James waited a moment expecting Lauren to ask the next obvious question of what exactly he figured out and nothing came. "Is everything OK, you seem a little out of it."

"Well," Lauren said slowly, "have you noticed that I haven't been feeling real great lately?"

"Yeah," James replied nervously, "but I thought that was just a cold or something."

"Actually I did too, but it's not and I've done some figuring out of my own."

Now James began to panic thinking she had some sort of condition that was potentially serious, or worse. "My God, what is it?"

Lauren paused for a second and crinkled her face before speaking. "It would appear as though we will be adding to our own stable in about eight months. I'm pregnant, thus the reason I haven't been feeling so well."

James wasn't sure what to say, he simply stood there with his mouth gaping, relieved but in shock. The idea of telling Lauren about Sing fell from his mind. "We're going to have another baby. Holy shit! I can't believe it." He paced back and forth in front of Lauren with a giant grin on his face. Lauren remained seated, laughing at him.

"You going to be alright there, Dad?" she inquired, "you're looking a little spastic right at the moment and kind of freakin' me out."

"I can't help it, I had no idea. How did this happen?"

Seeing an opening that was impossible to turn down, Lauren responded with her best two-bit comment. "The postman my dear, how else do you think."

The remark caused James to laugh. As Lauren got up from her chair James grabbed her hands, looked into her eyes and smiled. "That's great news Honey, great news. You know, I really think things are turning around. Everything's going to be alright, you wait and see."

Chapter 35

~

AUGUST 3

Night began to fall on Western New York as Jack, Michael and James gathered around the kitchen table. The entire pot of coffee Margaret had made sat nearly empty, but as of yet, the threesome had resolved nothing. The conversation went round and round about how to proceed next. One thing that popped up several times was the Travers. It was a million-dollar race, run annually at Saratoga for 3-year-olds, with the winner netting a hefty $600,000. It usually drew a deep field, the best of the best. Hardly a spot for a horse who hadn't won all year, but it was the only race that would give them the money to stave off the bank. It was clearly their last hope. As a group they still believed that Sing had enough talent to compete.

Michael had tried everything he knew. Nothing seemed to work. Sometimes it was in the paddock, sometimes it wasn't until they hit the track, sometimes during the race itself, but Sing always found a way to mess things up. "I've given up trying to figure him out," Michael admitted. "I just don't know what else to do."

"Well," Jack replied, "we have no choice. We have less than 30 days and no other options. And he just ran a nice race against a horse that was a strong Derby contender before his injury. Hell, their final time was better than the Jim Dandy or the Haskell." Those being the major prep races for the Travers. "I say we enter him in and hope for the best."

"And who do you think will ride him?" Michael shot back at Jack. "Bejarano has a ride on the Preakness winner and there's no way a top jockey will take him. That may have been a tough allowance race, but he didn't win. Hasn't won all year." The room fell silent for a moment. Then James, who had been sitting silently at the kitchen table, looked up slowly.

"I know who should ride him," he said in a manner that was unmistakably different from normal. Even Margaret, having just entered the room, knew there must have been a tremendous amount of thought behind what James was about to say. James was a jokester, almost always leading with a wisecrack, but not this time. The gravity of the situation wasn't lost on anyone. "There's only one person that has ever been able to get this horse to settle." Everyone in the room hung on James' words, waiting for him to reveal his profound thought. "Manny," he continued, "Manny needs to ride him".

"What...?" Michael asked. "You have got to be kidding. He hasn't ridden regularly since Tampa, however many years ago that was. And he probably hasn't had 50 total mounts since he came up here."

Jack was quick to cut off Michael's outburst. "James' right," he said, stopping Michael in his tracks. "I've never seen a human and a horse have such a bond. That horse reacts to that boy and the only time he does run well is when that boy's on him. Having said that, I realize we'll look like damn fools running an allowance horse in the Travers, with a jockey who's more suited to be the pony boy. But I don't have time to worry about what other people think. I'm about to be kicked off my own land. If this makes me look like a fool, so be it, we'll be out of the game anyway. It's a risk I'm willing to take. We have to run him there, and Manny needs to be the one riding him."

Feeling the need to further explain his thoughts, James jumped back into the conversation. "I've been studying that horse for months now. I keep coming back to the same thing. When Manny's by his side, he's fine. And when he's not, well, that's when everything goes to hell. I'm not quite sure what it is, but he puts him at ease. That's the bottom line."

Michael couldn't disagree and every horse in the race would have to carry 126 pounds, so Manny would be able to make the weight necessary to ride. "You realize," Michael stated matter of factly, "that you're putting this farm in the hands of an exercise rider, in the biggest race of our lives?"

Jack paused for a moment glancing at James, who nodded his approval. "I can't think of another rider in the world that would care more about this farm than that boy."

AUGUST 6

"Well," Janet said as she hung up the phone, "I've got to say something now." She turned around hearing Jack and Mary coming into the kitchen. Her smile was so broad that even the kids knew something was up.

"Why are you so happy, Mom?" Jack asked.

"Now why do you think I'm so happy?" Janet asked.

"Because you're smiling and you usually don't smile that much?" Jack countered with Mary nodding her head in agreement.

Janet was slightly offended by Jack's analysis, though she recognized he was probably correct. Hey, she thought, you try spending every waking hour with you two clowns. She quickly put that out of her mind and tried to show her other "happy" side. "How would you guys like it if I went to school with you three days a week and worked in the office?"

Mary responded immediately, loudly exclaiming, "Cool Mom!" Jack on the other hand displayed a little trepidation. He smiled, but his level of excitement wasn't quite that of his sister. Jack, like many boys, occasionally found himself in trouble at school and having his mother stationed within the same building did not present a pleasant picture. Thoughts of being sent to the office to feel the wrath of both the principal and his Mom danced in his head as he solemnly exited the kitchen.

Janet was preparing dinner when Michael came home. He was a sullen man, beaten down over the course of the last seven months. Janet understood this and was waffling back and forth on how best to tell him about the job. Then Mary came barging in.

"Daddy," she screamed before giving him a big hug. As she released her hug she kindly added, "Mommy's going to come to our school and work," and then promptly left the room, her work complete.

Janet cringed, that was not one of the scenarios she was mulling over. Michael looked up at her with questioning eyes. Well, ready or not, it was time to share the news.

"I didn't want to say anything until I knew something definite," Janet said, looking at Michael to determine his reaction. Michael's face portrayed no emotion, good or bad, so she continued. "Back the last day of school when I picked up the kids, a friend of mine who works there said there might be an opening part time in the office. I told them to let me know, that I might be interested. Sure enough they called. So I went over there a week or so ago to interview and lo and behold, they offered me the job." When she was finished she shrugged her shoulders and smiled. "What do you think?"

What could Michael say? He was about to lose most of the horses he had under his control, he'd given up on figuring out Sing, his brother and his dad were naming jockeys for him and his family was about to lose their farm. At this moment Janet could have said just about anything and he would've gone along with it. "How many hours a week is it?"

"It would be three days a week, about six hours per day. Basically the normal school hours so it wouldn't interfere with watching the kids afterward." The enthusiasm shown through her voice and Michael felt it.

"Actually," he said, "that sounds like a perfect fit and I'm afraid we may need the money come September. I think you should take it if you haven't already."

Janet could barely contain her excitement. "I haven't accepted it yet. I wanted to talk to you first to make sure you were OK with it."

Just then Jack and Mary came in looking for a snack. "What do you think guys? Do you think Mom should come and work at the school with you?" Michael asked.

Mary once again showed how keen she was on the idea by jumping up and down while yelling "yeah" over and over again. Jack slowly walked over to his dad and whispered in his ear.

"If I get in trouble at school, will they go tell Mom?"

This brought a long needed smile and a little laugh to Michael. Something that was way overdue. "Don't worry bud, I don't think they'll tell Mom if you get in trouble."

The relief on Jack's face spoke a million words. And with that dilemma solved, Jack now accepted his mom's new appointment. He turned to her while smiling and said, "I'm glad you're going to be working at the school too, Mom."

Janet, still trying to quell her emotions, told her family she would call the school tomorrow and let them know. She, like Michael, appeared to be starting a new chapter in her life.

AUGUST 7

Around 8:30 a.m. two trucks and an SUV pulled into the O'Briens' driveway, each of which was tan colored and had Benson Realty plastered all over it. Jack worked in his usual spot at the barn and Margaret and Sarah lingered in the kitchen. They all heard the vehicles pulling in and parking near the house, so they went to investigate. Not that it was any surprise. All three knew and were expecting the surveyors to come out today and map the property.

Six men exited the three vehicles and walked toward the house. Jack whistled to them and the men stopped in their tracks. When they turned toward him he waved his hand indicating he was the one they needed. So the men changed direction and began walking down the hill toward the barn. They met up about halfway between the two structures. One of the men stepped forward and introduced himself.

"Good morning, I'm Eugene Hallinan with Benson Realty. You must be Jack O'Brien."

"I am," said Jack, firmly shaking the man's extended hand.

"I hope it's not a problem we're here today? This shouldn't take more than a few hours. I expect we should be out of your hair by midday or so."

Jack laughed inside. It's a problem alright, but what the hell am I supposed to do about it? "No it's no problem at all. Take all the time you need."

Having gotten the approval, the lead man turned to his crew and began issuing orders. As he was in the middle of pointing one of the men to the far corner of the property, Jack spoke up again.

"There is one thing you could do for me." The man turned and responded, "sure."

"Could you work it up two different ways? One price, if I were to sell the entire property, house and all. And a second for only 40 of the 50 acres, leaving us the house and 10 contiguous acres."

"Sure, we could do that," he said in a reserved tone, realizing this wasn't someone's investment property they were selling, it was their home. "Assuming everything goes smoothly out here, we should have an offer ready in a couple days."

After thanking the man Jack walked up the drive toward the house where Margaret and Sarah had come out to observe. As Jack approached, the two women watched the crews disperse to their respective locations, notebooks and survey equipment in tow.

"How long is this going to take?" asked Margaret.

"They said they should be done by around mid-day."

If you didn't know any better, seeing a group of men surveying a property would seem harmless. But for Jack, Margaret and even Sarah, what those men were doing was tearing the heart out of a family. Sarah turned and began walking back into the house. "I can't watch this."

Margaret put her hand on Jack's back. "I think I'm going to head back in too. You coming?"

Jack looked at his wife and kissed her on the top of her head. "I'll be in shortly Dear." He felt as though he needed to stay and watch, despite how it made his gut feel. As if he was standing up to the beast, rather than turning tail and running back inside. Whether it made any sense to anyone else didn't matter, Jack wasn't even sure it made any sense to him. But his conscience required it and that's all he knew. If nothing else, it made him feel as though he still had some fight in him and that is worth more than words can express.

Chapter 36

~

AUGUST 10

When the call came, Jack was at the barn doing, as Margaret likes to say, whatever it is he does. Normally she would have simply taken a message and told him later, but it was Benson Realty and she knew Jack was waiting for their call. They agreed to hold on the line while she went to get him. After a few minutes Jack arrived at the house and picked up the phone "Jack O'Brien here."

"Mr. O'Brien this is Eugene Hallinan, I have our proposals. I thought I would give them to you over the phone and then mail the originals this afternoon. That way, if you have any questions we can go over them now."

"Fair enough," said Jack. "What did you come up with?"

"For just the forty acres alone we would offer $200,000 and for the entire property, house and all, we would offer you $400,000."

As soon as he heard $400,000 Jack smelled a rat. That was exactly what they owed to the bank and he was sure this property was worth more than that. Somebody tipped these guys off, though it's hard to believe Ron would do such a thing. Jack decided to press Benson Realty for some answers. "That seems lower than I was expecting. How did you come up with that figure?"

"Well, it really is a nice piece of property, but we ran into some issues with the creek that runs through it and the slope of some of the hills. We'll either need to do a lot of land moving or substantially scale back the number of houses we'd put in. Of course, in either case we'll end up losing. It's less revenue in one scenario and more expenses in the other. So you understand why we needed to drop the offer down a little."

Jack said "yeah", but no he didn't understand. That was an excuse because they knew they could get away with one. Jack had no real leverage. Jack knew it, and apparently so did they. "Alright, what's my timeframe on this thing?"

"I'll drop it in the mail today and you have 30 days from the date of the letter to accept. If you have any questions once you've received it just let me know. My name and number will be on the letter."

"OK," Jack hung up the phone, disgusted with it all. It's bad enough I have to sell the place, he thought, but that offer was insulting.

Margaret was sitting at the table with him during the entire call so she could see the numbers he'd written down. They were forcing them to sell the whole property and that was all there was to it. She got up from her chair and headed toward the coffee maker. "How about I make us a fresh pot of coffee."

Looking up from the sheet of paper where he'd written the figures, Jack gazed into Margaret's knowing eyes, "That would be great."

Margaret and Jack drained their first cups of coffee when the phone rang again. Jack was closest so he picked up the receiver, "O'Brien residence."

"Jack, Bobby Gillner here, how are things?"

"Hey Bobby, not too bad, how's everything on your end?"

"Good, good thanks. Hey, sorry I haven't got back in touch with you until now. The owners I had in mind for your horse had to do some figuring first."

"Oh, I was wondering. Just thought it was probably a no go," Jack said.

"No, not at all. I liked what I saw. The owners really want to run one at Saratoga and they were waiting to see about another horse they have. They've only got two horses, one is still in training and the other has a shin so he needs some time. They wanted to find out the extent of the injury before making a move. As it is the horse will be fine but will need a month off. So I told them I knew of one that might be for sale and should be ready to run again before the end of the meet."

"Did they have a figure in mind?" Jack inquired.

"Sure do, they said they would give you $75,000 for him."

Jack was surprised at the offer, which was about fifty more than he expected to get around the Finger Lakes area. "That's a nice offer. When do they want to know by?"

"They'd like to hear something back by Monday. Give you the weekend to mull it over. That way they can pursue some other options if it doesn't go through."

"I understand. That's fair enough. I'll give you a call on Monday and let you know."

"Good enough, I'll wait to hear from you then. Have a good weekend."

"Thanks Bobby, you do the same." Jack hung up the phone again and sat back down. 'Funny game, a horse is worth $75,000, the farm that raised him is only worth $400,000...' With this offer now on the table, there might be a little bit more to think about.

Rather than go back outside, Jack opted to stay around and run numbers again. Once he had hashed things out, he emerged from his study and summoned Margaret into the kitchen. "Alright Mother I've been through the numbers. I'd like to hear your thoughts on what you think we should do".

Margaret sat down and looked at Jack's chicken-scratched numbers. "I may need a translation on what you've written down here."

Jack looked down at what he'd written and made a funny face understanding the extent of Margaret's plight. "Sorry about that. Let me just tell you where we are. They've offered us $200,000 for the 40 acres alone and $400,000 for the entire property, which is exactly what we owe to the bank. We've also got an offer on Sing for $75,000, which we need to respond to by Monday. The offers on the house are good for 30 days, so we don't need to make any quick decisions there. As far as the other horses, if we were to start selling them we could probably get another

$100,000. If word got out that we were in financial trouble and it turned into a fire sale, then that would probably drop to about $60,000."

Margaret scribbled down some "legible" notes as Jack ran the numbers. When he finished, she studied what was in front of her to try to figure out where they were. Feeling like she had a grasp of the situation, she began the discussion. "So if we decide to sell Sing then the Travers is out and so is our only chance at winning any substantial purse money. Which in turn means we'd have to sell at least the 40 acres."

Jack responded with a simple "correct."

"Now if we chose to keep Sing, then what are the various scenarios we're looking at?" Margaret posed.

Taking a second to run through everything, Jack took a breath and glanced at the ceiling while preparing his exposition. Once ready, he lowered his head and looked at Margaret.

"If we keep him," he said before pausing, "and run him in the Travers, then how he does will have a huge effect on what happens next. If he finished second, the purse money would be $200,000, less jocks' percentage, which Manny would probably give right back to us, and some nomination fees. Combined with the $200,000 for the 40 acres, we're paid off. From there we could trim down the horses since we wouldn't have a barn to keep them in any more. We could probably keep some and just pay to have them boarded somewhere.

"If he were to run third, the purse money would be $100,000. Combine that with the sale of the 40 acres gives us $300,000. From there we could again trim down the herd and we could probably get a good price for Sing as well. At any point, we shouldn't have any trouble getting the final $100,000.

"If he finishes any worse than third, then I think we'd have no choice but to sell the whole property. The purse money wouldn't be enough and Sing's value would be back down to $25,000 if we sold him around here and maybe $50,000 to someone downstate."

Margaret scribbled down the numbers, underlining some and circling others, then reviewed what she'd written. Satisfied, she looked at Jack. "So we could end this thing this weekend by selling Sing and signing the offer on the whole property. From there we start selling the other horses. In the end we pay off the bank and have around $175,000."

"And no place to live," Jack added curtly.

Margaret wasn't fazed. "We could buy a little cottage along Canandaigua Lake and retire there." She waited for Jack to respond, but he knew better so she continued. "Or we could sell Sing, sell the 40 acres and then the rest of the horses. That would get us $275,000 for Sing and the 40 acres and hopefully another $100,000 for the other horses. From there we would be only $25,000 short, but I'm sure we could work some sort of deal from there."

Jack nodded his head in agreement, but said nothing. Margaret waited a second and then picked it up again. "Of course by selling all the horses, we put Michael and James in a very tough place. Though I guess if we lose the farm, they're there anyway."

"Yeah."

"So, if we don't sell Sing now, then we are banking on him to run a huge race in the Travers."

"In a nutshell, yes," Jack said.

"There is one scenario you didn't mention," Margaret added.

Jack, not sure of what he'd forgotten looked at her quizzically.

"What if Sing wins the race?" she asked.

That thought had entered Jack's mind, but he didn't want to say it out loud, not to her, not to anyone. Now Margaret forced it. "If he were to win, we sell nothing," Jack said. "And we dance in the streets…"

Margaret looked him in the eyes. "You really think he could do it, don't you?"

It seemed such a long shot that Jack didn't want to admit it, but yes he did. Margaret made the realist acknowledge the highly improbable. "Don't ask me why, but yes I think he has a shot."

"Well Jack O'Brien, I think you need to give this all some thought over the next couple days and we can talk about it again Monday morning. I'll think about it too, but this decision is yours to make. I'm with you, no matter which way you go. Understood?"

Jack smiled at the most blessed woman he'd ever seen, a family's burden resting squarely on his shoulders. "Understood."

Chapter 37

~

AUGUST 12

WITH NOT MUCH TO DO on a lazy summer afternoon, Lauren decided to go look at baby clothes. It was certainly a little premature, but a little window shopping never hurt anyone. Besides, it had been a long time since she'd checked out what was new in baby fashions. Already having a girl, Lauren was kind of hoping this one would be a boy. Not just for her, but for James as well. She knew James would love having a boy to follow him around. Although she had to admit, the boy clothes were never anywhere near as fun. As she was rummaging through the clothes' racks with Sydney by her side she looked up to see a familiar face, her sister-in-law Janet. She was lucky in the grocery store to have avoided Henry Livingston, but today she would have no such luck. Janet had already seen her and was on her way with Jack and Mary in tow.

"Lauren, funny running into you here."

Lauren's mind was racing a mile a minute trying to come up with a good excuse as to why she was perusing baby clothes. Moments away from a full-fledged panic, Lauren suddenly came upon the easy answer. "A friend of mine is having a baby shower soon so I thought I'd see if I could find something".

"Oh that's nice. Is she having a boy or a girl?"

Crap, another question thought Lauren. Luckily she was in character now and more able to think quickly. "She doesn't know yet, which makes it kind of tough." Not wanting to field any more questions Lauren deftly changed the subject to one that was on everyone's mind. "What do you think will happen with the farm?"

Janet bought right into it and changed her facial expression to one of concern. "I'm hoping for the best, but it doesn't look good. Michael is really down about it. How is James doing?"

"He's doing OK. He's not ready to give up the ship quite yet, but yeah, it certainly doesn't look very good. I can't imagine what their dad will do if they have to give up the place."

Janet shook her head. "I know it. I can't picture him anywhere but that farm."

A thought crossed Lauren's mind to mention something about Michael having taken in three new horses. But just as quickly she realized that conversation would most likely wind back around to Janet and Michael's finances which, at this point in time, were probably hurting. It might also lead to where James fit in with the business, the answer of which may be nowhere. Altogether, nothing pleasant could come from verbalizing her thought, so she said nothing and searched her brain for another, less depressing, topic. "Have you been to Canandaigua lately?"

"No why?"

"Oh, you've got to go by and take a look at the lake front."

"Why's that?"

"Remember the other side of the road from the beach, there used to be a trailer park."

"Yes, I never could figure that one out, quite a location for a trailer park. I heard they were finally getting rid of it. Did they?"

"Sure did. They took all the trailers, along with every tree, bush and twig in sight. It's a giant empty lot. Now all you see is the back of that shopping center that butts up to it. It's ridiculous looking."

"No kidding, the trees too. Why did they take them down, are they building anything?"

"No, and it doesn't sound like anything is coming soon. I don't know why they let them do it. Why not leave the trees? They'd obscure the view of the shopping center and make it look kind of like a park. It would've been decent looking. Now it looks horrible."

"Who knows? You can't trust developers, and it always seems like they've got someone in their pocket these days."

"That's the truth," Lauren agreed. A sudden silence signaled the conversation had run its course and Lauren felt as though she'd dodged the pregnancy bullet. Now all she had to do was find a way out of the surprise meeting, which she did in the form of the children.

The three cousins, excited to see one another, had begun a game of chase in and around the racks of clothes. "I should grab Sydney and get going before things get out of control. It was nice to see you again."

"You too, I imagine we'll be seeing each other again shortly. Michael said if they do run Sing in the Travers we'll probably all go down to see it."

"Yeah, James said the same thing." Lauren stopped for a moment pointing for Sydney to come back. "Alright, well let's hope it doesn't come down to this one race. I'll see you soon."

"Yeah really, I'm not sure I'll be able to take the stress if it does," replied Janet, now moving in search of her two.

AUGUST 13

By the time Monday morning came around the decision whether to sell Sing had long since been made. Neither Margaret nor Jack had made mention of it, but both knew what they wanted to do. After a quiet breakfast Margaret cleared the table of plates leaving Jack alone with his coffee cup. "Well," he asked, "what are your thoughts on Sing?"

Margaret continued to load the sink, throwing the ball back into Jack's court. "I told you before, this is your call. Whatever you think is best I'll support you." Jack sighed but agreed. Margaret turned from the sink, still scraping a butter plate, awaiting Jack's response.

Jack stared at the bottom of his coffee cup, as if wanting to quiz his brain one last time. Then he slowly nodded his head, as if his brain had answered and looked at Margaret. "I don't want to sell him. I want to wait and run him in the Travers. If it turns out poorly, then we sell the whole place and walk away. I've thought about it and I don't want half a farm, not if I can help it. I want all of it or none of it. I won't sit here and look at a bunch of houses on my fields." His voice was firm and gave the impression that he was certain of his choice.

Margaret thought about asking him if he was sure, but years of marriage told her there was no need. "Good," she said, "that's what I was hoping you'd say."

So there it was, one roll of the dice for the future of the farm. In the end, it wasn't really that tough a question to answer. Jack had spent the weekend combing his mind for some guidance, something he could latch onto. He found it in a picture on his dresser. The same picture he'd seen a little more than a month ago. Once again, he travelled back in time. He recalled the desperate situations, the first desperate situations of his life, the kind that make you or ruin you. Back then it wasn't a piece of property at stake, it was men's lives. Jack was young and daring then, not the gray-hair old man he is today. But those bold courses of action saved many lives and won him several medals. He believed they had a chance in the Travers, it was time for one more bold plan.

With Sing's status settled, Jack went to the phone and dialed Bobby Gillner's number. After Bobby answered Jack jumped directly to the heart of the matter. "We've decided to keep Sing in our stable for now."

"Damn, that's too bad. Not for you I guess, but I have to say I was looking forward to getting my hands on him."

"Yeah, I can understand that," Jack said, "But we feel like we may have pinpointed a couple of his issues and are anxious to see if it pans out."

"I know what you mean, Jack. You don't want to pass him on if you feel like you've just had a breakthrough. Do you plan on running him again over here?"

Jack wasn't sure how to respond to the question. He wanted to tell Bobby they were planning on running in the Travers, but he couldn't. It sounded too foolish. "Yeah, I think we will," he finally said, opting to keep it simple, yet truthful.

"I'll keep my eyes out for his next outing. And if you do decide to sell him, let me know. I don't know if these owners would still be interested, but I'm sure I could find someone."

"Thanks Bobby, I appreciate that. It was good to touch base with you again after all these years."

"You too Jack, you too. Don't be a stranger alright?"

"Alright." Jack hung up the phone and made up his mind that no matter how things turned out, he would make sure to rekindle some old friendships he'd let fall away.

One friend, whose relationship remained strong despite the circumstances, was Ron Dombrowski. Ron sat in his office dying to know if there were any new developments with the O'Briens' farm. He knew the realty company scheduled their appointment for last week and figured Jack should have an offer pretty soon, if not already. By late morning Ron couldn't wait any longer and dialed Jack.

Jack sat at the kitchen table with the paper's business section and Margaret, seated across from him, the front section. Although Jack's eyes moved from word to word, he couldn't have described anything about the article. The thought of running Sing in the Travers made it impossible to focus. Jack read the same sentence for the third time when the phone rang. "Jack it's Ron, any news?"

"Hey Ron, yeah the realty company came out last week and made us an offer. Did you ever tell them how much we owed the bank?" Jack didn't want to accuse Ron of anything, but he needed to ask the question. He wanted to clear up whether it was pure coincidence or what.

"God no. I never mentioned a word about what was owed. Why do you ask?"

"Well, I asked for two proposals. One for the whole property and one for just 40 acres. The one for 40 acres was $200,000 and the one for the whole property was $400,000, exactly what we owe you guys. It just seemed very odd to me and I thought the offers were a little low."

"That does seem very odd, and low. I was expecting it to be more in the $600,000 range."

"Yeah, we figured it would be at least $500,000. Do you think it would make sense to have someone else come out and appraise the property?"

"I certainly know of a couple of good appraisers," Ron said, "but I don't think it will do any good."

"No?" Jack said, surprised at the answer.

"No. The problem is there's no one else in the market to buy. None of the banks are doing much lending, so unless you've got cash, you're out of luck." Ron heard a disappointed sigh on the other side of the line. "As of right now, Benson is the only developer buying. Unfortunately, you're not the only guy in trouble and a bunch of us in the office have been beating the bushes trying to find some other buyers. So far it's been a dead end."

"Sounds like I'm screwed."

"I don't want to say that, but yeah, it doesn't look good."

"Any idea how the other offers have been?" Jack asked.

"Actually, they've been a little on the low side too. I hadn't given it much thought, since none of the clients were mine, but I think pretty much everyone's been a little disappointed. It kind of makes me wonder." Ron paused a second. Things around the office had been deteriorating, morale was way down and there were talk of layoffs. The possibility of someone leaking information for their own benefit was tough to imagine, but in this climate, it could happen. "I'd hate to think someone in this office has been talking to them, but something definitely seems off."

"You guys aren't allowed to do that, are you?"

"No," Ron said unequivocally. "All your information with us is confidential. The only way we can give it out is if you give us permission or if we're compelled by law for some reason."

"I didn't think you could, but I'll tell you, it does seem awfully strange. My gut says something ain't right."

Ron agreed, his gut feeling the same. "I think it's time I do some checking around."

"Well don't go getting yourself in trouble or anything, Ron. But I'd have to admit, I'd be interested to find out if someone passed our information on to them. And I'd bet I could find a lawyer that'd be interested too."

"I'll see what I can do," Ron said. "Do you have any idea what you'll do?"

Jack had balked at the idea of telling Bobby Gillner about their plans, but for some reason he didn't mind saying something to Ron about it. Perhaps it was because Ron was a horse racing novice and wouldn't think they were absolutely crazy. "Funny you say that. We just decided today that we're going to run one of our horses in the Travers. How he runs will determine what we do."

Now, although Ron wasn't much into horse racing, even he knew the Travers was a big race. "Do you have a chance of winning?"

"It's going to be a long shot, but we think it's worth a try. If he wins, then we can pay back everything we owe. If he finishes second or third, then we can probably get away with selling only the 40 acres, though I really don't want to do that, I'm all or nothing, you know that. Anything worse than third and we're done."

This was it, thought Ron, their last gasp. "Well, I wish you good luck then Jack. You know I'll be rooting for you."

"Thanks Ron. I'll talk to you soon."

As Ron hung up, he began to think about the offers Jack had received. Something didn't smell right, but who in his office would've talked to Benson Realty about it. As Ron was running through the list of people who had access to Jack's information, Henry Livingston came strolling by on the way to his office. That was it, it was that S.O.B. "Henry The Ain't." He knew what was going on and how much they owed. And he would have known the details on all the other farmers in the same predicament.

Somehow Ron had to find proof. And if he did, and it was him, so help him God for there would be hell to pay.

AUGUST 14

For the first time in a while, Jack, Margaret and Sarah sat together at the kitchen table eating dinner. Perceptive to the farm's difficult financial situation, Sarah realized early in the summer that her getting a "real" job would be far better than staying on the farm and helping out. She still lent a hand now and then, but spent most of her days at the tack shop. It turned out to be easier work anyway. Between work and spending time with old friends, she wasn't around much, so she appreciated the times she sat down to a nice dinner with her parents. She also knew in less than three weeks, unless something big happened, the farm would be gone. That fact began to weigh more and more heavily on her over the past half month. And tonight, those building emotions came spilling out.

"Have you guys figured out what you're going to do yet?" Sarah asked.

Margaret and Jack looked at one another, realizing they hadn't really kept Sarah, or any of the other children for that matter, up to date with things. And Jack would have been wise to allow Margaret to answer the question, but instead he took the lead and responded first. "At this point, it looks like there's a good chance we'll have to sell at least a part of the farm," Jack said.

Sarah maintained her composure, but didn't at all like what she'd heard, so she pressed further. "When will you know for sure? You only have until the end of the month, don't you?"

"Well," Jack said rolling the last of his brussels sprouts around his plate, "we plan to run Sing in the Travers on the 25th. How he does will tell us what we need to do."

"But I thought he hadn't run very well so far this year. What if he doesn't run well again?" Sarah's voice began to exude the fear that welled up inside her. Next to her at the table Margaret sat quietly, not liking where the conversation was going, but choosing to remain silent and hoping Jack would smooth things over.

Jack, always the straight talker, did no such thing and gave her the unadulterated truth. "If he runs poorly then we'll probably be forced to sell the entire farm, house and all."

Hearing how desperate things were, Sarah's eyes started to fill with tears and she turned toward her mother for comfort. Margaret grabbed for her hand while simultaneously scowling at Jack. Jack said, "Well, it's the truth." While Margaret was playing her motherly role, Jack, realizing his mistake, tried to remedy his previous comment.

"Honey, don't worry, something inside me tells me everything will be OK. It has to be, I need to work around the horses, I can't deal with people." Though poignantly accurate, it did little to help.

Margaret, still miffed at Jack for his bluntness, attempted to lighten the mood by using him as the butt of a joke. "Jack dear, you realize horses have the mentality of a 3-year-old child, which I can only assume is why you get along with them so well."

The remark had its intended response. The saddened mood in the room was momentarily lifted as both Sarah and Margaret began laughing. Jack, who was on his way to the sink, said nothing. Fighting back the urge to toss his plate, he placed it in the sink and headed for the door. He didn't appreciate what she was saying, but he understood her intention. The best thing to do now was to leave before he got pissed off.

"I'm sorry dear," Margaret continued, eyeing Jack's demeanor, "but seriously, if things end badly, maybe we can get you a job at a daycare facility. You can spend some quality time amongst your peers."

Sarah laughed again, her fear quelled, at least for the time being.

Chapter 38

~

AUGUST 17

THE TWO BROTHERS WATCHED AS their trainee came bounding down the stretch with an insurmountable lead. Neither showed much emotion until the horse made it under the wire. Then, James turned to Michael and shook his hand, "We're rolling now," he said enthusiastically.

It was their second winner of the day, to go along with a third with another horse. They sent three horses to the races and each one collected a paycheck, an all-around good day. But Michael still recognized it was only a drop in proverbial feed bucket, so his enthusiasm what somewhat curbed. "Yeah, that's great and all, but it's probably too little too late."

"Come on now, we need to stay positive."

"Stay positive? Seriously? Maybe you think Sing's got more of a chance than I do, but I just don't see it. I don't understand how you can be upbeat right now?"

"I don't know," James said, not truly sure himself. "I just feel like things are beginning to turn in our favor. The good karma is back on our side, the momentum is building."

"James," Michael said, as if to give James a reality check, "the farm will likely be gone in two weeks."

"No Michael, I'm not buying it yet. I can't explain it, but I feel better about this then I have for long time."

"I wish I could feel the same," Michael said, with resignation, "but I don't."

"Well, it's not over yet, so don't give up on me." The pair entered the winner's circle and James grabbed the horse's bridle. A second later the picture was taken. "Hey," he said, starting the horse toward the test barn, "I'll stop by Mom and Dad's on my way home and let them know how we did."

"OK," Michael said with indifference, "I planned on calling over, but that's fine with me."

And a call would have been fine, but James wanted to see his parents. He was itching to share the news about Lauren, but didn't want to tell everyone quite yet and this was a perfect excuse to go past the farm. He figured some good news would be welcome around the farm about now. Even though James couldn't verbalize it with Michael, he believed deep down that the worst was over and better times were coming. The two wins today only strengthened his faith.

James pulled onto the farm and immediately walked toward the barn assuming that's where his Dad would be. As he approached he could hear Jack and Margaret yelling back and forth to one another, neither understanding what the other was saying. Of course, he could hear both of them perfectly well and laughed as he entered the barn. Margaret saw him first and stopped what she was doing.

"Hi Honey, what are you doing here?"

"Actually what I'm doing is getting a good laugh out of you and Dad. Are the two of you deaf or what?"

Margaret laughed at the comment, realizing how funny it must have been to have listened to their attempted conversation. As Jack arrived to where they were standing she pointed to him and said, "I can't help it, the man mumbles. Nobody can understand what he says."

Jack took a deep breath, "anyway" he added with a dismissive tone before turning to James. "What brings you out here?"

"I thought I would come out and let you know how the horses ran today. We ended the day with two wins and a third."

"Oh beautiful," said Margaret. "But you came all the way out here for that? You could have just called."

"In fact, I do have some other news I thought I'd share." Jack and Margaret looked at him bewildered. "Remember at the Fourth of July picnic Mom, you were talking about us having more kids and I made the comment about Lauren being baron? Well, as it turns out, she's not." James paused a moment to see if Margaret was catching on. The wide-eyed expression she made indicated it was beginning to click. "That's right, we just found out she's pregnant."

As James expected, his mom was elated. "Are you kidding? Oh my God, that's wonderful," she said as she leapt forward and hugged James.

Waiting for the embrace to end Jack extended his arm to shake James' hand. "Congratulations son, that certainly is good news."

"Lauren and I didn't plan on telling anyone yet, so no one else knows, but we thought you guys could use some good news."

Margaret responded first. "Don't worry we won't say anything, but that is such exciting news."

Jack laughed as Margaret began clapping. He looked at James, "you realize this may kill your mother if she has to keep quiet about this?"

Margaret took a swat at Jack. "Oh, shut up Jack, it will not."

"Try to keep it under wraps for a little while anyway," James pleaded with her. "She has a doctor appointment in a few weeks and if everything goes well, maybe we'll let it out then."

"I can hold out until then," Margaret said. "Are you guys hoping for a boy or girl?"

"It would be nice to have a boy, but we know what to expect if it's a girl. Either way it's probably our last."

"So you say," Jack said. "But you never know what might happen."

"That may be true. Let's just say it's our intention to stop at two. With two we can play man-to-man. Add that third and we're forced to go to a zone defense."

Margaret rolled her eyes. "Nice analogy son, but we had three. Remember your brother and sister?"

"I know Mom, but you didn't work. We do, and at this point I'm hoping both of us still have jobs when the baby's born."

"Well, no need to worry about a third at this moment," Margaret said, waving her hand in the air. "What about names, have you given any thought to names yet?"

"No Mom, not yet."

Margaret continued throwing questions at James, he did his best to answer them and the threesome stood talking about the thrilling news forgetting, if only for a while, the deadline looming just 14 days away.

AUGUST 18

Michael stood in the bleachers near the finish line watching Sing and Manny warm up. On his walkie-talkie he called to James who was Mac, keeping close tabs on Sing. "Let me know when you're ready."

"They're set now," James replied.

Michael turned to Steve Tordone, the clocker who times all the official workouts. This would be Sing's last officially timed workout before the Travers. "Sing So Long, five eighths," Michael said. Timex, that's what they called Tordone, acknowledged it, "gottcha." Sing would run at near full speed for five eighths of a mile. Michael was hoping to see Sing run the distance in exactly one minute, the same basic time he had prior to his last race. He picked up his binoculars and watched Sing break into stride. He could see Sing moving fluidly from one pole to the next. 'God he looks great,' thought Michael. No matter what happened during the race, he knew this horse was the most amazing animal he had ever had the "pleasure" of training, though the frustration made it hard to use the word pleasure. As Sing neared the finish line, Michael gazed down at his own stopwatch, pushing the stop button as Sing's nose crossed the wire. In disbelief, Michael turned to Timex. "What'd you get?"

With a broad smile, Timex said, "58 flat, whew."

"Shit, that's what I thought." Immediately, Michael picked up his walkie-talkie and yelled into it. "James!"

"What's up boss?" James casually replied.

Annoyed by James' relaxed tone, Michael quickly shot back at him, "What the hell was Manny doing, does he have any idea how fast they went? I didn't want that horse using himself up."

"It couldn't have been too fast, they just passed me and the horse is barely breathing. The way he sounded, it was more like a Sunday stroll."

Michael jumped back at James again, "58 flat!" All Michael could hear was the sound of James laughing, a half laugh, part whistle, like he had seen a pretty girl and found a hundred-dollar bill at the same time.

"Our work is done here," James calmly said to his brother.

Michael put down the walkie-talkie and let out a long breath. James was right, the horse was ready. The time had come. One week from to-day they would get their shot. Michael started down the steps on his way back to the barn. He wanted to make sure to meet Sing and Manny when they arrived after cooling out. As he passed Timex, the clocker clicked his watch for another set of workers "Give em hell next week." Michael smiled and shook his head, trying to keep the thought out of his mind, wondering what they'd gotten themselves into.

AUGUST 23

From along the rail Jack watched the last of the morning workouts come to an end. He told Michael he would be out about 9:30, but chose to arrive about an hour earlier. Not to get in the way, but rather to enjoy the quiet sound of horses going through their morning exercises. He found, especially in the morning, a rekindled love of the track and its workings. He had grown weary of it years ago, but those things he didn't like seemed to have faded away to the recesses of his mind. If things didn't end well with the farm, maybe coming back to work around the track might not be so bad. Jack looked down at his watch as the thuds of a single horse's pounding hooves faded in the distance. It was time to head over to the barn.

Michael, James and Manny sat together cleaning tack, each on a beat-up old rickety chair, each with a bucket between their feet. The trio formed a semi-circle, heads bowed. "You boys look like three army cooks peeling potatoes," Jack said, uncharacteristically upbeat. Nobody answered, just a few "heys" filled the air. No one other than Michael knew he was coming. They had decided to wait until now to tell Manny he would be riding Sing in the Travers. They thought it might be overwhelming, so telling him as late as possible seemed like a good idea. Hell, Michael wanted to wait until post time. James, not realizing what Michael and Jack were up to, asked Jack what he was doing out here this morning. "I thought we should go over the plans for this weekend," Jack answered.

Then it hit James. He smiled and motioned toward Manny. Manny noticed James' gesture and started to get nervous. "Hey, you guys aren't going to make me stay here again are you? That's not fair, I want to go too, you know."

The three O'Briens began to laugh, but it was James, unable to hold it in, who spoke first. "Don't worry Manny, you're going this time." Manny let out a sigh of relief, as Michael and Jack continued to smile waiting for James to drop the bombshell. "In fact," said James, "you are going to be riding him in the Travers."

Manny was dumbfounded, he wanted to ask James to repeat what he'd said, but when he opened his mouth nothing came out.

"Well man, say something," implored James. "You've got a mount in the Travers Stakes at Saratoga. What do you have to say for yourself?"

Manny finally composed himself, still in disbelief. "Why are you having me ride him? I don't understand."

James opened his mouth to speak again, but Jack held up his hand for him to wait, deciding he should be the one to let Manny know how he'd been chosen. "Manny, we've been trying to figure this horse out for more than a year now. The only time he seems at ease is when you're either with him or on him. You have a bond with him and I know you know that. I also know you can ride. You're a smart rider and we trust you. We want you to be the one to get it done for us."

Manny was taken aback by the commentary. This was the second time Jack had made some very personal and praising comments toward him. He couldn't believe Jack held such faith in him. Manny wasn't sure how to respond, so he just said what he felt. "I'd be honored."

Jack and James moved in to shake Manny's hand and pat him on the back. Only Michael remained at arm's length, still not sure this was the best move for the barn, or more appropriately, the family. But he knew it wasn't his call to make. If this is how his dad wanted to proceed, then so be it. He owned the horse. Paid the bills. It was Jack's race to lose. His farm to lose.

It took a couple of hours for the magnitude of the situation to hit Manny. He would be riding in the biggest race of his life with the fate of the farm resting squarely on his and Sing's shoulders. The weight of that realization was immense. As Manny packed what few things he would need while he was gone, the urge to talk to someone overpowered him. He paced around his apartment, which suddenly felt so small, like the confines of a prison cell. He needed to talk through things and the horses wouldn't cut it. He needed to free his mind. Wish for his dad, there was only one call, one party that would be interested and excited to hear the news, his aunt and uncle in Florida. Their exchanging of letters, now countless, had established a close and wonderful relationship. They would help him talk through everything and give him the reassurance he needed.

As Manny picked up the phone and began dialing, he realized the contrast between now and a half a year earlier. Six months ago he was terrified of contacting his aunt and uncle and now he was praying they were home to take his call. As each ring passed Manny's heart sank until suddenly the ringing stopped and a familiar voice answered. Within seconds, Manny's aunt had the phone in the kitchen and his uncle had the phone in the upstairs' bedroom, both listening and saying little.

Manny spent the next 20 minutes filling them in on everything that had happened, barely drawing a breath. He told them about the desperate times the O'Briens had found themselves in and that this was their last hope to save the farm and that he was charged with guiding Sing to victory. Manny never let on how scared he was about the farm or the race, but his voice betrayed him and it became obvious to his aunt and uncle. And it was his aunt who stepped forward to take control of the conversation. Although she had no children of her own, she seemed, like most women, to have some innate motherly instinct. When she spoke, her voice was calm and her tone heartening. "So you ride him every day then."

"Oh yeah, he gets some sort of exercise each day. It depends when he raced last and if he's preparing for another one, but I get on him every day."

"You must know him real well then, don't you?"

"Yeah, absolutely. I'm used to all his little tricks and stuff," Manny said with a little laugh. "And a lot of times I'll go back and see him in the afternoon and groom him or something. He likes the company."

"I'd bet he's really fond of you, giving him all that attention."

"I think he is. He does seem to perk up when I come around. He's a horse and all, but he definitely acts different for me than for anybody else."

The questions were simple, but the answers echoed much more. The call lasted nearly an hour, but seemed like much less. When it was finally coming to an end Manny began to wonder if this woman was like his mother. She was after all her sister and the more Manny got to know her, the more she was able to soothe him.

"You know Manny, I didn't know your dad very well, but I heard he was a wonderful horseman and had great instincts," she said. "I expect you are an awful lot like him. You know this horse, you just need to trust your instincts and things will work out. Have faith in yourself."

His aunt's words struck home, reassuring his frightened mind. Maybe she was right. Manny always knew he had a way with horses, he just needed to believe in himself. He thanked her for the kind words and said goodbye. Tomorrow they would head to Saratoga and a date with destiny.

Chapter 39

~

AUGUST 24

MICHAEL AND JAMES PACKED THE truck and trailer with everything necessary except Sing, who was munching hay in his stall. Manny stood at the stall door, watching Sing eat, waiting for the word to go and wishing he could be more like Sing, oblivious to what it all meant. The phrase "ignorance is bliss" suddenly became crystal clear.

Inside the trailer James checked and doubled checked everything. To forget something or bring the wrong item could cause problems, or if nothing else, added stress, and there was no room for error on this trip. Meanwhile, Jack and Margaret were huddled with Michael going over what needed to be done the next couple of days while the boys and Manny were gone. When James stepped out of the trailer Michael looked at him. No words were spoken, the question already known.

"We're all set," James said.

Feeling as though everything was in order, Michael called to Manny, "let's go." Manny and Sing emerged side by side. As if out for a stroll they walked up the ramp and Sing took his place in the trailer. Manny secured Sing's halter while James and Michael raised and secured the ramp. After Manny tied the hay net he slid out the side door and latched it closed. They were ready to go.

The group of five came together at the front of the truck. Hugs and handshakes alternated from one person to another. A farewell square dance rotating partner to partner. Hugs and hands, hands and hugs. The words goodbye and good luck echoed with each embrace. They were solemn and heartfelt, everyone understanding the fate of the farm rested on the success of their journey. Manny thought about his new role on this trip. No longer simply a groom, there to assist. He would be front and center and it weighed heavily upon him. Margaret hugged him and wished him luck. Jack extended his hand, firmly grabbing hold of Manny's. "Good luck Manny."

Manny, knowing what was entrusted of him, gave Jack's hand a sturdy shake. "I'll do my best Mr. O'Brien."

"I know," Jack said. "I know."

Seeing the sincerity in Manny's eyes, it hit Jack the burden they were putting on the young rider. Jack knew his response needed to relay the confidence he felt in him. He continued his firm grasp of Manny's hand and placed his free hand on Manny's shoulder, his hold solid. "You've never given us anything less Manny. If our horse has any chance at all, it's with you riding him."

The words had their intended effect. It was important for Manny to know he was chosen, and not because there were no other choices, but because they had confidence in his ability. "Thank you, Mr. O'Brien."

As Manny turned to climb aboard the truck Jack called out to him. "And Manny," Jack said waiting for Manny to turn around; "I think you've known me long enough, call me Jack." Manny smiled and climbed in.

The truck slowly pulled away with Margaret and Jack standing together, waving in the background, Jack wondering if he'd just sent them off to slaughter. "I should be with them." Margaret looked at Jack, "I chose to make this our final stand. If it goes bad, I should be there to take responsibility."

Margaret moved to face him. "No Jack, your place is here. We may call them boys, but those are three men we just sent on their way. Let them do what they've trained to do. They don't need their dad helping them anymore. You've fought your battles, let them fight this one. For all of us."

Jack looked away from Margaret and at the truck, growing smaller and smaller in the distance.

About the time the O'Briens' trailer was pulling out of Finger Lakes, Ron Dombrowski walked from his office over to Henry Livingston's. Since that phone call with Jack, Ron had been searching for some evidence someone had leaked information to Benson Realty. Thus far, every lead and every person he spoke to led the trail back to one individual, Henry Livingston. Ron had made up his mind, today marked the day he would confront him. As he approached Henry's office he noticed the door was shut. Ron stopped at Henry's assistant's desk. The woman sitting before him continued with her work, never glancing in Ron's direction.

She's as big an S.O.B. as he is, thought Ron. "Is our fearless leader in today?" he asked.

The assistant's answer was devoid of emotion. "If you mean Mr. Livingston, then no, he is out for the day. He'll be in on Monday."

"He's quite a worker isn't he?" Ron replied, trying to shake the unfeeling zombie Henry employed as his assistant. But she would have none of it and kept punching at her keyboard as if hearing nothing. Disgusted, Ron turned to leave, but as he did a handwritten message caught his eye. The name on the note was the evidence he had been searching for. The note read "call Bob from Benson Realty...a question about another property." Ron reached down and grabbed the note.

The assistant, finally acknowledging his presence, grabbed for the note. "Hey, you can't do that," she yelled.

Ron looked at the note and threw it back at her. "What business does he have with Benson Realty?" When no answer was forthcoming, Ron pressed on. "He's telling them what people owe isn't he? He's cutting some sort of deal with them?" The assistant refused to respond to the questions. "He is, isn't he? Isn't he?" At this point the assistant stood up and bustled to the ladies' room to escape. Ron considered following her in, but chose not to. That was enough for today; the mystery informant had been revealed. But Monday, when Henry returns, Ron thought to himself, we'll have a little face to face and see what the bastard has to say.

On his way back to his office, Ron realized that a confrontation surely wouldn't resolve anything, so the next question was who, above Henry, could he talk to? There wasn't anyone within the bank who he trusted to take action. Then it dawned on Ron. The newspapers would probably love such a story. *The big bank giving it to the little guy.* Maybe this weekend he should take the time to organize his facts and write it. On Monday, assuming the conversation with Henry goes nowhere, give the papers a call and fill them in on the machinations. A wry smile began to form on Ron's face. That should make things real interesting for him, he thought, exactly what a prick like him needs.

Pulling onto the grounds of Saratoga, Manny swung his head from one direction to the other in an effort not to miss anything. The forest green barns with slate roofs, the raked shedrows, and the flowers and ferns hanging from hooks in the wooden beams left little doubt this was no ordinary race track. He was in awe.

Their assigned stall was located across Union Avenue next to the Oklahoma training track. It was relatively quiet as they pulled in, the morning workouts completed. Most of the horsemen already stationed at the track took the opportunity to get a bite to eat, call owners, maybe catch a 15 minute nap, as they waited for the day's races to begin. Michael brought the truck to a halt and the three men got out and prepared to unload their precious cargo.

Manny walked Sing down the ramp, both with their eyes wide open trying to take it all in. Sing halted as he stepped on solid ground, put his nose to the ground and snorted several times. When everything checked out, he allowed Manny to continue walking him around, his ears pricked at attention.

"Well, it looks like he took the trip fine. Why don't you let him stretch his legs a minute and then put him in his stall," Michael said. "I'm going to go over and let them know we're here."

"Will do," replied Manny. Meanwhile, James unloaded the traps and prepared Sing's stall. Manny waited for James to emerge from inside the stall so as not to yell. "This place is something, isn't it James?"

James smiled and looked around. "It sure is. This is your first time here, isn't it?"

"Yeah, I've seen it on television a bunch of times, but never been here in person. It's even better in person."

James stopped what he was doing and leaned against the truck. He gazed toward the sky as if reflecting on things. "I got to come here as a kid with Dad. I'll never forget it. I was about 10 or so and Dad had a horse running in an allowance race. I kind of helped out, but mainly stayed with Mom. She took me all over the place, all through the track. You'll have to make sure to wander around while we're here. The place really is something special."

"How did your horse do?" asked Manny.

"To be honest I don't really remember. I don't think he won, I would remember that, but he may have finished in the money. Dad was happy so it couldn't have been too bad."

Manny pulled on Sing's shank and took him into his stall. Once Manny unhooked the shank, Sing immediately dropped his head and began sniffing around. From end to end he went, trying to determine who had been there before him. Who left this unfamiliar scent? Manny slid past the preoccupied animal, patting his backside on the way. As Manny hung Sing's shank on the stall door, he raised his eyebrows toward James. "Let's hope your dad feels the same after this race."

James laughed, "Don't fret about that yet, too much time. How about you, what's your first memory of Saratoga?"

"I found out what Saratoga was back in 1998. A bunch of us watched the Travers. They showed a lot of pictures of the paddock and the people at the picnic tables. It looked like a really cool place. A heck of a lot different than Tampa Bay Downs," Manny said reminiscing about the discovery.

"1998. Who won the Travers that year?" James asked.

Manny's voice picked up as he began to describe the scene. "That was the year Coronado's Quest, Victory Gallop and Raffie's Majesty all hit the wire together. I remember we were all screaming, no one could tell who won. I knew then, at some point I had to come see the place. It just took me a few more years than I thought."

Then the light bulb went on in James' head. "That's right, I remember that one now. Coronado's Quest ended up barely hanging on, Mike Smith draped on him like a blanket. That was a good one."

The two men stood there, each enjoying the memory. After a couple minutes of silence the mood changed back to the seriousness of the situation. "James," Manny asked, "what will happen to me if we lose tomorrow? I have no idea where I'll go or what I'll do."

James, like his father earlier that day, hadn't really comprehended what losing the farm meant to Manny. It was his home too and their business was Manny's livelihood also. It never occurred to James that Manny didn't really know where he stood. "Sorry Manny, it didn't dawn on me before. I guess no one talked to you about how you fit in, did they?" Manny put his head down and slowly shook it from side to side. "Hey listen," James said, "I know I speak for everyone in the family when I say this. You're one of us now, you're an O'Brien, the little Spanish brother we never had. I don't care what your name is or whose blood runs through your veins. And when this is over, no matter what happens, you'll be taken care of." After a brief pause, James continued with a hint of sarcasm. "Whether you like it or not, you're part of the family now."

Manny laughed and thought about what James had said. He was part of the family. It was true and to think otherwise would be ignoring the facts. They trusted him on Sing in the biggest race of their lives, Jack's gracious comments and faith in him, Margaret always treating him like he was one of their own and now James straight out telling him. He was one of them, accepted for who he was. "Thank you, James. That really means a lot to me."

James smiled and patted Manny on the back, his sincerity evident, "No problem."

Just then Michael came walking back to the barn. "Sing all set?" he asked. When James and Manny gave him an affirmative nod, he continued. "OK, why don't we go store our stuff first. After that we can come back here. I want to make sure at least one of us is here all the time. I also want to walk him over to the paddock once during the day. I figure it will help get him ready for tomorrow."

When it appeared Michael was through James told him it sounded good. Then he turned toward Manny. "I think Manny should stay with him the most. I mean, most horses have a goat or a donkey or something to put them at ease. Sing here has a Manny."

James and Manny laughed.

"Ha ha ha," Manny countered.

Michael rolled his eyes, "You two about ready? It's like working with two kids."

The comment had no effect as James and Manny were used to it. "Whose place is this we're staying at?" inquired James.

"An old trainer buddy of dad's. He's letting us use the house he rents for tonight and tomorrow. He's apparently volunteered to stay with someone else," said Michael. James and Manny agreed it was awful nice of him. Ready, the three climbed aboard the truck and headed for their temporary quarters at Bobby Gillner's house.

Once they'd chosen their respective rooms and dropped their bags in the dated Victorian on Ludlow Street, the boys returned to the track. They found Sing quietly watching the comings and goings, the previous trip to Saratoga undoubtedly having a positive effect on his behavior. After each scarfing down a Hatties Chicken Sandwich for lunch, they pulled Sing out of his stall and made their way toward the paddock. The races for the day were already being run so the crowd had grown, big and lively, which was exactly what Michael wanted.

"Nice size crowd today," Michael said, as they walked along the horse path, following the field for the fourth race. White fencing on either side of the path kept the pedestrians at bay and allowed for an unimpeded walk, though some fans liked to hang over rails periodically.

"It'll be about double this tomorrow," James said. "Probably good to get him some schooling today."

"That's what I was thinking when I planned this."

"How long do you want to stay in the paddock for?" asked James.

"The horses for this race will leave the paddock with about 10 minutes to post, I think we can leave after that, so he doesn't hear the race call. Let's go to the corner by the Big Red Spring, it's the quietest spot and hangout until they've left and then we can bring him back."

"Sounds like a plan."

As the paddock buzzed with activity, Michael, James, Manny and Sing hung near a tree in the far corner. "What do you think Manny?" said James.

"I *was* enjoying checking the place out and watching the horses and everything," he said, before pausing momentarily, "but that was until the jockeys came out. Seeing them – John Velezquez, Castellano, Bejarano... makes me feel kind of uneasy, enfermo."

"That's gonna be you tomorrow afternoon, buddy." James said, not realizing exactly how Manny felt.

"Please, I know."

Now grasping Manny's mood, James changed his tone. "Don't sweat it yet Manny, we've got a lot of time between now and then. Some great athlete once said, 'Don't worry about being nervous because you'll be nervous, turn it into energy...' Or something like that. Just keep your mind focused on Sing and making sure he stays calm. That's where your head needs to be. He needs to be our focus."

"Yeah, yeah, will do," Manny said, clearly a bit tense.

Michael looked at James who raised his eyebrows. Both realized then, they had more than just a horse to keep relaxed before the race. "Alright, they're heading out. Let's head back to the barn," said Michael.

The next few hours were spent watching and wagering on the remaining races, though always near the barn and Sing. Manny took James' words to heart and seemed dedicated to keeping Sing content, thus himself with it. Grooming, walking, grazing, talking, anything to pass the time and keep the mind occupied. And for the most part, it worked. Whether it's their beauty or their strength is unknown, but it's been said, the health of a man can be measured by the time he spends with his horse. Today, that benefit may have gone both ways.

The last race ended at 6:00 and Sing was resting comfortably, so the boys headed home, stopping at Boston Market for some takeout on the way. They ate in silence, each pre-occupied. Manny picked at his mashed potatoes and green beans, partially out of nerves and partially to make sure he made weight. After dinner Manny watched the US take on Honduras in World Cup qualifying match. Having grown up loving the sport, Manny sat glued to the television for a solid two hours, satisfied with the 1-1 draw as only a soccer fan can be. James and Michael, on the contrary, were bored to death, not caring a lick about soccer, deciding instead to go to the Parting Glass for a couple of pints. Michael, two Smithwicks. James, two pints of Guinness and an Anchor Steam.

The soccer game ended at 9:30, about the time Michael and James returned, the beer quenching their thirsts and quelling some of their nerves. All three were exhausted from the miles and stress of the road trip and ready for good night sleep, something they each prayed they could get.

Chapter 40

~

AUGUST 25 – TRAVERS DAY

Manny opened the door of the microwave, the only light to guide him around the kitchen. He searched in vain for the main switch, wondering why the builder hadn't put it in plain sight. When the lights suddenly came on he spun around to see James strolling in. "You up too?" James asked.

"Yeah, I didn't sleep worth a darn," replied Manny.

"I can understand that. I think we're all a little on edge. I'm anxious to get over there and get this day started."

"Me too," said Manny, "me too."

James looked at the clock on the microwave; it read 4:25. "Well, another 13 hours and it will be almost post time." The expected post time for the race was 5:37 p.m.

Looking at the clock Manny moaned, "Why do I think this is going to be the longest 13 hours of my life?"

James laughed "yeah, this could be a long one. The rest of the crew is due in about 11:30 this morning. Michael and I will come back here and meet them. You may want to just stay over at the track with Sing. No sense battling the traffic twice. I expect it'll be chaos around here when they arrive."

"That's probably a good idea," Manny agreed. "You want to head over now and get things started?"

"Sure. I'll tell Michael we're going and that he can meet us in an hour or so." Conveniently, the house they were staying in was close enough to the barn so that Michael could walk over once he was ready to go. After informing Michael, James and Manny drove over to feed and check on Sing. Sing appeared to have come through the night well, so James gave him his limited race-day rations, a scoop of oats and sweet feed. The plan was to have Manny take him out for a jog to stretch his legs once he'd had some time to digest breakfast. Merely a slow trot and another walk around the paddock was all they wanted, nothing major and hopefully nothing exciting.

Having patiently waited the long hour since feeding time, Manny sat comfortably atop Sing. They walked slowly toward their destination, a mile and an eighth dirt oval, encountering a strange aura as they went, one that seemed to arrive out of nowhere.

It was a warm and humid August morning, common to Upstate New York in late summer, where the temperature and dew point come together. The result is a fine mist that hangs in the air and today the entire track was cloaked in it. It felt eerie and calming all at the same time. This morning's activities were as busy as any other, but a silence hung in the air as if attached to the mist itself. No one dared speak too loudly or move too quickly, lest they upset Mother Nature. It appeared as though she was still sleeping, not ready to wake and face the day's events.

Horses appeared from the mist, galloping, and then just as suddenly they disappeared. Only the sound of their hooves pounding the dirt let you know of their existence. In the distance the grandstand's lights gave off a supernatural glow revealing a faint outline to the massive structure, silent and ghostly.

As far as Manny was concerned the mist made for a perfect morning. It allowed him to hide from the terrifying reality he faced, like a child pulling the blanket over his head during a storm. Not that anyone would pay attention to the two unknowns making their way toward the track. They were one more horse and rider out for a morning workout, nondescript and unrecognizable.

Arriving at the track's entrance Manny and Sing waited for a set of Todd Pletcher's to go by, like soldiers, they marched past, big and imposing, like Gods. Sing stood quietly, waiting for Manny's signal to proceed. Once clear, Manny urged him forward. Slowly they trotted their way around the oval, an easy jog, just enough to loosen up. Sing moved smoothly and attentively, also intrigued by the mystic scene, yet not uneasy. He, like Manny, took comfort in his companion, each knowing and trusting the other, a well-trained team having done this same thing countless times before. Their unusual bond, forged over months and months of daily contact.

Feeling at ease and lulled by the rhythmic beat of Sing's hoofs hitting the ground, Manny reflected on his life, where he'd been and where he was going. The "been" part was known, but where he was going was shrouded in as much mist as the air in front of him. It was hard to fathom in a matter of hours he would be riding this horse he'd grown so fond of, for a family he dared almost call his own, with the fate of the farm on the line. The mist, aiding his subconscious, made it feel like a dream. He looked down at Sing's muscled neck and chest, running his hand through Sing's mane. Manny knew it was a moment to savor. It was a once in a lifetime event with a once in a lifetime horse. He had learned long ago there were no certainties in life and the winds of fortune were sometimes cruel. His years had brought him moments of great joy and tremendous sorrow. Today had the potential to add one more moment to his list. One thing was assured; it would not be just another day. Only whether it ended in joy or sorrow remained to be seen.

When Manny was satisfied Sing had done enough, the pair walked back across Union Avenue to their barn. They returned to Sing's stall to find Michael and James anxiously waiting. "How'd he do?" inquired Michael.

"Good," Manny answered. "He felt real good, didn't spook at anything. Acted like a complete professional."

"Excellent," Michael said relieved. James held Sing as Manny dismounted and Michael ran his hands up and down Sing's legs. He felt no heat and saw nothing amiss. "Let's give him a bath and then let him graze a bit. After that, in his stall until the race."

James nodded his understanding, "Sounds good."

"I'll go get the bucket and hose," Manny said, as Michael unhooked Sing's girth. James, standing face to face with Sing, carefully pulled the bridle from his mouth, leaving the reins still around his neck. He then put on Sing's halter, the shank already attached. Sing, for his part, stood motionless, even graciously lowering his head. Once the halter was secured, James removed the reins from around Sing's neck. Moments later, Manny returned and he and Michael began soaping up their star player. Sing paid no attention to his bathers, he was busy trying to grab the shank from James.

"Hey Manny," James said, "How do you get this horse to stop. He's driving me nuts with this."

Manny smiled, refusing to make eye contact with James. He didn't lie well and knew James would call him on it if he saw his face. "Uh, I don't know. He never does that to me."

"You serious? He does it with me all the time." Manny didn't respond, instead he kept moving toward Sing's hind end and away from James, a faint smile remaining on his face.

With Michael and Manny bathing Sing together it didn't take long before the job was complete. Once over, Manny relieved James of holding Sing and walked him over to some green grass around the trees. Michael and James waited by the stall, admiring Sing. Freshly washed, his copper colored coat exhibited a nice sheen. He was fit, ready and looked like a million. After about 15 minutes of grazing Michael called them back and Sing went quietly into his stall. Their jobs complete, Michael and James returned to the house to shower and prepare for their families' arrival, leaving Manny to sit alone with Sing, pondering what the day might bring.

About the time their two sons were driving back to their temporary Saratoga quarters, Jack and Margaret were wrapping up the morning activities as fill-ins at Finger Lakes. After this, they planned to return home and take care of the horses there. Once those horses were tended to they needed to run to the local farm and garden to get supplies. It was a nice busy morning and that was no coincidence. Jack and Margaret knew the race would be hanging over them all day. The more time they had to think about it, the slower the day would go.

"We all set here?" asked Margaret.

"I think so," Jack responded, looking up and down the barn area for anything out of place. "Let's head back and take care of the others." Margaret agreed and began walking toward the truck. "I'm curious how things are going for the boys."

"So am I," added Margaret.

"Maybe we should call down there?" Jack said in a tone that was more pleading than it was inquiring.

Margaret knew that wasn't necessary. "If anything has happened, we'll have a message on the machine when we get home. If not, then we can just wait until this afternoon. If we haven't heard anything by 1 or 2 o'clock, then we can give them a call. Besides, we don't have much planned for this afternoon and Lord knows we're going to need something to occupy us."

She was correct as usual, thought Jack. "You're probably right. I'm sure it's going fine." At least he hoped so.

Back at their borrowed house James and Michael were slowly getting ready for the impending arrival of their loved ones. Neither found any real need to rush. Like Jack and Margaret, they knew that they had a lot of time to go before the race and waiting around doing nothing could drive a sane man crazy. Michael used the down time to read the *Racing Form*, or moreover, study the *Racing Form*. He searched for any advantage against his competition. What was their weakness? Who were the he front runners, who sat back, who closed from way back. If there was a way to beat them, he'd find it buried in the numbers.

James on the other hand tried to focus on something besides the race. He read too, but let his mind wander into the world of David Baldacci's *The Hit*. Who was the good guy? Who could be trusted? Those unanswered questions occupying all his thought. Right up until 11:30 that is, when a pair of vans pulled into the driveway. Then, mayhem.

The kids ran in and began wandering the house checking out their new accommodations. Michael and James went out to meet their wives and help carry the suitcases. As James reached Lauren, he noticed she had an unsatisfied look on her face. "This is it? I was kind of hoping we'd be staying in one of those Victorian mansions on Union Avenue or North Broadway. Those are some nice houses."

"True, but those weren't quite in the budget. We opted for the economy Victorian instead. Didn't want you getting accustomed to a life of luxury since we might be living in a shack after this."

Lauren laughed, "Uh huh, I hear you."

Meanwhile, Michael stood staring at the back of the van. "How many suitcases did you bring?"

"Hey, you never know what you're going to need. I like to come prepared," Janet countered.

"You realize this is only one overnight don't you?"

"Of course, I would have added at least another suitcase for a second night." Michael shook his head and yanked the giant suitcase from the back of the van.

As Janet walked toward the house Lauren came up beside her. "They're all the same aren't they?" eliciting a laugh from Janet.

From behind Lauren's van, James struggled with a similar problem. "Hey Honey," he yelled, "what did you pack in here, rocks? This thing weighs a ton. Probably going to throw my back out."

Lauren looked at Janet before yelling back to James. "Stop whining you nancy. I tossed that thing into the van with one hand." The two women stopped and listened for a reply. Only a small mumble could be heard. "That's what I thought," added Lauren with a laugh.

Once all the luggage made it in they wasted no time in getting dressed for the big day. Michael helped little Jack tie his tie, which Jack insisted he must wear for such an occasion, while Janet fastened a bow in Mary's hair as a final touch. Win or lose, they were going to look good. As Michael was kneeling in front of little Jack tightening his tie Jack looked straight at his dad. "Dad," Jack said as if preparing to enlighten his father.

"Yes," replied Michael.

"I think we're going to win today and Grandma and Grandpa will keep the farm."

Michael looked directly into Jack's eyes and then at Janet, who had stopped what she was doing astonished at what Jack had said. "Well, don't get your hopes too high Bud, this is going to be a very tough race. I'm not sure how much of a chance we have."

Undeterred by his dad's words Little Jack continued. "I know Dad, but I have a feeling he'll win."

Michael stood up having finished his work on Jack's tie. He smiled at Jack, "Let's hope you're right Bud, that would be great wouldn't it."

"Yeah," answered Jack letting out a big grin, "it would be great."

Janet and Mary walked over to where Michael and Jack stood. Janet smiled and looked down at her young son, touching his face with her hand. She knelt down and hugged him without saying a word.

Back at the barn Sing relaxed, alternating between napping and looking out his stall door. A groom walked by at a pace that implied he was in no hurry. He carried a bucket in one hand and had a halter slung over his shoulder. It was the first person Manny had seen for nearly half an hour. The shuffling of the passerby's feet caused one of Sing's stable mates to nicker, the first break in a prolonged silence. Manny sat in front of Sing's stall with a book in hand. Reading Manny found, like Michael and James, was a great way to entrench yourself in another world while putting off the reality of your own. Manny's choice, The Bourne Identity, chronicled the story of a man with amnesia trying desperately to uncover who he is. Engulfed in the action packed storyline, Manny didn't even notice the man walking toward him until he was right on top of him.

"So this is the long shot in the Travers today," the man asked.

Manny didn't exactly like the way it was put, but it was true. "Yup, that's Sing So Long."

Turning away from Sing and toward Manny, the questionable newcomer extended his arm to shake hands. "I'm Sean Clancy with the Saratoga Special. I was wondering who exactly this horse was. I tried to track you guys down yesterday, but you hadn't arrived yet. Do you think he has a chance?"

"Nice to meet you, I'm Manny Hernandez," Manny said, shaking hands. "We didn't get in until late morning yesterday. And as to whether or not I think he has a chance. Yes, I think he has an excellent chance," responded Manny with a certain confidence in his voice.

A look of surprise came over the journalist. "Oh, that was the other thing I was wondering about. Who is this jockey? It's too late for the Travers edition, but do you mind if I ask you a couple questions?"

"I guess not," answered Manny, not quite as confident as before.

"I saw you only had a handful of mounts all year. I was curious why, but I can see by your size you're probably a little bit too big to make the weight all the time."

"Yeah, I rode at Tampa for a couple years when I was younger, but I was in a bad spill and was out for a while. While I was rehabbing my knee, I grew a little more and put some weight on. And I guess things changed inside me. It didn't feel the same when I was ready to come back." Manny cut himself off, uncomfortable with how much he was sharing. After a brief pause, he began again. "Now, I couldn't get below 120 no matter how hard I tried." Manny shrugged his shoulders, "Part of me would love to ride full time, but I know there's just no way."

"You should consider becoming a steeplechase jockey," Sean quickly countered. "I used to be one before I retired and started doing this full time."

"You mean go over those jumps," Manny gasped, "no way, you have to be crazy to do that."

Sean laughed at the comment. "Why do you think I stopped and started this?" Manny smiled as Sean continued with the interview. "So, you really think you guys have a shot today?"

Manny reflected for a second, wanting to be sure to adequately convey his thoughts. Wondering if he was talking to a horseman or a journalist, Manny gazed toward Sing's stall as he began. "I don't think Sing has run anywhere near his best race yet. We all believe he can run with the best 3-year-olds out there. The only problem has been his inability to settle himself. He always seems to work himself up. Sometimes it's before the race, sometimes during."

Taking a second to understand what the young rider had said, Sean figured that he'd just answered another of the questions. "I take it then, that's why you're riding him today?"

Manny was surprised at the interviewer's sharpness. "Basically yes. I ride him every morning and he seems to do well with me. I don't know what it is, but hopefully it means he will run his best race ever later today."

"Well I noticed his workout the other day was phenomenal."

"Yeah, he went real easy. Hopefully I won't do anything to mess things up during the race," Manny added.

Sean noticed the jockey had a tremendous amount of faith in the horse, but not as much in himself. "Hey, don't worry about yourself. You know the horse and that's important. It's a long race, keep him relaxed and out of trouble. When it's time, let him run. Best horse usually wins."

Manny smiled at the ex-steeplechase jockey turned newspaper man. "It does sound easy when you say it like that."

Extending his arm one more time, Sean shook Manny's hand. "You'll do fine," he said adding a smile. "Trust me, I'm a writer." This in turn brought a smile to Manny's face. "And good luck. I'll be rooting for you." "Thanks."

Back at the house James and Lauren were almost set to go. Sydney had been readied first and was now playing with Mary. Lauren glanced at James and asked him to zip up the back of her sundress. When James didn't respond Lauren tilted her head slightly and slowly repeated the question. This time James acknowledged and came behind her. "Is everything OK honey?" she asked. "You seem a little lost in thought."

"Yeah, yeah everything is fine. I was just thinking about Manny."

"What about?" Lauren asked.

"Well, you, Janet and all the kids have come in and are with us. Manny is basically alone and doesn't have anyone. I'm worried he may feel left out." James paused for a moment before continuing. "He has a heavy burden to carry for this family today and I don't want it overwhelming him. He's a great guy and I feel like he should be with us."

Just then two screaming girls came running through. Lauren looked at James, "Yes, this surely would have a calming effect on him."

James laughed, "not at this moment, but you know what I mean."

"I do," she said. "But you have to remember he grew up differently than we did. He spent a lot of time by himself and is probably pretty comfortable being alone. I would think joining this whole group wouldn't do anything more than unnerve him."

"Maybe you're right. I just want to make sure he understands he's not alone and we're here if he needs us."

"James, something tells me he already knows," Lauren said. She took a look at James, straightened his hair and stepped back. "There, now you look ready to go win yourself a Travers."

Chapter 41

"Manny?" James said, not seeing Manny sitting in his usual spot in front of the stall.

Suddenly a head popped out of Sing's stall. "Hey James, what are you doing here?"

"I thought I would come by and relieve you for a while. With all the kids and wives squawking, it's maddening. I needed to get away for a bit and figured you may want to leave and get something to eat. Michael can handle the crew for the time being."

"Sure," Manny said, not exactly knowing what to do with himself, knowing there was no way he could eat.

"It's about 12:30 now. Do you want to come back in about an hour or so?"

"Yeah, that sounds good. I'll see you then."

With James standing guard and Sing resting quietly, Manny decided to take a walk. Perhaps it'll be good to be away from the track for a while, he figured, occupy his head with other Saratoga sights. And just down Union Avenue, Manny found Congress Park. A wonderful little place nestled in the middle of town. Inside its borders lies several peaceful ponds, a couple of monuments to those who'd served their country and a building from the 1800's that was once a raucous casino, but now serves as a quiet museum. The park's tranquility belies the commotion that surrounds Travers Day in Saratoga. It's the perfect spot to stop and think. To let your thoughts drift back to days gone by. To shelter yourself from the mayhem. The sound of water spraying from a pond's fountain and the soft quacks from the park's inhabitants provided the perfect backdrop to help relax Manny's racing mind.

He meandered about the park for a while before deciding to sit down on one of the park benches. As he sat down he took note of a mother and her young child. A little boy, probably no more than 3 or 4 years old Manny figured, was running after some of the ducks. His mom, sitting on a blanket in the grass, was busy talking on her cell phone. Faint memories surfaced of Manny and his mom. He couldn't remember an actual event; it was more of a feeling, the warm feeling of his mom holding his hand as they walked along the countryside. It made Manny feel safe, secure. The sound of a child's screech broke Manny from his daydream. A smile came across his face watching the scene unfold. The boy grabbed his mother's phone from her hands and darted for the pond and threw the phone in. Mom, in utter horror, froze not knowing what to do next. The boy, proud of his accomplishment, began a celebratory dance. It reminded Manny of a football player after a touchdown. A chase ensued ending in a swift spank. That was followed with Mom wading into the pond in an attempt to salvage her phone. Manny found it all quite comical, but with the episode concluded and having seen everything in the park, Manny figured it was a good time to wander back toward the track, maybe try to eat something and watch the early races.

A bite to eat, thought Manny. Tough question. He had been diligent with his weight and knew he had at least a couple pounds to spare, but would his nerves allow it? They still had over 4 hours to go and his stomach already felt tight. He put his hand over his stomach and rubbed it gently, wincing as he did so. Why couldn't they make this race earlier, Manny wondered, I'm not going to make it until 5:30.

On his way up the hill leaving the park, Manny found the day's copy of the Saratoga Special and thought about his new friend Sean Clancy. The front cover displayed pictures of the Kentucky Derby winner The Sarge and the Preakness winner Elusive Empire. The caption read "The Grudge Match." The two horses had run first and second in the Derby and Preakness, each winning one. After two grueling races, neither decided to run in the Belmont which was won by Go At Dawn. Unfortunately for Go At Dawn, a training injury sidelined him shortly after his victory and would keep him out of action until the fall. Manny was thankful that Go At Dawn was not available to race, but it was little consolation knowing he had to face the Derby and Preakness winners. Both horses took some time off and made their comebacks in early August. Elusive Empire won the Haskell at Monmouth and The Sarge won the Jim Dandy right here at Saratoga. Now they were set to renew their rivalry – The Grudge Match. Five more competitive horses decided to challenge the big boys. Manny and Sing made eight. A daunting task. Manny continued reading the article as he walked down Union Ave. The article detailed the feats of all those involved, especially the top two. It wasn't until the very last line that Manny saw his horse's name. "Also running will be long shot Sing So Long trained by Michael O'Brien and ridden by Manny Hernandez." Manny stopped walking and said aloud, as if Sing were standing next to him, "We're an also ran before the race has even started." Also ran being the term used to describe the horses who don't finish in the top three of a given race. Manny knew what they thought of his horse and it angered him, but he began to think maybe they were right. The accomplishments of the other entrants were hard to ignore. What real chance did they have?

As he stood on the corner a man on his way to the races stopped and said "that big green one was Sam Riddle's house. He owned the greatest horse ever, Man o' War." At first Manny had no idea what this man was talking about, but then realized, the way he had been standing made it look like he was staring at this giant house. Manny just smiled and nodded. Man o' War, now there was a racehorse. He only lost one race in his entire career. Then it hit Manny like a thousand-pound hammer. As if he suddenly had some sort of epiphany. The only race Man o' War lost was to a horse named Upset right here at Saratoga. It helped tag Saratoga as The Graveyard of Favorites, along with coining a sports phrase used to this day. The racing gods were speaking to him. This was the place where it was supposed to come together. *This* racetrack, *this* day, *this* horse. It seemed as if his entire life since his father's death had been leading him somewhere, but he could never figure out where. Perhaps, this was it, this was his destiny. The convergence of his lost life, the O'Briens' hard luck and one magical horse. Those lingering doubts he'd felt abruptly disappeared. An air of confidence began to fall upon him. No one gave them a chance, he thought. But they had the horse, a very good one and today he would prove it. As far as Manny was concerned, he and Sing were about to give the horse racing world the shock of their lives.

Renewed, Manny began to make his way along the track fence toward the main entrance. From the fence line he watched a father and his son getting a drink of water from the Big Red Spring, a Saratoga icon. Water comes from the natural springs below the ground fresh for the patrons to enjoy, which very few really do and the boy, after taking a large gulp, quickly understood why. The sulfur taste is hard for some to stomach. Realizing his mistake, the boy spit out what he had not already swallowed. Of course he did so right into his father's face, who'd made the mistake of kneeling in front of his son. The father jumped back, shaking his head and pulling his wet shirt from his chest. Manny broke into laughter; he couldn't wait until he had a family. He longed for the day he would be surrounded by a wife and children. He wasn't sure how many children, but at least four he figured. "That will have to wait," Manny said to himself. "Today, I have only one purpose." Of course, Manny thought, I don't even have a girlfriend and that's a whole other issue. With that, Manny passed through the turnstiles and re-entered the hallowed grounds of Saratoga Race Track.

As Manny neared the barn, he was surprised to see Michael, rather than James, standing nearby. "What happened to James?"

"He just went back to the seats. I wasn't going to let him be the only one to get some peace and quiet."

Manny laughed. Understandable. "How's Sing?"

"He seems fine. How are you doing?"

"I'm a bit nervous," Manny said smiling, "but I'm OK."

Satisfied with the current state of affairs, Michael said goodbye to Manny and began walking back to his seat. Glancing down at his watch he noted the time, 1:40, two hours before they would need to begin prepping for the race and about four until the race itself. Still a long way to go, he thought. He pulled out his cell phone and dialed his parents. He knew his dad was probably chomping at the bit.

Jack answered the phone on the first ring.

"Dad, it's Michael. How's everything back there?"

In a voice that sounded of equal measures of anxiety and irritation, Jack jumped right in. "About time you called, everything here is fine, what's the story *there?*"

Realizing he should have called earlier, Michael apologized. "Sorry about that, it's been a busy day so far. But everything is going well. Sing is resting in his stall and hasn't acted up yet. Manny is spending a lot of time with him, so assuming you guys are right, that should help. I'm on my way back to the seats from checking on him now."

"Good, good," Jack said, his voice changing to a calmer tone. "We've got to get that horse to the track without any problems. We can't afford to have him riled. Not today."

"I know Dad, I know. We're doing everything we can to keep him quiet, trust me."

"I know you are." Not wanting to harp on what everyone already knew, Jack decided he'd said enough. "Well if anything comes up give me a call, I'm not going anywhere."

"OK Dad, will do. If not before, I'm sure I'll talk to you after the race."

"Alright," Jack paused before continuing, "and Michael."

"Yeah?"

"Not that saying this has helped yet, but, good luck."

"Thanks Dad." Michael closed his phone and entered the clubhouse to wait out the next couple hours.

Looking at the clock, Jack sighed, way too much time before the race. He looked at Margaret, "I'm going out to ride the tractor."

"Where?" queried Margaret.

"I have no idea, around I guess. Hopefully something will need fixing. Otherwise I have no idea what I'll do for the next four hours." With that Jack walked out the door.

Margaret not knowing what she would do scanned the kitchen for something in need of work. She found nothing. "OK, well," she mumbled, then it struck her, "with Daniel and Nicole coming over maybe I'll make some sort of dessert for us." Having come up with something to occupy her she smiled; that should keep me busy, at least for a little while anyway.

The only O'Brien who properly planned for the long boring wait was Sarah. She had managed to schedule work at the tack shop from 8:00 this morning until 4:00 this afternoon. Saturdays were always busy so it should keep her mind from wandering toward the dark thoughts. She took a peek at her watch; 2:00, two hours to go. So far, a lot of foot traffic had passed through the shop and hopefully the next two hours would be the same. The way she figured it, if she leaves work at 4:00 it will take about 30 minutes to get home. That would only leave one hour before the race and they would have race coverage on television to help take up that hour. Glancing around the shop she noticed a couple eyeing new saddles. Here we go, she thought as she moved toward them, back to work.

Manny looked down at his watch, knowing he had to be in the jocks' room at least two hours before post time, it was exactly three o'clock. He stood up and stretched his arms, then turned toward the stall to see Sing staring right back at him. "I don't know what you think, but this has to be the slowest day ever, eh boy." Sing offered no response. The day slowly crept by, luckily Manny's book, which happened to be both good and long, helped him keep his mind elsewhere. A mind that remained positive, ready to ride.

The tote board standing in the middle of the Saratoga infield posted 3:20 as the time of day. James, draining a last gulp of a draft beer, turned toward Michael and pointed toward the board. "Looks like time to go."

Although already aware of the time, having been counting the minutes, Michael looked up as if to confirm. "Alright, let's get going."

Both men faced their respective family members and made sure they were going to be fine for the next two hours. The wives assured them they would. "OK, we'll see you just before the race," declared James. They leapt down the stairs and headed toward the barn to prepare Sing for the biggest race of his life.

Manny got out of his chair when he saw Michael and James coming down the shedrow. "Hey Manny, we'll take over from here," Michael said.

"Sounds good. I think I'll head for the jocks' room and get changed." Patting Sing's head, James asked "how's he doing?"

"He's been as quiet as can be. He slept for a while. Been looking out the stall door the rest of the time," answered Manny.

James smiled at Manny "how are *you* doing?"

Letting out a deep breath, Manny replied, "up until this point I've been fine, but with you guys showing up." Manny paused and made a funny face. "I'm not sure I'm feeling so good."

James laughed and Michael smirked. "Don't worry," James said, "go get dressed and try to keep yourself busy for the next hour and a half. We'll meet you in the paddock, try to come out early, with your valet, couldn't hurt for you to be around Sing for as long as possible. And you might want to move quickly, I think you're supposed to be checking in in about 5 minutes."

"Alright, I'll see you in the paddock." Manny picked up his book and rubbed Sing's nose, giving him a long, sincere look. He was Sing's groom, his exercise rider and today, his jockey. Manny turned from the stall and headed to the jocks' room. There was just over two hours to post time.

After tooling around for as long as he possibly could, Jack came inside and headed for the shower. Another vain attempt at passing time. They say the shower is a great place to think and although Jack wasn't so sure about that, a random thought did enter his mind while there. Once he'd dried off and changed, his random thought sent him into their dark and dusty attic. Carefully he stepped from spot to spot, trying hard not to crush anything. Their attic, like most, overflowed with what some called memories and others called junk. Scanning the contents, Jack waited for a clue before proceeding on. In the distance, he noticed a baseball bat leaning against a dusty old box. He looked down and visually marked the path he would take. Step by step he made his way over to the box.

He grabbed the bat and looked at the barrel, Easton, 28.5 ounces. Taking a firm grip, Jack held it as if ready to take a swing, poised and ready, then, inexplicably put it back down. Taking a closer look at the label, he opened the box the bat had been leaning on, causing a small cloud of dust to blow up at him. He waved his hand in front of his face and coughed, trying to dispel the cloud. Once the dust settled, Jack gazed inside. Little league supplies from many years ago. Memories. He reached in and began extricating the contents. Each item contained a small piece of his sons' childhood. Jack smiled, they were good times. He laughed thinking of the many times he yelled at Michael, James and especially Daniel – a flower picker instead of a ball player – to pay attention. Ah Daniel, it didn't take long to know that boy wasn't going to be an athlete. He reached down again and pulled out his old coach's cap. He smacked the dust off with his free hand and put it on. It fit snuggly, just as it had back then. It used to be a good luck charm. He took it off his head and studied at it, then turned from the box and began retracing his steps out of the attic, the hat still in his hand, and him hoping there was a little luck left in her.

Inside the jocks' room, Manny wandered about aimlessly. He'd signed in and went over to his assigned valet's corner, made sure all his gear was there and then wondered 'what do I do now?' The facilities were much nicer than at Finger Lakes or Tampa, but it was still a locker room, that place where athletes try desperately to pass time before doing what it is they came to do. For a jockey riding nine races a day, it was nothing more than a dress room, for a kid riding his first Travers, it was a torture chamber. At one of the numerous tables filling the room, four jockeys played a round of Racehorse Rummy, the game in full flight, the players' animated banter making up most of the room's noise. Manny walked over and watched for a couple minutes. He didn't know the participants, and though they made eye contact with him, none made any effort to acknowledge his presence. Manny was an outsider, a newbie passing through who didn't merit recognition. It didn't take more than a couple minutes of being ignored before Manny started to feel awkward, out of place. The room, though plenty big enough, began to feel tiny and Manny claustrophobic. His first thought was to leave, go somewhere, but where? Just then, a side door opened and in strolled Bejarano and Velazquez. Manny wasn't sure where the door led to, but he went to check it out. To his surprise, and delight, it opened to the little fenced courtyard available only to valets and jockeys. Stepping outside, the fresh air provided an immediate relief. He found an empty picnic table and sat down, opening *The Daily Racing Form* for another look at the Travers, making mental notes of inside speed, stalkers, closers.

It was not more than a few minutes past 5:00 when Daniel and Nicole entered the kitchen at the farm. As they walked to the living room Daniel spotted three pies sitting on the kitchen counter. How many people are coming over, he wondered? Once they entered the living room he was surprised to see his dad already there, his eyes glued to the television. Margaret came and greeted the pair. "Hey Mom, what's with all the pies?"

Margaret waved her hand at him "don't ask."

Shrugging his shoulders, Daniel pointed Nicole to the opposite end of the couch from where Sarah sat. She was also watching the coverage. Realizing he couldn't get anyone's direct attention, he decided to throw out the question for anyone to answer. "Have they shown them yet?"

Again to his surprise, it was Jack who answered. "Bits and pieces, but you can't tell much. I'm hoping to get a better look so we can see how he's doing."

"How much time before the race?" Daniel asked.

This time Sarah answered. "About a half hour."

Daniel sat back and began to watch the action. Within a couple minutes he decided he couldn't just sit there any longer. He stood up and walked toward the kitchen. Looking at his mom as he went, he asked "What kind of pies are those anyway?"

Chapter 42

⁓

MICHAEL HAD BEEN DREADING THE walk from the barn to the paddock for days despite having made the exact same walk the day before. Today though, he expected there would be about twice as many people, which meant double the number hanging over the fence gawking at the horses as they went passed. And that meant a much greater chance something would go wrong. As they marched along, Michael realized the crowd was even larger than he had envisioned. He swore the entire racing world was standing along the fence line watching the procession. Michael stood to Sing's left as they walked, holding the shank in his right hand and a bucket and sponge in his left. James was stationed to Sing's right holding a second shank. Up until now, Michael had been suspect of exactly how much Manny contributed to Sing remaining calm, but at this moment, all he could think was how nice it would be to have him walking alongside.

Further up the line, Michael spotted a young boy abruptly hop up onto the fence. Fortunately, it happened in front of Elusive Empire, who was surrounded by an entire entourage of grooms and assistants. The horse's trainer barked at the boy, indicating in no uncertain terms to get his backside off the fence, which the boy did with a look of fear in his eyes. Not that it bothered Michael any. Whatever the guy said worked and that's all that counts. That it terrified the boy and upset his mother meant nothing to Michael. Only Sing mattered.

The walk continued ever so slowly for what seemed a growing eternity. But the crowd, aside from the boy, was respectful of the high-strung

Thoroughbreds and stood quietly. Finally, Michael saw the paddock in the distance. There it is, not too much further he mumbled. Then without warning they stopped. Michael felt himself heating up and wanted to yell to keep them moving, they were so close. But he knew to yell was to risk setting off Sing and he surely didn't want to be the one to screw things up. Not to mention it probably wouldn't do an ounce of good. He tightened his grip on the shank, anticipating trouble. "Can you see anything?" he asked James, his voice stressed.

James tilted his head back and forth. "No, nothing at all."

A few of the horses began to dance, but Sing remained quiet, his ears pricked, surveying the activity. Then whatever it was that stopped them cleared and they began to move again. One by one the horses entered the paddock and with it a safe distance from the mass of spectators, the clicking, like crickets, of the photographers' cameras. Once inside, Michael breathed a healthy sigh of relief. So far so good, he said to James, who also let out a large sigh.

In the corner of the jockey's room Manny sat buttoning up his white and green silks. Other than a casual hello from some of the other jockeys, Manny hadn't spoken to anyone. As he sat there alone he noticed, out of the corner of his eye, a figure approaching him. He slowly spun around to find a very recognizable retired jockey standing beside him. It was Pat Day. The Hall of Fame jockey who'd retired several years ago and was now an ambassador for the Race Track Chaplaincy.

"How are you doing son?" the Hall of Famer asked as he sat down beside Manny.

Already nervous enough about the race, Manny was barely able to speak to one of the most famous jockeys he'd ever seen ride. "Ahh, OK I guess. I'm actually a little bit nervous."

Pat chuckled at the comment. "Yeah that's understandable. I used to get good and nervous before a big race."

Amazed such a great jockey, known to the racing world as "Patient Pat" because of his ability to sit chilly on a horse until just the right time, could get nervous before a race. "You used to get nervous?" Manny asked.

"Sure," Pat poignantly replied. "I think anyone who says they don't is either lying or just doesn't care."

Manny was shocked at this revelation. "What about being nauseous? Did you ever feel nauseous?"

Laughing, the ex-jockey patted Manny on the back. "Yes, that too. In fact," Pat snickered, "I remember before my first Derby, my legs were shaking so much I could barely stand. Oh boy was I ever nervous." As Manny reflected, Pat shared various stories of other times he'd been terrified. It seemed what Manny was feeling was as normal as riding itself. Focus on the horse, Pat said, shift your thoughts away from everything but the horse. Pat ended the conversation by offering him some words of encouragement. "Just remember, you're out there to ride *your* race. You can't be afraid to make a mistake, don't second guess yourself. Trust your instincts and you'll be fine."

After listening to what the veteran of more than 8,800 winning rides said, Manny thanked him.

"It was a pleasure meeting you," Pat said. "Good luck and God bless you."

Finishing buttoning his silks, Manny gazed at the clock on the wall. He still had 10 minutes before they clanged the bell that traditionally called the jockeys from their quarters. No sense waiting until then, he thought. He put on his helmet, grabbed his whip and headed for the exit, as ready as he was ever going to be.

Michael stood by one of the large elm trees as James walked Sing around the stone dust path that circled the trees. In the distance James could see an odds board. Without bothering to look at what Sing's current odds were, he searched for the display that listed how many minutes to post. He finally found it; 25 minutes to go. It had been a long day to this point, but nothing had gone awry....yet. They needed another uneventful 15 minutes to get Sing and Manny to the track.

The sight of Manny strolling toward the tree threw Michael at first. He scanned the rest of the paddock but didn't see any other jockeys. "Aren't you a little early?"

"Yeah, but I was going stir crazy in there. I figured it would be more interesting out here."

"I'm not sure I'd call interesting, but it's definitely a sight to see," Michael said, glad that Manny was again close to Sing, but still unable to calm his own strained nerves. As they stood side by side, Michael stared intently at his horse walking in circles in front of him and Manny stared just as intently at the throngs of people now lining the paddock.

'What a mass of humanity,' thought Manny. 'There must be thousands of them. I never rode in front of a crowd like this at Tampa.' Nor had he ever been to a venue that drew this number of spectators. He couldn't help but marvel, and be frightened, at the sight. This is the big league, exciting and intimidating. Contemplating the sheer numbers of people watching can unnerve the less confident. Feeling himself becoming more nervous, Manny repeatedly told himself, remember what Mr. Day said, ride your race, trust your instincts. Confidence is the key to making good judgments. Manny knew this and tried to keep his from wavering. When he looked at Sing he felt good. When he looked at the crowd and the competition he faltered. It made him wonder if his decision to come out early wasn't such a good one.

Like some form of compulsive disorder, Michael couldn't help but look again at the odds board for the minutes until post time. Two minutes since the last time he checked. Which was two minutes since the time before that. He knew he had to relax, but he couldn't. There was too much at stake. Sing was about to face the toughest field he'd ever seen. If he were to act up, lose focus, expend virtually any non-productive energy at all, the race would be doomed before the start. Michael had worried since arriving in Saratoga, better than 30 hours ago. The pressure seemed to increase as each hour passed, starting with this morning's workout. They had made it through the morning, through the day, to the paddock and now were within minutes of getting him to the track, all without incident. Like a pressure cooker that kept on building, the intensity was becoming nearly unbearable. A slight breeze kicked up and Michael felt it cool him off. It was only then he realized how much he was sweating. It's warm out, but not *that* bad, he thought. God, when are they going to get them out there? He looked again at the board.

Under normal circumstances James probably would have played with Sing as they walked circles around the trees. Maybe grab his tongue, or play a game of tug Sing seems to enjoy so much, or just fiddle with him some. But today was not the day to risk Sing's unpredictable behavior. If something went wrong, he, like Michael, didn't want it to be for something stupid he did. So professionalism ruled the day. He walked, patted Sing gently and spoke to him quietly, doing everything he could to keep him relaxed. And it worked, or appeared to anyway. But then again, it could be all the activity keeping him occupied and have nothing to do with me, thought James. Either way, it doesn't matter, as long as he remains like this, we'll be good to go.

As James contemplated the mental workings of his horse, a crew of valets entered the paddock, saddles and cloths in hand. Time to tack up the competitors. For most horses, it was no big deal, and it never bothered Sing before. But this was Sing and all bets were off. So Michael took the saddle cloth from the valet and gently placed it over Sing's back, being careful not to make any sudden movements. Then, as softly as possible, he laid the saddle atop the cloth, just behind the withers. All the while, James kept a firm hold of Sing and Manny stood just to his right, slowly stroking his head. As Michael cinched up the girth, Sing continued to look around, oblivious to Michael. After confirming the saddle was on tight, Michael motioned to James, his job done and another possible calamity averted.

James took Sing and began walking around the tree once again. As they finished their first lap, Sing stopped dead in his tracks. James waited a moment, not wanting to upset him, then clucked softly and pulled on the shank. Sing jerked his head upward, but then started to move forward. Michael watched the incident, saying nothing. Both men felt their luck was surely running out and hoped the call for riders up would come soon. Sure enough, mere moments later, as if they had willed it, the horses stationed to their front began to line up. "Here we go old boy," James said to Sing as he brought him in line behind Elusive Empire. To their rear, Luzinski and his handler also came into line. "Not too much longer now."

Seeing James lead Sing away from the tree jolted Manny from his daze. Knowing that's his cue, Manny followed James to their spot in line. When all the horses had assumed their positions, the paddock judge gave a loud yell so everyone could hear. "Riders up!" Manny came along the side of Sing and lifted his left leg, like he had done for so many mornings, so few afternoons. Michael standing at the ready grabbed Manny's leg and in one swift motion tossed Manny up and into the saddle. Sing never flinched a muscle and that didn't go unnoticed by Michael.

Looking up at Manny, Michael began to speak. "When Dad told us you would ride him today, I thought he was crazy." He suddenly paused and gently patted Sing on the neck. Manny, wondering where Michael was going with this, said nothing. It didn't take more than a few seconds before Michael, having collected his thoughts, continued. "But he was right. No one knows this horse like you. He doesn't run for anyone but you." Michael paused again, letting the weight of what he'd just said sink in. "I've got him as ready as I can. Now it's in your hands. I know you can do it Manny."

Manny looked down at Michael as they began the walk out of the paddock to the main track. He knew it must have taken a lot for Michael to admit that. Manny could only think of one thing to say. "Thank you, Michael."

Michael nodded. "Try to get him to relax early on. The pace should be fast. Your best bet would be to try to stay off the front runners and then get one big run late. He'll get the distance, don't worry about that."

Manny listened to the instructions and said "OK."

While they were leaving the paddock and making their way to the main track, Sam the Bugler began to play the call to the post. Manny could feel the butterflies in his stomach begin to well up again. This was it, he thought. He took a deep breath and ran his hand down Sing's mane over and over again. Whether it was meant more to calm Sing or himself was unknown, though it was probably the latter. James passed Sing to the pony boy and slapped Manny on the leg. The two locked eyes, "good luck brother," James said.

Manny's response exuded a confidence and fervor that he'd never shown before, "I'll see you at the finish line."

James smiled as he watched Sing move off into the post parade. Despite being done with his job, he just stood there, moved by the whole experience. The horse, his family, his friend, this race. He felt the gravity of it all and savored it.

"You ready?" Michael asked.

"Yeah. Oh, yeah," James said, snapping back to the here and now.

They turned, ducked under the plastic white chain by the paddock chute and tried to navigate through the crowd to their seats, Michael leading the way, relieved his part was over.

After placing the wooden carving board on the coffee table, Manny's aunt glanced at the television and was startled to see horses being led from the paddock. "Hurry up, they're showing the horses walking," she yelled.

From inside the kitchen, Manny's uncle came scurrying, two large glasses of iced tea in hand, ready to wash down the waiting cheese and crackers. "Could you grab a couple of coasters?" he asked.

Once the coasters were in place and the drinks set, the couple sat down, just in time to see the post parade introductions. One by one, each horse and rider, their names listed below them, were shown to the viewing audience. "I can't believe we never went to see him ride when he lived here," Manny's aunt said, regret filling her voice.

"Well, there are probably a lot of things we should've done while he was here. Nothing we can do about it now. And besides, everything seems to have turned out pretty well in the end." He took hold of her hand and smiled. She returned his smile, acknowledging his point.

They turned their attention back to the broadcast the same moment the camera moved to Manny and Sing. "There he is, there he is," cried Manny's aunt. The image lasted no more than 4 seconds before it skipped to the next horse, but it was long enough to make an indelible impression. Seeing Manny atop his horse on national television made Manny's aunt feel something she'd never felt before. Maybe it wasn't the same thing a mother would feel, but it stirred something within, enough to make her eyes nearly tear up. She was proud of her nephew and the man he'd become. He looked strong and sure. Your mother would be proud of you, she thought to herself, thank you for bringing us back into your life.

"Wow, he certainly looks like he belongs up there, doesn't he?" Manny's uncle said, staring intently at the television.

"Yes," she responded softly, "he does."

Not until Manny broke from the post parade and began warming up Sing did his butterflies start to fade. Now he had something familiar to focus his attention on. Focus on the horse, that's what Mr. Day said, focus on the horse. He took his time and allowed Sing to warm up at his own pace. Thus far, even with the immense crowds, Sing had behaved beautifully. Manny paid close attention to his horse's movements and after several minutes of warming up, he knew Sing was ready to go.

As patrons scurried about trying to get their wagers in, Michael and James, along with their wives and children, stood impatiently at their seats. The question of whether their horse belonged, whether Manny was the answer to his behavior and whether the farm would remain in the family, would be answered in less than 5 minutes. All their time and effort, all the preparation were about to be put to the test. Kids and adults grew restless, waiting for the final act to commence.

"When are they going to run?" Jack asked Michael.

Knowing her husband was completely pre-occupied and not wanting him disturbed, Janet quickly answered. "Quiet honey, they're getting ready to go in the gate now."

The pomp and circumstance that so often accompanies big races and is so wonderful for the masses was tantamount to torture for the O'Briens. As much as they individually wanted to enjoy it, they couldn't. The stakes were simply too high.

Michael put down his binoculars and looked toward James. "He warmed up well and looks good. They'll be no excuses today."

James kept his binoculars at his eyes, following every footstep Sing took, anxious for him to get in the gate. "Yeah, he looks comfortable. No excuses."

The horses began to make their way toward the starting gate. Manny decided to keep Sing as close to the inside rail as possible, steering clear of the fans lining the outer rail; no reason to risk anything now. Once they made it to within 30 feet of the gate the assistant starters grabbed hold of the runners and waited for their turn to load. As they waited patiently, Manny looked at Sing's neck and shoulders, then his back, to see if he had worked up a sweat. Despite the warm temperatures, Sing remained perfectly dry. He didn't appear nervous or washed out. He appeared the exact opposite. His ears were pricked and his nostrils were flaring. Sing looked like he was on a mission, like he had something to prove.

The assistant starter began to walk forward pulling Sing into position. The O'Briens had one shot to save the farm and as the gate doors closed behind Sing it was their final round entering the chamber.

Chapter 43

⁓

Silence descended upon the O'Brien household as the last of the horses entered the starting gate. The time had finally arrived. In just over two minutes the fate of the farm would be determined. Jack sat on the love-seat by himself, his old ball cap propped up against a pillow, unnoticed by the rest of the room. Daniel, Nicole and Sarah shared the couch on the opposite side of the television to Jack. Only Margaret stood, behind but centered between both pieces. She knew she wouldn't be able to sit still and didn't want to bother Jack. It was only when the gates flew open that she finally stopped pacing.

The horses broke from the gate with a powerful thrust. Manny held on tight as Sing bolted forward. After a couple of strides, Manny released his stranglehold on Sing's mane and balanced himself in the irons. Sing's break from the gate had gone without incident. There is always that chance some other horse will swing in either direction and knock you sideways, but they all broke cleanly today.

Moving forward Manny faced his first important decision. Up until this race Sing had always jumped out to the front early and been a part of those horses dictating the pace. Today, Sing was moving well but falling back behind the front runners. Manny wondered whether he should push Sing to run in the lead pack where he ran in his previous races? The race was one mile and a quarter, one full trip around the oval plus another eighth of a mile; a long way to go. Farther than Sing, much less Manny, had ever gone. Feeling it was more important to have Sing comfortable, Manny opted to allow Sing to go at his own speed, thereby making his first critical decision.

From their seats in the clubhouse Michael, James and their contingent watched the horses go under the wire for the first time. The two trainers were surprised to see their horse dropping back in the pack, though they were glad to see Manny deftly guiding him to the rail in an effort to save as much ground as possible. As the horses made their way around the first turn Sing continued his retreat.

Michael leaned toward James but continued holding his binoculars locked on Sing. "What do you make of this?"

Lowering his binoculars and looking at the first split time, a quarter mile in 23 1/5 seconds, on the toteboard, James responded. "Not sure. Going pretty fast up front, could keep pace if he wanted. Is traveling comfortably."

"Glad he's not up with that first group. He'd never make the mile and a quarter. You're right, he looks relaxed. Maybe this is how he's supposed to run, just never been settled before." Dumbfounded the two men watched as their horse loped along toward the rear.

Standing inside the clubhouse, Bobby Gillner watched on one of the many television monitors showing the race. With him stood dozens of other patrons, none of which he knew. The race promised to be a good one, with most of the field having a legitimate chance to win. Definitely a race worth seeing. He would have liked to be out front watching, but there were way too many fans to find his usual spot and he certainly didn't want to watch it in the box seats with his owners. So inside he stood.

The race started as he expected, the scheduled pace setters Defconthree and Luzinski running out front. To Bobby's surprise the pair was joined by Luca Toni, a horse who usually came from further back. That was the spot he figured to see Sing. Like Michael and James, he noted the split times and decided the lead was not where you wanted to be. Speed in average races is one thing, speed in the Travers is another. He glanced at his ticket, studied it. The date, the race number, the horse number and the amount. If felt strange to hold a betting slip again, since he couldn't even remember the last time he'd placed a wager. Years at the track taught him to stay away from the betting windows. Spending almost every day at the track, it's easy to toss a few bucks down here and there and then next thing you know you've spent a small bundle. It's like Vegas, they give you huge deals just to get you in the door because they know, once you're in, you're going to spend money. Many years ago, after getting himself in some financial trouble, Bobby realized he needed to exert more self-discipline. Since then, he very rarely bet, though he did offer up advice when asked.

The advice he gave out, to more people than he could even count, was to never, ever bet with your heart. Do not let your emotions make your decisions, not when it comes to money. Yet, for all his talk and discipline, Bobby stood there, holding a $50 win ticket, for an incredible long-shot simply because, well sure he did like the horse, but more because it was owned by an old friend. A friend who desperately needed the win.

Coasting down the backstretch, Manny took stock of the other horses. Three horses prompted the fast pace about 12 lengths in front of Sing. About 3 lengths behind them sat the next three horses, including The Sarge and Elusive Empire. It was another 9 lengths back to Sing and then another 5 lengths to the last of the eight. One of Manny's greatest strengths had always been his ability to judge how fast he was going, at least in the morning. He could tell based on Sing's pace the horses leading the race were going at a rate they couldn't maintain. He knew – hoped – eventually all three would fade.

That would leave the three horses following in the second flight in prime position to pounce on the lead. They were the ones Manny and Sing had to worry about. Manny had to hope the pace of the second flight, slower than the first but still strong, was enough to take something out of them. If it was, then that group would begin to tire coming down the stretch and give Sing his chance to pounce. Whether or not it would pan out was unknown, but Manny knew one thing for sure, he had a whole lot of horse moving comfortably underneath him.

Anne Dombrowski sat on the couch flipping channels as Ron entered the room. "Stop," Ron shouted as Anne skimmed from channel to channel. "Quick, go back one," he said hurriedly. Anne flipped the channel back. Realizing it was a horse race, of which she had no interest, she got up from the couch and headed to the kitchen. Ron had forgotten today was the Travers. How he had forgotten he didn't know. All he could think about yesterday was that the O'Briens' farm would be foreclosed on in exactly one week. Not even sure if this was the race, Ron turned up the volume, tuning in to the announcer's call. The calls of horse after horse echoed from the television, until Ron finally heard "And longshot Sing So Long has only one horse beat so far and that's stretch running Magic Way." In that instant Ron knew it was indeed the Travers and things were not looking good. As he stood staring at the set, he felt like he was watching the death of a friend. He knew down the road only a short distance, a family was watching the same race and watching their farm fade away before their eyes. He sat down on the couch in the spot his wife had just vacated, his face sinking into his hands.

The five individuals gathered at the O'Brien house watched quietly as their horse continued to fall back until he was no longer in the picture. Fortunately for Jack, he had seen enough of Sing to know he was relaxed and running at his own pace. He also knew if Sing were to have any chance he would need to begin his rally soon. If Sing didn't appear on the screen by the time the horses were making their way around the far turn, the race might be over for him. A thought that was already crossing the minds of the other four O'Briens watching the telecast.

After James had put down his binoculars during the early stages of the race Sydney requested that he pick her up. Which, he naturally obliged. From that point on, James intermittently switched between watching the big screen located near the tote board, which gave the television view, and the live action way back along the backstretch. Since Sing was not shown in the television view, every few seconds he would steal a glance and mentally gauge the distance by which Sing trailed.

James hated the margin from the leader to Sing, but as the horses began to make their way around the far turn Sing began to close ground. James quickly lifted his binoculars, shifting Sydney so he could hold her with one hand. He focused in on Manny, who sat completely still on Sing. He hadn't asked Sing for anything. Sing was closing in the other runners on his own. James' heart began to beat faster.

"Look James!" exclaimed Lauren, "he's catching them."

James, and track announcer Tom Durkin, already knew it. James could also see what was coming on the horizon. He was beginning to tense up and turned to Lauren. "Take her, take her, please." Lauren grabbed Sydney, noting the expression on James' face. Her calm and laid-back husband was about to show her a competitive side she'd never seen before.

The sound of "and longshot Sing So Long is beginning to hit his best stride," coming from the television broke Ron from his melancholy state. He looked up, and although the view was from a distance, Ron could clearly see the green and white O'Brien silks closing on the other horses, moving swiftly along the rail. "Come on horse," Ron whispered, lifting himself from the couch.

In front of him, Manny could see the leaders beginning to fall apart. Luca Toni had already dropped out of it and Defconthree and Luzinski were slowing down. Behind them The Sarge, Elusive Empire and Cry of Dixie who'd been tracking the leaders prepared to join the fray. Manny also recognized the second flight of three horses was swinging wide in an effort to overtake the pacesetters. This put five horses sitting directly in front of Sing and forced Manny to make his most critical decision of the race.

There was no way to go directly through the horses in front of him, so Manny had to decide whether to go around them like the others, or stay along the rail and hope for it to open up. Speeding along at 40 miles per hour, there was little time for thought. Decisions needed to be made in seconds, split-seconds. Manny's mind raced in search of an answer. If he were to swing wide, it would certainly keep him out of trouble, but he would lose ground and it would probably compromise his best chance of winning. On the other hand, if he were to stay along the rail and then shoot through, the ground he saved might be enough to win the race. If nothing else, it would give him his best chance to win. But if a hole didn't open up, then any chance he had would be lost. It was a gamble that could make or break the race, and the farm.

As Sing continued to close ground on the horses in front, Manny's time to make his decision went from seconds to fractions. No one would blame him for going wide, but if he got cut off trying to stay along the rail, it would clearly be viewed as the wrong decision. This decision needed to be made correctly, and it needed to be made now, there was no more time to analyze. The conversation he'd had with Pat Day shot through his head, then time was up.

Chapter 44

~

"THERE HE IS!" YELLED SARAH as Sing finally came into view Daniel sprung from the couch pointing at the screen. "I see him!"

"Yes, come on Sing!" Margaret screamed, shooting a glance toward Jack who remained silent.

It was too early for cheering, thought Jack, but what he saw gave him hope. Sing was still moving easily and closing the gap at the same time. He also saw the wall of horses in front of him and knew Manny had a decision to make. 'What do you see, Manny. What do you see,' Jack said to himself, 'be smart now.'

"Swing out. Why doesn't he swing out?" pleaded Daniel. "He needs to swing him out."

"Patience!" barked Jack, immediately quieting Daniel. No longer able to contain himself, Jack rose from the loveseat, inching toward the television, moving with the motion of the race, never once taking his eyes off Manny who was trying desperately to hold Sing back, lest he run up on the horses in front of him. "That's it Manny, stay on the rail. It'll open. It'll open. Wait, wait, wait."

Manny clutched the reins, tugging, struggling to keep Sing from running up on Luzinski who impeded their progress. Doubts waged war about his choice to stay along the rail, should he have gone wide. As the turn ended and the straightaway began, Manny knew his one chance needed to happen now. "Now, dammit now." He focused intently on Luzinski to his front and as that horse's momentum began taking him away from the rail, Manny saw it happening, 'They always come off the rail,' he said to himself. Here it comes. Here it comes.... There it is.

Releasing his hold on Sing's reins, Manny pushed Sing's head forward screaming "YAAAH" at the thousand-pound animal.

The view from the television offered the best vantage point to see the hole open. Jack, having seen more races than he could count, saw it first. Months of frustration and pent-up anger could no longer be held in check. Seeing Sing power through the opening triggered a wave of emotion Jack had been restraining. Holding nothing back he roared at the television. "RIDE EM BOY, RIDE EM. ONE TIME. ONE TIME."

Never in all the races he'd ridden had Manny felt such a surge of power. Manny's body, already pumped with adrenaline, sent another shot coursing through his veins. Lifting his arm, Manny gave Sing two sharp cracks of the whip letting him know the time to run had come. His horse responded by charging up the now opened rail. But waiting for the rail to open had cost Manny some time. He could see that The Sarge and Elusive Empire, running head and head, had gotten the jump on him and had pulled several lengths in front. The third horse, Cry of Dixie, who had been running with The Sarge and Elusive Empire, raced a length in front of Sing, but was clearly running out of gas. Manny knew that horse was of no concern to him; the other two were the target.

It was obvious to Michael as Sing charged up the rail taking over fourth, that within a matter of seconds he would move into third. He was amazed, seeing for the first time everything his horse had to offer. All his hard work, the early mornings, the countless hours, were finally paying off. For the first time he could recall, he smiled watching Sing run. Barely audible he mumbled to himself "run you son of a bitch, run!"

Margaret watched Sing take over third. Though not as experienced as Jack at watching races, she'd seen enough in her day to recognize what was happening. She could tell there was only one other horse behind Sing that was showing any kind of energy. It was Magic Way, who had trailed throughout the race. But Margaret was savvy enough to tell the horse posed no threat to Sing. That horse was picking up the pieces and at best would finish fourth. So as long as Manny didn't suddenly fall off, Sing should finish no worse than third and that meant they would at least be able to keep their house. Margaret made the sign of the cross, thanking God for that.

The two horses Sing needed to catch - the damn Grudge Match in The Saratoga Special - continued to run in tandem down the lane. They were beginning to drift from the middle of the track toward the rail still several lengths in front of Sing. As they passed the eighth pole Manny knew it was time to get Sing to switch leads and angle off the rail, giving him a clear shot at the leaders. Shifting his weight to the right and giving Sing a pair of left-handed cracks of the whip, Manny signaled what he wanted Sing to do, just like he had in all those morning gallops, all those breezes.

"He's switching leads," James screamed to Michael. Both men, fully aware of the troubles Sing had had switching leads, began to lean to the right hoping their own body English might help. At that moment, Sing leapt to his right lead, like an engineering marvel, sprockets sliding over gaskets, greased and automatic. Boom, another gear. His trainers let out a roar as Sing angled off the rail and took off.

The surge in power accompanying the lead change astounded Manny. He switched the whip to his right hand, moved it forward to let Sing look at it and then gave him a smack on his right side. Sing in turn stopped angling away from the rail and straightened his run. Now off the rail in the 3 path, Sing could run unabated to the wire. Manny looked at the leaders and gauged the distance to the finish line. He was beginning to close the gap, but time was running out and he wasn't gaining quick enough. "YAAH, YAAH," screamed Manny, giving Sing another smack.

From the clubhouse James watched Sing getting closer and closer to the leaders. He took his eyes off Sing for a moment and scanned ahead for the finish line measuring the distance between them. They had a sixteenth of a mile to go and Sing was still 2 lengths back. Like his father, he could no longer contain his emotions. Pumping his fist forward he began to yell with all he had. "COME ON MANNY, COME ON MANNY, GET HIM UP THERE, GET HIM UP THERE MANNY."

The Kentucky Derby winner and Preakness winner had been running head and head for better than three eighths of a mile and it was now taking its toll. Neither horse was giving an inch, but their pace had slowed considerably. Their jockeys riding against each other, not against a long-shot closing from the clouds. Not one of the O'Briens gathered at their Hemlock home remained seated. All five stood shouting at the television, screaming and praying to some racing God they hoped existed, their horse would get up in time.

Just before they hit the sixteenth pole Manny thought for sure they would never get there, but within three or four strides he could tell they were quitting in front of him. Pumping with every ounce of energy he could muster – desire overcoming style – Manny desperately urged Sing to give everything he had. He guessed he needed 10 more strides to catch them, 10 more jumps, but he knew there was probably only nine more coming. It's the jockey's death march, imploring and begging, while fatigue burns in the veins of horse and jockey. He had to get there, he couldn't come this close and not get there. Manny buried his head in Sing's neck, pushing Sing to extend his stride.

As the horses neared the wire a silence fell over Saratoga Race Track – 45,000 screaming, euphoric fans watched the three horses give everything they had. It was 1998 all over again, Ridan and Jaipur again, Man o' War and Upset.... but this time a farm, and the livelihood of those who owned it, hung in the balance. Two hundred and fifty miles away in Hemlock, on that very farm, the O'Briens' stood deafly quiet, their collective breaths held, a lucky hat resting on the floor.

Chapter 45

~⌇

THEY WERE THREE IN A line in the shadow of the wire. Manny pushed Sing's head down. They had to cross the line first, he had to get there. He stole a glance to his left. Two other horses, two other heads trying to hit the wire first. All three heads moving at different intervals. Three strides more. Almost there boy. Two more. COME ON SING. One more jump.

Under the wire they flew. They'd hit the wire so fast, Manny couldn't tell whose head got it, his face still buried in Sing's mane. Sing continued to run on, past his two rivals. From behind, Manny could hear the faint voices of two jocks.

"Who got it?"

"Got me."

The other jocks didn't know. Manny ran the last moments through his head again, trying to picture the moment they hit the wire. If these guys couldn't even tell, how could he, an exercise rider in the biggest race of his life. Impossible.

The silence at the O'Briens' house was broken by a collective gasp as the announcer yelled, "Photo finish, too close to call." And it was, even for those watching on television with the benefit of slow motion instant reply. Three horses bobbing up and down, together with the camera distance, the human eye simply couldn't process it.

"Who was it?" Daniel asked, his eyes darting around the room. "Somebody. Who won?"

The gathered group looked around at one another, waiting for one to declare something. Nothing came. Not even Jack ventured a guess. The television commentators began the discussion on whose head appeared to be down at the right moment. They were merely speculating, filling air-time, counting strides, "Inside, inside, middle, watch the last jump, ooooh. Maybe outside," as they watched the reply. They couldn't tell either. The fate of the farm would have to wait until the stewards examined the photo and declared the winner, further extending the torture.

Moments after the horses hit the wire, two trainers' wives looked to their husbands for the answer. Then James glanced at Michael and Michael at James. In a hushed tone Michael spoke. "I don't think he got there."

"How can you be sure? It was so close," Lauren said, not ready to bow in defeat.

"Not sure," Michael quickly countered. "I don't know…. I don't know, maybe. Lord knows we're due."

"Where's my coat?" James frantically asked. Janet pointed to his chair he'd knocked over during the wild finish. He quickly bent over, grabbed his sport coat and started beating the dust off it, all the while keeping one eye on the tote board. Janet held onto Sydney, who was still wide-eyed after watching her father.

"What do we do now?" Janet asked, holding a visibly shaken Mary, who couldn't understand why every important adult had just screamed. Jack, on the other hand, just kept asking "did Sing win, did Sing win, did Sing win." No one answered him, so he kept asking.

"We need to get down there," James said.

"Jack!" Michael yelled. When he realized he'd captured everyone's attention, including his scared little son, he lowered his voice, "We don't know yet. Look," he said, turning to the wives, "you guys stay here for minute and let us get down there and get Sing. Hopefully the crowd will thin out by the time you guys arrive. But don't come down there if he got beat, OK? It's gonna be bedlam down there right now."

"OK, you guys go, get going. We'll meet you in a couple minutes," Janet said, making a shooing motion. They didn't need to be told twice. Within seconds, they were half way down the steps, taking them two at a time.

Perched in front of his television, Ron stood there, his arms open and extended as if waiting for someone to hand him something. He, like the rest of the horse racing world, waited for the stewards to give the answer. Pleading, Ron spoke at the television, "One time baby. Give it to me just this one time."

"Are you talking to me?" Anne Dombrowski yelled from another room.

"No, no," Ron yelled back, "talking to myself." Even though the outcome of the race would have no financial effect on Ron, he knew the importance of this race on his life was immeasurable. He needed Jack to keep his farm almost as much as Jack needed it. The guilt he felt for his role in this tragedy would forever haunt him. In a quieter voice, Ron spoke again. "Come on, please, just this once."

As Manny jogged Sing back, he waited to hear the roar of the crowd. A roar that would signify the winner had been declared. A roar that would mean life, or death, to the farm. He heard nothing. Closing in, he saw Michael and James walking onto the track and headed for them.

"Hell of a ride," Michael said, attaching the shank to Sing.

"Thanks," replied Manny.

"You did great Manny. Unbelievable," added James.

"Thanks," Manny said again, still trying to figure out if they'd won. "Did they post it? Did we get it?"

James, having grabbed the shank from Michael began circling Sing as Michael unhooked the overgirth from Sing's belly, letting the elastic belt dangle. "Not posted yet, and neither of us could tell. It was *really* tight."

Michael stood outside the circle James made with Sing and Manny. Each of them periodically glanced at the tote board, waiting. Not more than 10 feet from Sing and the O'Briens were the connections of The Sarge and Elusive Empire, each also circling their horse. Also watching and waiting for the inevitable. Everyone wanting to see their number posted on top, each set of connections repeating their numbers, like the plea would somehow help. Number 2 for The Sarge and number 6 for Elusive Empire. Sing wore lucky number 7. How long the stewards would take, nobody knew. They were alone in a dark room, deliberating. The seconds dragged on.

"This is taking forever," James said, just as the crowd roared to life. James, Michael and Manny jerked their heads around to the board. The order of finish was posted; 6, 7, 2.

The house in Hemlock remained silent as the numbers were posted. No one knew what to say or how to feel. They finished second. Enough to keep their house, but not the whole farm. There was relief and yet utter disappointment. They came so close. Of course, they had to be proud of what they accomplished. Sing and Manny lost by a nose to a Derby winner and beat a Preakness winner. But they still lost, and everyone knew what that meant.

"Well, there it is," Jack said, staring at the television, his voice offering no hint of emotion. Then he let out a sardonic laugh. "This is almost impossible isn't it? After everything, as big as gamble as this was, we come up a nose short?" He looked directly at Margaret. "It's just not possible, is it?"

Margaret looked at Jack and shook her head. What could she say? She understood where Jack was coming from, hell, she felt it herself, but at her core she had an overwhelming need to say something positive. "The boys did great. Absolutely nothing to be ashamed of."

"Yeah, but it still stinks," Sarah said, her disappointment palpable.

Margaret didn't like being countered, but acknowledged her daughter's statement, "That may be true, but life isn't always fair, sometimes it sucks. No other way to put it."

Daniel and Nicole sat down. Despite having very little at stake, Daniel struggled with the result. Before the race, he fully expected Sing to finish in the back of the pack. He never really gave them much chance to save the farm. But as the horses charged toward the finish, he not only believed they could win, he wanted it with a passion he couldn't explain. Now it was over and somehow didn't seem just. He stared at the television, unable to turn away.

While Margaret, Sarah and Nicole debated things, Jack grabbed his cap off the floor and made his way out of the room and out the house. Margaret watched him go, but knew to say nothing. He needed time alone. Time to digest what had just happened, as well as what lie ahead.

Once he heard the door bang shut, Jack let loose. "Fuck, fuck, fuck," he yelled, slapping the cap with each curse. "One fucking neck, that's all I needed. Hell, probably not even that much." He groaned, then looked over the farm. The pastures, the barn, the lake, the beauty of it all. "Shit!"

With distress in his heart, Ron stood there, watching another horse, with connections he didn't know, walk into the winner's circle. It pained him enough that he grabbed the remote and turned off the set. Recalling the conversation he'd had with Jack, he knew at least they could remain in their house, if that's what they chose to do. But like the O'Briens, it seemed a hollow victory. Of course, the O'Briens had nothing they could do about it. Ron, on the other hand, did.

He walked out of the family room and into the den. Sitting down at the desk, he opened his laptop and turned it on. While it warmed up, he thought about everything that had happened over the last three months. He thought about the banking heads from downstate and about Henry Livingston. The deceit and injustice. He tried to imagine what Jack must be feeling at this moment, knowing he'd just lost the farm. It filled him with anger, which is exactly what he wanted. He needed to feel it, to build it inside of him, because he had an outlet for it. The computer at his fingertips would provide him what he needed. He began punching the keys. "To the editor – Rochester Post Standard."

As Janet, Lauren and the kids reached the apron the crowd roared to life. At first it startled them, but then simultaneously the women realized what it meant. They looked through the gathered spectators at the tote board. Their hearts sank, spotting Sing's number second. They looked at one another, ensuring the other knew what it meant. No words needed to be spoken, they both understood.

Just then little Jack spoke up. "Why did everyone yell Mom?"

Janet knew she had to tell him. She could try to avoid telling him Sing finished second, but he would certainly ask if the information wasn't forthcoming. "They posted who won," she said, but before she could even finish her sentence, Jack asked if it was Sing. "No honey, Sing finished second." The disappointment on Jack's face overwhelmed his mother. She picked him up and held him tight, fighting back the tears. "It's OK dear," she said, "he ran a great race and we should be very proud of him." Her words had little effect on the discouraged boy, his own tears now gushing.

Disregarding their husbands' orders, they continued their way, showing their owner credentials in order to get onto the track itself. They reached Michael and James as Manny pulled off his saddle and prepared to weigh in.

"Great ride, Manny," Lauren said.

Manny smiled the best he could, "Thanks."

Lauren walked with Sydney over to James and kissed him on the cheek. "You guys did great." James nodded and smiled, trying to cope with the outcome.

As James led Sing away, Lauren made it to Michael, but before she could say anything, little Jack, fighting back the tears, spoke up. "I'm sorry, Daddy. I was sure he would win."

Michael, like Lauren, was taken aback by their son's emotion. Michael knew at this moment his own feelings were irrelevant, what mattered was his son's well being. "Hey now, don't you worry about that. He almost had it. And he ran his heart out and that's what really matters." Knowing his dad was OK with the outcome, Jack's sad face began to transform, a slight smile emerging. "I, for one, am very happy with how he did. You should be too." Michael kissed Jack on the head, and then he kissed his wife and then his daughter before following behind James and Sing.

In Hemlock, Jack stood by the big oak tree admiring his land. In the distance the horses still out in the pasture grazed on the lush grass. The sun, beginning to head west, shimmered off the calm waters of Hemlock Lake. It was a peaceful scene. One unfortunately, not destined to last. But it surprised Jack he didn't feel worse. Fifteen minutes ago he was pissed they'd come so close. Yet now, in such a short time, he felt ready to redirect his attention. Maybe because he knew their chances were slim from the start. Or perhaps because the outcome validated his feelings for taking the risk, God loves a gambler. He couldn't pinpoint it. What he did know was his plan saved the house and proved their horse belonged with the best 3-year-olds around. Yes, Sing came close to winning, but Jack never lived in the world of 'what if.' He made decisions and lived with the consequences. That was who he is. The gamble came up short and life would continue on.

Jack placed his cap on his head, pulling it down snuggly. It was time to head back inside and check on his family.

Down in Florida, two novice horse racing fans went from being distraught early in the race to euphoric at its end. "That may have been the most exciting thing I've ever seen," Manny's uncle said.

"I know it," responded his aunt, "I just can't believe he almost won." She paused a moment, lost in thought before continuing on. "I can't remember what that means," she said, turning toward her husband. "Did Manny say they still get to keep the house or just part of the farm or what?"

"I'm not sure. I can't recall what he said, he was talking so fast, and honestly it didn't sound like they had a very good chance, so I didn't pay much attention."

"I'm going to give him a call and leave him a message. He probably won't be home until tomorrow sometime and I just can't wait that long."

She dialed Manny's number, struggling to wait for the beep. "Manny, it's Aunt Vickie. I know you're not home now, heck, I think you're still on your horse, but I had to call and leave you a message. We just had to say congratulations Manny! I know that you didn't win, but that was the most exciting thing your uncle and I have ever witnessed. We are so proud of you and I know your mom and dad are watching from heaven and couldn't be prouder. You did great, you really did. When things calm down for you give us a call. We'd love to hear all about it."

On his way through the clubhouse to the jocks' room fans reached out to shake Manny's hand and pat him on the back. Suddenly a young fan jumped in front of him and handed him a program and pen. For the first time in his life someone wanted his autograph. As he finished signing and handed it back to the boy, a picture adorning the clubhouse wall caught his attention. Focusing on the photo it dawned on him what it was. It was an old race photograph from 1919; a picture of Upset beating Man o' War. Manny stopped and stared. They'd come so close. He couldn't believe they'd lost. He thought it was their destiny to win. This day, this race. Still, he was proud. He knew he had every reason to hold his head high. He and Sing proved they belonged. He also knew it meant the O'Briens would probably keep Sing. He had to be worth more to them now. Selfish? Maybe, but so what. Sometimes you have to think about yourself and Sing meant more to Manny than he could ever tell. Another program was thrust in front of Manny. He happily signed it and smiled at the young fan. Then he turned and continued on his way shaking more hands as he went.

Standing inside the clubhouse, but away from the jockeys' path, Bobby Gillner watched the O'Brien Racing silks go past. His right hand closed into a fist, crumpling the now worthless betting slip into a ball. Then he smiled. It was worth the bet, even if he lost. He hadn't been that excited during a race in a long time, even with his own horses running.

The game can be a grind. The never-ending work, day after day. The rewards often coming few and far between. Bobby knew it was the reason for Jack retreating to his farm hideaway, tired of the grind. He hadn't reached that point yet, although he understood it. But races like the one today is why they all do it, why they get up before the sun every single day. The O'Briens sparred with the big boys and almost took them. They proved there is a place in this game for the little guy. And when you can trace your success back to something you did, it makes it especially worthwhile. Bobby thought about his friend. 'Jack you old dog,' Bobby whispered to himself, 'you got him figured out didn't you. No chance you'll sell him for $75,000 now, is there?' Bobby laughed out loud, making the patrons near him wonder if he were crazy, and then he headed for the exit, tossing his balled up ticket into a nearby trash can as he went.

Chapter 46

~

AUGUST 26

MICHAEL AND HIS FAMILY, ALONG with James and his, packed up their belongings and nibbled at a box of danishes and muffins from The Bread Basket, chatting intermittently as they did. The kids played quietly in the living room, having already eaten, as the adults prepared for the journey home. The conversations usually began lighthearted, about the kids or school or something mundane, but inevitably turned to the farm and the future. It was the elephant in the room and they couldn't escape it. They all knew the numbers and what second place meant. The farm was gone. But what about the horses? Who and how many would have to go was anyone's guess. The sound of Michael's cell phone ringing stopped everyone in their tracks. Michael looked at the number dialing in. It was one he knew well. Figuring this call would be for everyone, Michael yelled for James, the only adult not currently in the kitchen, and then picked up.

"Michael, it's your Dad."

"Hey Dad, hold on just a second, James is on the way in." When James arrived in the kitchen, Michael let Jack know. "OK Dad, we're all here and you're on speaker."

"OK, well, I probably should've called last night, but...last night...I don't know, last night was rough."

"It's alright Dad," Michael said, cutting him off, "we know. We felt the same."

"Yeah, that was tough to swallow. But, you guys did a hell of a job and your mom and I are real proud, real proud. You guys should be too."

Michael looked over at James "we are Dad."

"And Manny too. Absolutely great ride. Is he there?"

"Actually no, he's over with Sing."

"Well tell him I said he rode a great race."

"I will." Michael scanned the faces of James, Lauren and Janet. "Dad."

"Yeah."

"What happens now?"

The dreaded question, a question Jack wasn't sure of the answer to. "Nothing at the moment. Just bring it home and go about business as usual. I'll be in touch and let you know."

"OK."

"And again, great job. We'll see you soon."

As Michael turned off his phone he looked to the others. James was the first to speak. "What do you suppose that means?"

"Don't know. I figured he tell us to get back to Finger Lakes and start selling off. It's not like we have much time," Michael said. Somewhat confused, no one uttered a word. There weren't many options remaining, sell the horses, sell the farm, what else was there?

Manny stood in the stall doorway, his head completely inside the stall. Approaching from behind, James considered scaring him, but decided against it.

"Manny, how's our horse doing?"

"Good. He ate up everything this morning and seems full of energy."

"Excellent," Michael said, entering Sing's stall and leaning down to feel Sing's legs.

"Dad called this morning," James said, "he told us to tell you that you rode a great race. Said he was real proud of all of us."

Manny smiled. "That was the greatest race I've ever been in. I still can't believe we lost by a nose."

"Yeah," James said with faint resignation. "I feel like if I keep watching it, one of these times he'll get the nod. We were soooo close."

"So what happens now?" Manny said. "Did he say they would sell the farm? I hadn't thought about it much, but I need to find a place to live. I mean, I knew it might happen, but I wasn't really thinking about the dates. What do I do?" The realization that his home would disappear in a week had snuck up on Manny, leaving him panicked all of a sudden.

"To be honest, I hadn't thought about that either. But I wouldn't freak out yet. For one, there's no way they're going to tear down the barn that quick. Maybe the new owners will need someone to watch it for a while, who knows. And secondly, there's room in the house for you, or at our house for that matter." At least for the time being, James thought, realizing what he'd just said.

"That's true." Manny's smile returned, "Man, that really scared me for a minute."

Just then Michael ducked under the webbing of the stall and wiped his hands on the back of his jeans. "OK, he's seems in good shape. Let's gather up everything and get home."

Jack grabbed the kitchen phone off the hook and checked the clock. It was 2:00, as good a time as any to call. Bobby Gillner answered on the second ring. "Bobby, Jack O'Brien again."

"Jack," he said with a laugh, "man oh man, you almost pulled it off. Hell of a race."

"It was, wasn't it?" Jack said. "We came close."

"Sure did. So, for what do I have the pleasure this time?"

"Well, I wanted to talk to you about the horse again."

"Oh yeah, you're not still looking to sell him, are you?"

Jack paused a moment, hating what he was about to say. "Unfortunately, I think we may have to…" Jack filled Bobby in on everything that had happened and the main reason they ran Sing in the Travers.

"Wow," Bobby said, "that was a gutsy move, running him in the Travers. And to think you came within a nose of getting it all."

"You're telling me," Jack moaned. "But I figure the horse is definitely worth $200,000 after that. So if you can find someone willing to buy him for that by the end of the week, we'll let him go."

"I'd feel terrible taking him under the circumstances, but I'd hate to see you lose the farm. He's certainly a talented horse and if you're going to sell him, I'd like to be the person who buys him. Hell, Jack, stay in for a piece."

"That's exactly why I called you Bobby. It's a hell of a predicament."

"Sure is. Well, let me make some calls and I'll get back to you. It's probably too much for the guys that offered last time, but I have another client that's always interested in a stakes horse. And they don't mind buying in for partial. So, anyway, let me see what I can do."

"Thanks Bobby, I'll talk to you soon."

The plates were cleared and Margaret and Jack sat silently finishing off their post-dinner coffee. "I called Bobby Gillner today," Jack said.

Margaret had been waiting for Jack to say something about where things stood, but knew eventually he would. She was a patient woman and understood her husband. "And?"

"I told him that I'd sell Sing for $200,000 if he could find a buyer in the next few days."

If Margaret was surprised, she didn't show it. "Do you really want to do that?"

"Want and need, want and need..." he said "That horse has done an awful lot for us. I think we all feel a certain attachment to him. But this is a business and selling him would save this farm. The debt would be paid off, we could keep all the other horses, the boys would all have jobs and Manny would still have his room over the barn. It makes the most sense."

"Yes, it does," Margaret said. "But it doesn't feel right, does it?"

Jack took another sip of his coffee. "No dear, it doesn't. And I'll probably have to live with that the rest of my life."

"And if he doesn't sell, then I assume we sell the 40 acres?"

"That would be the only other option. It's either the horse or the farm as we know it."

AUGUST 27

Ron looked at his watch as he entered his office. It was 9:00 a.m., later than he'd arrived in some time. But there was a reason. After emailing the newspaper Saturday night, he received a phone call Sunday from a reporter. It so happened that the reporter had been working on a piece that weekend that posed the exact question Ron's email answered, or in the absence of actual proof, insinuated. A few weeks prior, when the first of the properties began to fall, there were allegations of kickbacks. Not just at Finger Lakes Savings and Loan, but a couple other banks as well. So the reporter had been digging and found some very questionable sales. He had no hard evidence, but something wasn't right and he tried in vain to get someone to talk. With times so tough, no one was willing to say anything that might jeopardize their job. That was until Ron. His email, and subsequent discussion, was the corroboration the reporter needed to send the story to print.

So Ron sat and read the paper this morning, something he usually did at the end of the day. His discussion with the reporter was supposed to be confidential, but he needed to be sure. Seeing his name in print would not be good. He was relieved to see it wasn't. As he reached his desk, he saw a sticky note attached to his monitor 'See me – HL.' Henry Livingston, what a way to start the day.

Ron entered Henry's office and immediately noticed the local section of the paper and its headline "Bankers and Developers Team Up Against Landowners." Showing no emotion, Ron said, "You wanted to see me?"

"Have you seen this article," Henry asked, pointing at the paper.

"No."

"No, haven't seen it, huh? That surprises me." Henry looked up at Ron. He was hoping to bait him into saying something, maybe confessing

306

to it. There was no way of proving it and accusing him of it could be grounds for lawsuit, especially in light of what he was about to say.

"I'm afraid I don't know what you're talking about Henry?"

"Well no matter. Look Ron, things have been really slow around here and we've lost a bunch of business. We need to downsize, so I'm letting you go." Henry said it with a hint of pleasure in his voice. "You have 15 minutes to pack up your belongings."

Ron looked at Henry with disgust that went beyond the border of hate. But he said nothing. He turned and walked out.

"Oh and be sure to leave the key to the office on your desk."

Ron silently went to his desk, grabbing an empty paper box on the way. He shoved everything that was his, and a few things that weren't, into the box in a heap. Only the pictures were delicately handled, gently put atop the mound. From inside his sport coat, Ron pulled out his key chain, removed the key and dropped it on the desk. The unmistakable pinging sound echoed throughout the office. Ron glanced around the place to see if anyone was looking. Like a scared prairie dog colony, everyone hid in their respective cubes, not wanting to risk looking out. Seeing no prying eyes, Ron opened his side drawer and grabbed every file he had. He picked up his photos, slid the files underneath, and walked out the door.

"I knew those bastards were dirty," Jack said, before taking another bite of sausage. "I hope somebody goes to jail for this."

"What are you talking about?" Margaret asked.

"This article," Jack said, pointing to the headline in the paper. "Some of these bankers are feeding information to the developers. The guy doesn't indicate he has any solid proof, but he apparently has some sources that are backing his claims. I'm thinking somebody's head is going to roll for this."

"Who's head? You mean someone that works there or the ones doing it?"

"I meant the people doing it," Jack said, raising his eyebrows. "But I guess it could be both."

"So do you think our property is one of the ones involved?"

"After the price they gave us, I guarantee it."

"Do you think that could help us in some way? Maybe get us more of an offer."

Jack thought about it for a minute. "No, I doubt it. If they know what we owe, then they know. There's no reason for them to change their offer. The only thing we could ever do is sue someone if we found out who gave out the information. Of course, the farm would be gone by then."

"Yeah well, I find out who it was, I'm suing," Margaret said with authority. "And I'm going after em for everything they've got." Jack couldn't remember the last time he'd seen such a fire in Margaret's eyes. As he took another bite of sausage, all he could think of was the adage – hell hath no fury like a woman scorned. God pity the man if she ever finds him.

Manny stood in his apartment relishing the orange glow of the setting sun, his ear now itself a reddish hue, having been on the phone with his aunt for nearly an hour. He gave all the details of the weekend, how nervous he'd been beforehand, the honor of meeting and talking to a Hall of Fame jockey, how thrilling the race was, and how it felt to come so close to winning, and yet not. It was a 36 hours etched in his memory forever.

"Oh Manny, to see you sitting up there and that horse, he was so beautiful."

"Aunt Vickie, he is the greatest horse I've ever ridden. He's unbelievable. And I'm not sure when we'll run him again, but I can't wait. I've always ridden him in the morning and, you know, that's great, but now that I've had a chance to really let him loose," Manny paused as if to catch his breath, "I'm dying to race him again. It was so awesome."

"Speaking of the future, what *is* happening with the farm? Your uncle and I were trying to remember what you said if you didn't win."

Manny sighed, "I think they'll have to sell part of the farm."

"Oh, that's terrible."

"Yeah. From what I understand, it'll be most of the pasture and the barn, but no one's said for sure. In fact, this may be the last time I call you from my apartment."

"Where will you go?" she said, shocked it may happen so soon. "I hope you have some place lined up."

"I talked to James this weekend about it. He said there's a room in the house here or even at his house. I didn't want to ask Jack and Margaret yet, since they haven't said anything, but I'm pretty sure they'll let me stay with them. They've been really great to me." It dawned on Manny as he said it that this wouldn't be the first time someone gave him shelter when he had nowhere else to go.

"They sound like wonderful people Manny, I'm sure they will. And if they don't, you're certainly welcome here."

"Thank you," Manny said, "And speaking of that, I want to thank you again for having taken me in and treated me so well. I owe you a lot."

"Manny, you really don't have to say that. It was our pleasure."

"Even so, it means a great deal to me and I won't forget it."

After saying goodbye, Manny stared out at the horses and lake, contemplating what a shame it would be littering this farm with another non-descript housing development, another "Deer Meadows" without any deer, or "Pond View" without any view.

AUGUST 28

Michael waited for Manny to get beyond the barn on his way to the track on one of the new horses from Belmont, before he approached James, who was busy mucking a stall. "Hey," Michael said, poking his head inside the stall, "you didn't speak to mom or dad last night did you?"

"No, I was going to ask if you had."

"No, I didn't either. Haven't spoken to them since Sunday morning."

"What do you suppose is going on?"

"Don't know. I would have thought they'd tell us by now to go ahead and spread the word. Why wait, there's no way we can pay to board them all over winter."

"How many do you think we'll have to get rid of?"

"I don't know, maybe half."

James debated whether or not he should broach the subject, but now seemed as good a time as any. "Think there'll be enough to keep me employed at the O'Brien Racing Stable? Or should I start looking for gainful employment elsewhere?"

Michael didn't smile. "Don't start looking yet. With Sing, we could probably make enough to keep both of us employed. Which brings me to my next thought."

Before Michael could convey it, James spoke, "You're thinking dad has a lead on Sing and that's why he hasn't said anything to us."

Michael frowned at James, having stolen his assertion. "That's what I'm thinking."

Both took the moment to digest what that meant, not so much to the farm, but to themselves. "I'm not sure how I really feel about that" James said. "I probably should be happy, I mean we keep the farm and all, but I hate the idea of losing Sing."

"I know, as frustrating as that horse has been, the taste of that last race isn't going to leave me anytime soon."

James nodded his head in agreement. Then his look became more sullen. "You think it's tough for us, what about Manny? I think he loves that horse more than life itself. This could kill him."

"You're right, but if it happens, he needs to think about it rationally. He keeps his job, his apartment and the family keeps the farm. It would be the right thing to do if they have the option."

"You're right," James acquiesced, "but it really sucks, you know?"

"Yeah, I know," Michael said, thinking about the fact he'd already begun looking for Sing's next race.

James went back to mucking the stall trying to reconcile what the loss of a horse that'd dominated his life for the last nine months would have on the entire "extended" family.

Jack stood by the phone with a questioning look on his face as Margaret entered the kitchen. "What's with the look?" Margaret asked.

"I just tried to call Ron to let him know what's going on." Jack stopped there, not completely finishing his thought.

"And?"

"They told me Ron is no longer there, would I like to speak to someone else."

A look of horror came over Margaret. "They fired him?"

"Sounds like it, doesn't it?"

"Why would they do that? He'd been with them for years."

"I have no idea, but I hope he didn't get himself in trouble trying to find out who ratted us out. This thing is bad enough. I'd feel terrible if we somehow caused him to get fired."

"Well, let's hope not," Margaret said, now sharing Jack's same expression.

"I might give him a call at home tomorrow if I don't hear from him."

"Speaking of hearing from people, when are you supposed to hear back from Bobby?"

Margaret's question brought Jack back to his own problems, working out the number of days in his head. "Probably soon. I figured he'd need a few days." He paused a moment before continuing. "Maybe I'll call him tomorrow too, get an idea where we stand." He glanced at the calendar on the wall, time was running short.

Chapter 47

~

AUGUST 29

MARGARET MADE HER WAY DOWN the upstairs hall as Sarah came out of the bathroom. Spotting her mother, Sarah called to her. "Mom."

"Yes," Margaret said, turning her attention to her daughter, who wore a definite look of concern.

After spending a couple of days digesting what the second place finish meant, Sarah seemed at ease with the outcome. But her sleep last night was interrupted by thoughts of two forsaken felines. "So what do we do with Parkway and Dixie now? I doubt Dad will let us bring them inside and it's not fair to just abandon them when those people come and tear down the barn. We have to do something, give them some sort of home."

Margaret, anticipating this moment might arrive and having already thought through exactly what to and what not to say, raised her hand to halt her daughter's appeal, then looked at her with a faint smile. "Don't worry about them dear, I'm way ahead of you. I figure your Dad is going to need a good-sized shed to keep all his tools and what-have-you in. And since we don't have one, I expect he'll build one. In fact, it wouldn't surprise me if he starts building one today. I'll bet we can talk him into putting in a little cat-door so they can come in and out. How does that sound?"

Once again, Margaret worked her magic and did it without raising any more questions. Sarah smiled and hugged her, relieved in the notion their lives weren't shattered, but would go on as before, even if slightly different. "Thank you, Mom."

Standing along the rail, Bobby Gillner watched the Saratoga morning workouts. It was a cool, pleasant morning, a sign that the New York summer was beginning to fade away. And a sign the meet was coming to an end. He loved it in Saratoga, especially the mornings and was always sad to leave. In the background, he could hear Mary Ryan giving color commentary as the horses ran past, entertaining the throngs of breakfast-eating spectators. A fun source of facts and information, Mary was staple at Saratoga, as is the morning breakfast crowd. Pleasant weather, delicious food, interesting commentary and the sight and sound of horses, what could be better?

Pulling out his cell phone, Bobby dialed a number and put the phone to his ear. "Doc, its Bobby, what did you come up with?" When the voice on the other end of the line finished, Bobby smiled. "Good, so you're officially in for 100. And I'm in for 50. All I need to do now is convince Jeff to get in for the other 50." Bobby paused, listening to the question. "Yes, I'm fairly certain I can talk him into it. I'll give him a call this afternoon and be back in touch. Oh, and be ready to stroke a check. We'll have to act quickly on this."

Margaret, a grocery bag in either hand, swung the kitchen door open, spotting Jack standing near the phone again, deep in thought. "I see you're near the phone again, what's going on now?"

"I just got off the phone with Bobby Gillner and I called Ron right before that, but nobody answered."

Margaret plopped the bags on the counter and wrestled with which question to ask, then decided on both. "What did Bobby say and did you leave a message for Ron?"

"Yes, I left a message for Ron. I let him know I'd called the bank and asked him to give me a call as soon as he can."

Margaret acknowledged the answer and was satisfied with the response. "OK, and what did Bobby have to say?"

"He said he had one investor for a hundred thousand and he planned on going in for fifty thousand himself. He's talking to another guy for the final fifty and if that guy balks, there's one other that might jump in. He did say he felt pretty confident they could get the two hundred thousand."

Margaret didn't need to look at the calendar to know the date. "He's aware of how much, or in this case, how little time we have?"

"Yeah, he knows. Even if we don't get the money for Sing until Monday, it should be fine. I'll give the bank two hundred on Friday and tell them I'll be back on Monday or Tuesday to pay off the remainder. They're not going to start the repossession that quick."

"Well I suppose not, but I wouldn't trust those bastards" Margaret said, pulling the groceries from the bag and wishing she didn't utter that word. "But it would be nice to have this done and behind us before the weekend."

Jack nodded his agreement and made his way over to assist his wife.

The office Ron sat in was in great contrast to that of the branch manager of his previous employer. This branch manager's office told a completely different story. As noted by the multiple pictures of his wife and children at various stages in their lives, the person who called this office his home was most certainly a family man. He was also committed to the bank as evidenced by the awards lining the book shelves. And even the casual observer could tell he was a man dedicated to helping his clients, demonstrated by the pictures of the man and his clients, hand in hand, smiling for the camera.

But Ron knew those things already after working with Joseph Danetti for six years before Joe left Finger Lakes Savings & Loan to go work for Ontario Community Bank. Joe had ambitions that didn't fall in line with a family run bank that practiced nepotism. So after gaining valuable experience, and working side by side with Ron, Joe left for greener pastures, or at least pastures with more grass. Ron was there today hoping there might be room on that green pasture for one more old horse.

"Ron, it's good to see you again. What's it been, since that networking event at the Marriott last April?"

"I think so," Ron said, very glad he'd made a point to talk to Joe during the event.

"That was a good time. I'm not sure it was worthwhile from a business standpoint, but it sure was fun."

"Yeah, they always put out a great spread. And I do tend to run into people I haven't seen in a while."

"Me too," Joe said, acknowledging maybe there was some benefit. "I'm glad you called and I'm sorry to hear about what happened." Ron smiled, but said nothing. "You know, had you called me a month ago, I'd have said there's nothing we can do for you. But with everything that's transpired between then and now, I think the landscape has definitely changed. And since the story in Monday's paper, we've been getting calls left and right from people looking to move their business." Ron began to get excited, hoping for the best, but again kept quiet. "It seems the people want to bank with someone small and local, and they don't want to be just a number. Who'd a thought, huh?" Joe said sarcastically.

Now, Ron had to say something. "I've been saying that for years. The numbers matter, but so do the people and they're the ones that refer the business."

"My sentiments exactly!" Joe agreed. Then he looked at Ron, returning to the reason they were there. "Regarding your situation…"

Ron waited, praying he would hear they wanted him, because if not, he had no idea where he would go from here. There were no other jobs out there for an old banker and that's all he'd ever done and the thought of flipping burgers didn't exactly appeal to him. He held his breath.

"I think we can bring you on, but I have to warn you, the position is really contingent upon us landing some of these loans. If we don't, I doubt we'll be able to support the position."

"That's more than fair," Ron said, thinking about the files he took from his office. "I'll make sure we get them."

"Well, I know how personable you are and I believe that's exactly what we need at a time like this. I'm confident things are going to work out well for the bank and for you."

"I am too," Ron said, extending his hand across the table.

Joe shook his hand, "Welcome aboard, when do you want to start?"

"Actually, I'd love to start today if possible. I'm not big on sitting at home and waiting."

Joe paused a moment, "Um, I guess that shouldn't be a problem and I love the get-up-and-go attitude. Let's go get you set-up."

Chapter 48

~

AUGUST 30

AFTER A SHORT DISCUSSION JACK hung up. Margaret had heard the phone ring, but only once, so she assumed Jack must've been downstairs to answer it. As she arrived in the kitchen she found Jack still standing next to the phone.

"Now who was that? And why does it seem like every time I come in here, you're just getting off the phone and have that funny look on your face?"

Without answering the question, and showing no emotion, Jack spoke. "Is Sarah still upstairs?" Margaret nodded yes. "Bring her down will you." Though confused, Margaret obliged Jack's request. Within a couple of minutes, Margaret and Sarah entered the kitchen. Before anyone said anything, Jack picked up the phone. "I have something I need to tell everyone. Let me get the boys on the phone and we'll do this all at once."

Margaret stood beside Sarah, curious about Jack's behavior. It had to have something to do with that call, she thought, and she had a feeling she knew who that may have been. But why didn't he just say something to her when she was there before? Why keep her in the dark too? She was dying to know what he had to say, but knew not to interrupt. He had a plan and there would be no veering from it.

As Jack began dialing, Sarah interrupted, "what about Daniel?"

Jack paused for a moment, having forgotten his youngest son. "I'll call him later." Focusing back on the phone, he continued dialing.

Michael sat at his desk, filling in workout times for the horses that had already gone, when his phone rang. Without looking at the number calling in he put it to his ear and answered.

"Michael, it's your dad."

"Hey Dad, what's going on."

"I've got news, are your brother and Manny around?"

"James is here, let me get him." Michael yelled for James, who was down at the other end of the barn. "Manny is out on the track."

"Alright, you can pass the news on when he gets back."

Jack's tone and words gave Michael no indication as to what the news would be. As James slowly made his way over, Michael yelled again. "Hurry up, dad is on the phone." Realizing this was the moment they'd been waiting for, James tossed a brush and rub rag on the ground and hustled to the tackroom. "OK Dad, he's here now."

"Is that thing on speaker? Can you both hear me?" Both boys said yes simultaneously. "Good. I have your mother and sister here with me. You're all getting this for the first time." No one listening had any idea what Jack was about to say, but they all knew tomorrow was the end of the line. As they waited for him to begin, each filled with an uneasy tension. Sarah fully expected to hear the farm was being carved up, and Michael and James turned toward Sing's stall, where he poked his head out and looked right back at them. Margaret believed she was the only one who knew what was definitely coming.

"By now, you boys must have figured why I didn't tell you to start advertising most of the horse stock for sale."

James and Michael stared at one another before Michael answered, "Yeah Dad, we guessed you had an offer on Sing."

"Your right," Jack said. Sarah, having no idea that was a consideration, was stunned. Michael and James lowered their heads, as if in reverend respect for a lost friend. "But we're not going to need to." Now, everyone stood shocked.

Margaret, feeling like she'd missed something the entire week, spoke up before Jack could continue. "You're going to sell the acreage?"

"No," Jack quickly replied, "not that either." Confused, no one said a word. "Ron Dombrowski, our banker, got fired from the bank on Monday. But then yesterday he got a job with Ontario Community and the first thing he did was convince them to give us a loan for the other $200,000. We don't need to sell Sing or the farm or any of the horses for that matter."

Sarah raised her hands in the air and screamed 'Yessss', then hugged her mother. Margaret, still flabbergasted at the change of events, hugged her daughter, and shot a glance at Jack. Jack knew the 'you owe me an explanation' look without even looking at her.

At the Finger Lakes barn, Michael and James bumped fists. "Great news Dad, absolutely awesome," James said.

"I'll tell you, when I got up this morning," Jack said, "I fully expected to tell everyone we were selling Sing. I literally just got off the phone with Ron. Apparently he snagged all of our information while he was cleaning out his office on Monday, so he had everything he needed. As long as he doesn't go to jail, it was simply a matter of convincing his new boss. Lucky for us, he did."

"Not that I want to sell Sing, at all even, but are you sure this is what you want to do?" Michael asked. "I'm sure it would be nice not to have any loan on the property after all this."

"Yes, I'm sure Michael," Jack said. "This is the right decision."

"Good," Michael said with a smile, "I've been scouting races for him already."

Feeling as though the moment had passed, Jack ended the call. "Alright, you two get back to work. Like you said, we're still not debt free, so go produce me some winners."

Michael and James smiled, 'yes sir' their only reply. As they stood there digesting the good news, Michael had a thought. "Now, do we tell Manny he almost lost Sing, or do we just skip that part?"

"I think he's been through quite enough," James said, "probably no harm in skipping that part."

With his *Daily Racing Form* spread out across the dining room table, Bobby Gillner stared intently at today's fourth race. A race in which he had a sure contender and after handicapping it, one he felt they could definitely win. While he played out in his mind how the race would probably unfold, his phone rang. His immediate hope was that it was a return call from an investor telling Bobby he had the $50,000, but as he reached over the paper to pick up his cell, he noted the number calling was Jack O'Brien's. "Jack, if you're calling to check in my progress, I had one guy back down, but I'm pretty sure I have another set to go. He just had to confirm something and should be calling back any time."

"Actually," Jack said, "that's not exactly why I'm calling."

Sensing something was up, Bobby snickered, "oh man, you're not pulling the plug on me again, are you?"

"You're not going to believe this; our banker got fired Monday, got a job with another bank yesterday and then got us a loan for the 200. Now we don't need to sell anything, including Sing."

Bobby laughed, "Jack, you're killing me, you realize that don't you."

"I'm so sorry Bobby. I feel terrible asking you twice to buy him and then reneging both times."

"Hey, Jack," Bobby said, his voice calm and unhurried, "don't worry about it. To be honest, I had mixed emotions about buying him anyway. When I saw him run the first time I thought he was a good horse, but no big deal when we didn't get him. But after that Travers, part of me really wanted to get my hands on him. But under the circumstances, you know, it just didn't feel right. Of course, at the same time, I'd rather get him than someone else. I don't know, either way it's tough, I guess I'm just glad you're keeping the farm."

"Thanks Bobby and I hope this won't cause you much trouble. Just tell your investors the owner is a flake and backed out." Bobby laughed again, especially knowing Jack as anything but. "When I called you, I really didn't think we had any choice, sell Sing or sell the farm, those were our only two options."

"Like I said Jack, don't sweat it. That farm and that horse mean far more to you than they ever will to anyone else, and that probably includes me. Of course, if he would have won the other day, that $50 win ticket might have changed that, but hell, Jack, it's right they stay with you."

Jack felt humbled by what Bobby said, the truth in his words and the consideration given. "I appreciate that Bobby, a lot. And keep your eye out next year, Saratoga's got some nice races for older horses. Maybe we'll ship in and see if we can't surprise the big boys one more time. I'll even pay you something for your house this time."

"No charge, buddy. And if you do send him over here, make sure you come along and spend a couple nights. And bring the wife too. I'll take you guys out for dinner, unless of course you win, then you're buying."

Jack laughed, "I will, I promise."

"Take care, Jack."

"You too Bobby, and thanks again for understanding."

Chapter 49

⁓

IT HAD BEEN A SEVEN day stretch Manny would never forget. A week ago he found out he'd be riding Sing in the Travers. That night, he could barely sleep thinking about what it meant, to him, and to the farm. The next 48 hours, well they were a nothing but a blur. Manny could barely recall anything that had happened, except the race, which was forever etched in his mind. But the outcome wasn't exactly as they'd hoped and it seemed certain the farm, and the apartment he was standing in, would go. Suddenly, even that took a dramatic turn.

When James and Michael told him this morning, he was, like the others, shocked. James told him he looked exactly as he had the previous Thursday when they gave him the Travers news. Manny didn't know what to say, but James naturally did. James, being James, said he had no idea what might transpire this coming week, but looked forward to next Thursday and hopefully another chance to spring something big on him. It was getting to be quite fun, as he put it. Manny begged him not to, his heart couldn't take much more.

Now, standing in his small and beloved apartment, Manny gazed out into the darkness. It was past midnight and despite being exhausted, he couldn't sleep. Life had handed him so many disappointments, so much pain, it was hard to grasp the amount of good fortune the past week had bestowed upon him. Sing had shown the world his ability and with it, what Manny meant to him. And Manny had proven his worth, to the family, to the world and most importantly, to himself. Now, everything he held dear in his life, the horse, the family, the farm, would remain with him. It felt too good to be true.

Unable to clear his mind, he'd gone down to see the horses, but there was too much in his head and the horses were more interested in their own sleep than his sleeplessness. Feeling like a nuisance, he returned upstairs and his mind continued to skip from the race to the farm to the apartment to the loan to the banker... Rather than lie back down, Manny pulled the loveseat over to the window and wrapped himself in a blanket. He stared out at the empty pasture and distant lake. The full moon cast a soft glow across the land and with it a peacefulness which could only be experienced in such a rural setting. The night's silence and beauty slowly went to work on him, easing his mind to a mere crawl, lulling him into his own darkness.

As he slept, he dreamt again of the race. His pulse raced as they charged the length of the stretch, striving to reach the finish line first. But this time there was no dramatic finish, no anxiety over the outcome. He simply stood with Sing well past the finish line. He couldn't tell how it ended, but it didn't seem to matter. He turned Sing around preparing to go to the unsaddling area when he felt a bizarre sensation, as if he were being watched. He looked along the rail for the ever present patrons, but saw no one. He turned to the infield, no one. No workers, no nothing. He was alone, yet the feeling remained. But at the same time it wasn't troublesome, actually it felt good, calming. The unknown sensation enveloped him like his blanket.

The sound of horses broke Manny from his dream. He lifted himself off the seat and stepped to the window. He walked slowly, his muscles still stiff from having slept half sitting up. He looked out the window at the partially risen sun. In the field below the newly let out horses were standing quietly, pointing toward his room, their ears at attention. Had they been calling him or each other, he wondered. He walked to his dresser and opened the top drawer, glancing at a letter he'd read so many times he'd memorized its words. He reached for it, touching, but not picking it up. The touch was all he needed.

Manny returned to the window, content. When his dad died he'd lost his identity, his direction in life, but as he stood there overlooking the mist coming off the deep green pastures, a scene he had witnessed countless times before, things were different. Today, he knew who he was, and he knew his mother and father were watching him and were proud of him. He wasn't alone and never would be again. The void he'd searched so long to fill was gone and his world would never be the same.

AUGUST 31

James knocking into the master bathroom door woke Lauren from her sleep. She noticed he was fully dressed and glanced over at the clock; 5:15 a.m. "You're up early aren't you?" she asked.

In a whisper, James responded. "Yeah, Michael wanted to take off today so he asked me to look after things."

"When was the last time he took a day off?"

"It's been a while," James said. He waited a moment before adding "It's nice to know he trusts me."

"I believe you've earned that," Lauren told him. She sat up and looked into his eyes. "I'm proud of you James. I hope you know that."

He walked over, leaned in and kissed his wife on her forehead.

She smiled as he began to leave the room. "What, no kiss on the lips?"

James turned his head back toward her and grinned. "Sorry honey, caca breath."

Lauren laughed. As James was about to leave the room she threw one more question at him. "By the way, what is Michael doing today anyway?"

"If I'm not mistaken, he's going school shopping with Janet and the kids," James answered with a broad smile.

Michael glanced at his watch, 10 minutes since the last time he checked. Holy Moses, he thought to himself, now *this* is work. The sound of Janet calling his name caught Michael's attention.

She was holding up a blouse. "What do you think of this?"

Michael, like most men, had zero fashion sense, but he smiled and as sincere as he could, answered the question. "That looks really nice. I like it."

"Yeah? Good. Maybe I'll wear it the first day of school," Janet said, excited to be joining the kids on their first day back and her first day in a long time. Scanning the store, Janet surmised they'd seen it all. "OK," she said, "I think we're done here."

Under his breath Michael whispered "thank God." He looked around to see where the kids had wandered off to while Janet went to pay for things. Having retrieved everyone, the foursome regrouped just outside the store. Michael, still on a high from their pseudo-victory in the Travers, and the fact they were done shopping, offered lunch out for everyone.

Janet and the kids responded with three cheers. It was nice to see Michael smiling and happy again, Janet thought, not that anyone would ever describe him as jovial. But anyway, it was good to have the family back to normal.

Rising from his seat Jack tossed the front section of the paper back onto the breakfast table. A follow-up to Monday's story made the front page. It appeared the SEC was checking into the allegations. Maybe the smoke did lead to a fire. For certain, somebody out there was feeling the heat and that was fine with Jack, the more the better. His only concern was making sure he made it to the bank on time. With the new loan Ron secured for them and the earnings from the Travers, they had enough to pay off Finger Lakes Savings and Loan. That meant they could keep the farm, along with Sing and the rest of the stable. And with Sing figured out – and his half-sister looking like she could run – the future looked brighter than it had in years. Jack patted the pocket of his blazer to make sure his checkbook was there. Ready to go.

"You sure do clean up nicely Jack O'Brien. I'll give you that," Margaret said.

"Thank you Mother," Jack responded dryly. "You don't think the tie is too much do you?"

Margaret smiled at him and winked. "It's perfect," she answered. As Jack turned to head for the door Margaret added, "It feels pretty good, doesn't it?"

"I'm not sure I can put it into words," Jack said with a smile.

"Well, thank Ron for me. Not that I'm sure you won't anyway, but let him know what he did saved us."

"Trust me, I will."

With that, Jack turned and left. As he was about to open the truck door, Margaret came outside and yelled to him. "Hey, why don't you invite Ron and Anne over for Labor Day? I think it would be nice to have them over after all this."

Jack agreed, it would be nice to put this chapter behind them and rekindle his friendship with Ron. As he pulled out of his driveway and headed down the road he glanced over, surveying the rolling hills of his property. Four horses, all relatives of Sing's, in the near pasture ran along the fence line, as if providing Jack with an escort. When Jack reached the end of the property, the horses angled off, turned down the hill and began galloping back, their job complete. Out of the blue he recalled the well-known phrase that says home is where the heart is. How lucky he was, Jack thought, to have his heart resting on 50 beautiful acres in the quiet country of the western Finger Lakes.

Made in the USA
Middletown, DE
06 June 2015